THE CANAL MURDERS

THE FEN MURDER MYSTERIES

CHRISTINA JAMES

www.bloodhoundbooks.com

Print ISBN 978-1-5040-7655-5

PRAISE FOR CHRISTINA JAMES

'We think this is a really exciting addition to the UK crime writing scene and look forward to reading DI Tim Yates' next case.'
— *LoveReading*

'An absorbing and generously written book...the police investigation is balanced by a more personal and emotional narrative, maintaining the reader's interest. It is this narrative that is ultimately more memorable.'
— *Euro Crime*

'A book that I would read again, not only because of the rich tapestry of images, dialogue and internal landscapes, but also the thoughtful use of the written word. I can't wait to read the next Tim Yates novel.'
— *Elaine Aldred*

'If you're after a complex plot with some political and illegal undertones, plenty of suspicious circumstances and some interesting historical content, then give this a try.'
— *Mean Streets*

'Cracking crime writing at its best.'
— *The Bookbag*

'Had me fairly engrossed at all times.'
— *Crimespace*

'A brilliant story, one of my favourites of the year.'
— *Books From Dusk Till Dawn*

ALSO BY CHRISTINA JAMES
PUBLISHED BY BLOODHOUND BOOKS

THE FEN MURDER MYSTERIES

The Sandringham Mystery (Book One)

To Max and Ruby and their very good friend, Emma. With love.

CHAPTER ONE

I t was a sharp, clear morning. The sun had long since risen and coloured the sky pink on the horizon. It was unseasonally chilly; the grass was damp with condensation and a light mist was just lifting.

Debbie Wicks had almost finished her newspaper round. She was cycling away from the close-built streets of terraced houses inhabited by the majority of her customers and was about to enter the scrubby grounds of Brooks' paint factory. This was her last call and it always made her uneasy. The factory was invariably deserted at this hour: the first employees didn't start arriving until seven forty-five, at least thirty minutes after Debbie had shoved the *Financial Times* and *The Sun* through the letterbox. The building was ugly, squat and flat-roofed, with mean little iron-framed windows. Management didn't see fit to leave some lights on at night, as the local copper had advised after the several occasions when kids had broken in for a spot of petty thieving. The porch was sometimes dimly lit by a single naked bulb, but the latest incumbent had ceased functioning at Christmas.

Debbie pedalled past the cast-iron gates, which had been

left open for so long they were immobilised by creeping tendrils of convolvulus and thorny blackberry runners, taking care to avoid the potholes in the badly-maintained factory road. She was fifteen, the eldest of three children. The Wicks family led a ramshackle sort of existence: her father was unskilled and worked at what jobs he could get when he felt like it: recently these had included bricklayer's mate, doing the heavy work for a local gardening firm and 'prepping' for a painter and decorator. The jobs never lasted very long; few ran their course, cut short by Derek Wicks' poor time-keeping or blatant absenteeism. Debbie's mother suffered from permanent depression; she just about managed the basics of housekeeping. It was left to Debbie to do the shopping, the ironing and most of the cooking and to ensure her brother and sister left for school each day looking more or less presentable. She needed the money from the paper round to buy clothes for herself, though keeping it for that purpose could be difficult: it wasn't unknown for her father to 'borrow' her earnings with the promise that he'd pay them back 'when his ship came in'. Debbie was ambitious and determined to make the most of her opportunities. She was bright at school, although finding the time to get her homework done was a constant struggle. She knew she had no hope of being allowed to stay at school after she was sixteen; she'd be expected to work to contribute to the family income. She had plans to apprentice herself to a hairdresser who'd encouraged her and study part-time for her A levels as well as her hairdressing qualification. Eventually she'd find a way of going to university. Meanwhile, she was desperate to move out of her parents' house; compared to her present home, a flat-share with other girls would spell sheer luxury. She was thinking about this as she dismounted from her bike and fished around in her canvas bag for the last two remaining newspapers.

Suddenly there was someone at her elbow. Her heart leapt

with fright. She put her hand to her throat, felt the blood pumping there.

'I'm sorry, I didn't mean to make you jump.' It was a soft voice, warm and lazy. 'It's a bit spooky here, isn't it? I wonder if you can help me. I've just bought a kitten and she's run away from me. I followed her here. She went round the side of that building and now I've lost her. I think she must be in those bushes over there. I'm late for work as it is. Will you come and help look for her?'

The first worker to arrive at Brooks' each morning was invariably Moira the cook. Tea had to be ready and waiting for the early shift. When she'd made it, she liked to get well on with the bacon sandwiches and scones for the mid-morning break. If her bus was on time, she could also manage to squeeze in a quick fag before anyone else arrived.

Moira was a key-holder. She was rummaging in her bag for the keys as she walked up the factory road, not looking where she was going. She'd almost reached the entrance when she stumbled on something and landed heavily on one knee. Slowly she got back on her feet and inspected the knee, which was already bleeding from a nasty cut. She saw that she'd tripped on the red bicycle lying in the porch, sending its rear wheel spinning.

'Which stupid fucker left that there?' she said aloud, trying to sound as belligerent as possible to cover her fear: she didn't recognise the bike and inside the porch it was very dark. She had a very cursory look round, but could see no one. She inserted the key, let herself in as quickly as she could and shut the door behind her, bolting it from the inside. When the first workers turned up, they'd have to bray on it if they wanted her to let them in.

CHAPTER TWO

Ricky MacFadyen was walking down Red Lion Street. He was carrying a parcel of fish and chips from Sheddy Turner's and eagerly anticipating consuming them.

As he turned the sharp dog-leg bend, he heard a woman scream. Someone else was shouting. Ricky saw that a small crowd had gathered near two men rolling around in the middle of the road. Each was punching the other vigorously, but one of them, clearly younger and stronger than the other, was giving his opponent a pasting. Blood was pouring from the latter's nose and the flesh surrounding both his eyes was already swelling.

Ricky dumped his parcel on a bollard, ran forwards and dived into the fray.

'Cut it out!' he said, grabbing the man who seemed to be getting the best of it and trying to haul him off.

The man stood up to face him foursquare. His clothes were casual but expensive. He was about six foot two and powerfully built. He was olive-skinned, with very black hair.

'Who the fuck do you think you are?'

The voice was rough. Ricky thought he detected a twang of Irish.

'I'm a police officer.'

Ricky groped in his breast pocket for ID.

'Oh, a copper, are you? And I'm the fucking Dalai Lama. Where's your helmet?'

The man landed two brisk punches on Ricky's nose and forehead before making a run for it. Ricky didn't chase after him: his assailant had caught him off guard and for a few seconds he couldn't take in what had happened. He looked at the man lying on the ground. He might be badly injured: the first priority was to help him. Ricky's own eyes were smarting with the pain. Gingerly, he put his hand up to his face. As far as he could tell, his nose wasn't bleeding.

The man on the ground rolled over and, supporting himself with his arms, slowly clambered to his knees. His nose was still streaming with blood. Ricky grabbed hold of his elbow.

'Can you stand, sir? I'll call an ambulance.'

Unsteadily, the man hoisted himself to his feet and, taking a handkerchief from his pocket, wiped some of the blood from his face.

'No ambulance!' he said. 'No fuss.'

A woman came out of the craft shop opposite carrying a folding chair. She set it up on the edge of the pavement. The injured man sat down heavily.

'Thank you,' he said.

'I'll fetch you a glass of water.'

The injured man gestured impatiently with his hand, as if to swat her away. For a moment he'd forgotten about Ricky, who took the opportunity to call for a squad car.

'Affray in Red Lion Street,' he said. 'This is DC MacFadyen. Backup needed, and an ambulance.'

Catching the last two sentences, the injured man glared at Ricky and immediately forced himself to his feet. He put his hand to his head and fell back on the chair again, closing his eyes.

'Steady, sir. Just hold on there for a little while.' Ricky raised his voice, making an effort to detain the bystanders, who were already beginning to melt away. 'I'm going to need a couple of witnesses. Did anyone see the whole incident?'

The six or seven people remaining, most of them men, muttered such excuses as that they'd just come to look when they'd heard 'something going off' as they sidled past him. Ricky was left with only a girl of about twelve and the female shopkeeper.

'I saw most of it,' said the shopkeeper. 'Poor Mr Fovargue!'

'You know him?'

'Yes, it's Jack Fovargue. *You* know – him as teaches the kids about soil and growing things. Such a nice man.'

Ricky knew nothing about this, but he didn't say so. The name 'Fovargue' sounded vaguely familiar. It was unusual enough to stick in the memory even if he'd only come across it in passing.

'Who started the fight?'

'Oh, not Mr Fovargue. He's a gentleman through and through! It was the other one as started it.'

'Do you know him, too?'

'No, I've never seen him before. A didicoi, I expect. They've been passing through in dribs and drabs lately, after that big fair they have up north.'

'You mean the Appleby Fair?'

'I suppose that's it, yes. Did you recognise him, Ellie?'

Ricky turned to the girl, who was standing quietly by his elbow, large solemn eyes fixed on Fovargue's swollen face.

'I think I've seen him before. I think he once came to Junior Soil Society.'

'To what?' said Ricky.

'Junior Soil Society,' said the woman, as reverently as if she'd just mentioned an Ivy League university. 'I told you: Mr Fovargue teaches the kids about looking after the land. He gets them interested in their heritage.' She switched to a lower key. 'This is Ellie. She's my daughter.'

Ricky nodded at Ellie.

'What's your name?' he said to the woman.

'Julia. Julia Withers.' She pointed at the name over the shop.

'Do I understand that you're prepared to make a statement, Mrs Withers?'

'Yes, of course I will.'

'No. No statements, no fuss,' said Jack Fovargue, suddenly opening his eyes as much as he could and erupting into life again.

A police car drew up alongside them. PC Giash Chakrabati jumped out. He was joined at the kerbside by PC Verity Tandy, his partner.

'DC MacFadyen! Are you all right?'

'Yes,' said Ricky. 'Why do you ask?'

'You've got a nasty cut above your right eye, sir. You may need a couple of stitches.'

'Seriously?' said Ricky, touching his eyebrow gingerly. 'I wasn't aware of it. It's this man who's really been hurt. I asked for an ambulance. Do you know if it's coming?'

'Your request was relayed. It shouldn't be long. Do you want me to take a statement while we're waiting? Do you feel up to talking to us, sir?'

Jack Fovargue settled himself more squarely in the chair and straightened his back. It was a struggle, but he managed it.

'Look,' he said, forcing a smile and speaking in a quiet and tautly even voice, 'I'm extremely grateful to you all, but I don't want any fuss. A hot bath and I'll be fine.'

'I'm sorry, sir, but I...'

The ambulance arrived, manoeuvring itself into position alongside the police car. The small group was joined by two male paramedics.

'Do you want us to move the car?' said Verity.

'That depends on the casualty. If he can get into a wheelchair, you're okay.'

'If you insist on taking me in the ambulance, I'm quite capable of walking to it,' said Jack Fovargue, attempting another smile. His voice trembled slightly, betraying irritation – or was it fear? 'But quite frankly,' he continued, 'as I've already said, I think you're making too much of this. I appreciate your concern, but I'll be fine.'

'You need to get yourself checked out, sir.'

'All right, I'll come with you.' He stood up. One of the paramedics offered his arm and Fovargue took it, clinging to it quite fiercely. He looked over his shoulder at Ricky and Mrs Withers. 'But no statements, please. It all looked much worse than it was. And I have absolutely no intention of pressing charges.'

CHAPTER THREE

D I Tim Yates was having a rough time. Over the past six months, there had been a spate of thefts of expensive farm machinery. It had started in the spring with the disappearance of several quads. Quads were a popular quarry for thieves – they were difficult to lock securely and it was relatively easy to spirit them away.

The quad thefts had begun in February, after the start of lambing. At first, Tim had regarded each incident as separate and unrelated – the quads had been stolen from different parts of the county and under differing circumstances. One had been taken from an open field where a farm hand had left it with the engine running while he rescued a ewe trapped in a bramble thicket. Another, also with the engine left running, was driven off while its owner bought cigarettes in a convenience store. More sinisterly, two others had been stolen from locked farm buildings when their owners were away. The thieves had rammed the doors and removed the quads. It was these two burglaries, which took place at separate farms during the same week, that had convinced Tim that he was dealing with a single group of organised criminals, not a scattered series of opportunistic petty thieves. The quads were probably being stolen to order.

But this was just the start of it. As spring turned into summer, expensive agricultural machines had gone missing from farms across South Lincolnshire and beyond. Irate farmers had reported the disappearance of ploughs and harrows, seed drills and muck-spreading equipment. One farmer had lost a generator; another a tractor. These incidents had only one thing in common: no one had ever seen the thieves at work, or even heard them as they made their getaway. Incredibly, even the man buying fags in the convenience store had caught no glimpse of the perpetrator.

With the arrival of the harvest season, the thefts had reached epidemic proportions. Tools and vehicles were being stolen on an almost daily basis. Superintendent Thornton had just received a report that a combine harvester had vanished and he was rapidly losing patience. Tim was in his office now, ostensibly to discuss a new plan of action, but in reality, to bear the brunt of one of Thornton's tirades.

'Do you know how much a combine harvester costs, Yates?'

'This was a secondhand one, sir. I'd say about fifty thousand.'

Superintendent Thornton paused for a couple of seconds.

It wasn't a bad guess.

'It's insured for sixty-five thousand. No doubt we'll be asked to confirm the theft to the insurance company. But that isn't the point. The point is that the farmer is doing his nut. He's got to get his harvest in and all the hireable harvesters are already out working. Apparently, either getting a new one or securing a hired one will take some time and in the meantime the harvest will rot. You do know who this farmer is, don't you, Yates?'

'I understand it's Mr T R Pack. He always calls himself 'T R', for some reason.'

'Yes, well, that's his prerogative. You must be aware that he's one of the wealthiest and most powerful farmers around here. And he's complained to the Lord Lieutenant of the county. He's told him that we've had six months to catch these criminals and made no progress whatsoever. The Lord Lieutenant's been on to the Chief Constable, and I don't need to tell you that he's not best pleased when he receives criticism of this nature. What a mess, Yates, what an unholy mess!'

Tim was diverted between feeling crestfallen by this attack on his own competence and trying to douse the small but obstinate flicker of amusement kindled by Thornton's use of hyperbole.

'I can't deny that Mr Pack has a point. We haven't made much progress, but it isn't for want of trying. This is a very clever gang, if it is a gang. We've tried laying various traps for them, but either they've been canny enough not to get caught out or they've not been operating in the right area at the time.'

'You mean *you've* not been operating in the right area at the time,' said the Superintendent truculently. 'And of course it must be a gang. What are you suggesting? A single individual working on his own? He'd need Herculean powers to nick some of this stuff on his tod, wouldn't he?'

'I don't think it is one person, sir. What I'm saying is that it might not be a conventional gang, either: there could be one individual or a small team of people masterminding a large number of petty crooks, villains they just bring in to do a job every so often and then tell to lie low for a while. I think it might be a cleverly-engineered network, in other words.'

The Superintendent tried not to look impressed.

'You could be right, Yates. However, neither I nor the Chief Constable – nor, I dare say, the Lord Lieutenant and Mr T R Pack – are interested in your ingenious theories. What we want is some action. I mean effective action. You need to catch some of these people pronto, Yates. I'm charging you with making at least one arrest by the end of the month. And, if I may say so, I'm behaving very generously under the circumstances. If you still haven't got anywhere in a couple of weeks' time, I shall have no option but to accept the Chief's suggestion that we draft in that team from Essex that's also been dealing with organised theft. And I don't need to tell you what that will do to my budget.'

'The Essex team has been successful, I assume?'

'I don't know the details, Yates. I can find out. But they can hardly have been less successful than we have, can they?'

CHAPTER FOUR

Tim was about to sit down at his desk to map out a new plan for catching the farm machinery thieves when he caught sight of Ricky MacFadyen coming up the stairs. Ricky's hair was dishevelled and his tie askew and, as he came closer, Tim could see that one of his eyes was almost closed, the skin surrounding it disfigured by a purplish-red swelling. There was dried blood above his right eyebrow. He was clutching a parcel wrapped in white paper.

'Christ, Ricky, what have you been up to? Are you all right?'

Ricky managed a pale grin. It turned into a grimace.

'I *am* all right – I think so, anyway. To answer your first question, I was breaking up a fight in Red Lion Street and got caught in the crossfire. My own fault, probably.'

'What sort of a fight?'

'How many sorts are there? It was quite vicious. I wasn't there at the start of it, but some thug picked a quarrel with a character called Jack Fovargue. Apparently Fovargue's quite well-known for the work that he does with kids – conservation or responsible farming, something like that. Have you heard of him?'

'Vaguely, but only because I remember the name. I wouldn't have been able to tell you what he did. What's happened to him? And the thug?'

'Fovargue's been taken to A & E, even though he didn't want to go, by the paramedics who answered my call. The thug got away – I had to stay with Fovargue and no one else seemed inclined to chase after him.'

'You got a good look at him, though – you'd recognise him again?'

'Yes, and so would at least half a dozen other people who were there, though only two of them have volunteered to give statements. Not that there's any point: Fovargue is pretty adamant that he doesn't want to press charges. His attitude to the whole thing struck me as odd – it was as if he was embarrassed by it, and anxious to put it behind him immediately. He could just have been suffering from shock, I suppose. The thug looked a bit like a gypsy, except that he was very well-dressed.'

'Whether or not we press charges may not be Fovargue's decision. The thug assaulted a police officer as well as Fovargue. That isn't something we'll be allowed to ignore. And, incidentally, I've known quite a few well-dressed gypsies. Or travellers, I think we're supposed to call them now.'

'I hadn't thought of it as an assault on me as a policeman, really – he couldn't have known from my appearance.'

'Did you tell him you were a police officer? The thug, I mean?'

'Yes. He didn't seem inclined to believe me. He said if I was a police officer, he was the 'fucking Dalai Lama', or something like that.'

'Ha! Anyway, he shouldn't be allowed to get away with it. You'd better go and see Fovargue. He may have changed his mind about pressing charges. If he hasn't, we need to find out why he doesn't want to. The likeliest explanation is that he knows the bloke who attacked him and has a reason for not taking it further. Whatever he thinks, if he knows who it was, we want a name.' Tim scrutinised Ricky's damaged face more closely. 'I take it you've been to A & E yourself? They haven't done a very good job of cleaning you up, have they?'

'I... er ... no. I decided to come straight back here. I didn't want to get in the ambulance with Fovargue or have to wait around in A & E, for that matter.'

'I can understand that, but you need to get yourself checked out. See if they'll give you an emergency appointment at the doctor's. Pull rank as a copper if necessary.'

'I hate doing that.'

'So do I, but sometimes it's the quickest way to get things done. Besides, you've been assaulted while on duty, so you deserve some kind of preferential treatment. Protecting our citizens, and all that.' Tim scrutinised Ricky's face. 'You're looking a bit pale under all that damage. Have you had anything to eat lately?'

'I'd only just bought these fish and chips! I was just on my way back from Sheddy's when the ruckus started.' Ricky felt the limp parcel that he was holding and dropped it on to Tim's desk. 'They'll be stone cold now!'

Tim stifled a laugh at Ricky's woebegone expression. He seemed much more concerned about the loss of his lunch than the mess that had been made of his face.

'Well, don't leave them on my desk. Kindly dispose of them somewhere they won't smell. Then I'll treat you to whatever they've got left in the canteen. It won't be up to much, but we should at least be able to get a few calories down you. Then you can take yourself off to the quack.'

'What about interviewing Fovargue?'

'It'll do tomorrow. It's unlikely that he's planning on going anywhere, isn't it? Better if he gets himself sorted out first. If he's as reluctant to talk as you say he is, we don't want him to wriggle out of it by accusing us of harassing him while he doesn't feel well.'

'I don't think he's that type. From what the woman who keeps the craft shop in Red Lion Street told me, he's an absolute pillar of the community, and well-liked, too.'

'Excellent. He'll see sense then, won't he, when you point out that it's an offence to strike a police officer? You can keep it pretty low key, but make sure you take someone with you.'

Ricky sighed. Something in Tim's tone told him that his boss had a hunch the interview wouldn't be plain sailing. Ricky suspected Tim was right and also realised his usual boundless optimism in the face of a challenge was rapidly deserting him. He'd probably feel better about it after he'd given his energy levels a boost. Purposefully, he picked up the packet of fish and chips and strode through to the kitchen to dump them in the bin. Then he headed for the canteen, Tim following in his wake.

CHAPTER FIVE

Davina Smith had been on the game for two years.

Like most of the other working girls in the small town of Worksop, she did it to fund her heroin habit. She'd hated being a sex worker at first, but now she'd settled in to the life she found it wasn't too bad. She had a half-decent flat and some nice clothes and she enjoyed the social life, such as it was: it consisted of the chance to talk to some of the more intelligent punters and the superficial camaraderie she'd established with the other girls. They were still rivals for business, but if the chips were down and there was danger she hoped they'd support each other. This was important for Davina, because, unlike most of the others, she hadn't caved in to being managed by a pimp. Several had tried it on, but Davina was still together enough to be able to tell them to piss off. The key to independence was getting a decent fee for her services. While she could manage this, she'd never be in debt to her dealer, so wouldn't be in need of 'protection'.

The great advantage of working alone was that she kept all her earnings. The drawback was that she was isolated; she saw other sex workers as they walked the streets, usually followed at

17

a discreet distance by their pimps, but once she was with a client there was no one to look out for her, not even in the self-serving, hit-and-miss style adopted by most pimps. She'd had a few scares: one punter had hit her in the face with the flat of his hand and another had made her strip and fastened her naked to railings on a bitter evening (she'd been rescued by a copper on his beat, so dazed with cold that she'd felt gratitude but no shame when he set her free). These experiences had made her wary of strangers. She preferred to go with regular clients, even if few paid generously and some made disgusting requests. She reasoned that it was better the devil you knew.

Davina stood out from the ordinary Worksop girls in other ways, too: she came from a 'good' home; had grown up in a nice house on the outskirts of the town. Her parents had divorced, but her mum had kept the house and got a good job in insurance. Davina had been a middle-of-the-roader at school, practical rather than academic, popular and 'with her head screwed on', as one of her teachers had said. She'd been destined for a career in nursing, which everyone thought would suit her. Instead she'd accepted a gift of Ecstasy at a pop concert and from that rapidly escalated to the hard stuff. At first, she'd stolen just from her mum, then from students at her college, to pay for her drugs. She'd been caught and the college had pressed charges. She'd been handed a suspended sentence and then kicked out of college. Her mum hadn't abandoned her, but Davina couldn't trust herself not to steal again if she went home. They still met up for coffee sometimes, but her mum's bleak face was getting harder and harder to bear. Not that she ever reproached Davina, but there was worry etched in every line.

Anyway, it was because she was posh that Davina was a favourite with the punters. They liked the way she spoke and the gentle little attentions that came naturally to her. Made them feel less squalid, probably – more as if it was a proper relationship.

It was Friday night and she was walking through the town centre now, watching out for a bloke called John who'd picked her up the last three or four Fridays. John was okay; he just wanted straight sex and always paid up without grumbling about the forty quid she asked for. She'd put the price up a bit for him: instinct had told her he'd be good for an extra tenner.

Winter was closing in; although it was barely 8pm, it had been dark for a couple of hours. Some of the shop windows were dimly lit, but as many had been boarded up, Davina stood for a while in the shadows of a derelict pub. It was the spot where she'd first met John. She'd give him ten minutes or so, to see if he showed up. She glanced across the street, saw Vicky with a bloke in tow, a stocky little guy. It wasn't John. She paced the pavement, a few steps one way, a few the other, not moving away from the old pub. A gust of wind powered round the corner. She shivered, drew her fake fur bomber jacket more closely around her. She was wearing knee-length boots, but under her short skirt her thighs were bare.

Tights were too much of an encumbrance.

A car passed her slowly and the driver wound down his window. She walked towards him.

'How much?' he said, grinning.

Too late, she saw there were two or three guys in the back, waving and jeering at her.

'The knave of hearts, he stole some tarts...' one of them chanted. She gave them the finger and walked rapidly away, past the shadowy pub and into a pedestrianised area protected from the road by a row of bollards. She hated kerb crawlers.

She was thinking about where to pitch next when she felt a light tap on her shoulder. She spun round.

'Hello,' said a soft voice. 'I'm glad I've caught you.'

CHAPTER SIX

A few months before, just before the farm vehicle thefts had started, Tim had been surprised by his wife, Katrin. Katrin often surprised him and usually delighted him with her surprises. However, he'd learnt that they did not always gratify them both in equal measure.

'Tim!' Katrin had said suddenly, when they'd settled down to a quiet evening after supper.

Tim had looked up immediately, an ignoble presentiment of fear striking his heart. When his wife invested this much energy in pronouncing his name, it was usually because she wished to discuss something of importance to herself (and possibly correspondingly disagreeable to him).

'Yes?'

'I've been thinking...'

'Go on.'

'Sophia starts school next year.'

'I know.'

'The thing is... just lately I've had the strong impression that my brain is getting rusty.'

'Your brain isn't rusty. You're the sharpest knife in the drawer.'

'Thanks! I'm flattered. But that very much depends on *whose* drawer, doesn't it? Anyway, I've been thinking...'

Tim had waited. Rather meanly, he'd offered her no encouragement to continue.

'I've been thinking I'd like to study for an MA.'

'You mean, go back to university?' Tim had tried to make his voice non-committal. He hadn't wanted to show Katrin how much he disliked the idea.

Katrin had laughed. She could read Tim like a book.

'Only part-time. And I'd mostly be studying remotely. I wouldn't be giving up my job or have to live away from home.'

Tim had stifled a sigh of relief.

'I think you should go for it. What do you want to study?'

'Criminology.'

'Criminology! Whatever for? You know far more about it already than a bunch of poncy academics.'

'In a haphazard way, maybe. But I've worked only on individual cases. I've never studied criminal psychology systematically. And if I had the qualification I could probably find a more interesting job.'

'Such as?'

'Well, criminal profiler, for example. I've always thought that must be really absorbing.'

Tim had laughed sardonically.

'Charlatans, most of them. Though I have met the odd one who had something useful to tell us.'

'I'm sure I could be one of the useful ones.'

'You could be. On the other hand, you could be bloody dull.'

'Thanks very much!'

'What I mean is, when you've got a job that demands results, there's an unspoken imperative to come up with something, even if the evidence gives you no fucking clue. And you wouldn't want to do that.'

'You mean, I'd be more likely to admit that I 'had no fucking clue'?'

'Precisely.'

Katrin had been silent for a moment. 'I'd still like to give it a try.'

'I've already told you to go for it,' Tim had said ungraciously.

Katrin had leaned across to kiss him. 'Thank you, Tim.'

'There's no need to thank me. Your instincts are usually right, which is why I usually go along with what you say. Just promise me you'll jack this in if it proves to be disappointing. There's no need to waste your time and money just to prove you can do it.'

'Okay, I promise.'

Tim had taken a while to reply. The turn the conversation had taken had triggered a new, unwelcome, chain of thought.

'How much does it cost, by the way?'

'Oh,' Katrin had said airily, gathering up coffee cups, 'I think it's... affordable.'

CHAPTER SEVEN

Having slept on it, Tim decided that he should himself accompany Ricky on his visit to Jack Fovargue's. Ricky's hunch that their attacker might have been a traveller was intriguing: one of the theories he was working on was that the farm vehicle thefts could have been co-ordinated by a group of travellers. That would explain why he could discern no geographical pattern to them and how the thieves had managed to be so elusive.

Silverdale Farm, the address supplied to Ricky by Fovargue, was a large, rather bleak, red-brick building. It was completely isolated, standing alone at the heart of Baston Fen. It had been extended several times in ways not always sympathetic to the original architectural style, which appeared to be Victorian Gothic. Tim guessed the house originated from the high Victorian period, which would make it more than a hundred and fifty years old. It was more elaborate than most farmhouses, but not grand enough to have been inhabited by an aristocrat. It could have started life as a wealthy gentleman's whim, a second residence for playing at farmers when he tired of 'town'.

The house had been built to the right of a track leading off the roughly cambered fenland road. The track continued well beyond the house itself: there were several outhouses and yards, as well as some rows of Dutch lights and some allotment-sized market garden plots. All of these looked as if they were well-cared-for. The area immediately in front of the house was rather more neglected, although this was probably because it had been turned into a play area for small children. It was littered with a miscellany of small bicycles, scooters and abandoned toys. There was no proper path leading to the front door. As he and Ricky picked their way across this obstacle course – and Tim was reflecting that it must degenerate into a muddy quagmire in the winter – he heard an engine in the distance. He thought it might be a motorcycle, but when he looked up he saw a quad disappearing over the horizon. It was purple, an unusual colour for a quad. Not one of the missing vehicles, then, unless it had been disguised: he was sure he would have remembered if one of them had been purple.

Ricky rang the doorbell. The door was opened by a well-built woman in her late thirties. She had thick, wavy auburn hair tied back in a ponytail and was wearing a matching jumper and cardigan. A single pearl was suspended from a gold chain round her neck. If it weren't for her jeans, she'd have been the living image of a stereotypical county-set wife.

'Good morning, Mrs Fovargue? I'm DC MacFadyen. I won't need to tell you that your husband was assaulted in the street in Spalding yesterday. This is Detective Inspector Yates. We're here to gather a few more details. And to check on how Mr Fovargue is, of course.'

'I'm afraid Jack's not here at the moment.' She directed her smile at Tim. Typical of this kind of woman, he thought: she invests all her energy in the most senior person present; doesn't bother with the juniors.

'Really?' Tim said, injecting surprise into his voice. 'Aren't you worried that he may not be well enough to go out just yet?'

Her rather forced social smile morphed into something softer, a look of indulgence, perhaps.

'You don't know Jack, Detective Inspector. It's impossible to keep him inside when he thinks he should be working. He's been gone for a couple of hours now. I don't know when he's planning to return, unfortunately. Otherwise I'd ask you if you wanted to wait.'

'That's very kind of you, Mrs Fovargue. We won't hang around today, as his plans seem to be so... fluid. Perhaps instead we can make an appointment to return when he *is* here?'

'I'm afraid that I don't manage Jack's diary, or even have access to it.' She paused and noticed Tim's raised eyebrow. 'Oh, I could if I wanted to. But Jack has so many irons in the fire, it's too confusing to try to keep up with him. I have enough to do with my work here and looking after the children.'

'Quite,' said Tim. 'Perhaps in that case you could supply us with his mobile number?'

She hesitated. Surely she wasn't going to try to pretend that she didn't know it?

'I can never remember it offhand. If you wait here, I'll fetch it for you.'

She disappeared into the house. Evidently there was still no question of asking them in. The two policemen stood waiting on the doorstep, a shrill wind whipping round their legs. Ricky tutted quietly and rolled his eyes at Tim. Tim threw him a grim look in return. He wasn't amused by this show of unhelpful helpfulness and he'd been perturbed by seeing the quad. He scanned the horizon, which lay beyond typical flat Fenland country of rich ploughed fields, the view unbroken for possibly five miles until at last obscured by a row of poplar trees.

It took Mrs Fovargue several minutes to return. When she

did, she looked flustered, her face red as if she'd had an argument with someone or been chastised. Tim reflected that she'd had time to call Fovargue and speak to him – if he really was out of the house. An alternative possibility was that he'd been there all the time and told her to get rid. It was a big enough house for them to have spoken in a distant room, unheard by their visitors.

'Here is the number. I've written it on a slip of paper for you. Don't be surprised if it goes to message. Jack has several phones, because there are so many businesses.'

'For which of the businesses is this number?'

'I forget. But it's the number he always tells me to call, if I need to speak to him,' she added brightly.

'That should work, then,' said Tim sardonically. 'Well, if that's everything...'

She began to close the door.

'Just one more thing, Mrs Fovargue.'

'Yes?' She was looking apprehensive now, struggling to regain the self-assurance with which she had first greeted them.

'When DC MacFadyen and I arrived, I thought I saw a purple quad. It was some distance away, heading out into the open fields over there. Does it belong to your husband?'

'I'm sorry, I can't help you with that. I don't have anything to do with the vehicles. I just know that there are many of them and they change hands all the time. One of Jack's businesses is about sourcing vehicles for people. Unusual vehicles, mostly – veteran tractors, that sort of thing. I'd say a purple quad was quite unusual, though, wouldn't you?' She gave a forced little laugh.

'Indeed. And I'd say that a company operating in this area to supply veteran vehicles was pretty unusual, too. In my experience, the farmers round here are a doggedly unsentimental bunch. They've got an eye on the bottom line, which means using the most efficient machinery they can get their hands on, not the sort of kit their parents and grandparents used. I'm surprised your husband can make a go of it.'

'Oh, well, the veteran vehicle business is national – even international, sometimes – not just local. And Jack would agree with you about the farmers in this area. He says they'd do anything to squeeze out a bit more profit. That's why he started his organic farming business: to show them that they don't have to murder the soil in the process. As you probably know, there's an educational division to it, as well. He gives classes to schoolchildren to teach them about the soil; sometimes visits schools, too. I help him with that.'

Her voice had recovered its aplomb. She clearly felt she was on stronger ground now.

'And is it part of his message that only old vehicles are good for the land?'

She gave a tinkly little laugh.

'Certainly not. But, although it's really the big farmers Jack wants to educate, so far he's had the most success with smallholders. Some of them are incomers, retired people or people seeking a new way of earning a living.'

'You mean, people in pursuit of the 'good life'?'

'That sort of thing, yes. And they can be quite sentimental, not just about organic farming, but also about the kinds of implements farmers used in the past. Someone once asked him if he could source some old tools and it just grew from there. Jack set the service up as a favour – he barely makes any money out of it. He's too nice, really.'

Tim managed to swallow the smart rejoinder that sprang to his lips. Mrs Fovargue was visibly more relaxed now she'd circumnavigated the tricky part of the conversation and he didn't want to put her on her guard again.

'I'm sure you're right,' he said. 'Here's my card. Please ask your husband to call me when he gets back today. And tell him that if this isn't convenient, I'll give him a call myself tomorrow. Thank you for your help, Mrs Fovargue.'

'My pleasure. My name's Susie, by the way, in case you want to speak to me again.'

CHAPTER EIGHT

Superintendent Thornton was waiting impatiently for Tim and Ricky to return to the station.

'There you are at last, Yates. I didn't expect your little jaunt to take half the day.'

Tim swallowed his annoyance while Ricky quickly made himself scarce, disappearing in quest of coffee.

'It's quite a long way to Baston Fen, sir, and I think we've been gone only a couple of hours. Did you want to discuss my new plans for catching the farm vehicle thieves?'

'Naturally I do want to talk to you about that, but something more urgent has come up just now. There's been a murder. I want everyone to attend a briefing.'

Tim was surprised that the Superintendent, usually cautious to a fault, was so quickly prepared to categorise a newly-discovered crime as murder. It was normal police practice to describe non-natural deaths as 'unexplained' or 'suspicious', at least until Forensics had done their work.

'A murder! Are we sure it's a murder, sir, or at this stage are we just looking at a suspicious death?'

Superintendent Thornton glowered at him.

"We' are quite certain it's a murder, Yates, unless you think that a suicide is capable of cutting off her own head and secreting it somewhere.'

'You mean that a headless corpse has been discovered?'

'That's precisely what I mean. Do you think it's rash of me to conclude that the poor woman's been murdered?'

'I... No. Where was she found?'

'Floating in the Fossdyke Canal.'

'But that's not on our patch.'

'I know that, Yates. But North Lincs have asked us to help if we can. Just to keep a watching brief at first and then see if we can throw light on any of the evidence, when they've gathered as much as they can. We might be able to help them to identify the woman, for example. It's not unheard of for people to travel from South to North Lincolnshire, is it?'

Tim ignored the question. 'They're quite sure it's a woman?'

'I believe so. There was considerable mutilation to the body, but the sexual organs were identifiable.'

'Sounds nasty.'

'It *is* nasty, Yates, very nasty. But there's no point in my standing here telling you what I know piecemeal. Michael Robinson's here from Lincoln to brief us. We've just been waiting for you and MacFadyen to return before we begin. Michael needs to get back to Lincoln as soon as he can.'

Tim's hackles rose slightly. He and DI Michael Robinson were exact contemporaries and had attended several police courses and conferences together. Michael was popular with most of his colleagues and had certainly managed to ingratiate himself with the top brass: Tim had no doubt that a glittering future lay ahead of him, one that would far outstrip Tim's own. Personally, Tim found Robinson both arrogant and patronising; worse than that, he'd noticed Robinson grabbed the credit for other people's good ideas and hard work whenever he could, though no one else seemed to have rumbled him. Sly bastard.

Tim followed Superintendent Thornton to the briefing room. Ricky MacFadyen slipped in after them, clutching a mug of coffee, just before Thornton closed the door. Most of their colleagues were already seated, talking quietly to each other as they waited. Tim was a little irked to see DS Juliet Armstrong standing at the front of the room, earnestly talking to DI Robinson. Surely she didn't like that twat?

Juliet glanced across at Tim and smiled before taking a seat in the front row. Following her gaze, Michael Robinson also saw him and came bustling down the room to greet him. As he drew level with Tim, he extended a large hand. Reluctantly, Tim held out his own hand to have it crushed too warmly for rather too many seconds.

'Good to see you, Timmo,' Robinson boomed. He had a square, pinkish face and dirty blond hair. Tim was a little over six feet tall, but still he had to look up to meet Robinson's eye. He squirmed inwardly at the nickname that Robinson had just invented.

'Good to see you, too, Mike. It must be at least a year since we last met.'

'Very probably – I don't remember. Dennis has been telling me about your problems with the vehicle thefts. Just give us a shout if you like. Two heads are better than one!'

Tim bridled visibly. He'd worked for Superintendent Thornton for almost seven years and never yet been invited to call him by his first name. Pointedly he looked across at Thornton, still hovering beside them, and raised an eyebrow, but his boss was beaming like a schoolmaster supervising two prize pupils. Whether or not he had permitted Robinson to call him 'Dennis', he clearly didn't resent the familiarity.

'I rather thought you were here so we could help *you*,' said Tim stiffly.

'What? Oh, yes. Never leave a stone unturned in a murder case, I always say. Or any serious crime, for that matter.'

'Quite so,' murmured Thornton, glaring at Tim.

'Well, let's get on with it, shall we? You'll need to get back to Lincoln double quick.'

'Considerate as ever, I see,' Robinson replied levelly. 'Right you are, then.'

He turned on his heel and strode back up to the front of the room. Superintendent Thornton followed in his wake and took the seat next to Juliet. Tim preferred to remain standing at the back.

Michael Robinson evidently intended to run the briefing like a tutorial. He paced up and down in front of the white board, waving a marker pen as he spoke.

'Good morning, everyone. Feel free to interrupt me if anything I say isn't clear. How many of you know the Fossdyke Canal?'

Andy Carstairs raised a hand as if he were indeed a student in class. Robinson waved the marker pen at him by way of encouragement.

'I used to go there as a kid. It's a kind of tourist spot. I think its proper name is the Fossdyke Navigation.'

For a moment DI Robinson looked disconcerted. Tim smirked. That would teach the didactic bastard.

'Quite right, though locally it's usually called the Fossdyke Canal, or just the Fossdyke. Originally it was built by the Romans, so it's an important part of Lincoln's heritage. It's been used commercially on and off to transport goods for the last two thousand years. It joins the River Trent to the High Bridge in Lincoln.'

Robinson flicked a switch and turned on the projector that

was mounted in the ceiling. A faint image appeared on the grey-painted wall.

'Oh dear,' he said, 'that doesn't show up very clearly, does it?'

'It'll work better if the blinds are down,' said Superintendent Thornton. 'DI Yates, would you do the honours?'

Tim took his time to saunter across to the rear window and press the switch that lowered the blind. Juliet got up to deal with the other window. Tim gave her a nod and a grateful thumbs-up.

'Cheers!' said Robinson. 'That's much better. Now, as you can see, there's a long stretch of towpath – about six miles of it – running from Lincoln to Saxilby.'

The image was much clearer now. It showed a map of the canal. The stretch of towpath to which Robinson had just referred was marked, together with some lock gates and a pub. It was a simple sketch map of the kind reproduced in tourist handbooks, rather than the more elaborate Ordnance Survey version. A red cross had been placed about halfway along it.

'The body was found just here,' Robinson continued, stabbing at the cross with his marker pen.

'When was it found, sir?' The question came from Giash Chakrabati. Robinson shot him an irritated look.

'I was just coming to that. The body was discovered yesterday afternoon, at 14.23, to be precise, by a cyclist who'd stopped for a break. He noticed what appeared to be a bundle of rags near the bank. When he'd taken a closer look, he cycled back to a fisherman he'd passed earlier to ask him to help. They raked the bundle in to the bank with the fisherman's gaff and managed to haul it out of the water. It was the headless body of a woman. As you can imagine, both were deeply shocked.'

'Do you know how long she'd been in the water?' Juliet asked.

'The body's still with the pathologist. He may be able to tell us more exactly, but his first impression is less than a week.'

'And the head?' said Tim. He was intrigued now and couldn't help getting involved. 'Is there any possibility that it's also in the canal?'

Robinson rolled the marker pen in his palm and appraised Tim for rather too long.

'Obviously there are frogmen searching the canal, and we'll arrange to have it dragged, too. But we don't have the head yet. I wouldn't have forgotten to mention it if we'd found it, DI Yates!'

A murmur of laughter rippled round the room. Tim flushed and gave Robinson a curt nod to acknowledge his reply. It was galling to hear his colleagues respond to Robinson's mockery, even though he knew that any light-hearted quip was always welcome to relieve the tension in a murder briefing. He'd often injected some humour into his own briefings; just not at someone else's expense, like that clever sod.

Juliet cleared her throat. Robinson looked across at her and immediately became serious again.

'Did you want to say something, DS Armstrong?' He was almost deferential.

'I was wondering... how was she decapitated? Can you tell what kind of implement was used?'

'That's a good question, with unfortunately a not very pretty answer. It wasn't a clean cut by any means. Again, we have to wait for Forensics to be more accurate, but first impressions are that it was hacked off quite roughly with a fairly crude instrument. Not something like a chainsaw, in other words; more probably, a knife or a hatchet. The murderer had several goes at it before he – or she, but not many women would have had the strength – succeeded.'

Juliet shuddered.

'Was the head cut off post mortem?'

'Probably. But at this stage I can't say for certain. Judging from the other wounds on the torso, I think it's likely she was already dead.'

'The body was clothed?' It was Andy Carstairs speaking. 'Yes. Fully clothed. She was wearing denim jeans and a long-sleeved shirt. And a short jacket. Her underwear didn't appear to have been disturbed. Of reasonable quality, but all chain store clothes. As such, hard to trace, of course. Only her shoes were missing.'

'Anything in the pockets? Anything at all that might help to identify her?' Andy continued.

'No, nothing. No keys, purse, mobile phone, anything like that; not even some loose change; and no handbag, though that might still be in the canal.'

'Any idea about her age?' Tim risked another question.

'Obviously it's more difficult to estimate her age when we don't have the head. Forensics should be able to help with that, too. Our best guess is that she was a young woman, not a teenager. Perhaps not more than twenty-five. Fairly slight build, though that doesn't help to guess her age.'

'Was she white?' Giash Chakrabati asked.

'Yes. Sorry, I should have mentioned that.'

'Have any young women been reported missing on your patch?' Tim again.

'No, not recently; and none on yours, either, according to Den... Superintendent Thornton.'

'I take it you haven't talked to the Press yet?' The Superintendent seized the mention of his name as his cue to butt in. Typical question from him, thought Tim: dealing with the media was never far from uppermost in his mind.

'No, but we're going to have to issue a bulletin soon. To tell you the truth, I'd really appreciate some advice on how to draft it,' Robinson said, with what Tim considered to be uncharacteristic humility. 'I usually try not to give too much away, but I probably can't avoid mentioning that the corpse is headless. We can't provide a proper description of the victim, for a start. But it's tricky: I don't want to create sensationalist headlines for the gutter press.'

'Quite so. I take your point.' Superintendent Thornton said unctuously. 'DS Armstrong is our expert on press releases. I'm sure she'll be happy to help you. If the briefing's over, you can use my office.'

'I think that's all I have to tell you for now,' said DI Robinson, putting down the marker pen. 'Thank you very much, everyone, for paying attention. I'll keep Superintendent Thornton posted as I learn more, of course.'

'In the meantime, keep your eyes peeled,' said the Superintendent severely to the room in general, himself catching as many eyes as he could as his team prepared to pack up and leave. 'Don't forget that anything suspicious, however small, that you happen to hear or see could help DI Robinson to solve this case.'

'Such as finding a head in a bag,' Tim heard one of the PCs mutter as he left the room. Despite himself, Tim couldn't help another smirk.

CHAPTER NINE

Juliet glanced at her watch as she and Michael Robinson toiled at the seventh draft of his statement for the press. It was almost 3pm and she needed to get away by 4 o'clock. She'd started work very early that morning to compensate for leaving early – not that Tim or Superintendent Thornton would ever have demanded this of her: in common with all her colleagues, she often put in twelve- or fourteen-hour days. But Juliet would have felt uncomfortable working a short day, as if she were cheating.

Robinson was sitting claustrophobically close to her. She could smell his (expensive) deodorant, which didn't quite conceal the tang of fresh sweat. Perhaps he'd been more nervous than he had appeared at the briefing. Juliet had met him only a few times. She knew Tim disliked him, but also that Superintendent Thornton went out of his way to shower him with praise, and suspected that the two circumstances were not unconnected. She had yet to form her own opinion of Robinson. He was quite unlike Tim, that was for sure, both in attitude and the way he went about things. There was a decided slickness about the way he talked which contrasted with his slow and meticulous take on practical detail. Juliet was aware that her own painstaking way of doing things was a good foil for Tim's more quixotic approach, but even she was beginning to feel exasperated as Robinson continued to chew over every word in the statement. For God's sake, she wanted to shout, how controversial can a preposition be?

She looked at her watch again. This time Robinson noticed. He pushed his yellow fringe out of his eyes and gave his forehead a rub.

'I'm sorry, am I keeping you from something?' He sounded affronted.

'Not really,' said Juliet. Then she changed her mind: she'd spent too many years of her working life suffering from her own politeness. 'I mean, not yet,' she added. 'But I do have to get away by four.'

'Something to do with this machinery theft muddle of Timmo's?'

Juliet bridled a little. Tim could – often did – irritate her, but she knew he was very worried about these crimes and had been working overtime for months to try to solve them.

'No, nothing to do with work. It's a personal matter.'

'Oh, hot date, then?'

'Not that either,' said Juliet, flushing. Robinson was nearer the truth than he guessed, but she had no intention of enlightening him. 'Shall we have another go at this? Perhaps start again from scratch?'

'Good idea. Look, I'm sorry this is taking so long. I'm no good with words – not written ones, anyway. Spoken word's okay: I'm told that I've mastered the gift of the gab.' He grinned like a schoolboy.

Juliet managed a weak smile in return. Correction, she thought to herself, he was like Tim in one respect: he knew when he'd overstepped the mark and wasn't above a bit of self-deprecation to make amends. She turned back to the computer screen and banged out a fresh couple of paragraphs, Robinson watching intently as the words appeared on the screen.

'You've cracked it! That one's perfect!'

Juliet quickly erased from her face an expression of disbelief. She certainly didn't want to indicate that she had anything less than full confidence in what she'd written, but she knew that, word for word, the statement was virtually identical to the first one she'd drafted two hours previously.

'Great! I knew we'd get there in the end,' she said, standing up. 'If you'll excuse me, I'd like to catch up with Tim again before I leave.'

'Sure,' he said, 'and thank you, Juliet – much appreciated.'

'My pleasure,' she responded, as she made for the door. She was almost through it when he called after her. 'I hope you enjoy yourself! If you can't be good, be careful!'

She flicked a quick look of contempt over her shoulder. Unrepentantly, DI Robinson winked.

CHAPTER TEN

Superintendent Thornton instantly regretted his generosity in lending his office to DI Robinson. As soon as he had received the complaints from the Lord Lieutenant and the Chief Constable he'd resolved to distance himself from DI Yates as much as he could, in case the whole damned farm vehicle thing blew up into a row. If someone's head was going to roll, he'd do his best to make sure it wasn't his own. He'd therefore have preferred it if he'd been sitting behind his own desk preserving an official gulf between them when considering Tim's revised plan of action. As it was, he was obliged to sit alongside Tim in the open-plan area in a manner which, from his present perspective, might be considered overly egalitarian.

Tim sensed his mood and became correspondingly deferential.

'Should I begin, sir?'

'Well, I'm not sitting here for the good of my health,' Thornton snapped.

Tim swallowed.

'Picking up on what we said yesterday, we can find no pattern to the vehicle thefts, in terms of location, the types of machinery stolen – except that more quads have disappeared than any other kind of vehicle – or victims. As you know, sir, some of the victims have been quite wealthy farmers, others just small-holders or amateur gardeners who use quads when working on their allotments.'

'The last lot are just boys playing with expensive toys, if you ask me,' Superintendent Thornton commented severely.

'I'm inclined to agree, sir,' said Tim carefully, 'or girls, in some cases. But that doesn't make those thefts any less culpable.'

'You don't need to tell me that,' said Thornton belligerently. 'Carry on.'

'I've been thinking of the cases of car theft I've had to deal with over the years. I'd say there are four broad groups: kids twocking for kicks, who will as often as not set fire to the vehicle after a joy ride, criminals, who steal cars to commit specific crimes and then abandon them, and then what you might call the professionals: two kinds of organised gang, the ones who disguise stolen cars, often of the same marque, by respraying, removing engine serial numbers, etc. and sell them on; and those who steal to order, for prearranged clients. We can forget about the first group: these crimes are not being committed by kids; not a single one of the vehicles has been found, either intact or burnt out. Theft to support crime is unlikely – I can't think of a more conspicuous or inept getaway vehicle than a quad, unless it's a tractor. That leaves the two more organised types. Given the wide geographical spread of the thefts, I think that stealing to order is more likely than stealing for resale to punters.'

'In other words, you don't think the criminals are using a makeover garage or some kind of remodelling facility?'

'No. It's more likely that the stuff is being nicked to order and moved out of the county quickly, perhaps to somewhere else in the UK, perhaps abroad.'

Superintendent Thornton spent a few moments letting Tim's ideas sink in. He'd converted his supercilious air to something approaching enthusiasm.

'Okay. Well, assuming you're right about all this, Yates – and I suppose your hypotheses are as good as any – who are the culprits? That's what I want to know. No more beating about the bush.'

'If I could tell you that with certainty, we wouldn't be sitting here talking about them. If you're asking whether I can come up with some names of suspects, the answer, unfortunately, is no. But I've thought a lot about generic suspects...'

'"Generic suspects", Yates? What are they?'

'I mean, the kinds of background the suspects are likely to come from. The more I think about it, the more likely I believe it is that they are travellers...'

'Not very original, that, is it, Yates? Most coppers latch on to the travelling community when they're casting around for someone to blame. And you'll have to tread carefully: as you're aware, Romanies are quite respected in this area. They've been working on the land here for a long time.'

'I'd say there was a world of difference between the kind of Romanies you're talking about and some of the travelling families who pass through here. But hear me out: if my theory that we're looking for a small organised gang operating a much larger web of thieves is correct, travellers would fit the profile exactly. They keep on the move, so are hard to pin down, and have a huge network of contacts, both of other travellers and others who work with them as they're passing through.'

'Are you aware of any travelling families 'passing through', as you put it?'

'I hadn't been until yesterday, when Ricky MacFadyen said that the man who attacked him and Jack Fovargue was probably a traveller. Which reminds me, when Ricky and I visited

Fovargue's place today, I saw a purple quad disappearing into the distance.'

'How is that significant, Yates? Are any of the missing quads purple?'

'Certainly none when they were stolen – and I didn't really think this was one of the stolen vehicles. What did strike me was the size of the enterprise Fovargue runs out there. He has fingers in all sorts of pies and it's quite a slick operation. He can't have been short of cash when he set it all up.'

'Pillar of society, though, isn't he, Yates? A lover of the Earth, local philanthropist and all that?'

'So we've been told.'

'How did your interview with him go?'

'He was out, according to his wife, though we had a suspicion that he was hiding in the house and had told her to say so.'

'Why would he do that?'

'I don't know, but yesterday, as you are aware, he was very reluctant to discuss the incident in Red Lion Street. It was almost as if he was afraid of something.'

'You're arranging to go back, make an appointment or something?'

'Yes. I've asked him to call me before the end of the day. If he doesn't, we'll call him. I'd like permission to investigate all his activities while I'm there, sir.'

'Are you asking me for a warrant?'

'I suppose I am.'

'Well, the answer is no, Yates, at least not on this first occasion. You may ask him to show you round, if you like, and see whether he co-operates. But don't lose sight of the fact that, first and foremost, you're visiting him as the victim of a crime. You'll have to keep that entirely separate from any other investigations you may see fit to pursue. Otherwise, he might have grounds for complaint.'

Tim tried not to sigh.

'And we appear to have got a bit sidetracked, don't we, Yates? Since I assume you're not suggesting that Fovargue is the mastermind of this network you've conjured up, I advise you to deal with him as quickly as possible and get back to focusing on the job in hand.'

CHAPTER ELEVEN

Juliet closed the door of her flat behind her and leaned against it for several seconds. It was only a few minutes past four – she still had plenty of time. There had been moments during the course of the afternoon when she'd believed that she'd never get away from the station, but finally she'd pulled it off. She should have been feeling elated. Instead, her mood was downbeat, both sad and apprehensive. She couldn't explain why, except that the unsavoury details that DI Robinson had disclosed about the headless corpse had depressed her, while writing his interminable press release had left her inexpressibly weary. She'd have given anything for a long, hot bath followed by a lazy evening on the sofa, curled up with a book and a gin and tonic.

She gave herself a stern shake and began rapidly to peel off her clothes, chiding herself for her own contrariness. For months she'd been lamenting her lack of a social life; now she had a date, all she could do was hanker after an evening by herself. She deserved to be lonely.

Briskly, she gathered up the bundle of discarded clothes and took them with her into the bathroom, dropping all but the trousers and sweater into the laundry basket. She turned the shower to the hottest setting she could bear and stood under the pulsing jet of water for several long minutes, exorcising the filth of the murder. When she finally stepped out she felt cleaner and wider awake, but knowing that she'd had no success in banishing the subdued mood.

Although she was wearing her hair shorter these days, her mass of thick, dark curls was still unruly and hard to dry. She was rubbing it vigorously with a towel when the doorbell rang. Panicking slightly, she peered at her watch, which she'd left on the side of the hand basin. It said four thirty-five: he wouldn't be there for another twenty-five minutes. She'd specifically told him not to come early. Deciding to ignore the caller, she wound the towel round her head turban-style and padded from the bathroom to her bedroom.

She dropped the towel on to a chair and began to drag a comb through her wet hair. She was sitting on the spindly stool that faced her wardrobe unit, a streamlined piece of Scandinavian furniture combining cupboards, shelves and a mirror which ran almost the full length of the stud wall. Hearing a slight sound, she turned to look at the window. A shock jolted through her. She screamed. Immediately, the face and upper body of the boy who had been peering at her through the glass receded. She could hear his footsteps as he ran away.

She scrabbled in the drawers for underwear, struggling into her bra and pants as quickly as she could, and pulled on a sweater and some jeans. She was barely dressed when there came a banging at her door.

'Juliet! Is everything all right in there?'

She recognised the voice of Alice Buck, the woman who lived in the flat opposite hers. She'd been ashamed of the scream immediately it had escaped from her lips. The last thing she wanted was to have to explain it to someone else. However, she knew that Mrs Buck, who was both nosy and well-meaning, wouldn't give up until she'd answered. Admirable, really, she supposed.

Barefoot, she flung open the door, still feeling a little shaky. Alice Buck was a big woman in her sixties with an old-fashioned reluctance to wear 'good' clothes at home. She was also an enthusiastic smoker. She was standing on Juliet's doormat, a fag held poised in the fingers of her right hand, while with her left she hitched up a pair of ancient brown trousers made of some clingy synthetic material that delineated her generous contours with cruel precision.

'You all right, ducky? I thought I heard you calling for help.'

'I'm fine, thanks,' said Juliet stiffly. 'I thought I saw someone staring at me through the window, but I could have been mistaken.'

'Not been on the bottle, have you?' Alice cackled at her own joke.

'No, of course not.'

'You was probably right, then,' said Alice, more serious now. 'I've seen one or two weird people hanging round here just lately.'

'What sort of people?'

'Oh, I don't know: didis, probably. Mostly young lads, with one or two older blokes. Could have been casing the flats. I wish them joy if they break into mine.'

'Why's that?' Juliet asked dutifully, knowing this was expected of her.

'Nothing worth pinching!' Alice replied triumphantly. 'Not even a decent telly! Sometimes it pays to be poor.'

'Well, let me know if you see any of them again.'

'I will do, duck. Going to report it to the police, are you?'

. . .

Alice Buck had just taken a long draw on her cigarette. Now her laughter at another joke even wittier than her first spluttered into a paroxysm of coughing.

'Are you okay?' said Juliet anxiously.

'Yes. Don't mind me. I should have given up the fags years ago. Still, there has to be some pleasures in life, doesn't there? I'll push off now. I just come to check that you was okay yourself.'

'Thank you. I...'

Over Mrs Buck's shoulder, Juliet caught sight of a tall bearded figure coming up the steps. He noticed her at the same moment.

'Oh, God!' Juliet breathed, painfully aware of her bare feet, unmade-up face and, above all, the tangle of semi-dry hair that was beginning to frizz out in a halo around her head.

Mrs Buck turned round and took the measure of Juliet's visitor. She scrutinised every inch of him, from his brown suede boots to his beard and long, wavy hair.

'Well, I can see you've got company, so I'll push off now,' she said. She grinned at the man and disappeared into her own flat.

'Hello, Juliet. It's great to see you. Is everything all right?'

'Hi,' Juliet responded, trying to inject some warmth into her voice. 'I'm sorry I'm not quite ready yet. I've had a bit of a setback. It won't take me too long, though, if I can just get my hair to dry. Do you want to come in?'

Jake Fidler smiled uncertainly.

'Well, yes, if you don't mind.'

CHAPTER TWELVE

Tim and Ricky were at Silverdale Farm again, again waiting for someone to answer the door. To Tim's surprise, Fovargue had called him late the previous afternoon and suggested they might like to return the next morning. He'd even apologised for their earlier wasted journey.

Despite this promise of co-operation, they now found themselves facing a closed front door. They had been standing on the wrong side of it for quite a while. Tim had just pushed the bell for the third time.

'He'd better not be having us on,' he muttered to Ricky, leaning on the button for a good thirty seconds. 'If we don't get anywhere this time I shall lose patience.'

As if on cue, someone called out 'Just a minute!' and began, by degrees, to jerk open the door, which appeared to be sticking. Gradually Jack Fovargue's compact figure was revealed.

'Good morning! DI Yates, I take it?' He advanced a few steps and held out his hand, which Tim shook briefly. As his wife had yesterday, he chose to ignore Ricky.

'Yes, DI Tim Yates, South Lincs police. DC MacFadyen you know already.'

Fovargue mimed a startled double-take as if he'd only just noticed Ricky. He held out his hand again.

'My guardian angel!' he said, chuckling. 'I must thank you. I'm sorry you got caught up in all that. Not too much damage done, I hope?'

'No,' said Ricky, 'just a bit of a sore face, that's all. How are you yourself, sir? You took more of a pasting than I did.'

'Right as a trivet.' Fovargue laughed again. 'I told you I would be. It takes more than a drunken lout to get the better of me. But you'd better come in, both of you. Don't stand there on the step.'

He made a waving gesture over one shoulder and stood back to let them past him.

They found themselves in a large square kitchen. Although it was quite a warm day, the wood-burning stove, set in what looked like the recess originally created for a kitchen range, had been lit and was chucking out heat. Fovargue pointed to the shabby but comfortable-looking sofa that stood in front of it. 'Take a seat near the stove. I love the old house, but most days it's chilly inside these thick walls.'

Fat beads of perspiration were already appearing on Ricky's forehead. As yet, Tim himself felt no discomfort, but he knew that shortly the heat would become oppressive. Both policemen sat down on the sofa as directed. As Tim was hoping they would get the interview over with quickly, it dawned on him that this was probably the same result that Fovargue's overbearing hospitality was intended to achieve.

'Well,' said Fovargue, as if they were complete strangers who'd wandered in on him by mistake. 'What can I do for you?'

'I'm sure you know why we're here, Mr Fovargue,' Tim said, injecting as much warmth into his voice as he could. 'It's about the assault on you and DC MacFadyen two days ago. As I told your wife yesterday.'

'I'm truly grateful for your concern,' said Fovargue, his expression so open and guileless that it seemed unquestionably genuine. 'And so is my wife. But I think I had already mentioned to... er... DC MacFadyen... that I don't wish to press charges. Being set upon by a young hothead is not a pleasant experience, but I'm a busy man. I don't want the distraction of having to take this further. I'm sure you will understand.'

'Whether or not I understand your reasoning is immaterial, sir. The fact is that a police officer was also assaulted during the affray. Even if you don't want to press charges, that can't be ignored. As my boss has very forcefully pointed out.'

'Oh, dear,' said Fovargue. 'We are in the soup, then, aren't we?' The comment seemed strangely flippant.

'I don't know what you mean by that, sir. Let's just start at the beginning, shall we? Did you know your assailant?'

'No, never seen him before in my life.'

'Okay. What were you doing in Spalding that morning?'

'I'd been to the information centre at Springfields, to settle the final details about some soil appreciation courses I'm doing there. I made a detour to Red Lion Street because I wanted to book a meal for myself and my wife. She's very keen on the Indian restaurant there.'

'I see. So you were just walking along the street minding your own business?'

'Precisely that, yes.'

'What time of day was it?'

'I think it was getting on for one o'clock. DC MacFadyen can probably verify? He turned up a few minutes later.'

Ricky nodded at Tim. Tim didn't show it, but he was annoyed. Ricky's alacrity in confirming Fovargue's story almost felt like a betrayal.

'Tell us what happened next. In as much detail as you can

remember, sir. For example, did your attacker jump you from behind or did he meet you head on?'

'He... I think he was passing me on the pavement and jolted in to me as he went by. Then he started swearing and told me to look where I was going. I said there was no need for that kind of language, we'd both misjudged the narrowness of the pavement. Then he suddenly socked me one. I had no idea it was coming.'

'You retaliated?'

'I'm a peaceable man, DI Yates. I disapprove of physical violence. But yes, of course I retaliated, when some bloke had just jumped me for no good reason. What would you have done?'

'Probably much the same as you did, sir, but I'm not the one who's making the statement. I understand that a 'proper' fight ensued, with both of you lashing out at each other. Would you agree that's a fair representation of the facts?'

'I suppose so. To be entirely honest with you, I'm a bit vague about the sequence of events after he first laid into me.'

'What's the next thing you can remember clearly?'

'Being escorted into the hospital by the paramedic.'

Tim's inner sardonic smile tickled into life. Fovargue would say that, of course.

'Are you saying you can't recall the details of the fight?'

'No, I'm afraid not. Sorry.'

'For how many minutes would you say you had been fighting when DC MacFadyen arrived and broke it up?'

'Not all that long. Perhaps for two or three minutes, maybe even less. I was aware that people were stopping to watch. It was embarrassing.' Tim noted that although Fovargue claimed to be unable to describe his attacker he could perfectly recall his reaction to the onlookers.

'Indeed, I can imagine. According to DC MacFadyen, he pitched in and pulled your attacker off you. Thwarted of the opportunity to carry on hammering you, the man socked it to DC MacFadyen instead. Is that right?'

Fovargue shrugged.

'I was feeling pretty disorientated by that stage. If that's what DC MacFadyen says, I have no reason to disbelieve him.'

'Quite.' Tim shot a sidelong glance at Ricky. Normally, DC MacFadyen was placid to the point of inertia, but at present he was looking extremely riled. Tim threw him a quick smile, encouraging him to humour Fovargue.

'And the attacker?' Tim continued.

'Sorry... what do you mean?'

'Your attacker. Can we have a description?'

'I've already told you – I didn't know him.'

'Yes, you have, Mr Fovargue, and I'm sure you're telling the truth.' Tim gave Fovargue a straight look, which was returned unflinchingly. 'But you must have noticed what he looked like: he got much too close to you for comfort. How would you describe him?'

Fovargue was silent for a few seconds.

'I think he was a biker,' he said at last.

'A biker?'

'Yes. There have been several gangs of them in the area recently. I'm sure you police must know about them,' Fovargue added smoothly.

'We're alerted to all sorts of things, Mr Fovargue. What intrigues me now is why you think he was a biker. Did you see him with a motorbike?'

'No, but he struck me as the type...'

'Was he wearing or carrying a helmet?'

'I'm not sure. No, I don't think so.'

'In DC MacFadyen's own statement, he notes you said you thought the man could have been a traveller. He agrees that was a reasonable assumption on your part.'

'That may have been my original view. I've had time to think about it since.'

'But you're unable to provide a detailed description of what he looked like?'

'I'm afraid so.' Jack Fovargue shrugged and smiled apologetically. Tim decided to change tack.

'It's disappointing that you can't remember what happened more clearly. Thank you for your time, anyway, sir. As you see, DC MacFadyen has been taking notes. Perhaps you'd like to look over the statement and sign it if you agree it's correct?'

'Certainly. Will that be all?'

'Not quite,' said Tim. 'I take it that all the outbuildings beyond the house are yours?'

'Yes. I run several businesses from here, as I believe Susie told you.'

'Yes, she did. It all sounds fascinating. She told us you more or less fell into the second-hand farm machinery business by accident.'

'I prefer to call it a vintage tools business. But yes, I started it when someone asked me to source an authentic '30s horse-plough.'

'How many businesses do you have altogether?'

'Four. They're not all run entirely separately. I started by growing organic vegetables to sell. That's why I bought the house and the land that came with it – you'll have noticed there's quite a lot of land. Then I got involved with societies dedicated to protecting the soil – some of them international. I don't know how interested you are in farming, DI Yates?'

'I'm not an expert, but I guess everyone who works in South Lincolnshire has picked up some farming knowledge.'

'You're probably aware, then, that although the soil around here is incredibly rich and fertile, the farmers don't expend much effort on looking after it properly?'

'I can't say I've given it that much thought, but I suppose I've always known the big Lincolnshire farmers farm intensively. It follows that they must use commercial fertilisers and weed-killers, that sort of thing. They probably don't see why they shouldn't: as you say, the soil is excellent: rich enough to take what they might throw at it, if I can put it like that.'

'You're right: that's a good summary of the typical big shot's attitude. But it's mistaken. Farmers can't keep on pounding away at the soil forever. Eventually it will fail. It's not just what they put on the soil that's damaging it, it's the methods they use. Farmers in Norfolk have long been losing top-soil to dust storms, after ripping up hedgerows. It hasn't happened here yet, but it will if no action is taken. That's why I set up the Silverdale Soil Appreciation Society.'

'It's mostly for children, isn't it?' said Ricky, remembering what the woman who kept the craft shop in Red Lion Street had said.

'It's for anyone who's interested. We have a range of subgroups. But we've had more success with children than adults so far, mainly because both the schools and the local scout troop have shown an interest. Susie does some of the work with children.'

'Do the children come here?'

'Occasionally. One of the barns is laid out with seats and we keep the equipment we've invented to show what's happening to the soil in there. But mostly we take the stuff out with us and go to see them. Silverdale's too remote to attract many visitors.'

'So, there's the organic farming, the vintage vehicles business and the soil appreciation stuff. But you said there are four businesses?'

'There's also the tankers.'

'What are they for?'

'We own a couple of sewage tankers. We empty cesspits,

both domestic and commercial ones: there are still a surprising number in South Lincolnshire. It's actually the most profitable of the businesses, but that's not why I started it...'

'Let me guess,' said Tim. 'It was because other tanker companies were damaging the environment with chemicals.'

'You got it. Why are you so interested in the businesses?'

'You probably know there's been an outbreak of theft of agricultural vehicles over the past few months. It's been reported on local television and in the papers. Actually, *outbreak*'s putting it mildly: it's been more like an epidemic.'

'Yes, I've read about it: some of the farming bigwigs have been banging their drums, haven't they? Tough for you. But I don't see what it has to do with me.'

'I'm not suggesting it does have anything to do with you, directly. But since your activities all relate to farming, I wondered if maybe you've seen or heard anything that might help us?'

'Not that I can think of. The farm machinery I deal in is all antique. Thirty years old, at least.'

'I understand that. But this is a big property and, presumably, you have quite a few staff?'

'The workforce varies, depending on the time of year. Sometimes there are up to thirty people on the payroll; in the winter, maybe half that. Josh Marriott sees to it all. He's my farm manager. But I still don't understand what you're driving at. And we keep a tight ship here. Josh would know if there was anything underhand going on.' Fovargue succeeded in keeping his tone smooth, his voice well-modulated, but Tim noticed he'd begun to clench and unclench his hands.

'We're not singling you out, Mr Fovargue. We've been systematically making enquiries throughout the county. As you've pointed out, so far we've drawn a blank. A property like this would be ideal for temporarily concealing stolen goods in transit, but I'm not suggesting for a moment that's what's happening. Silverdale Farm's not exactly at the top of our list of suspects. But I thought I saw a purple quad on the Fen when we visited yesterday, which set me thinking. Probably it didn't mean anything at all and, as far as we know, none of the missing quads is purple. I mentioned it to your wife: she may have told you.'

'No, she didn't, but Susie's not your woman when it comes to vehicles. She's not interested in them, other than knowing whether they'll provide a means of getting from A to B. But you're sure it was a purple quad? It seems unlikely. We do own a quad here, but it's army surplus. Khaki, in other words.'

'Perhaps that was it, then,' said Tim. 'I could have been mistaken about the colour. In any case, we'd like your permission to take a look round the whole property. Just as a routine check. We can get a warrant if you prefer it.'

'Absolutely no need for that. I'd be delighted to show you round.'

Fovargue's next action belied his words. He suddenly seemed startled and made a show of consulting his watch.

'Christ, is that the time? But we can't do it now, I'm afraid. I should have left ten minutes ago: I'm going to be late for my next meeting now. Can you come back tomorrow? In the meantime, I'll line Josh up, tell him that you're coming. He'll be better at explaining how it all works than I am and he knows all the people working here, if you want to ask him about any of them.'

'Yes, we can come tomorrow,' said Tim, 'but we'd appreciate it if you'd take the time to read and sign the statement now. While your words are still fresh in your mind.'

Jack Fovargue held out his hand impatiently for the written statement Ricky was offering him and cursorily speed-read the whole two pages in a few seconds. He grabbed a pen from the table and scrawled a signature at the bottom of the second page.

'There you are,' he said. 'Good luck with your investigations. Now I really must show you out. Sorry to be so abrupt.'

CHAPTER THIRTEEN

The day had been relatively warm for the time of year, but it had rained in the afternoon and as evening approached, the mist had begun to rise from the damp earth, curling along the roads and settling in ghostly ribbons a few feet off the ground. The short bus journey was unpleasant: obliged to stand, she'd been hemmed in by a man in a filthy donkey jacket to her left and a mean-looking teenage boy who exuded BO to her right. The floor of the bus was wet with the rain that had dripped from half-closed umbrellas. Everyone was ill-tempered: each time the vehicle stopped, departing passengers pushed and shoved their way to the exit door, while new ones crammed in at the front, flashing passes at the driver and elbowing their way into whatever spaces they could find.

Bored and tired, she gazed disconsolately out of the rear window, peering into the night. A car was crawling along behind the bus. She'd first noticed it a few stops before. Each time the bus shuddered to a halt, the car stopped, too. It was odd that the driver didn't want to overtake. She couldn't see him clearly, but she could tell he wasn't an old man. Yet even Feliks didn't drive as cautiously as that.

Thinking of Feliks shook her out of her daydream. She hadn't been paying proper attention to the landmarks as they passed, or even playing her usual game of counting the numbers of stops before she reached hers. Now she could see that the bus was heading for open country, which must mean that she should have got off at the last stop. Feliks would have been sitting there in the lay-by, waiting for her. He'd have been worried when she didn't appear. She was impatient to call him, ask him to wait, tell him she'd get off the bus as soon as she could and walk back to him, but both her arms were pinioned, squashed into contorted positions by her fellow passengers. There was no chance she'd be able to remove the phone from her bag and talk to Feliks. She decided she'd get off the bus anyway: there was no point in travelling miles out of her way. If Feliks had already gone home, he wouldn't mind returning to the lay-by to fetch her.

Shaking free her right arm, she managed to stretch out far enough to ring the bell. Immediately, the driver stamped on the brake, throwing all those standing off balance.

'Fucking hell!' said the man in the donkey jacket, giving her a filthy look. Several others were glaring at her, too. Flushed with shame, she squeezed her way under the arms gripping the hanging straps and stepped over bulky shopping bags to reach the door. As the people standing closest to it reluctantly made way for her, the driver hollered at her.

'Try that trick again, love, and you'll get the rough edge of my tongue. This is a request stop only. I need a bit more warning than a couple of fucking seconds.'

'I'm sorry.' She'd tried to call back to him, but her throat felt so constricted that she was sure he couldn't have heard her. She climbed off the bus, the doors immediately swinging shut behind her, and stood at the side of the road to watch as it lurched out of sight, a moving rectangle of bright light growing smaller and smaller until it disappeared, leaving her in darkness. Belatedly, she realised there were no street lights on this stretch of road and she didn't know how far she'd have to walk back to the lay-by. She cursed her own impulsiveness: she'd been so concerned about not upsetting Feliks that she hadn't thought about the danger of walking alone in the dark. She knew Feliks would have wanted only for her to keep safe. She scrabbled in her bag for her phone, called him and told him to look out for her along the road. Then she set off.

'Hello.' The voice made her jump. It was a man's voice, softly-spoken and well-modulated. Nevertheless, she was terrified. She looked up, appalled, and saw the car that had been following the bus. She should have noticed that it hadn't driven past her. The driver had lowered the front passenger window and was stretching across to speak to her.

'Don't be afraid. I only want to help you. It's a nasty evening, and you're looking a bit lost.'

CHAPTER FOURTEEN

Juliet climbed into Jake Fidler's emerald green Skoda hatchback. It was more than half an hour since he'd turned up on her doorstep hot on the heels of her mystery peeping Tom. In the time which had intervened, she'd settled him in her kitchen with a glass of wine while she'd retreated to the bedroom to make a fierce attack on her damp curls, discarded the jeans and jumper for cream trousers and a smart black silk blouse, and applied a very modest amount of make-up. When she'd emerged, Jake had given her an appreciative look and insisted that she spent a few minutes relaxing with a small glass of wine for herself. They had plenty of time, he'd reassured her; he was always pathologically early and was sorry he'd arrived before she was ready. He was even sorrier – and inwardly outraged, though he didn't want to spoil the evening by dwelling on it – that she'd been the victim of some warped street urchin. Jake's whole life was devoted to children and adolescents, some of them very disturbed indeed, but that didn't mean he would condone bad behaviour from them.

Juliet was feeling more relaxed now, though still a little apprehensive about how the evening might unfold.

'Nice car,' she said, as he took her jacket from her and hung it on a peg above one of the rear doors. 'Somehow I thought you'd be driving an old banger.'

'You credit me with being more altruistic than I really am,' he said. 'But if what you really mean is you're surprised I can afford it, you've got a point. My salary doesn't run to vehicles like this. I'm ashamed to have to admit to a wealthy aunt who's only too happy to help out. I need a decent car for ferrying kids about – at least, that's how I justified accepting it.'

'But it's true that you do,' said Juliet. 'You must spend half your life taking kids somewhere: to sports fixtures, or to keep doctor's and dentist's appointments.'

'Or to A & E.' Jake smiled wryly. 'Children in care seem to need more hospital visits than average.'

Jake had just been appointed the warden of the children's home in Spalding. He'd been acting warden for several months while his predecessor recovered from surgery and had only recently been given the permanent post after the latter finally decided that he didn't want to return.

'Why do you think that is?' asked Juliet. 'Is it perhaps because when a large group of children live together they take more knocks than kids who grow up in an ordinary family?'

'I suppose there may be an element of truth in that, though, professionally speaking, I'm not sure I should admit to it. We do try to recreate a home atmosphere as much as possible, and we certainly take a lot of trouble over their safety.'

'Oh, I didn't mean...'

Jake laughed.

'I know you didn't. Anyway, it's a fair point. They may get knocked about more than children living in a smaller household. Then there's self-harm. As you know, we look after quite a few disturbed kids and they're likelier than average to hurt themselves. But I think the biggest reason we take children to hospital more often than the average mum and dad is because they draw attention to themselves.'

'You mean, they pretend to be ill or injured?'

'Yep. It's a classic ploy. Either they are genuinely hurt and they make out the injury is worse than it is, or they just fake it. If one of these kids tells you he has swallowed a razor blade or says she's pushed a bead up her nose, even if you suspect they're lying, you can't afford to take the risk.'

'It seems a bit of an extreme way to get noticed. And I imagine it's followed by plenty of the wrong sort of attention, once you've rumbled them. No doubt you give them what for, for wasting everyone's time?'

'Depends on the kid. Some do it out of boredom or sheer devilry, but with others it's a plea for help. We always take a very considered view on it. If the kid's sick, we have to deal with it appropriately, nip it in the bud. Otherwise, it's a trait they'll take with them into adolescence and beyond and, believe me, it will be ten times worse by then. Some people will do anything for fame; sometimes it's confined within their own social group, but often it's more ambitious than that. Psychologists think modern serial killers may be motivated by a compulsion to be famous – or notorious, I suppose I mean. But you'll know more about that than I do.'

'I've come across that theory,' said Juliet slowly, 'but I'm not sure I believe it. Several times I've been at close quarters with a serial killer's handiwork – too close – and I'd say the sense of escalating frenzy with which they carry out each successive crime, if they're not caught, points to something more than a desire to be noticed. It's a compulsion, an urge to mutilate and degrade that far outstrips the desire to kill.'

'That in itself could be a cry for help. Perhaps they want to be caught, so that they have to stop.'

Juliet laughed.

'And you say you're not altruistic! That's the most gullible excuse I've ever heard for committing a vicious and terrifying crime!'

'I don't mean to be gullible. I just like to take an all-round view of things.'

Juliet settled back in her seat. She was beginning to enjoy herself. They talked of other things for a while. They were heading for the Cambridge Arts Theatre. Jake had been given some tickets by a friend who'd had to go away on business unexpectedly – or that was what he said when he'd called Juliet to ask her if she was interested in seeing *Travesties*. She'd been surprised – she hadn't seen Jake for almost a year – and her first instinct was to decline the invitation. But then she'd thought, why not? It was only a trip to the theatre, after all; it didn't have to go any further than that. She couldn't remember the last time she'd watched a play.

They drove in companionable silence for a while through pleasant country villages to avoid, Jake said, the horrors of the A14, until they were some eight miles from Cambridge. It was growing dark. The road was busy, and Juliet, herself a careful motorist, was watching it intently, but, she hoped, without Jake noticing. She didn't want him to think she was a bossy back seat driver. His driving was fine, but when she suddenly drew breath sharply and grabbed his arm he stamped down on the brake, causing the car following them to sound a sharp blast on its horn.

'God! What did you do that for?' he said.

'I'm sorry,' said Juliet. 'It was just that roadside shrine. It took me unawares.'

Jake peered into the murk of the bushes that edged the road.

'What roadside shrine? I can't see anything.'

'No, we've passed it now. I hadn't seen it before, but I remember reading about it. Someone's still putting flowers on it.'

'What's it for?'

'It was erected by the husband of a woman who disappeared near that spot. She got off a bus at the wrong stop and vanished. It took him quite a while to persuade the council to let him build the shrine. That's why I remember it: the story made the national papers. And we were asked to distribute some of the missing person posters. He was Polish, I think – they both were – or perhaps from another Eastern European country.'

'Maybe she just did a runner.'

'Unlikely. They were a devoted couple, apparently. And the police found traces of blood at the scene, matching her blood group. It's likely she was murdered, but they haven't managed to find a body.'

'No chance it was the husband?'

'Again unlikely. He waited for her at the right bus stop and then when she didn't show up he went home. She called him when she realised what she'd done and asked him to fetch her. A neighbour saw him hurrying out again at exactly the time he gave in his statement. The phone records stacked up, too. When he reached the stretch of road where she'd said she would be, she was nowhere to be seen. He was convinced straight away that she'd come to harm. He said she'd never have left the road when she knew he was going to meet her.'

'A sad story. Can you remember her name?'

'Not her surname. It was something unpronounceable. I think her first name was Irina. And he was called Feliks – I remember that, because it seemed so inappropriate for a man who was in perpetual mourning. Still is, if those flowers are anything to go by.'

'When did all this happen?'

'Not recently. Four or five years ago, at a guess. You know how your memory can play tricks – it could have been a bit longer than that.'

CHAPTER FIFTEEN

'**E**verything all right?' Katrin asked, after Tim had walked through the door without shouting a greeting. He turned straight into the living-room and slumped down on the sofa – she heard the thump as it shifted a little and hit the wall. She emerged from the kitchen, wiping her hands on a tea towel. Tim was sprawled on the sofa, his eyes closed.

'What's the matter? Aren't you feeling well?'

'I'm not ill. I've just had a bloody awful day.'

'What's happened?'

'Among other things, a woman's body's been found in the Fossdyke Canal.'

'That's not your problem, is it? It's on the North Lincs patch, surely?'

'It is, but of course we're all expected to co-operate. If co-operate's the right word for how that prat Michael Robinson behaves.'

'Oh, I understand what's got to you now. You don't like him, do you?'

'Do you?'

'Not especially. I don't dislike him as much as you do.'

'No, women don't seem to be able to see through him. He had Juliet eating out of his hand today.' Katrin let out a shout of laughter.

'Oh, really, Tim, is that what's at the bottom of it? Juliet wasn't giving you her undivided attention for a change?'

'You know damn well that Juliet's been able to spare me little energy since she got the DS's job. However, Thornton told her to drop everything this afternoon so that she could help Robinson draft a press release. It seems he's not up to it himself. Thornton was all over him – even let him use his office while Juliet was working with him.'

'Meaning Superintendent Thornton can't see through Michael, either?'

'So it would seem. He was almost fawning on the guy. The boot was on the other foot when it came to me. I just got a bollocking for not making any progress with the farm vehicle thefts. It seems that some smart Alec in the Essex force has offered to help out. Thornton's given me another couple of weeks to get somewhere and if I can't he's going to draft this character in to replace me on the case.'

The smile immediately faded from Katrin's face. She knew how worried Tim was about the stolen vehicles and how much effort he'd put in to trying to solve the case. It had already cost him many late evenings at work and an even larger number of sleepless nights.

'That *is* unfair.'

'Well, as we both know, life isn't fair. Let's have a drink. Gin and tonic?'

'I'll fetch them in a minute. First, tell me a bit more about the murder victim. Do you think she was local?'

'No one knows yet. For one thing, she's headless; for another, there are virtually no other clues to her identity. Her clothes were not distinctive. There was no handbag and she had no means of identification on her. And they haven't been able to find the head yet. We'll probably only have fingerprints to identify her, unless we already have her DNA on record. That'll be difficult if she doesn't have a record and no one reports her missing.'

'What do you mean, "they haven't been able to find the head"? What happened to her head?'

'I don't know what happened to it, but it certainly wasn't attached to the body. It had been hacked off, quite crudely, apparently. It could still be in the dyke. They're sending frogmen to search for it.'

'How strange...'

'You can say that again. It's the first murder case I've been involved in where the victim didn't have a head.'

'Of course that's strange, but it isn't what I meant. When I went in to the college today...'

'I'm sorry, love, I forgot all about your tutorial. How did it go?'

Katrin mainly studied for her criminology course online, via distance learning facilities, but occasionally she met other students from South Lincolnshire for a face-to-face tutorial. They met at the WEA college in Holbeach.

'Fine. I really enjoyed it. But what was strange was that we were discussing serial killers and someone mentioned the Burnley Knifeman. Do you remember the case?'

'Only vaguely. Remind me about it.'

'His name was Stephen Jenkins. He was a student at Burnley College – a bit of an eternal student, actually. I can't remember his exact age, but I think he was over thirty. He'd been a young tearaway – he was sent to a youth offenders' centre before he'd officially left school. A dead-end kid, but then his mum married a local businessman with plenty of money. The businessman set Jenkins up in a flat with an allowance, on condition that he either got a job or continued his education. Jenkins had no intention of working, so he kept on enrolling for different courses at the college. I don't know if he ever qualified for anything, but I don't suppose his stepfather cared. He just wanted to keep Jenkins out of his hair.'

'It's coming back to me now. How long ago was it?'

'When the first body was found? About six years ago. I can look it up if you're interested. He killed at least three people altogether. They were all dumped in the canal. All stabbed. The first two were local prostitutes who led such chaotic lives that they probably wouldn't have been missed. The third victim was a schoolgirl. The police theory was that either Jenkins thought she was a prostitute, too, and panicked when he realised she wasn't, or that he sexually assaulted her and then killed her to shut her up. Either way, he must have had to get rid of her body in a hurry, because she wasn't decapitated like the others. Her body was the first of the three to be found, even though the evidence shows pretty conclusively that she was the last one to be killed. Police dragged the canal, then, and that's when they found the two headless prostitutes' bodies, weighted with stones and dropped in the canal in a very remote spot. As I said, they might never have been discovered if Jenkins hadn't killed the schoolgirl and thrown her into a shallow part of the canal, almost in the town centre. She wasn't weighted down and she didn't sink.'

'How did they catch Jenkins?'

'Someone had seen him hanging around the canal – he was one of those killers that can't resist going back to the scene. The police searched his flat and found the knife, which still had on it traces of the blood of both the schoolgirl – I think her name was Tara something – and one of the prostitutes. And he'd been put in the young offenders' prison for knife crimes. He didn't even try to protest his innocence. Don't you think it's a coincidence that we should have been talking about him today, just when you were finding out about someone else who'd been decapitated?'

'I don't like coincidences,' said Tim, 'but I'm not sure that this qualifies as one. I hope not, anyway. If Michael Robinson finds other bodies in the Fossdyke, I may have to eat my words.'

'Well, it *is* interesting – and at least you've perked up a bit now.'

'I'll perk up even more if we have that gin and tonic. Do you want me to fix it?'

'No, I'll do it. You'll put too much gin in it. I always feel as if my throat's been cut when you make it.'

CHAPTER SIXTEEN

A s Tim and Ricky turned off the Fenland road and drew to a halt at the top of the track that led to Silverdale Farm and the outbuildings beyond, Josh Marriott suddenly emerged from the dense undergrowth that grew in the lea of the steep-banked dyke that abutted both road and track. As if responding to a cue, Jack Fovargue came sauntering across his ill-kept lawn to greet them all. The two men met a few feet ahead of the car in which the policemen were sitting.

Tim was watching them carefully. They appeared to exchange no words, which seemed a little odd. Fovargue caught Tim's eye and smiled, inviting them to get out of the car with the same extravagant beckoning gesture that he'd employed when he'd ushered them into his kitchen the previous day. Marriott had kept his head down until that point, but now he raised it and grinned uncertainly. Tim had seen that look on other occasions: at once shifty, suspicious and conciliatory, it spelt form as plainly as if Marriott had had 'old lag' stamped across his forehead.

'It might be worth checking Marriott out when we get back to the station,' Ricky muttered, sotto voce.

'Exactly what I was thinking. Come on, let's see what they've got to show us – and keep an eye out for anything they might be trying to hide.'

'Hello,' said Jack Fovargue, as they joined him. 'Bang on time, I see.'

'Good morning, Mr Fovargue. We do try not to keep people waiting if we can help it.'

'This is Josh Marriott,' said Fovargue with a flourish, like an impresario introducing a prize-fighter. 'Josh, this is DI Yates and... er... DC McFadden. Got to dash myself, I'm afraid. I'll leave them in your capable hands.'

As if taking the introduction literally, Marriott extended a huge beefy paw. 'Pleased to meet you,' he said.

Tim nodded and took the outstretched hand, trying not to wince as Marriott crushed his fingers. Marriott released them as suddenly as he'd grabbed them. He didn't offer to shake hands with Ricky.

'Well, I'll love you and leave you, then,' said Fovargue, who was already nimbly hot-footing it back to the house.

There was a short but awkward silence. Marriott seemed to have no inkling of how to proceed beyond the most basic of social niceties.

'It's good of you to spare the time to show us round,' Tim said at length.

'Just following orders,' said Marriott gruffly. Then, either remembering his manners or some previous instruction, he attempted another unconvincing smile. 'Where do you want to start?'

Tim shrugged.

'We're in your hands,' he said. 'We'd like to see how all the businesses operate. If you want to show us them in the order that works best for you, that'll be fine.'

'I thought you was more interested in the vehicles?'

'We're certainly interested in the vehicles. But we'd like to get an understanding of how all the businesses work together.'

'Why's that, then?'

'Mostly for routine purposes – we do our best to get a working knowledge of all the farms and businesses in our area, and we don't know much about Mr Fovargue's enterprises. But we are also concerned for his personal safety. As I'm sure you know, he was beaten up quite badly a couple of days ago. And then there's our more general concern about farm vehicle security in South Lincolnshire at present. There have been several robberies of farm machinery and other agricultural vehicles – quads, in particular. We're trying to help the owners of such vehicles tighten up on security. We wouldn't want Mr Fovargue to become the next victim.'

'Right.' It was difficult to imagine how anyone could imbue a single syllable with such a lack of conviction.

There was another pause. Marriott seemed to be engrossed in thought.

'Okay,' he said. 'I think I've got it. We'll start with the outside stuff first – the Dutch lights and the organic market garden. Then we can go inside to take a look at the vintage machinery and the soil appreciation stuff. I don't know much about that, by the way. It's Jack's and Susie's baby.' Marriott sniffed. 'Not exactly in my line. Then I can show you the tanker business. There's just fields beyond that – nothing of interest for you there.'

'That sounds like a good plan,' said Tim cheerfully, wondering what Fovargue's 'line' really was.

Without acknowledging Tim's reply, Marriott began trudging up the track. Tim and Ricky followed. Marriott didn't appear to be moving quickly, but he was taking long strides. They struggled to keep up with him.

He stopped at the first structures they encountered, a

substantial row of Dutch lights, and slid open the door of the one nearest to them. One half of it was almost empty, containing only plastic pots of herbs arranged in rows on steel trestles. The other half contained tomato vines, strung from floor to ceiling. Most were heavy with fruit.

'Looks like a good crop,' said Tim. 'Purple and yellow ones, as well as red. Are they unusual varieties?'

'The proper word is 'heritage',' said Marriott, over-accentuating the aspirate. He didn't exactly sneer, but it was clear that his esteem for the cultivation of fancy plants pretty much matched his enthusiasm for soil appreciation. 'They do quite well – people will pay through the nose for them. The tomatoes is just about all that's left in here at this time of year. Earlier there's lettuce and spring onions and that as well.'

Tim had been paying attention, but now his concentration drifted: he'd caught a glimpse of a young woman leaving through the rear door of the huge greenhouse.

'How many staff work in this part of the business?'

'They're mostly casuals. Students in the summer, some older schoolchildren, mums with kids who want to earn a few quid. That sort of thing. They've mostly been laid off now. We've a couple of labourers who work the year round.'

'Is that one of them?' Tim pointed at the retreating back of the young woman.

Josh Marriott smiled sardonically.

'Not her. She's an eek-ologist, or some such. She's from the university, doing some kind of project about the soil. Been in here collecting samples, I should think. Doesn't get her hands dirty otherwise.'

'That's interesting,' said Tim evenly. 'How long is she here for?'

'Until Christmas. Then she has to go back to school, write up whatever it is she's been collecting stuff about.'

'What's her name?'

'Martha. Martha Johnson. D'you want to talk to her?'

'Not especially.'

'Well, we'll probably run into her later on. She works in the Soil Appreciation shed. She's taken over the little office in there. Dead cosy. She won't stay out here for too long.'

Marriott led them back out the way they'd come. Beyond the Dutch lights were a dozen large raised beds, set out in groups of three on either side of the path.

'Some of this stuff's experimental,' said Marriott. 'Rare types of asparagus and herbs and that. Some of it's just bog standard – Brussels and other greens. As you can see, some of them are part-empty now, but there's usually summat growing all the year round. We sell vegetable boxes until just after Christmas.'

'You don't have any root crops?'

'Yeah, we do. They're right over there, nearest the boundary. They grow out in the fields. The taties have mostly been lifted now and we'll be digging up the carrots soon, but the swedes and turnips stay in the ground until they're needed. The cabbages, too.'

Marriott paused in front of a long, low outbuilding. 'This is the shed where all the soil appreciation stuff goes on, if you're interested. You want me to ask Martha Johnson to show you it?'

'Perhaps on the way back,' said Tim. They had now almost reached an area of flagged yard. It stood in front of another shed, bigger than the 'soil appreciation' one. There were farming implements arranged on the flagstones, laid out carefully, almost as if for a museum display.

'This is where the vintage vehicles are renovated?'

'Yep,' said Marriott. 'There's some money in that. Stuff you see out here, people buy it as ornaments for their gardens. Small ploughs and water-pumps, that type of thing. The bigger things are inside.' He pointed a grimy index-finger at the heavy double doors, which were closed.

'May we take a look?'

The question seemed to worry Marriott.

'If you want,' he said. 'There isn't owt new in there, though – no quads and such. Has to be at least thirty years old. That's according to the boss. There's some as says twenty years is old enough for vintage, but he's a bit of a stickler.'

'We would like a quick look round, if that's all right with you.'

'Sure,' said Marriott, scowling. 'I'll just get the key. It's in the office. You can wait here. I shan't be long.'

He headed back towards the soil appreciation shed. Ricky wandered on to the yard area and began to examine the farming implements.

'Some of these were made much longer than thirty years ago,' he said. 'My granddad had a little plough like this that he'd made into a feature in his garden. He said it had belonged to his granddad originally.'

'I think Marriott was talking about the motor vehicles when he said thirty years. They're probably much easier to date than these tools. I doubt if the tools have brand-names or serial numbers, that type of thing. Many of them will have been made in local blacksmiths' forges.'

'None the worse for that, though,' said Ricky. 'Look how beautifully these ploughshares have been turned.'

Josh Marriott reappeared as suddenly as he'd left, clutching a knot of rope from which several keys were swinging. His mood seemed to have improved during his short absence.

'Martha Johnson says she'll stay until you're ready to look at what she does in there. She was going to knock off early today, but not for any particular reason.'

'We don't want to hold her up...'

'I wouldn't worry about that. It won't hurt her to do summat useful for a change.'

He selected a key and inserted it into the giant padlock that secured the iron bar on the shed door. The padlock yielded easily. Marriott turned, frowning, to a keypad set into the lintel.

'Let's hope I can remember the fucking code,' he muttered to himself. 'Boss keeps on changing it. It's a right pain.'

Ponderously, he pressed four of the keys, so slowly that Tim feared that even if he had the correct code the device would time out. There was a clicking sound.

'Got it!' Marriott said triumphantly. He seized one of the tall brass handles set into the door and pulled. It glided noiselessly to his left. The door to the right then yielded just as effortlessly. He stepped into the shed and snapped on a series of lights. As Tim and Ricky followed him inside, the whole shed lit up, illuminated by several rows of 'Chinese coolie hat' light fittings.

It had been set up like a showroom. Each of the vehicles it contained had been restored as far as possible to its original condition. Some, presumably the best or the most valuable ones, had been set on plinths or had their rear wheels raised on jacks to display them to better effect. There were several tractors, two Land Rovers and an ancient combine harvester.

There was also an old cattle truck and some sheep trailers. Interspersed with the vehicles were some larger auxiliary tools – bigger ploughs than the ones outside, harrows, crop-spraying attachments and potato hoppers.

'Wow!' said Ricky. 'This is fantastic!'

Tim wasn't as interested in farming as his DC was, but he could still see how much loving care – not to mention hard cash – must have been put into this collection. A monster of a vehicle standing in the corner by the door took his eye. It was mostly concealed by a tarpaulin, but its long narrow chimney was a giveaway.

'Is that a traction engine?' he asked.

'Yep. That's not for sale, though. The boss likes it. He takes it to shows sometimes, as a draw for the kids. They come over to look at the engine and he gets them interested in the soil.'

'There's a beautiful old motorbike here,' said Ricky, admiration and envy vying with each other as he spoke. 'I think it's a genuine BSA B32. They stopped making them in the 1950s.'

'I didn't know you knew so much about motorbikes,' Tim said. 'I'm impressed!'

'Yes, well that one's not for sale, either,' said Marriott. 'Boss likes it to run around on. It's one of his hobbies, tinkering with it.'

'But most of the rest of these vehicles are for sale, I take it?'

'That's right.'

'How do you sell them? Not many people can happen on this place by chance.'

'They're advertised to collectors in various ways: websites, newsletters, that type of thing. A lot of people as buys them get to know the boss and Susie through the soil appreciation business first. Purists, I think the word is: they don't just want to look after the land, they want to break their backs doing it in the same way as our ancestors did.' Marriott let out a snort of laughter. 'Best of it is, our ancestors didn't give a damn. Any shortcuts they could take, they would do. And who could blame them for that?'

It was by far the longest speech he'd made since they'd met him. It left Tim wondering why Josh Marriott wanted to work for Jack Fovargue at all: he seemed to feel nothing but derision for most of the principles that Fovargue held dear.

''Course,' Marriott continued reflectively, 'a lot of the old vehicles and tools is sourced to order. They pass through here quite quickly then. But some of this stuff has been here a good while.'

'That's a ferocious looking thing,' said Ricky, pointing to a massive jack-hoe hanging on the wall. It had been mounted beside a rack containing maybe two dozen billhooks of different sizes. Further along, some pitchforks had also been fastened to the wall.

'Yep, it's a jack hoe. All the things with sharp blades are fixed up above where kids can't reach them. We get kids looking round sometimes. Then there are the boss's own, of course.'

Tim went deeper into the shed to take a closer look at the pitchforks.

'Some of these look very old to me,' he said. 'I'd say they were nineteenth century.'

Josh Marriott shrugged. 'Could be,' he said laconically.

Tim had almost reached the back wall of the shed. The left-hand corner was darker than the rest of the building. Looking up, he saw that the bulbs had been removed from the four of the coolie-hat shades that would have illuminated the area.

There was a vehicle standing in that corner, pressed up against the back wall, as far against it as it could be. Like the traction engine, it was swathed in a black tarpaulin, but it was much smaller – probably a small car – and no part of it was protruding. Tim moved along a little further to take a closer look.

'There's nowt over there,' Josh Marriott called after him hurriedly. 'Just some bits and pieces for repairs.'

'It's quite dark here,' Tim replied, trying to soothe the man by not showing that his curiosity had been aroused.

'Lights in that bit must have gone. I'll get them fixed,' Josh said dismissively.

Tim decided not to mention that the four light bulbs had

clearly been removed. He wouldn't antagonise Josh by attempting to remove the tarpaulin himself, but he would ask what lay beneath it and see what kind of answer he could get.

'What's in the corner there?'

'I told you, just some spare parts.'

'It looks like a whole vehicle to me.'

'It ain't whole. It's an old car that the boss uses for spares, that's all. Half of it's gone now.'

'It looks to me as if there's quite a lot of it left.'

'From its shape it looks as if it might be an old Morris Minor,' said Ricky, who had come to join Tim. 'I'm surprised you can use them for spares for farm vehicles.'

Josh Marriott shrugged again.

'Don't ask me. Not my baby. I've got strict instructions to leave that as it is. Not that I'd be able to show it you, even if I wanted.'

'Oh. Why's that?'

Josh gestured triumphantly at the tarpaulin. 'Padlocked,' he said.

Tim moved a couple of steps closer to whatever had been packaged under the cover. It enabled him to see that the black canvas was indeed criss-crossed with several galvanised wire ropes. At all the main intersections of each of these padlocks had been fitted.

Tim decided not to press it. Instead, he met Marriott's eye and grinned.

'Quite a little Aladdin's cave, this, isn't it?' he said jovially. Obviously relieved, Marriott nodded his head vigorously. 'Bit of a crank, the boss,' he said, as if in confidence. 'But it's all above board. You can take my word for that.'

'I'm sure I can,' said Tim seriously. He dared not look behind him, knowing that Ricky would be there, valiantly stifling a laugh.

'Now, have we done in here?' Marriott continued.

'I think so. Is there anything else you'd like to see, DC MacFadyen?'

'I don't think so,' said Ricky, who, when he emerged into natural light again, had become very red in the face.

CHAPTER SEVENTEEN

Juliet had arrived at work late, having stayed at home to take a call from Michael Robinson, who'd said he wanted further advice on how to deal with the media prior to another press conference he'd arranged early that morning. When she reached the station, Tim and Ricky had already left for Silverdale Farm. Andy Carstairs was going out, too, and she saw him only briefly before he disappeared.

She was grateful that she'd therefore be able to spend a few hours on her own, catching up with paperwork and trying not to think too much about the meaning of the previous evening's events. She knew how curious her colleagues could be, and how mercilessly Tim, in particular, would quiz her if he thought she was withholding something of interest about herself. The fact that he had no right to pry into her private life didn't seem to occur to him (though, to be fair, he had always entrusted her with a great deal of personal information about himself). She didn't resent Tim's inquisitiveness: she just felt unequal to dealing with it now. Her mind was in too much of a turmoil for her to be able to articulate even the briefest account.

She had barely had time to seat herself at her work station before a voice came booming over the banisters.

'Ah, Armstrong, good morning! I was afraid you were off sick, or something. Could you come up here? There's something I need your help with.'

Juliet prickled immediately. Of course she'd co-operate by helping Superintendent Thornton; workwise, she'd do just about anything for him that didn't compromise her integrity. But how dare he suggest casually that she might be 'off sick, or something'? She, who had not taken a day's sick leave since she'd been in hospital with Weil's disease almost four years previously and never asked for time off, except annual leave, on any other pretext whatsoever. She thought about taking issue with Thornton, pointing out the injustice of his remark, but decided that at present she didn't have the energy to carry it through. She resolved to raise it on another occasion, when she felt mentally stronger.

She stood up slowly and had just reached the foot of the stairs when the Superintendent's phone rang.

'Ah... perhaps you'd better wait until I've taken this call, Armstrong. I think I know what it's about: I've been expecting it. I'll give you a shout when I'm ready.'

'Just send me a quick e-mail, sir. That would be easiest.' She saw a flicker of horror crossing Superintendent Thornton's face before he retreated back into his office. Beleaguered as she was by her own emotions, Juliet smiled despite them.

She was nearly back at her desk before she realised she had had nothing to drink that morning except a glass of water and turned into the small, galley-like kitchen to fill the kettle. While she was waiting for it to boil she ran rapidly over the previous night's events in her mind.

The evening had got off to an unpromising start with the appearance of the young lout at her window and Jake Fidler's arrival while she was still in an agitated state, with her hair wet, no make-up and wearing ancient clothes. He hadn't seemed to mind any of this – though he had been annoyed about the intruder – and the trip to Cambridge had been one of the most enjoyable car journeys she could ever remember. She had worried she'd spoilt it a little by talking too much about the victim commemorated by the roadside shrine – it was the copper in her coming out and she knew it could be unsettling – but again he'd taken it in his stride. They'd quickly forgotten about it when they reached the theatre and settled down to enjoy the play, which had been spectacularly good. Then they'd gone for a simple one-course meal in an Italian restaurant. Then he'd driven her home. And then he'd kissed her.

That was all. She hadn't invited him in and he hadn't suggested that she should do so. He'd kissed her, watched her into the flat, and then driven away. It was as simple and unremarkable as that.

At least, it would have been simple and unremarkable for most women. For Juliet, it was as if she'd been plunged into an earthquake. The fact was, she'd enjoyed that kiss very much indeed. And, like a teenager obsessed with her first boyfriend, she could think of little else besides when she might see Jake Fidler again.

Juliet was thirty-six. There'd been other boyfriends, but for four years or more her most intense relationships had been with women. At the beginning of that period she'd arrived at the conclusion that she was gay, although acknowledging it continued to make her uneasy. This wasn't because she was ashamed of her sexuality. It was, however, true that although she had derived a great deal of pleasure – and, ultimately, also much pain – from the time she'd spent with her female partners, she had also known, almost from the start, that each of those relationships had lacked something. She was still trying to understand exactly what she was searching for to attain fulfilment. Despite the euphoria triggered by the previous night's date, she was not naïve enough to think that Jake Fidler could provide her with all the answers. Instead, a new thought was growing in the back of her mind: a most unwelcome one. If there was one thing of which she was certain, it was that there could be nothing more beautiful or desirable than fidelity. Although, generally speaking, she was both liberal and tolerant in her views, she was unwavering in her opinion that those who cheated on their partners deserved only the most profound contempt. How ironical – not to say tragic – it would be to discover that she was bisexual, and needed a partner from either sex.

'Armstrong!'

Superintendent Thornton's voice broke through her thoughts. Preoccupied though she had been, she noticed immediately that his tone was different from when he'd summoned her a few minutes before. He sounded... panic-stricken.

'Armstrong! Are you there? I need you to come up. NOW!'

CHAPTER EIGHTEEN

Tim was about to discover what made Josh Marriott tick. He and Ricky had just been taken to the next part of the Silverdale Farm development. It consisted of another yard – this one tarmacked, and not nearly as pristine as the first – on which two tanker lorries had been parked. A small hut, evidently fashioned from a much older structure, stood at one corner of the yard. A large space separated the two lorries. Josh Marriott pointed to it.

'That one's out on a job,' he said. Tim noted that he'd become more authoritative and decidedly more affable as soon as they reached this place.

'This is mostly what I do,' said Marriott. 'I oversee the rest of it, but this is where I do the grafting: matching the tankers to jobs and sometimes taking them out myself. It's proper work: I can't think of owt more worthwhile.'

'The tankers are booked out to empty cesspits?' Tim asked.

'That's the bulk of the work. Cesspits and septic tanks – there is a difference, though most people don't know it. We do other pumping jobs as well – blocked drains, flooded roads, you name it. Emergencies, often. But there's lots of houses in this part of the world that isn't on mains sewage. Deep in the Fens, there's even places that still have earth closets.'

'You say there are three tankers?'

'Aye. Nathan's out on a job with the one as goes there. It's not a big job – that tanker's smaller than the others.'

'Is Nathan one of the permanent farm hands you told us about?'

Marriott threw him a withering look.

'Not him. This is skilled work. You need to know what you're doing with the gear and you have to get what it's all about. Septic tanks is delicate things – they run on microbes, you've to be careful not to upset the balance.'

'Fascinating!' said Tim. 'But who *is* Nathan, then?'

'He's subcontracted from a company based out Peterborough way. Sometimes we have two subcontracted blokes – usually in the winter, when there's more work. Nathan's been working for us for six months, which is longer than usual. I'm trying to persuade the boss that it's not just a blip, that the business is growing. If he agrees, we could take Nathan on permanent, like. He's a good worker.'

'Where is he at the moment?'

'He's out Twenty way. There's a couple of houses there as shares a cesspit. We're called out to empty it every twelve weeks or so.'

'That must be an expensive business. For the owners, I mean.'

Josh Marriott grinned.

'You're right there. You wouldn't want to buy a house with a cesspit unless you'd got plenty of dosh. Even a septic tank'll cost you. Still, one bloke's meat...'

'What did you say the difference is between cesspits and septic tanks?'

'I didn't, but if you're interested, a cesspit is just a holding tank. It contains raw sewage, which has to be pumped out when it's filled up. A septic tank still needs emptying, but it has a bit of a sewage treatment system. Nothing fancy, but the microbes I mentioned help to break the sewage down and there's some basic drainage for the liquid effluent. It's called a soakaway. Septic tanks are cheaper to run, because they only need emptying about once a year, but you can get into a right mess with them. You've to have regular soakaway tests done, to make sure the soil isn't getting contaminated. Right up the boss's street, that is, of course. He started the tanker business because he was dead keen on people getting it all done properly.'

'Do you carry out these soakaway tests as well?'

'Not officially. It's done by the Environment Agency. But folk as uses our services regularly stands a good chance of passing the tests. And unofficially we can do a sort of pre-test, tell them whether they're likely to pass or not.'

'Isn't that much the same sort of testing that Martha Johnson does to the soil here?'

Josh Marriott scowled.

'In a way, I suppose. She's just a tinkerer, though.' He put on a mincing voice. 'That last lot of compost was far too acidic, we really must try to get a better balance.'

Ricky grinned. Tim could see that Marriott's no-nonsense attitude appealed to him.

'Talking of Martha Johnson,' said Tim, 'we'd better not keep her waiting too much longer. There's nothing else to see here, is there?'

'Only the root crops you asked about. They're in the fields beyond that dyke.'

'How many fields are there?'

'Just four. Two abreast and then another two abreast. About eight acres altogether.'

'Mr Fovargue told me that there's a quad.'

'Yes, it's a bit of a clapped-out old thing. Army surplus, I think. It's beside the shed where Martha is, if you want to see it.'

'We will take a look, thanks, though if it's as battered as you say it's unlikely to be of interest. I assume the tanker lorries are incapacitated when they're not in use?'

'Yeah, but who's going to take one of those? They'd have to be really full of shit!'

Marriott cackled at his own joke.

'You're right,' said Ricky, smiling. 'But carry on incapacitating them, all the same. We're working on the theory that some of the missing vehicles are being stolen to order. And I imagine these tankers aren't cheap.'

'Coming back to quads,' said Tim. 'Have you ever seen anyone who doesn't belong here riding a quad across this land?'

'Can't say I have. But the local kids get everywhere. I can tell you I've had to clear off kids riding those little dirt bikes sometimes. Some kids are given quads, too, or they nick 'em.'

'You're right,' said Tim, 'although I don't think we're looking for joy-riders.'

Josh Marriott gave Tim one of his shifty looks.

'Let's go and see milady, shall we? Otherwise she'll be pulling a long face when we get in there.'

Tim had been in Martha Johnson's presence for less than a minute when he understood why Marriott found her so irritating. She was a chirpy little woman, rather old-fashioned for someone who hadn't yet reached thirty, and relentlessly cheerful, but in a superior kind of way. However, what he found most striking about her was not her demeanour, but her uncanny resemblance to Susie Fovargue. She could have been a pocket version of Susie or her daughter, except that Susie was only a few years older. Sister? He wondered if he could find out without asking her directly.

'...so we take samples of all the soil types regularly,' she was saying. 'We make all our own compost, and we mix it differently according to what's being grown. Each of the Dutch lights and the raised beds has different mixes. What we're looking for is the optimum blend for each type of crop. And sustainability, obviously. That's at the very heart of what we do.' She nodded enthusiastically and gave a chirruping little laugh, her auburn curls bobbing.

'What about the fields?' said Ricky.

'Which fields do you mean?'

'The ones out beyond the tanker yard. Where the root crops are being grown.'

'Oh, we don't bother too much about those,' said Martha, her laughter tinkling away again. 'This is an experimental station.'

'But I thought one of the purposes of the soil appreciation society was to test the soil for the farms round here, see if the farming methods used are stripping it of nutrients.'

'Certainly we'll do that, for those who are interested,' said Martha briskly. 'Unfortunately, it's mostly the small market gardeners and what you might call third-agers – incomers who've retired young – who really care. The big farmers don't have much compunction about what they're doing to the land. They'll pay for it one day, of course.' She accompanied her last words with a long trill, as if delighted by the prospect of a local Armageddon.

'Why not test Mr Fovargue's fields, in that case? It's the nearest he comes to 'big farming'.'

'Oh, I may very well do, if I have time. Not that it'll benefit anyone very much, because we don't publish any results. I wouldn't be averse to it, myself, but Jack thinks it would be a bad idea to get into naming and shaming, if the big farmers do ask us to do some testing eventually.'

'I'm sure he's right about that,' said Tim, thinking of the Lord Lieutenant and the pompous and belligerent Mr T R Pack. 'You seem to be very committed to your work,' he added. 'It's an unusual choice of profession. How did you come to be involved with the soil? Are you a farmer's daughter?'

'Oh, no, I'm afraid I'm much more boring than that!' Tim braced himself for the inevitable laugh. 'My father's a clergyman.' (That explains her self-satisfiedness, and the slightly unworldly old-fashionedness of the woman, Tim observed to himself.) 'And I'm not especially local: I come from North Lincs. I have no connections with this area except through the soil appreciation society. There's a network of them across Europe, you know. I became interested after reading a newspaper article about them. Mr Fovargue asked the university for a student to carry out some tests here and, as I'd already enrolled for my Masters, it fitted perfectly! I shall write up the work I'm doing here for my dissertation.'

'Which university?' asked Tim.

'Lincoln.'

Ricky was not alone in recognising the glance of condescension that flickered across Tim's face. Martha Johnson was quick to disabuse him.

'For my current research, that is. For my first degree I studied at Cambridge.'

Ricky turned away, hiding his grin.

'I didn't know they taught agricultural subjects at Cambridge. It must be a relatively recent thing.'

'Oh, I studied in quite a different discipline then. Two disciplines, actually: I did joint honours in Anthropology and History.' The laugh tinkled away. 'Actually, it was because of Anthropology that I became interested in all this. I did some work on early cultivation methods, how they affected the way people developed, that sort of thing.'

'Indeed,' said Tim. 'You must be very clever, as well as dedicated.'

'Oh, I wouldn't say that!' she giggled. 'But I do try hard. I had to try *very* hard to get this job. There was quite a lot of external competition. And not, I think, complete unanimity *internally* about my appointment.'

She gave Josh Marriott a pointed stare. He glared back at her, but Tim noticed that he was the first to look away. Tim's estimation of Ms Johnson rose a couple of notches.

'Anyway, I'm here now, and I do realise how lucky I am. Not just to be able to do the work on the soil, but to work here. This farm is very ancient, you know. It's marked on the maps that the Dutch drainage engineers drew up in the seventeenth century. And there are several old buildings! Just the sort of thing I like.'

'The actual farmhouse is mid-Victorian, isn't it?'

'The part you see has a Victorian façade. It's been built in front of a much earlier structure – bits of it are certainly seventeenth century, probably older. And there was a cottage where this shed stands now. There's not much of it left to see, but the outhouse at the side is still pretty much intact. It was originally a dairy. And the foundations of the cottage were used again when they erected this shed. They're still here, including the old cesspit. Not used now, of course.'

'You must find that interesting,' Ricky said to Marriott, trying to draw him back into the conversation.

'Needs filling in, as far as I'm concerned. I told you, cesspits is bad news. Old ones even worse. In this area they get flooded sometimes.'

'How do you know so much about the history of this place?' Tim asked Martha Johnson.

'Oh, Jack – Mr Fovargue – has collected as many records as he can. He knew I was interested, so he showed them to me. He doesn't want to get rid of the cesspit – he says it adds to the character of the farm, even though no one sees it.' Tim waited for the laugh, but this time it didn't come. Martha Johnson's mood had changed: she was suddenly very subdued.

'Would you like me to show you some of the testing techniques?' Her voice was formal now, almost clinical.

'They haven't got all day, and neither have I,' Marriott growled, surprising Tim with the harshness of his tone. 'If you've seen all you want, I'll walk back to your car with you. I can show you the quad on your way out.'

'Thanks, but...'

Tim's mobile began to ring. Superintendent Thornton's number flashed up on the screen. Thornton, who detested mobiles, rarely called Tim when he was out.

'I'd better take this call. It may be urgent.'

He stepped outside the shed. It had started to rain and a brisk wind was whipping round the side of the building.

'Yates? Where are you? You need to get back here, and quickly.'

'I'm at Silverdale Farm. Has something happened?'

'Yes, Yates, something *has* happened. The divers have been searching that river – lock – canal – the place where the headless body was found.'

'You mean the Fossdyke Canal?'

'Yes, that, exactly.'

'Have they found her head?'

'No, unfortunately. It's worse than that. They've found two more bodies.'

'Headless?'

'One of them is. There can't be any doubt about it, Yates: it's the work of a serial killer. Michael has asked for you to be seconded to the case, and of course I've agreed. He's asked for Armstrong, too, but we'll have to see about that.'

'What about the farm vehicle thefts?'

'What about them, Yates? Don't you think a murder enquiry's more important? Besides, MacFadyen can take charge. He's up to speed with it, isn't he?'

'Yes, but...'

'Just get back here, Yates, will you?'

CHAPTER NINETEEN

Juliet was the first person Tim saw when he arrived back at the police station. She had removed her spectacles and her face was pushed up close to her computer screen. She was concentrating intently. Tim had seen her like that before – it gave away that she was examining scene-of-crime photographs.

'Have Lincoln sent over some photographs already? That was quick!'

'Just these few, of the young girl...'

'Yates! Come up here, will you?'

'I'll see you later,' said Tim. 'You can show me the photos, tell me what you make of them.'

Superintendent Thornton was seated behind his desk when Tim entered his office, looking both important and annoyed. 'I expect you to come to me to be briefed about a major case, not consult your subordinates.'

'I wasn't asking Juliet – DS Armstrong – to brief me, sir. I was just interested in the photographs she has up on her screen. Lincoln have sent them quickly.'

'All right, Yates, we'll overlook it, shall we. This is no time to be petty. You're right, the photographs have come through quickly, but only of the latest victims. What did Armstrong tell you?'

'Nothing at all, sir. We barely spoke. She was just mentioning a young girl... she didn't even finish the sentence.'

'Yes, well that young girl is Michael's first priority. He needs to find out who she is... was. If at all possible, the parents must be notified before the media get hold of the story and the parents have to suffer the misery of putting two and two together.'

'I'm sure you're right, sir, but would you mind starting at the beginning? I'm a bit confused about what's happened.'

The Superintendent sighed and began again, enunciating his words slowly and carefully, as if humouring a willing but backward child.

'You will remember, Yates, that Michael came here to brief us because a body had been discovered in the Fossdyke... dyke... er, whatever it is.'

'Canal.'

'Yes, yes, the Fossdyke Canal. And you will remember that the body was without its head; and that the head was missing. In fact, I think it was you yourself, Yates, who enquired whether North Lincs intended to search the canal to see if the head could be found. Which of course they did. Michael had a dredger and two police frogmen detailed to the spot yesterday afternoon, I must say with admirable efficiency. They worked for a few hours yesterday, apparently without finding anything, and returned this morning at first light. The man operating the dredger arrived first and set to work immediately. The frogmen arrived a bit later and entered the water some distance away from him, for obvious reasons.'

'They didn't want to get entangled with the dredger?'

'Indeed. I believe they'd decided to work along the stretch of the canal where the dredger had been the day before, hoping that it might have dislodged something of interest.'

Like a disembodied head, Tim thought, without saying the words aloud.

'Well, the uncanny thing is that the dredger pilot and one of the frogmen each found something at practically the same time. The dredger pilot realised that he'd dislodged a large mass of some kind. And, even before he'd dived, the frogman noticed a young girl's body floating in the water.'

'Floating?' said Tim. 'How long had it been there?'

'Michael's still waiting for Forensics to send in their report. But we're more or less certain that she'd been there for only a few hours.'

'You mean she was killed and dumped in the canal last night?'

'Either then or in the early hours of this morning.'

'And she's intact? I mean, none of her body parts are missing?'

'As I said, we don't have a pathologist's report yet. But visibly she's 'intact', as you put it. She hasn't been decapitated, if that's what you meant. I must admit it was one of the first things I asked Michael myself.'

'Christ!' said Tim. 'A young girl! That's terrible. Do we know how young? I know we'll be waiting for the path lab to tell us exactly,' he added, pre-empting a further comment from Thornton about this.

'Quite,' said the Superintendent again. 'But we can hazard a guess. Michael says he's pretty certain she's a schoolgirl – he'd put her age at about fourteen.'

'Was she wearing a school uniform?'

'I don't think so.'

'And no girls from the area have been reported missing?'

'Not yet. It's almost certain to happen in due course.'

'What about the other body? The one found by the dredgerman? I'm assuming from what you've already told me that it *was* a body,' said Tim.

'Yes, indeed. And this one appears to be much like the first one – the one found first, I mean. It appears to have been in the water for some time; it was weighted down with rocks; it's that of a young woman (but not a girl) and it's dressed in chain store clothes. No jewellery or other possessions that could aid identification. And the head has been hacked off.'

'I don't mean this question to sound flippant, but is there any sign of either of the heads?'

'No. They're both still missing. Of course, the canal search has been halted now. It will be resumed in due course.'

'We actually have no reason to believe that the death of the young girl is linked to that of the two murders, do we? We're not even yet certain that she was murdered?'

'It's correct that her cause of death has yet to be established, but it's likely she was murdered. I don't get the drift of your thinking.'

'The two women were almost certainly killed by the same person. He... or she, though I doubt it was a she... could either have been watching or alerted to the fact that the first woman's body had been found when DI Robinson issued his press release. My money's on the second. Whoever it was will therefore have known there was a good chance of the second woman's body being found quite soon afterwards. Even if the killer is one of those who enjoys notoriety, why risk getting caught by dumping a third body in the same place? And whether or not it was the same killer, how did they manage to dump the girl without being seen? Even if she was a suicide, and unconnected with the murders, how did she manage it? I'm assuming there was a police guard on that stretch of water last night.'

Superintendent Thornton looked uncomfortable.

'I wouldn't know about that, Yates. You'll have to ask Michael when you see him. I've said I'll free you up to report to him later this afternoon. That's all right with you, isn't it?'

'"Report" to him, sir? But we're both on the same rank. I hadn't envisaged...'

'It's Michael's investigation and he's asked for you to be seconded to it. So yes, you will be reporting to him, Yates. As I've already said, there's no time at present for pettiness. You know yourself there can only be one SIO. Too many cooks, and all that.'

The Superintendent consulted his watch.

'You won't need to leave for Lincoln for an hour or so, so I suggest you make best use of the time by briefing MacFadyen as fully as you can about the farm vehicle thefts. You'd better include Armstrong in the briefing, as well and, come to think of it, it might be a good idea for me to sit in. Then I'll have more idea about what to say to the Lord Lieutenant.'

'I thought you said DI Robinson had asked for DS Armstrong to be seconded to the case as well.'

'He has, but I haven't made up my mind about that yet. Always willing to help, but he can't have all the outstanding members of my team. I've already agreed to loan Ms Gardner's services as well.'

Tim was left none the wiser about whether in the Superintendent's estimation he was ranked with Juliet and Patti Gardner as 'outstanding'.

CHAPTER TWENTY

T im was seething as he descended the stairs to the open-plan area. He'd wanted to bemoan Thornton's insensitivity to Juliet under the pretext of asking to look at the photographs again, but as he approached he saw that she was deep in conversation with someone on the phone. Ricky was seated at his own work station, to her left, and Juliet, looking uncomfortable, had moved her chair as far away from his as she could. She was holding her left hand against her face, evidently to shield her words from Ricky, and she'd flushed a brilliant scarlet. Ricky, for his part, was stolidly leafing through some files, apparently unaware of the embarrassment he was causing – though there was no guarantee he wasn't listening. Recently Tim had come to appreciate Ricky more. There was more subtlety concealed within his blubbery exterior than he was generally given credit for. Tim himself was mightily curious; Juliet rarely took personal calls at work. To whom could she be speaking? He sat down on a spare chair some distance away from her and took out his mobile, pretending to check his emails.

'Yes... no,' Juliet was saying. 'No, not tonight, I can't – there's a new case I have to work on. Yes, it is. I can't tell you that. Yes, of course. No, I really do want to. What about the weekend? I can't promise – it depends on how this case pans out, but I should be able to take some time off on Saturday. No, I don't mind – I understand your job is demanding, too.' She glanced up and saw Tim. He had his head bent over his mobile, but she knew him too well not to believe that he wasn't drinking in her every word. 'Look, I've got to go now. I'll call you later.'

'Everything all right?' said Tim as soon as she'd put down the phone.

'Yes,' she said curtly. 'Why do you ask?'

'No reason. You just seem a bit... flustered, that's all.'

'I don't do flustered.' Juliet's voice was cold. 'How did you get on with Superintendent Thornton?'

Ricky raised his head from the folder. So he probably had been listening, Tim thought.

Tim glanced up the stairs. Thornton's door was closed. Tim could see him through the glass, talking to someone on the phone. Tim knew therefore he could get away with being pretty indiscreet to Juliet about Thornton's briefing, but there was still Ricky to consider. Tim fondly believed that Juliet was the only one of his subordinates who understood the tensions of his relationship with Thornton.

'It was a short briefing, but to the point. You'll know as much about what's happened as I do – more, since you've been studying those photographs.' He looked across at Ricky, to include him in the conversation. 'They have found two more bodies, but apparently they died in different circumstances. One, another woman's, is headless and decomposing. The other's that of a young girl. It appears to have entered the water after the first body was discovered yesterday. Not necessarily murdered, as the Superintendent points out, but probably. No identities known of any of them.'

'How old was the girl?'

'We're waiting for Forensics to tell us.' Tim turned to Juliet. 'How old would you say she was, from the photographs?'

'Not more than fourteen or fifteen. Unless she's very small for her age.'

'Superintendent Thornton says DI Robinson thinks she was a schoolgirl.'

'If she was murdered,' said Ricky slowly, turning the idea over in his mind, 'why dump her in a spot where there's major police activity going on? The killer would know that the body would likely be discovered very quickly.'

'Precisely my own thoughts. It's possible that he – or she – was unaware that the other body had been found, though I doubt that. Whether it was the same killer or somebody different, I think they chose that place deliberately. With the intention, as you say, of the girl's body being discovered almost immediately.'

Superintendent Thornton came clattering down the stairs.

'I've already told you, Yates, we don't know yet whether that girl was murdered. It doesn't do to make wild conjectures. Now, are you ready for this briefing? You only have forty minutes or so before you need to get off.'

Juliet caught Tim's eye and smiled sympathetically. It was a small gesture, but he appreciated it. He was very fond of Juliet – to him she was like a little sister (sometimes also a big sister) as well as being the most dependable and loyal colleague he'd ever had. He wondered again about the awkward conversation she'd been engaged in a few minutes before and hoped she was taking proper care of herself. He'd hate her to get seriously hurt.

CHAPTER TWENTY-ONE

When Tim arrived at Lincoln police station later that day, he was shocked at the change in Michael Robinson. Robinson's customary bluff camaraderie, which irritated Tim by being both patronising and, he felt, frequently tinged with suppressed aggression, had vanished. Robinson was a ghastly colour: his face had taken on a greenish hue and the skin below his eyes was bruised and baggy. His shirt was crumpled and looked suspiciously like the one he had been wearing the day before. He shook Tim's hand warmly, the macho vice-like grip abandoned.

'Tim,' he said. 'Am I glad to see you. Thanks for coming.'

It was on the tip of Tim's tongue to point out that his presence was hardly voluntary, but he stopped himself in time. It would be stupid to quit while he was winning. Instead, he decided to polish his newly-acquired halo.

'My pleasure, Michael,' he said briskly. 'How are you? You look bushed, as if you've been up all night.'

'I have, pretty much. But that doesn't bother me – we've all done it at times like this, haven't we? It's finding the body of that young girl that's got to me.'

Tim nodded sympathetically.

'It's always worse when it's a child. You never get hardened to it.'

They were in Michael Robinson's office, which was both long and wide: rather a grand room for someone of his rank. Superintendent Thornton might have adopted a more ironical attitude towards his protégé if he'd seen the trappings with which he surrounded himself. Robinson began to pace the length of the room now, compulsively curling and uncurling the fingers of both hands as he walked.

'Are you really okay?' Tim asked. 'Let me get you some coffee. Or perhaps you should go home for a shower and a couple of hours' kip before we make a start?'

'No time for that. Coffee would be great – there's some in the pot over there. It just needs pouring.'

Tim went over to the coffee-maker Robinson had indicated and poured out two cups of coffee.

'Sugar or milk?'

'No, just neat, thanks.' Robinson's hand shook as he took the cup. Some of the coffee spilled into the saucer.

'Michael, what *is* wrong with you? Believe me, nobody knows better than me the pressures of a murder investigation and what they can do to you, but if you'll forgive me for saying so, you seem to be barely holding it together. You weren't like this yesterday.'

Robinson put down the cup of coffee, plonked himself heavily into a chair and rubbed his eyes with both hands.

'You're right, it isn't just the investigation. The fact is, I've made a terrible mistake.'

Tim took the seat opposite him.

'What kind of mistake? You've not had any sleep – it's probably not as bad as you think.'

'I've been careless, slapdash. When the newspapers get hold of the story, they'll have a field day.'

'You're beginning to sound like Thor... my boss, now. What have you done? And how do you know the media will find out?'

'Oh, they'll find out all right; as will the Chief Constable, the kid's parents and just about anyone else you can think of who might have a passing interest in the case. The thing is, I didn't detail anyone to guard the crime scene at the canal last night.'

'You mean you left a new crime scene unprotected?'

'Yes. It wasn't a conscious decision – I could pretend I considered it, but I didn't. It's a remote spot, and I could say we were pretty certain that any further evidence would be in the canal and not on the bank, and so on. I'm sure that's what the Chief Constable will tell me to say publicly when he gives me a bollocking. But the fact is, I just forgot.'

Tim nodded sympathetically.

'It's the sort of thing I'd forget, if I didn't have someone like Juliet to remind me. Anyway, there's quite a lot of credibility in those points you just made, if the story does break.'

'Yes, but they're not the nub of it, are they? When the papers latch on to it, they're going to say that if a police guard had been there, the kid might have been saved. The killer would have got windy, dumped her while she was still alive and run for it.'

'That's making assumptions about all sorts of things. First of all, we don't know that she was murdered...'

'Come off it, Tim. I know kids of that age do top themselves, but do you really think she would have gone there to do it? You don't think she'll turn out to be a suicide, do you?'

'No,' Tim admitted. 'No, I don't. But if she was murdered, the chances are she was already dead when the killer took her to the canal. Forensics might be on your side there.'

'I agree it'll help if they can prove she was killed somewhere else. But you know what reporters are like: this will give them the chance to concoct a juicy story about police negligence and they won't be too particular about whether all the facts fit.'

There was a long silence. Tim knew that Robinson was right: the press would have a field day. And there was no way they could prevent the story getting out: three murders in the same place, one of them possibly preventable. Journalists' entire careers had been built on less. A small gremlin deep inside him was quietly sniggering: he couldn't help feeling an element of schadenfreude as Robinson described his predicament. He banished it sternly. As he'd admitted with perfect honesty, long before now he would almost certainly have been in the same jam himself if he hadn't been supported by such an efficient team, particularly Juliet.

The only constructive thing he could do to help Robinson would be to change the subject.

'You're going to have to forget about all that for the moment, Michael. You're probably right that the media will sniff out the error, but we'll cross that bridge when we come to it. For now, we must focus on the case. I know we're waiting for Forensics and all the rest of it, but what's your first reaction? Assuming the girl was murdered, do you think all three deaths are linked?'

Robinson sat up. He was obviously making an effort to concentrate. He seemed calmer now he'd got his confession off his chest.

'The two headless bodies must have been dumped by the same perpetrator; that's a no-brainer. The chances of two murderers mutilating two young women in the same way and chucking them into the same canal at exactly the same spot are zilch. I don't know what to think about the girl. I've been puzzling it over. The likeliest explanation, it seems to me, is that her killer knew that we'd found the first headless body – that wouldn't be difficult: I'd had a press conference, for God's sake – and deliberately dumped her at the same place. But then he would have had to know that the crime scene had been left unguarded – unless he just took a chance on it, or approached it carefully until he was sure. If all that's correct, his only reason for dumping her there must have been to draw attention to himself. And it suggests that he's local. That doesn't necessarily mean that the girl's killer is the same person that killed the two women. But it doesn't look like a copycat crime, either. However she died, she wasn't decapitated.'

'Those are precisely my own conclusions,' said Tim. He paused for a moment. Something that Robinson had just said had triggered a recent memory, though he couldn't quite catch it. He'd have to let it niggle away until it rose to the surface again. 'Now,' he continued, 'Superintendent Thornton has agreed that I should be seconded to this case. I don't know how open-ended that arrangement will be: Thornton has a habit of giving with one hand and taking away with the other.'

'Really?' Michael Robinson seemed genuinely astonished.

'Yes, well forget I said that. The point I'm making is that I'll help you in every possible way while I'm here, but it may not be for as long as either of us would like. How do you want to work it? Naturally, you'll be the SIO. As he says, there can't be two of us.'

'Actually, I was thinking we could be joint SIOs. You've been involved in more murder cases than I have. I can benefit from your experience.'

Tim could hardly believe his ears. Robinson's self-confidence must have taken a greater knock from the mistake he'd made than Tim would have thought possible. That the error would be lurking away in the background, and inevitably revealed at some stage, undoubtedly with unpleasant consequences for them both, made the offer less attractive than it might have been, but there was no way he would kow-tow to Robinson as a subordinate if there was an alternative.

'Okay,' he said. 'I'll go along with that.'

CHAPTER TWENTY-TWO

Juliet had listened dutifully to Tim's briefing about the vehicle thefts, taking notes in her usual meticulous way. So far, she hadn't been much involved in this investigation, although she'd attended a few of the other briefings during the course of the several months in which it had been running. Ricky MacFadyen was Tim's chosen second-in-command for it, and Andy Carstairs had put in a considerable amount of time, too. Juliet had been happy to let them get on with it: it wasn't the sort of case that really interested her. Tramping across muddy fields and interviewing boorish farmers enraged by the theft of their vehicles definitely wasn't her thing.

She'd hoped that DI Robinson's request for both herself and Tim to be seconded to the murder enquiry would be granted, while quite aware that Superintendent Thornton couldn't be expected to spare two of his most senior members of staff when he had a major investigation of his own to deal with – especially now that the beady eye of the Chief Constable was firmly fixed on the latter. When Thornton had called her to his office that morning it had been to ask her to help draft a diplomatic reply to the Chief Constable and Lord Lieutenant; and her unceremonious dismissal had been because he'd thought it was the Chief Constable calling him again. Instead, the call had been from DI Robinson, to inform him of the discovery of the other two bodies.

After Tim's briefing, she'd stayed behind to ask the Superintendent if he still wanted her to help draft the letter. 'All in good time, Armstrong,' he'd said, smoothly. 'I'm not sure we'll need to bother with that letter now. I'm about to phone the Chief Constable again, to let him know that Lincoln has asked if Yates can help with the murder enquiry, and of course I've agreed.'

He was about to bustle away when he paused and added:

'No doubt I'll have to reassure him that we can cope with two major cases at once. That's where you come in, Armstrong. I want you to spend most of your time on the farm vehicles thefts, make sure that MacFadyen's bang on the money, leaving no stone unturned, etcetera. I particularly want you to make sure that he deploys the uniforms effectively: I don't think he's too hot on that. Obviously I can't afford to let Michael have both you and Yates in Lincoln, but I give you permission to spend any spare time you may have to support him with desk work. Those photographs he sent over, for example. You're welcome to study them, pick up any details of interest and report back to him: you're good at that sort of thing. There'll be other photographs coming later.'

'Yes, sir. Thank you.'

Juliet was seeing red as the Superintendent hurried away. Unlike Tim, she wasn't usually irked by Thornton's politicising and his constant manoeuvrings to impress those in high places. His ploys were so transparent, at least to his subordinates, that she tended to regard them with amusement. On this occasion, however, the Superintendent's words had infuriated her. Fine for him to boast of his support for two major investigations at the same time while she undertook the drudgery of what amounted to two full-time jobs.

She remained alone in the briefing room for a few minutes until she felt calmer. When she emerged, she was surprised to find Patti Gardner waiting for her outside. She'd been so absorbed in her thoughts she hadn't seen Patti through the glass set in the door.

'Hello,' Patti said. 'Have you got a minute? I didn't like to disturb you while you were in there. You looked so serious.'

Although she admired Patti for her professionalism, Juliet wasn't a big fan of her personally. She told herself she couldn't really put her finger on why that was, but knew she was being disingenuous: the truth was she could see that Patti made Tim feel uncomfortable whenever they were in the same room together and suspected that the SOCO leader had in the past tried to entangle him unsuccessfully in an affair. This was, in fact, quite a long way from the truth, although Juliet was correct in her surmise that Tim had never been unfaithful to Katrin. It was unlike her to take Tim's part against someone else without knowing the details, but she found Patti's habitual severity, combined with the nobly injured look she often assumed in Tim's presence, singularly unattractive.

She gave Patti an appraising look, noticing she was even gaunter than last time they'd met, her hair yet more brutally cropped. Patti could only be a few years older than herself, but she seemed to be heading rapidly towards an ascetic and embittered middle age. Perhaps there was a lesson to be learnt there.

'Patti! It's nice to see you. I can't remember when we last met. I'm afraid you've missed Tim. He's on his way to Lincoln, to help with DI Robinson's murder case. I thought you'd been seconded to it, too?'

Did she imagine that a shadow crossed Patti's face when she

mentioned Tim's name? If so, it was only very fleeting. Patti gave her a warm smile, which softened her features, providing a pale glimpse of the beautiful young woman she'd once been.

'I have. That's why I'm here – there are a few loose ends I need to tie up before I go back to Lincoln. I just wanted to know if you'd made anything of the photos DI Robinson sent earlier.'

'In what sense?'

'I wondered if you'd ever seen anything like it before.'

'I've seen plenty of dead girls and young women – though I'm sure not as many as you have – and even more photos of them. Should I have picked up something different about these?'

'Just asking: I don't really know what I'm expecting you to say, when it comes down to it. I've got a hunch there's something strange about the crime, that's all. I wondered if the photos had triggered a similar reaction in you.'

'You think she was murdered, then? Not a suicide?'

'Obviously I'm not a pathologist. We need a proper path report: Professor Salkeld's on his way to Lincoln now. Hopefully he'll be able to tell us the cause of death. But yes, I'm quite certain she was murdered. Stabbed, to be precise. The body has multiple stab wounds. But her clothes are intact. That's one of the things I find strange.'

'I couldn't have known that, given that the wounds are concealed by her clothes, but I had noticed her clothes weren't damaged – you took some excellent close-up photos – which is why I was trying to keep an open mind about whether she'd been murdered.'

'The killer must have removed her clothes to stab her and then replaced them afterwards. What could have been the reason behind that?'

'The obvious answer is that he'd made her take off her clothes before he raped her. Then he killed her and dressed the body again before he dumped it.'

'I'd thought of that. Obviously, Professor Salkeld will examine her for signs of penetration. I think it's likely that he'll conclude she wasn't raped, though.'

'Why do you say that?'

'I haven't touched her clothing more than I can help, because I don't want to destroy any evidence. But she's still wearing her underwear and it doesn't look as if it's been tampered with. That's rarely the case with rape, if the victim's murdered afterwards – usually the underwear has been damaged; more often than not, it's missing or found lying discarded somewhere nearby.'

'I admit that would be more typical. But all that suggests to me is the killer's better than most at covering his tracks.'

'If that's what he was trying to do, why dump her there at all? Unless he's totally cut off from the outside world, he will have known that that stretch of the canal would be crawling with police today. If he wanted to avoid detection, that's the last place you'd expect him to choose.'

'You're right; that same thought had crossed my mind. I don't know the answer, though. I'm sorry that I can't be any more help now, but I'll keep on thinking about it. As you say, Professor Salkeld's report may give us more to go on. What about the other two bodies?'

'The Lincoln SOCO team photographed them in situ – well, almost in situ, only a short time in each case after they'd been pulled out of the canal. They've been taken to the morgue now. I'm going there myself, to take more photographs as Professor Salkeld carries out the autopsy. We'll have to work on them quickly – I don't know how fast they'll deteriorate, even under refrigeration. It depends on how long they've been in the water.'

'Take some close-ups of their necks, will you? If we could

establish what was used to hack off the heads it might give us a lead.'

'Sure, I'd do that anyway, as a matter of routine. Don't expect miracles, though, and be cautious about interpreting the evidence. Decaying flesh can be misleading.'

'I take it both heads are still missing?'

'They were when I checked an hour or so ago. The team working at the scene haven't found anything else since the second body was dredged up – neither the heads nor any effects that might have belonged to the victims. If we can't identify the two women from their DNA, I'm not sure what sort of progress can be made with finding out who they are.'

'I think what's most likely to happen next is that the girl's parents will report her missing. Then we'll find out who she is.'

'I agree, but that won't necessarily help with the other two. I'm far from convinced that her death is linked to theirs.'

Juliet had half-expected Tim to call her once his first briefing with DI Robinson had taken place. She decided she would wait at her desk until six-thirty, making best use of the time by going over the vehicle thefts dossier in more detail. Ricky had compiled a separate folder of 'at risk' properties that the police had visited as part of their enquiries. It mostly contained short accounts listing the vehicles maintained at individual farms and smallholdings and the advice offered to their owners on how to protect them from theft. Working through this as well, she quickly recognised its true purpose: it was designed to act as an insurance policy for the police, enabling them to show the Chief Constable, or anyone else who might ask, that every possible precaution had been taken to prevent more thefts.

Most of these reports were barely a page in length and boringly repetitive. However, her attention was grabbed by the latest of them, Ricky's account of his and Tim's visit to Silverdale Farm, which Ricky had filed only that afternoon. It was several pages long and went into some detail about the nature of Fovargue's businesses and the many vehicles associated with them. Ricky had noted in the margin that the vehicle inventory was incomplete: he'd not had the opportunity to list all the vintage vehicles. Even without them, Fovargue's vehicle holdings were impressive: Ricky had recorded that two Land Rovers, three tanker wagons, two tractors, a quad, a motorbike and a traction engine were all kept in working order on the site, to be used by Fovargue and his employees in the running of his four businesses. Additional to these were the dozen or so uncatalogued vehicles, most of which Ricky thought were functional, although mostly not DVLA-registered, and the numerous farm implements for sale, some of which were motorised. He'd also noted that the stringency of security measures at the farm varied considerably: the house and larger buildings were fitted with sophisticated locking systems and alarms, but several valuable vehicles and many agricultural tools were left standing outside at all times. There were no perimeter fences except those that acted as boundaries to the fields that lay far beyond. The farm and its various yards and outbuildings could easily be accessed from the road. No advice had yet been offered on improving the security arrangements, as Jack Fovargue had not been present during the inspection (Ricky had not added that DI Yates had had to leave the farm in a hurry).

Looking up Silverdale Farm on Google Maps, Juliet could see how remote it was. There were no other dwellings within about a five-mile radius, and it was almost eight miles to the nearest village. It would be a perfect sitting duck for thieves intent on stealing vehicles: she was surprised that apparently no attempts had yet been made to purloin some of its assets. She would tell Ricky to keep it under surveillance for a while. She scribbled a few notes to remind herself, closed the folder and looked at her watch: it was six-thirty-five. If Tim wanted to speak to her, he'd have to wait until tomorrow now, or call her mobile. She shut down her computer, put a few things into her handbag and prepared to leave for the day.

She'd barely closed the outside door behind her when someone touched her elbow. Turning sharply, she was surprised to find Jake Fidler standing there.

'Jake! You almost made me jump out of my skin. I thought we'd agreed not to meet until the weekend.'

'I wanted to see you before then.'

He searched her face. She saw that his own was pinched with cold, his expression apprehensive.

'How long have you been standing there?'

'Only since six. I thought that was when you said you'd be leaving today.'

'It was, but I had to wait... for a call. A call that never came, actually.' She let out a forced little laugh.

'Come for a coffee?'

'I... oh, all right.' She knew she sounded ungracious, as if she'd agreed because she could think of no suitable excuse. It would be more accurate to say that Jake's unexpected ambush had panicked her. 'The café over the road?'

He nodded; together they crossed the road in silence. 'There's a seat in the window,' he said. 'You take it and I'll fetch the drinks. What would you like?'

'A cup of tea would be great,' she replied, trying to sound brighter.

Only a few people were sitting in the café, individuals all sitting at separate tables. The lone waitress was pointedly spraying the unoccupied ones with a detergent gun and polishing them vigorously. Seeing Jake standing at the counter, she took her time in moving across to him.

'They close at seven,' he said to Juliet, when he returned with a tray set with two battered metal individual teapots and two thick white pottery cups. 'Time enough to have a chat.'

'How did you manage to get away from work? You said you were on duty this evening.'

'I am, but I've got someone to cover me for an hour. More like two hours, now,' he added. 'It's okay – they're reliable. The favour I owe them just got bigger, that's all.'

'You could have waited to see me. I didn't realise I had such pulling power!' Juliet tried to joke. His earnestness was making her uncomfortable. Her hand was resting on the table and he placed his own over it. Gently she drew it back to her lap, putting her other hand on top of it.

'What's the matter, Juliet?' His voice was bleak. She forced herself to meet his eyes and could read the anguish there. 'We had such a good time last night – at least I did, and I thought you did, too. What's changed? Why are you giving me the brush-off today? Have I done something to offend you?'

To her horror, Juliet found herself choking back tears. She looked down at her hands.

'It's nothing to do with you!' she said, taking a sip of her tea. 'It's entirely my own fault.' She swallowed hard. 'I should have told you this before. I'm gay.'

He remained both silent and motionless until, eventually, she felt compelled to look up again. His eyes were full of compassion.

'Okay,' he said, 'if you say you're gay, I'm not going to contradict you. I'll respect you just as much if it's true. But you'll have to forgive me for saying that I find it very difficult to believe.'

Juliet bristled immediately. She already felt humiliated and, despite his reassuring words, thought she'd probably just diminished herself in his eyes.

'Are you saying I don't know my own mind?'

'I'm saying that sexuality can be a strange thing. It's sometimes difficult to interpret. Many straight men are attracted to other men to some extent, without it making them gay. I'm guessing the same goes for women, too. It's a hypothetical attraction: it's like many people of both sexes 'fancying' other people's partners without actually wanting to commit adultery.'

'I don't understand what you're saying.'

'I'm probably not making much sense, even to myself. What I'm trying to say is that last night wasn't fake. I know you felt like that, too.'

Juliet nodded miserably.

'Yes, but I don't understand it. It's more than four years since I had a boyfriend, and all my relationships with men have been awkward.'

'But you've had girlfriends since?'

'Yes, several, but none of those relationships has worked out, either.'

'Why do you think that is?'

'Oh, for various reasons – different ones in each case. Some of them have hardly got off the ground. If they've had anything in common, it's that all have been... lacking in something, somehow.'

'I'll try not to be too pleased about that. I'm not going to pretend that I'm the answer to a maiden's prayers.' He put on a falsetto voice for the last sentence. Juliet found herself smiling briefly before she became grave again.

'That's just it,' she said. 'What if you are part of the answer, and someone else is the rest of it?'

'You're afraid that you might be bi?'

'Yes. It would be my worst nightmare – it's against everything I stand for.'

'What do you mean?'

'I believe in fidelity. I've always known that if I found the right person to love, I'd want to commit to them entirely. That doesn't square with loving two people, does it?' Her hand flew up to her face, as if shielding her from the anguish. Jake seized it and held it tight in his.

'Juliet,' he said. 'If that's all that's worrying you, I'm happy to take a chance on it. And, just to make it clear, the chance I'd be taking would be on us, not you and someone else. I reckon I'd be pretty tolerant about it if you needed someone else as well. I'm only asking you to give us a go, that's all: get to know each other better. We can cross any other bridges if we come to them.'

CHAPTER TWENTY-THREE

It was the middle of the evening. Tim was driving home from Lincoln and had covered about half the distance before he remembered that he hadn't called Katrin to let her know he'd be late. His conscience pricked him, but he decided it would be pointless to stop and call her now: he'd be home in less than half an hour.

As he swung the car into his drive, he saw that Katrin hadn't drawn the curtains, although by now it was quite dark. Hearing the noise of the engine, she came to the window and looked out. He could see from her expression that she wasn't in a good mood. Mentally he was preparing his apology as he hurried from the car into the house.

'Katrin, I'm really sorry, I...'

'Where have you been, Tim? You could have called me. I kept Sophia up for ages because you said you'd see her before she went to bed. I know you've got a lot on your mind with the vehicle thefts, but it's not as if it's a murder case...'

'It is a murder case, now,' Tim interrupted, 'I've been seconded to Michael Robinson's murder investigation. I've been with him in Lincoln this afternoon. That's why I'm so late. I'm sorry – I meant to call you.'

Katrin was immediately sympathetic.

'Oh, Tim, I'm sorry about that. Superintendent Thornton can be very insensitive sometimes. He must know that you'll hate working for Michael. And what about your own case?'

'I'll tell you more about Michael later: it's not as bad as it sounds, but I must admit I thought the same as you, when Thornton first told me. Michael's asked me to be joint SIO; I'm not reporting to him...'

'That doesn't sound like him!'

'No, although he has a reason for it. And he's got a lot on his plate now. They've found two more bodies in the Fossdyke Canal...'

'That's extraordinary, after what we were talking about yesterday!'

'I know – the odd thing is, I didn't remember the connection you'd made until I was on my way home. Can you tell me again about those old murders – the ones in Bolton, I think you said?'

'It was Burnley. The killer's name was Stephen Jenkins. He was studying criminology – or supposed to be. His stepfather was supporting him, I think on condition that he kept out of his mother's way. He killed and decapitated two prostitutes and then he killed a schoolgirl. He seems to have borne a grudge against prostitutes – I don't need to tell you that it's a trait shared by many serial killers. It was assumed that Jenkins had been exploited by prostitutes, or that he felt irresistibly drawn to using them and then felt disgusted with himself. He maintained his right to silence both when being questioned by the police and throughout a very long trial: he made no attempt to explain his actions and resisted his defence's dogged attempts to suggest mitigating circumstances – disturbed childhood, diminished responsibility, all that sort of thing. Claiming he felt remorse was a non-starter. But you haven't started at the beginning, Tim. You say there were three bodies in the Fossdyke. Were the victims all women? Was either of the others decapitated?'

'They were all women. All young, but one was just a child – a girl in her early teens. The other women had been decapitated, but the girl hadn't.'

Involuntarily, a shiver ran through Katrin's body from head to foot, as if someone had pumped ice into her veins. She wrapped her arms around herself. Earlier she had lit the fire. It was burning low now and she drew closer to the modest blaze.

'Katrin?'

'This is uncanny. It's as if you're describing the Jenkins crime all over again. Have you found the heads of the two women?'

'No. We haven't given up looking for them yet. Were the heads of Jenkins' victims ever found?'

'One of them was, eventually. Buried on the canal path, I think. I can check. Jenkins never admitted to the murders – or denied them, for that matter – but apparently he was furious when the head was found, threw some kind of violent tantrum. He was in prison by then. The police had already identified the victims, but I imagine they were glad that when it was confirmed that the head belonged to the person they thought it did. They found out who the girl was almost immediately, but they couldn't begin to guess at his motive for killing her There was no evidence that he was a paedophile.'

'What else do you know about him? Was he the usual loner?'

'He was a misfit rather than a loner. He did have some friends, both at the college and working in the town. He also had a girlfriend. She had no inkling that he was violent – or so she claimed. The police suspected that he'd been responsible for several vicious attacks on local women before he actually killed, though I don't think they proved it.'

'Probably didn't need to. He's serving an indefinite tariff, isn't he?'

'Yes. His defence tried to get him put in Broadmoor. He was examined by two psychiatrists, who both concluded he was sane. The judge said he was extremely dangerous and posed a significant threat to women.'

'Perceptive of him!'

'Yes, but you know as well as I do that kind of formal summing up serves a purpose: it means he's unlikely to be released unless he can prove he's both remorseful and no longer a danger.'

'He hasn't applied for parole?'

'I can check, but it's unlikely he'd be allowed to. The crimes took place only six years ago. And as I've just said, he's made no attempt to fulfil the requirement for parole.'

'Agreed. I'm just trying to establish there's no possibility at all that Jenkins could be involved in the Fossdyke murders, once we know when they're likely to have happened – that he wasn't out on licence at the time. The strangest thing from my perspective is the young girl, in both cases. Why did these two girls die?'

'Was the body of the young girl at the Fossdyke weighted down?'

'No, she was found floating in the canal. And probably only put there last night, which is also odd: if the same person killed all three, he was taking a big risk by going back.'

'But had the bodies of the two women been weighted? With stones, maybe?'

'Yes, although he made a better job of it with the second one. She was still at the bottom of the canal. It seems that a bag of stones had been tied to the first one and worked loose over time. Her body was found by a fisherman, partly risen to the surface. The girl had been chucked in, probably by someone in a hurry, and didn't sink.'

'This gets weirder! The girl that Jenkins killed had been hurled into the canal in haste, as well. Her body was visible from the bank. It was only when police divers went in to retrieve it that they found the first of Jenkins' other two victims. Her body had also risen to the surface – it was partially obscured by some reeds. It had broken free of the weights – a bag of stones.'

'Why do you think Jenkins killed the girl?'

'He was a psychopath. Arguably, you don't need any other explanation; but she wasn't his usual type of victim. If the police are right about the other assaults, all the women he attacked were prostitutes except her. My guess is that she'd found out something about him and he was afraid she might expose him in some way – though I seem to remember there was no evidence that he knew her.'

'Would you mind collecting all the stuff you have on the Jenkins case and sending it to me? It's bound to give us some clues about the Fossdyke murders.'

'You're thinking they're copycat crimes?'

'It's rather obvious, isn't it? Too obvious, in fact. I think that's what we're meant to think, but the truth of it is probably something quite different. Even so, the Jenkins case is the best lead we have – we've found precious little else to go on, except the bodies.'

'Sure, I can gather the stuff together for you. It won't take me long. Now, what was it you were saying about Michael? Has he blotted his copybook at last? I'm all agog.'

CHAPTER TWENTY-FOUR

To her own surprise, Juliet had slept well. In one sense, the conversation she'd had with Jake Fidler had resolved nothing, but his sensitive yet pragmatic words had calmed her and helped her to reach a more balanced perspective. It had enabled her to understand that in the past she had repeatedly made the foolish mistake of taking a mental leap forward each time she met somebody new, trying to figure out where the relationship might lead and how she felt about that. This time, she would live each day as it came and just enjoy Jake's company, no strings attached. That was all Jake had asked for and would place no pressures on either of them. She felt as if a great yoke had been lifted from her shoulders. The next morning, she arrived at the station with a clear head and considerably more energy than she'd been able to summon the previous day. She was surprised to see Ricky already seated at his workstation. An owl rather than a lark, he usually struggled in the mornings, but frequently made it up by working late into the night.

'Hi, Ricky. What's the matter with you? Unable to sleep?'

'You're very bright and brisk this morning,' he replied brusquely.

'And you're much grumpier than usual. Is something wrong?'

'Not *wrong*, exactly. It's this bloody vehicle case. The more I think about it, the less it makes sense.'

'The mysteries of the criminal mind! But are you talking about something specific?'

'Yes and no. I've been looking at similar crimes. Nationally, there's a spate of organised vehicle thefts every few years, though this is the first I can find in South Lincolnshire. Others have been centred on most of the adjacent counties – with the exception of Lancashire – Derbyshire, Humberside, a smaller scam around Nottingham a couple of years ago – but I don't think that can be significant. What intrigues me more is that there's been a strong pattern to all the others, both with regard to the types of vehicle nicked and the MO in nicking them. That's how the villains got caught, in every case: they became too predictable.'

'Perhaps our villains are just a lot cleverer – "Lincolnshire: the county whose criminals have the highest IQ."'

'Very funny! You *are* in a good mood this morning, aren't you! But my point is that the police found it easy to anticipate what the thieves were going to do next because that's the nature of the business, not because they were stupid. If you steal vehicles to order, you have to set up some pretty robust distribution channels, which means both trusting a large number of other crooks and having the wherewithal to shift big plant and machinery quickly. It's hard to conceal an operation like that over a period of time, and mostly they can't – so the police nab them. The other thing is, in vehicle terms, what's been taken in Lincolnshire is a real ragbag of stuff. Usually, these thieves are specialists – it cuts down the risk, as there are fewer clients, and they probably don't have the bandwidth to diversify, if that's the right word. So you get one lot nicking road-building equipment, another lot nicking tractors, and so on. Compare that with our list of stolen vehicles: several tractors, some very valuable, others less so; several quads, a combine harvester, two vans, a jeep and a whole catalogue of other bits of farming kit, such as harrows, ploughs and seed-drills. Where's the similarity between those?'

'Well, aside from some of the quads, they were all taken from farms or smallholdings.'

'Yes, but that proves my point: farming's pretty much what people do around here, but that encompasses a huge range of activities and our thieves seem to have tapped into most of them. Who can their clients be and how do they manage to spirit this stuff away so quickly?'

'Perhaps they don't have clients.'

'You mean, it's all just being hoarded somewhere? But what would be the point of that? And where is it? In a bloody great aircraft hangar that nobody has noticed?' Ricky's voice had grown louder with each word of this last sentence.

'Relax, Ricky, I was being flippant. I agree that these vehicles must have a pre-arranged buyer. What you're saying now is helpful, too, it's making me think a bit differently about the case. And thank you for the dossier and the visits folder: I worked through them yesterday and they've brought me up to date nicely.'

Ricky was immediately mollified; his face broke into a grin. Praise from Juliet was rare these days.

'Just one other thing. Although a lot of the victims were wealthy – most of the farmers in South Lincs have a few bob to knock together – Mr Pack is the only one you could really call stinking rich. He belongs to a small elite of local farming moguls, four or five families at the most. And he's the only one of them who's been stung.'

'Perhaps the others have taken better security precautions. Perhaps they've even listened to what we've told them about protecting their property! I take it we've visited them all?'

'Yes; and you could be right. But there might also be other reasons: maybe Pack was targeted because someone bears him a grudge.'

Juliet paused to consider this, her head on one side. 'Maybe. He's not a very pleasant person. But I bet he's an even less pleasant enemy.'

'Precisely! Even the most reckless thief would think twice about taking him on. Look what's happened since his combine harvester was stolen: he's stirred up the local farming community even more, convinced the Chief Constable we're not trying hard enough, caused a storm in the media and made Superintendent Thornton run around like a blue-arsed fly. He'd already lost a motorbike, and he was pretty peeved about that. If I was the villains, I'd be shit-scared by now. I'd certainly think more than twice about lifting anything else for a good time.'

'If they lie low for a while that could help us, although it'll also make them more difficult to catch. Are you saying they made a mistake when they stole from Mr Pack? That if they'd known who he was, they'd have left him alone?'

'Yep, that's what I think.'

'That's quite clever,' said Juliet slowly. 'There's also another possibility: that the thieves are thumbing their noses both at us and at Pack, as a local establishment figure. That they're tempting fate and daring us to catch them. Or perhaps they just don't like him.'

Ricky hadn't answered when a familiar voice, at present sounding exasperated, accosted them both.

'Good morning, Armstrong, MacFadyen. I trust you are planning your day and not just gossiping down there. I expect you both to be running around like – what was the term – blue-arsed flies!' He gave a short, humourless laugh.

Juliet had to work hard to suppress a smile.

'Yes, sir,' she said demurely. 'I was just complimenting DC MacFadyen on how up-to-date he's kept the dossier on the farm vehicle thefts. We're on our way out now. We're going to Silverdale Farm again. It's my opinion Mr Fovargue's a sitting duck for one of these thefts. He wasn't there for a security briefing yesterday, so we're going back to do it today.'

'That's admirable,' said Superintendent Thornton drily, 'and I'm pleased to know that MacFadyen is doing something a little more conducive to getting results than keeping his dossier up to date. May I ask why you both need to go?'

Thinking quickly, Juliet decided to rely on her reputation for being a bit fey.

'I'd like to see Silverdale Farm for myself, sir. I've got a hunch that there's something strange going on there. It may even be something that can help us crack this case.'

'Oh, well, don't let me squash one of your hunches. We all know how useful they've been in the past.' There was just enough irony in the Superintendent's voice to indicate that he was no pushover. All the same, he had already turned back up the stairs to retreat to his office.

'I didn't know we were going to Silverdale Farm today,' said Ricky, when he'd gone.

'I'd already decided to ask you to go after I read your report last night. I hadn't thought of coming too. That was a spur of the moment decision!'

Ricky grinned again.

CHAPTER TWENTY-FIVE

K atrin already had several downloaded files about the Stephen Jenkins murders, so was able to pass them on to Tim quickly. She told him she'd look for more information the following day.

What Tim was most interested in was the manner in which Jenkins had killed his victims. The pathologists' reports weren't among the files Katrin had on her computer. When she could get hold of them they might yield additional information, but the official account of the trial was detailed enough to be going on with. Each of the corpses had been examined by a different pathologist; all three had arrived at the same conclusion about the victim's cause of death: in their opinion, both women and the girl had died from multiple stab wounds. This was indisputable in the case of the girl, whose name was Tanya Jones, more a matter of probability where the two women were concerned. There was an outside chance that they had been decapitated while still alive, but none of the pathologists believed this. Medical evidence suggested that at least one of the women had had her head hacked off some time after she died. 'Hacked' was the appropriate word: Jenkins had almost certainly used a rusty hacksaw that was later retrieved from the canal.

Jenkins had done a good job of cleaning up, but nevertheless forensic tests carried out in the bathroom of his flat revealed small shards of bone and some blood, suggesting that he'd cut the heads off the bodies there, possibly having killed his victims somewhere else. More traces of blood were found on the landing outside the flat, but this could have been deposited either when he moved the bodies into the flat or moved them out again afterwards. The girl's blood was not found either inside or outside the flat, nor was there any other evidence that she'd been there. It seemed likely that she'd been killed on the canal path, or perhaps somewhere else altogether and then transported to the canal, in either instance without entering the flat.

The reason for her death had puzzled the prosecution: the only explanation they could think of was either that she'd stumbled on Jenkins while he was disposing of one of the bodies or she'd found out something about him that could lead to the discovery of his crimes. Tim wasn't entirely convinced about this. Men like Jenkins developed a taste for killing: Tanya Jones may just have been in the wrong place at the wrong time.

Tim was now on his way back to Lincoln, planning to arrive as soon as he could after Professor Salkeld started work on the autopsies again. He knew Salkeld had intended to carry out the young girl's autopsy the previous evening. He'd been asked to focus on her first in the hope of finding clues to help establish her identity. Tim assumed that the Professor hadn't found anything too exciting: if he had, he would have been sure to call Michael or Tim himself.

It was Tim's first visit to the morgue in Lincoln. He didn't like morgues, and this one was possibly the most dingy and cheerless he'd ever visited. The staff, however, were helpful.

Jerry, the male assistant who greeted him, assumed that he'd come to watch the autopsies through the observation window, but when he explained that he'd like to be present in the mortuary room, Jerry was happy to sort out some scrubs for him. As Tim was putting them on, Jerry went to ask the Professor's permission to admit him.

'Professor Salkeld says you can go in,' he said guardedly, when he returned. The tone of his voice made Tim look up and catch his eye.

'And?' he said.

Jerry smiled.

'Is it that obvious? Well, perhaps I should warn you that he's not in a very good mood today.'

'He never is,' said Tim. 'Don't worry, I'm used to him.'

'DI Yates!' said the Professor sardonically, as Tim entered his inner sanctum. 'To what do I owe the pleasure? Except for your natural propensity to get in my hair on occasions such as this, I mean.'

'Good morning, Professor Salkeld. I know I get in your hair sometimes. I promise to behave today. I wondered if you'd let me watch, perhaps at the same time talk to you about the autopsy on the girl you carried out last night?'

'I think that might be a trifle confusing for Paula, don't you? She's supposed to be taking down notes from what I say about this cadaver, not last night's.'

'Who?' said Tim. He looked beyond the Professor and noticed for the first time the young woman perched on a stool close to the top of the gurney bearing the victim's remains. She was holding a notebook. A camera stood on the bench in front of her.

'Hello, Paula.' Tim gave her a brief nod and turned back to the Professor. 'Well, perhaps I can watch you for a bit and talk to you about last night's autopsy when you take a break.'

The Professor sighed deeply.

'No peace for the wicked,' he said. 'I take it you know what the term 'break' means? It refers to time off, usually brief. As in a break from work.'

'If you're too busy, I can come back...'

'Perish the thought!' said Professor Salkeld. 'You'll still be in my hair if I know you're coming back. Let's get it over with, shall we?'

'Thank you,' said Tim. Although not as squeamish as some of his colleagues, he didn't enjoy post-mortems. He watched cautiously as the Professor slit the torso of the body from the crotch almost to the neck, then plunged his hand into the cavity he'd made and pulled out a large dull red organ.

'Her liver?'

The Professor plopped the mass into a steel dish and prodded at it with a latexed finger, peering at it closely.

'Aye,' he said. 'Not in very good shape, either. It's quite inflamed – see here – and considerably bigger than it should be.'

'Alcohol?'

'Possibly, though it doesn't have the classic oak-leaf appearance associated with cirrhosis. My money's on drugs. Heroin, to be precise.'

'An addict?'

The Professor straightened up and turned to face him.

'How many people do you know of who take heroin and aren't addicts?'

'Stupid question, I suppose.'

'Aye.'

'Can you tell how old she was?'

'I can't be very exact. It would be much easier if she'd kept her head.' The Professor chuckled grimly at his own gallows joke. 'Probably quite young, but she's no teenager. I'd put the age range at twenty-five to thirty-five.'

Tim thought back to the court report he'd been reading the previous evening. Both Stephen Jenkins' decapitated victims had been in their late twenties.

'Interesting.'

'Why's that?' said Professor Salkeld suspiciously. 'Most serial killers' victims are young women, aren't they?'

'I supposed that's generally correct, though there are other groups at risk as well: children and gay men, for example, sometimes the very elderly. But I wasn't referring to the demographic so much as the overall profile of the case.'

'Come again? You're getting almost as good at using big words as I am.' This observation seemed to lift Professor Salkeld's mood. Capitalising on the change, Tim smiled self-deprecatingly.

'Sorry, I didn't mean to sound like a criminologist. What I meant was, there are some unusual aspects of this crime that makes it like another set of murders that were committed six or so years ago. It was Katrin who first spotted the similarities.'

Professor Salkeld was continuing to make steady progress, delving several times into the cavity to extract more organs from the body and placing them methodically in steel dishes for Paula to photograph. Tim could tell, however, that his curiosity had been piqued.

'Aha. You policemen are keen on seeing patterns in things, aren't you? Which murders would those be, then? I don't recall having worked on anything like this before.'

Tim forbore to point out that the Professor wasn't the only pathologist operating in the country.

'They weren't committed in this region. I've been reading about the case I mean – there were three pathologists working on it, none of whose names I recognised.'

'Yes, but which case was it?'

'Does the name Stephen Jenkins ring any bells?'

The Professor paused, holding his scalpel aloft in mid-air.

'Stephen Jenkins? Vaguely. I half-recollect that there was an outcry when he was sentenced, because he was suspected of being involved in several other assaults and the police decided not to pursue it further.'

'You're right, but that was after he was sentenced. Do you remember any details about the case itself?'

'Six years ago, you say? No, I'm afraid I don't – but I wasn't... myself then. It may have passed me by.'

Tim remembered that around the time he'd joined the South Lincs force someone had told him that Professor Salkeld had lost his wife in tragic circumstances. He knew no more about it – the Professor was a man who liked to keep his personal and professional lives entirely separate – but Tim assumed this was what he was referring to now.

'You may just have been too busy,' he said brightly, side-stepping the subject. 'As I said, I spent some time yesterday evening reading up on the Jenkins case. Jenkins murdered two prostitutes and decapitated them before throwing them into the canal in Burnley, at a spot not far from where he lived. The heads of one of the women was subsequently found, buried close to the canal path; the other woman's head was never found. Jenkins' third victim was a schoolgirl, who wasn't decapitated. According to the pathologists' reports, all three died of multiple stab wounds.'

Professor Salkeld let out a low whistle.

'I have to admit there's something in this notion of yours,' he said. 'Paula, let's knock off for a while. Give the man the break he's been after since he arrived. We'll have some tea, talk a bit more about the lassie we worked on yesterday.'

'Tea would be great,' said Tim, bestowing one of his winning smiles on Paula.

'Aye, well, she's not the tea-lady,' said Professor Salkeld, with some severity, 'but I'm sure she'll show you where the stuff is kept so you can make your own.'

Tim had the good grace to look abashed, even though Paula then made tea for all of them anyway. The morgue didn't boast a proper staff room, but a modest rest area had been half-walled off from the rest of the mortuary room. It was furnished with a few easy chairs, as well as a sink, a kettle and a small fridge. As it was part of the operating room, it was kept at the same chilly temperature. Tim was grateful to be able to wrap his hands around the mug of hot tea.

'Now,' said Professor Salkeld, 'don't tell me any more about your Jenkins case just yet, because I don't want to rush to conclusions. Let's focus on the wee lassie we opened up last night. She probably was stabbed to death, though some marks on her neck suggested that her killer may have tried to strangle her first. It's difficult to say, but she didn't lose as much blood from the stab wounds as might have been expected. She did lose some blood, though. My guess is that he tried to strangle her, she lost consciousness and then he finished it off with the stabbing. There are a couple of odd features: the first was picked up by Ms Gardner, when she made a preliminary examination at the scene. The girl wasn't wearing the clothes she was found in when she was stabbed. Either she had been wearing other clothes which the killer discarded and replaced, or she was naked when he stabbed her, except for her knickers. We can't know for sure if she was wearing the same ones when she died, but my best guess is she was. I can tell you she wasn't sexually assaulted.'

'I don't understand why the killer would want to change her clothes.'

'That's been puzzling me, too, but maybe you hold the key to it, if you're right about it being a copycat murder. If you want me to, I can get hold of the autopsy report of the girl killed by your Stephen Jenkins, see if it can throw further light on it for us.'

'Thank you. I'd really appreciate that.'

'It's my job,' said the Professor gruffly, brushing off gratitude as he always did. 'After what you've told me, it would be remiss of me not to suggest it. The girl was probably Roma, by the way.'

'Roma? You mean she was a gypsy?'

'If you like. I prefer the term Roma. I can't be certain, but she has all the characteristics. If the parents don't come forward, we will establish more about her background by carrying out blood and DNA tests.'

'Is that the other odd thing you mentioned?'

'No. Why would it be? Plenty of Roma in this area, either living here or passing through. If I'd said Inuit, you might have had a point. The other odd feature was that there was nothing frenzied about the knife blows, even though there were thirteen of them. Knife crime is both barbaric and, unless the perpetrator is totally depraved, requires some courage. Unlike firing a gun or launching a missile, even running someone over with a car, it necessitates physical contact. Perpetrators therefore have to psych themselves up to it, often making themselves go berserk in the process. It's as if they're at once horrified by what they're doing and determined to see it through. Hence they often use unnecessary force and may keep on stabbing the victim after it's clear that he or she is dead. Sometimes they stop only when the knife blade breaks in the victim's body. This killer didn't subject the girl to that kind of attack. Although he stabbed her thirteen times, the knife entered her body gently, almost tenderly. Unique in my experience.'

CHAPTER TWENTY-SIX

Juliet and Ricky had driven to Silverdale Farm in Juliet's car. She had turned across the dyke and was reversing the car so that it faced the house when a Smart Car came hurtling past and parked diametrically opposite to them, as close to the house as its driver could go. The driver, a woman, spent a couple of minutes talking to someone on her mobile before getting out of the car. Her long chestnut hair had been tied back with a scarf. She was wearing a light blue herring-bone suit and knee-length boots.

'It's Susie Fovargue,' said Ricky.

'I don't remember seeing that car she's driving in your inventory.'

'I don't think it is on the list. She was out when I came with DI Yates.'

Juliet didn't comment. She knew that Ricky would already be feeling embarrassed about not having asked about other vehicles owned by, but not at, the farm when he visited the day before.

Susie Fovargue looked across at them, then back at the house, as if undecided whether to speak to them or go inside and shut the door. Eventually she decided on the former course of action, picking her way along the muddy track with care. Her expression was not welcoming. Juliet thought that she looked the part of the landed lady – expensive if rather dowdy clothes, discreet accessories and just a touch of make-up.

'Shall I introduce you?' Ricky asked.

'I think you'd better. We should get out of the car.'

'DC MacFarlane,' Susie Fovargue said coldly, as she reached them. 'I thought it was you again. What's the matter now? I understood that Josh Marriott showed you around yesterday, as requested.' The last two words were spoken with pointed emphasis.

Ricky didn't correct her by re-stating his name. He understood her continuing failure to recall it accurately was merely a game she was playing to demonstrate how insignificant he was.

'He did. He was very helpful to both DI Yates and myself. Unfortunately, DI Yates was called away early to an emergency and has been taken off the vehicle thefts case now.'

'The vehicle thefts? Yes, I believe you did mention them before. But I thought you and DI Yates came to quiz Jack about the man who assaulted him.'

'We did. But when DI Yates understood how many vehicles you keep here, he thought...'

'I'm DS Armstrong,' Juliet cut in crisply. 'I'm working on the vehicle thefts with DC MacFadyen now. We're here because we'd like to give you some advice on making your property more secure.'

Susie Fovargue shrugged. She didn't take Juliet's out-stretched hand.

'That sort of thing doesn't really concern me. You'd better talk to Jack, if he's around – or Josh.'

'You'll forgive me for saying that it should concern you, Mrs Fovargue. That's a nice car you're driving – new by the look of it? Although most of the thefts we've been investigating are of farm vehicles, it's unlikely that the thieves would turn up their noses at a car like that, if they came upon it. And this place is very isolated.'

'I suppose it *is* rather a nice car,' Susie Fovargue said, as if reflectively, though with just enough smugness in her tone to annoy Juliet. 'You're right – Jack only bought it earlier this year. I have no idea why. I didn't ask for it.'

'It's your vehicle, then, Mrs Fovargue? Are you the only driver?'

'I suppose you could say it belongs to me. Jack uses it sometimes, but I need it most of the time for the children.'

'What does your husband drive?'

Susie Fovargue laughed.

'Oh, anything and everything. He tends to use the van that belongs to his organic farm quite a bit. As you have discovered, there are quite a lot of vehicles here.'

'Not all of them registered for road use, I believe,' said Ricky.

Her smile faded quicker than it had appeared.

'Perhaps not, but I'm sure he wouldn't take them out illegally. And they really aren't my affair. If you'll excuse me, I'm in rather a hurry. I'm visiting a primary school in an hour or so and I need to go in to make sure the children are okay. There's a woman from Bourne who's come to look after them, but I need to give her some instructions.'

'Of course,' said Juliet. 'If we can find Mr Marriott, do we have your permission to discuss improving the security with him?'

'If you want to. I don't know how co-operative he'll be. Josh is the sort of person who'll lie in wait for thieves and give them a

141

good pasting, rather than spend money on expensive security devices.'

'Is that so?' said Ricky quickly. 'In that case, we need to talk to him quite urgently, because if he takes matters into his own hands like that he'll easily overstep what the law allows.'

'Indeed,' said Juliet. 'The term 'reasonable force' is not a very precise one, but most judges interpret it in favour of the person it's used against, not the person who uses it, however provoked they may have been.'

'Yes, well that's just typical, isn't it? Anyway, I was only joking. Feel free to find Josh and bend his ear if you want to.'

'Thank you. Just one other thing before you go: you said we could talk to your husband 'if he's around'. Don't you know whether he's here or not today?'

'As you have seen, I've just been out myself. Jack and I lead very busy lives. We often work together, but we aren't always in each other's pockets. He's spent a lot of time out delivering some of the vintage stuff lately. He may be doing that again now. Or he may be here. I don't know.'

She frowned, as if she disapproved of these activities.

'I take it you went out earlier this morning? That you weren't away overnight?'

'I don't like to leave the children overnight.'

'Of course not. What about your husband? Did he sleep here last night?'

Susie Fovargue hesitated very briefly before she replied.

'I have no reason to suppose he didn't. As it happens, I went to bed very early myself.'

Juliet nodded.

'Thank you.'

Susie Fovargue wasn't listening. Her attention had been diverted to the scooter which had just appeared at the entrance to the farm. She let out a sigh that sounded more like a snarl.

'Here comes that silly girl, late, as usual.' She stepped into the centre of the track and held out her hand. The young woman on the scooter halted and pushed up the visor on her helmet. Ricky recognised her: it was Martha Johnson. He also noted again the uncanny resemblance between her and Mrs Fovargue.

'You're very late,' said Susie, tapping her watch. Martha appeared to be unfazed by her hostility.

'I worked late yesterday: I was supposed to be leaving at lunchtime and I stayed to talk to the policemen about what we do,' said Martha coolly, fixing Ricky with her clear blue eyes. He felt obliged to offer some support.

'That's correct, she did,' he said. 'She was most helpful.'

'Well, I'm glad she's good at something,' said Susie. 'Perhaps she can help you find Josh. I'll leave you all to it.'

She walked away quickly, taking the most direct route to her front door by crossing the scrubby lawn. She no longer seemed to care about getting mud on her boots.

CHAPTER TWENTY-SEVEN

'Hello, Timmo,' said Michael Robinson, when Tim met him after his tea break with Professor Salkeld and Paula. 'I thought you'd get here a bit earlier than this.' Tim saw at once that most of the contrition that Robinson had shown on the previous day had evaporated.

'I've been with Professor Salkeld at the morgue.'

'Ah, yes. The autopsy on the girl. Cause of death was multiple stab wounds, as we'd thought. I take it he told you that?'

'Yes; I didn't know he'd told you, as well. He didn't mention it.'

'I asked him to call me last night. I suppose he took it as a foregone conclusion that you'd realise. I am the SIO and it is my patch, after all. But I know you're big buddies with him.'

Tim understood immediately that Robinson was trying to claw back his seniority on the case. He was glad he'd accepted his offer to lead jointly the previous evening, but perplexed about why Robinson had returned to his usual bumptious self. Surely the prospect of being found negligent was still hanging over him?

'I don't think Professor Salkeld has "big buddies",' said Tim mildly. 'You seem to be much happier today. I told you you'd feel better once you'd slept on it.'

'I *am* feeling better, but it's mainly thanks to your boss. I spoke to him this morning – confided in him, actually – and he told me not to worry. He said that everyone makes the odd little slip. Plus, Salkeld says the girl had probably been dead for a couple of days, so if there'd been a police guard at the canal it wouldn't have saved her.'

Tim was flabbergasted. Had Superintendent Thornton, probably of all the policemen in the country the most attuned to the dangers of adverse reports in the media, really suggested to Michael Robinson that his 'little slip' was unimportant? That the girl had died two days before her body was thrown into the canal was news to him, but he supposed he had forgotten to ask the Professor about this detail.

'Well, if calling Superintendent Thornton put your mind at rest, I'm glad. It'll help us both to concentrate better on the case.'

'I didn't call him, actually, he called me. He wanted to know where you were. I told him you hadn't arrived here yet.'

'You told him I was at the morgue?'

'No, I didn't know that, did I? I said you must have got held up somewhere and I was sure you would be here soon.' Making an effort, Tim didn't lose his temper, but he was unable to keep the sarcasm out of his voice when he replied.

'Thanks for that. Did he say what he wanted?'

'Yes. He wanted to speak to us both, actually. He's not convinced about the joint SIO idea. He says it looks stronger to have just one SIO. No buck passing then, no question of too many cooks, etcetera.'

'Well, that's tough, because you've already sent out the press release now. And it says we're joint SIOs. Going back on your plans so soon after you've issued a public statement looks much weaker than sharing responsibilities.'

DI Robinson had the grace to look awkward.

'The press release did say that, didn't it? I read it through myself.'

'Yes, it did say that, originally. But just before I issued it, I... deleted that bit. I wasn't sure about it. I already knew what Dennis's thoughts on it were, you see.'

Tim had to make a yet more Herculean attempt at keeping his temper. The spirits of Katrin and Juliet, both standing invisibly at his elbow, told him that losing his dignity over status for a very temporary secondment would not be worthwhile.

'Okay,' he said, as flippantly as he could, 'that's fine by me. As I told you, Thornton probably won't let me stay here for very long, anyway, so it's probably for the best. So, what would you like me to do now, boss?'

'Well, in a minute I'd like you to go to the marina at the end of the Fossdyke Canal and find out how many people slept on their boats there on Monday night. The body was dumped on the other side of the lock, but it's possible the killer entered via the towpath that skirts the marina. Someone may have noticed someone struggling with a bulky weight. But first I want to run an idea past you.'

'Oh?' said Tim. He was conscious of the tingling in his cheeks and hoped his face hadn't flushed scarlet. Robinson had made him livid.

'Yes. Do you remember the Stephen Jenkins case?'

'Yes,' said Tim. 'And it's struck me that there are similarities between Jenkins' crimes and what we're dealing with now.'

'Got there before you, Timmo! I spoke to Dennis about it. I think he's asked someone to do some research into the Jenkins case for me. I think it might even be Katrin, actually.

Lucky to have her, aren't you? It'd be nice if I had my own personal researcher on tap.'

'It looks as if you've managed to abduct mine, in any case. But, officially, Katrin isn't employed by me. Did Thorn... the Superintendent really offer her services, just like that? He usually puts a fierce guard on all his support staff.'

'Yes, well you just need to be a bit more adept at how you handle him, don't you? I think Dennis is quite highly-strung and I've noticed you rubbing him up the wrong way a couple of times. Anyway, I've got to get on now. I need to prepare another press release, get someone to produce a passable sketch of the girl who was thrown into the canal. I'll probably ask Patti to do it: I seem to remember she's turned out some quite good drawings sometimes.'

'And you'll want Juliet to help you with the press release?' said Tim, his voice spiked with irony.

'If you insist, Timmo. Thank you. And only if she can spare the time, of course.'

CHAPTER TWENTY-EIGHT

Tim was still smarting from his encounter with Michael Robinson. He'd driven to the Fossdyke Canal as instructed, despite being in no mood to interview the residents at the marina. He had encountered boat-owners before and was unimpressed: the ones with the swankier vessels were suavely up their own backsides, while those who owned old tubs tended to be scruffy, contentious and often with a propensity to sail close to the law in petty ways that made them secretive and uncooperative.

As he parked his car, he saw a man standing on the bank some distance from him. He was on the marina side of the lock-gates but staring towards the area beyond the lock where police divers were still working. Tim was amused to see a uniformed policeman stationed close by. Robinson wouldn't make that mistake again in a hurry. The policeman, however, seemed to be inhabiting a world of his own. He hadn't noticed the man.

The man turned and glanced across at Tim, then walked away rapidly, disappearing down a track close by to where he'd been standing. Something about the way he moved looked familiar. Tim couldn't quite put his finger on it: the man had a strange loping gait, at once hurried and fussy. Tim shrugged: the man was probably of no account, likely just a local being nosy. What was of more interest was that he'd just shown Tim a third approach route to the canal bank. The police had assumed it could be reached only from the marina or from the fairly substantial track that gave access to the canal some two hundred yards beyond the spot where the bodies had been fished from the water. This third route was closer both to that place and to the main road. He decided to inspect it more closely.

Although Tim was quick to reach the point where the man had been standing, the latter's departure was yet more nimble. There was no sign of him on the footpath down which he'd disappeared, which sloped sharply until it reached the highway. The short expanse of road that Tim could see was also deserted but he could hear an engine starting up, the noise rapidly moving further away. The vehicle sounded more like a van than a car.

Tim was about to clamber down the path when a rough voice accosted him.

'Oi! You! What you think you're doing down there?'

Tim turned to find a short but heavily-built man wearing sturdy gumboots lumbering towards him. He had long grey hair flowing from a greasy flat cap and a very ruddy complexion. One of the scruffier boat-owners, Tim guessed. He was in no mood to humour the man. He whipped out his ID and flashed it under the man's nose as the latter drew to a halt at Tim's shoulder.

'DI Yates, South Lincs Police,' he said. 'I'm working on the murder investigation. I assume you know that three bodies have been pulled from the canal here? One of them, the one just found yesterday, was that of a young girl.'

'We've heard something about it; ain't got no details,' said the man sulkily. 'Police come snooping round here quite a bit, but they never tell us owt.'

'What's your name?'

The man hesitated, as if revealing his name might get him into trouble.

'Donald,' he said at length. 'Donald Hyde.'

'Why did you appear to be so annoyed just now, Mr Hyde? What did you think I was trying to do?'

'I didn't know what you was trying to do, but I could see you as you was going to go down yon track.'

Tim had to strain to make out his words. He spoke with a broad Lincolnshire accent.

'Isn't that allowed?'

'It ain't a proper track at all. It's been made by kids pushing through the bushes, little bleeders. We've a kind of residents' group 'ere, trying to put a stop to it. We don't want a load of kids streeling through 'ere of a night.'

Tim suppressed a smile at Hyde's use of the phrase 'residents' group'. It sounded incongruously civic, coming from a man like him.

'I can sympathise with that, Mr Hyde. It's quite a remote spot and I'm sure you deserve some peace in the evenings. How long would you say it is since they started doing it?'

'You mean hanging around, or coming up through yon way?'

'Is there a difference?'

'Aye, we've always been plagued by kids. But they only thought of coming up that way this summer. June time, I'd say. Not long before the schools finished.'

'Thank you, that's extremely helpful. Now, if you'll excuse me for a few minutes, I just need to check out this track. I won't make it any bigger: in fact, if what I think is correct, we'll be sealing it off, which will probably help you. Then I'd like to come and have a further word with you, if that's okay.'

'I suppose it'll have to be. My boat's green. Sweet Pea, her's called.'

Tim had to work hard not to grin.

'Thank you,' he said.

'I'll put the kettle on,' the old man said gruffly. 'By the way, ain't we got no coppers ussen?'

'I'm sorry?' said Tim. 'Could you say that again? I didn't quite understand.'

'You said *South* Lincs Police,' Donald Hyde enunciated slowly and loudly. 'What's up with our own coppers?'

'Oh, I see what you mean. It's normal in murder investigations for several forces to be involved. Usually they require more manpower than a single force can provide, particularly if it's a rural one.'

'Uh. Well, that's your story. We're probably lucky to have you, anyway. The coppers round 'ere are a useless lot of buggers.'

He turned and began to stomp back towards the marina.

Still smiling, Tim turned back to the track. It was quite steep and very rudimentary, having been fashioned mainly by breaking the branches on the shrubs that grew on the sheltered side of the bank. As Tim picked his way through foliage and roots, he dislodged drifts of earth which scudded away, some getting trapped in the shrubs further down, some making it all the way to the road.

The road, when he reached it, was quite empty: there were no vehicles, either parked or moving, to be seen in either direction. Turning, he looked back up at the top of the bank. The path he had scrambled down was steep. It would be hard but not impossible to climb it while carrying a body from the road up to the top. He began to climb it again himself, going slowly so that he could inspect the undergrowth closely as he went. He found a few loose fibres clinging to the scrubby bushes, and bagged them carefully, though he knew that it was more likely that they'd been left by the kids who had been causing a nuisance than from the clothes of either the schoolgirl or her killer.

The last part of the track was particularly steep, with a precarious-looking overhang at the top. Tim placed his hands on the path beyond it and braced his arms to lever himself across the overhang. The manoeuvre succeeded in launching him on to the path, though he caught some of the clods of grass and earth with his feet as he did so, causing them to break away and collect in a heap at the first dogleg of the track.

Tim stood up and brushed the worst of the dirt off his trousers. His hands were grubby, too. He hoped Donald Hyde might be willing to dispense soap and water as well as tea. Heading back towards the marina, he scanned its horseshoe-shaped artificial basin for a boat painted green. Most of the vessels were painted white or blue and white. At first, he failed to spot Sweet Pea because he'd assumed she was a houseboat. Having worked systematically through all the houseboats, he started on the cabin cruisers. There were fewer of these, but they were much larger than the houseboats. He doubted, however, if any of them was permanently inhabited. Every last one of them shrieked 'rich man's weekend toy'. Unsurprisingly, none of them was green.

Finally, his eye fell on a dilapidated narrow-boat that had been moored at the very edge of the marina. It was floating low in the water and partly obscured by a weeping willow tree. It was too far away for him to be able to read the name painted on the bow, but as soon as he saw it he was certain that the narrow-boat was Sweet Pea. As if on cue, Donald Hyde appeared on the deck and waved. Tim waved back and started walking towards him.

'You've tekken yer time,' said Hyde reprovingly, as Tim

climbed aboard the narrow-boat. Something about his new host intimidated Tim into apologising.

'Yes, I'm sorry, I wanted to follow that track to the bottom, see exactly where it led. I've got quite mucky, actually – I wonder if I could wash my hands?'

'Aye, there's a sink down below. No hot water this time of day, mind.'

'That's all right,' said Tim. 'Cold water and a bit of soap is fine.'

'There's washing-up liquid,' said Hyde doubtfully.

'That's fine,' Tim repeated.

Hyde stood aside and pointed to the steep steps that led below. Tim began his descent, a little apprehensive of what he might find in the cabin. He'd heard tales of the unspeakable squalor allowed to fester in some of these inhabited vessels.

He needn't have worried. Hyde's living quarters, although sparse to the point of being austere, were neat and well-kept. A kettle was steaming gently on the cooker. Two mugs had been set out on the draining board beside it. The stainless steel sink was spotlessly clean.

Hyde followed him down.

'There's sink,' he said gruffly. 'I'll fetch thee a towel.'

'No need,' said Tim quickly. 'I can improvise.'

Hyde took him at his word and, having poured boiling water into the two cups, used a spoon to squeeze the teabags they contained before removing the latter and setting the cups down on the table. He then settled himself on one of the bench seats and indicated a carton on the table.

'Help yerself to milk. It's UHT.'

Having washed his hands and dried them approximately on a paper tissue, Tim took the bench seat opposite, forcing his legs into the cramped space between the seat and the table.

'Do you live alone, Mr Hyde?'

'On and off.'

'What does that mean?' said Tim, trying to lighten the question with a smile.

'What it says. Missus died a few years back. I've a lady friend, but 'er's none too keen on the boat, leastways unless weather's good. So 'er comes sometimes, when it suits 'er.'

'When was she last here?'

'Earlier in the summer. We take the boat for some rides out when she's 'ere.'

'So the boat's here most of the time when you're alone?'

'Aye. Except when it needs some work doing on it. Mostly I do that 'ere, too, but for big jobs it has to be tekken somewhere else.'

'I imagine you notice what's going on outside more when you're alone?'

'Maybe. 'Ard for me to say.'

'You said there was a 'residents' group'. How many people belong to it?'

'Just the five or six of us as mostly lives 'ere.'

'Was it because of the children you set it up?'

'What children?' Hyde gave Tim a blank look.

'The children who've been making a nuisance of themselves.'

'Oh, those kids. Pikey kids, they are, in the main. No, it was while before that. Mainly to stop fly-tipping. People dumping stuff in the canal.'

'That's very public-spirited of you.'

Tim found himself on the receiving end of another blank look.

'Aye. Well, the shit they dump gets stuck in the propellers, see?'

'So what do you do, Mr Hyde, when you discover someone

trying to offload their rubbish here, or the kids come marauding? Do you call the police?'

Donald Hyde let out a merry laugh. Momentarily, it made him look like Father Christmas.

'Not likely! We don't want that lot round 'ere. Useless, anyway, as I said. No, if we manage to get anywhere near those folk, we put the fear of God into them, that's all.'

'You do know it's against the law to threaten people?'

'We don't threaten,' said Hyde, with a vehemence that told Tim he should change the subject. He wasn't there to do the local constabulary's job for them, after all.

'You say these kids are 'pikeys'. How do you know that?'

'Pretty obvious. They come in big groups, all ages, even tidders. Often mebbe skippin' school.'

'Do they look ill cared-for?'

'Scruffy, tha means?' Hyde barked a short sarcastic laugh. 'Naw. What give you that idea? Allus dressed reet smart, though that don't mean they ain't grufty. And t'faathers mebbe nicked clouts, tha knows.'

Tim just about got the gist of this. He noted that Hyde's dialect had broadened considerably since he'd suggested the barge-dweller might be capable of breaking the law.

'Why do you suppose they like to come here?'

'To rile us. And all kids like canals.'

'That's true. Tell me, over the last few days – or perhaps weeks – have you ever seen a teenage girl with them? A bit older than the others, maybe, but quite small for her age?'

Donald Hyde shrugged.

'I can't say as any of 'em stands out. She the girl you was talking about – the one dumped in t' watter?'

'Yes. We haven't been able to identify her yet. Did you hear or see anything unusual the night before last?'

Hyde barely paused to consider the question.

'Can't say as I did. Reet quiet, as I remember. No kids, that's so.'

'Thank you. Well, if you remember anything later, here's my card. I'd be grateful if you'd call me. Do you have a phone?'

'No, but there's a one in t' club'ouse. There was three bodies, you say?'

'Yes, but the others have been in the water for some time. We will want to make enquiries about them in this area, but we need more information about them first. We may be able to find out who they were, too. For the moment, I'd be grateful if you'd introduce me to the other boat-owners who spend the night here regularly, and anyone else you know of who might have been staying overnight on Monday.'

Daniel Hyde nodded. 'Drink up, then.'

Tim took the carton of UHT milk and poured a splash of the liquid into his tea, where it hovered on the surface of the beverage, coagulating unpromisingly. Seizing the mug bravely, he took a sip. The fluid was disgusting: strong and bitter, it tasted of brackish water mixed with sour curds. It took all his willpower not to spit it out on the table.

He was wondering how he was going to negotiate the rest of the mugful without giving offence when the ringing of his mobile saved him. He pulled it from his pocket with more alacrity than he'd usually have shown during a possible witness interview, especially when the caller was Superintendent Thornton.

'Superintendent Thornton! Is something wrong?'

'What a question! Yes, it most certainly is, Yates, and I'm not just referring to the three murders that you're investigating, which I would suggest are 'wrong' enough. Someone's been killed on our patch now. I want you to get yourself back here straight away.'

'But...' Tim was aware that Donald Hyde was listening

avidly, his head cocked like an ancient cockatoo's. The phone was not in speak mode, but Thornton tended to shout when he was agitated.

'If it's Robinson you're worried about, I'll tell him I need you here.'

'Yes, sir,' said Tim. He hadn't been thinking about DI Robinson: the last hour or so he'd spent at the marina had been so fascinating that he'd forgotten how much he was smarting when he'd arrived there. Well, Robinson would get what he deserved more quickly than Tim could have hoped: he could run the case on his own now, and good luck to him.

CHAPTER TWENTY-NINE

'Is there anything else you'd like to see?' said Martha Johnson to Ricky, once Susie Fovargue had disappeared into her house. 'I know you had to cut your visit short yesterday. Perhaps you'd like another look-round today? I don't think Josh is here, but I'm pretty familiar with everything myself.'

'DS Armstrong's concerned about improving the security of the vehicles here. This place is obviously very remote and there are a lot of vehicles, even if they're not all on the road. And we've just discovered there's at least one that we didn't list when we took the inventory yesterday.'

'You mean Susie's car? I did think about that after you'd gone. She was out in it yesterday, which is how it got over-looked. The most nickable of the lot, I'd say.'

'Quite possibly you're right. Do you happen to know where Mrs Fovargue went yesterday?' asked Juliet.

Martha Johnson smiled. It was a curious, cat-like smile. It suggested she was not as naïve as she appeared.

'Susie wouldn't confide in me. She doesn't like me.'

'She does make that rather obvious. Do you know why?'

'Oh, it could be any number of reasons.' Again, the cat-like smile. 'Do you want to look round again?'

'That would be helpful,' said Ricky. 'It may help us to provide better practical advice on security. No offence, but we don't need to look at the greenhouses and the soil stuff again. Just the vehicles. Can you get into the big shed where DI Yates and I saw all the vintage stuff?'

'Yes, no problem. There's a complete set of keys in the office.'

'That's poor security, for a start,' said Juliet, 'unless they're locked in a safe?'

'No, they're just hanging on hooks. But you haven't seen the office yet: it's in one of the big sheds. The doors would have to be rammed with a tank to get them open after they've been shut and locked.'

'Stranger things have happened,' said Juliet.

They followed her along the farm lane. As Marriott had the previous day, she led them to the tanker lorries that stood on a large square of concrete not far from the fence, beyond which were the open fields also owned by Fovargue.

Today all three tankers were parked in a row. From above the middle one a jet of water could be seen at intervals, springing skywards; rivulets of water were running off the concrete and gathering in muddy trickles in the dust of the lane.

'Looks as if Nathan's back,' Martha Johnson said briskly. As she spoke, a very young man emerged from behind the tanker. He was engaged in hosing it down and evidently hadn't noticed them. He was dressed in waterproofs and waders and had a sou'wester pulled down low on his forehead. Martha walked right up to him before he saw her. He swung round as she jumped nimbly out of the way, narrowly avoiding a soaking.

'Hey, steady on, you frit me, creeping about. You could be wet through by now!'

He was smiling broadly at her, peering up from under the hat, as he turned off the hose at the nozzle. Then Juliet and Ricky, still standing at the edge of the concrete, came into his line of vision and he knitted his brows.

'You've brought company, I see. Summat to do with your work?'

'No, they're police officers. They want to give us some advice on vehicle security.'

Juliet, who was never comfortable when being talked about in the third person, moved quickly across the concrete to join them. Ricky followed.

'I'm DS Armstrong,' she said, 'and this is DC MacFadyen. You'll be aware there's been a series of vehicle thefts in this part of the world. It's been nearly a year since it started.'

'Yep, I've heard about it. But you ain't suggesting someone's going to try to steal one of these, are you?' He gestured at the tankers, his right hand still encased in an outsized rubber glove.

'Organised thieves will steal anything to order. I agree that this type of vehicle isn't likely to be first on their list, but it's still worth being careful. I suppose it's not practical to keep them inside, is it?'

'Not a cat in 'ell's chance. No space 'ere, in any case. The sheds is all taken up with other parts of the business. They're immobilised when they're parked up, though.'

'I'll make a note to ask Mr Fovargue if the security arrangements for them can be improved.'

'Right you are, then.' Despite his accommodating words, Juliet thought she saw a powerful grimace of contempt cross Nathan's face. Meant for the police in general, she wondered, or perhaps just for his employer?

'What's your surname, Nathan?'

'Buckland. Why do you want to know?'

'Just for our records. We're keeping a note of everyone we've talked to about vehicle security.'

'Watching your backs, then?'

'Something like that.' Juliet gave him a smile, trying to rekindle the one she'd seen him give Martha. He turned away.

'If that's all, I'll be getting on. Josh wants all these hosed down today.'

'Where is Josh?' said Juliet.

Nathan paused to give her a level look.

'How should I know? He's my boss – he doesn't ask my permission when he goes off somewhere. He's not here today, that's all I can tell you.'

'Thank you, that's helpful,' said Juliet, as she turned to walk back to the lane. Again, Ricky followed, but not before he'd seen Martha whispering a few words to Nathan before she rejoined them.

'Do you like Nathan?' he asked her, as they headed for the bigger of the two sheds.

'I don't see all that much of him. Josh says he's a good worker. He seems okay to me. Nice to see someone like him getting on.'

'Why do you say that?'

She hesitated for a moment.

'Not for any particular reason. I just like people to do well, that's all. The clergyman's daughter in me coming out, maybe.' She threw him one of her smiles: it looked more like a challenge than a gesture of friendliness.

'I'll need to fetch the keys for the big shed from my office. I'll just run on ahead. I won't keep you waiting long.'

Juliet had been walking ahead of them both. She was startled to see Martha Johnson suddenly sprint past her.

'Where's she off to?'

'Just to find the keys to that shed. She'll be back in no time.'

'What a strange set-up this is. I can't make up my mind whether it's very enterprising in a nutty sort of way, or that the 'businesses' simply don't stack up.'

'You mean they might be an elaborate front to conceal some less worthy activities?'

'The thought had crossed my mind. What does Tim think?'

'I'm not sure. I do know he finds it difficult to understand why Fovargue is so highly thought of round here. But his reputation's mainly based on the soil appreciation stuff and we haven't dug into that much. It's all about lectures and taking soil samples: not a lot to do with vehicles.'

'Maybe we should go to one of his lectures, see what he talks about.'

'Should be easy enough: both Fovargue and Susie seem to do a lot of lecturing. She focuses more on schools than he does; he talks to farmers' clubs and WIs, that sort of thing. They both go to agricultural shows.'

'Can you find out more about where they're going, say, in the next couple of weeks?'

'There's loads of stuff about them on their website; it must include information about events.' Ricky paused. 'I've been thinking about Nathan Buckland. I can't be absolutely certain, but I'm ninety per cent sure that he's the guy who floored Fovargue in Red Lion Street. He looks different wearing waterproofs and that hat, so I didn't recognise him when we were talking to him. But the more I think about it, the more I think it is him.'

'If you're right, it doesn't make sense. Why would Fovargue continue to employ someone who had assaulted him?'

'No idea, but Fovargue was very reluctant to pursue an assault case. He said he wouldn't be bringing charges, and in fact he seemed desperate for us to drop it. It was only because the guy took a pop at me, too, and Superintendent Thornton said it wasn't up to Fovargue to decide, that he agreed to go along with it. I wouldn't say he was helpful, though, even if he appeared to co-operate. And something that was peculiar about his tale was that first he said he thought the attacker was a traveller, then he changed that to biker.'

'Did you think the attacker looked like a traveller?'

'I think it was Buckland; he looks like a traveller, doesn't he?'

'Hard to tell with all that rig on... she's coming back now. Let's pick up on this later.'

Martha Johnson had reappeared, clutching a bunch of keys in one hand. She undid the padlock and punched in the key code with considerably more panache, Ricky thought, than Marriott had shown the day before. The doors of the great shed slid open. Martha turned on the lights.

'Gosh, is that an old traction engine?' said Juliet, immediately spotting the tarpaulin-shrouded monster just inside the shed.

'Yep. But I guess all traction engines are old – I haven't heard of any new ones being made lately. Josh's pride and joy, that is.'

'Do you know much about the tools and vehicles in here?'

'Not a great deal. He's shown me round a couple of times, told me the history of some of them. A lot of the things that pass through here are bought to order and sold on quickly, as soon as they've been cleaned up and, if necessary, repaired. Then there are others that have been here for years. Truth be told, I think he gets quite attached to them. He'd sell them if he found a buyer, of course, but he doesn't really want that to happen.'

'You seem to know a lot about what Mr Fovargue thinks.'

'He talks to me quite a bit. I'm lucky – I work in the part of the business that's closest to his heart. That's why I think we get on so well. We hit it off straight away.'

Ricky had been inspecting the tools fixed to the wall, but he circled back now to join in the conversation.

'Your appointment's only temporary, though, isn't it? Josh Marriott said you'd be here until Christmas.'

'Possibly,' Martha Johnson said, her open expression suddenly shutting down. 'But maybe not. Jack wants to give the soil appreciation work a much higher profile. He says he may be able to find a permanent post for me.'

I wonder how Mrs Fovargue feels about that, Juliet thought silently. Aloud she said, 'I remember those old tractors. There were still some around when I was a kid. Death traps, really: there was no safety bar, so if the driver rolled over he was pretty certain to be crushed.'

'There probably weren't many deaths of that kind round here – the fields are too flat. But I understand it does make them difficult to sell, unless they're bought by a museum or an exhibition. By law they must have roll bars fitted before they can be used again. And Jack doesn't like doing that: he says it spoils the integrity of the vehicle.'

Juliet glanced at Ricky, who was having to work hard to keep a straight face. She remembered that Ricky came from a family of small-time farmers and market gardeners. Doubtless the 'integrity' of the vehicles they used didn't come very high on their list of priorities.

'What's that over there?' Juliet asked. Unlike Josh Marriott on the previous day, Martha had switched on all the lights, including those illuminating the back of the shed. Juliet had just noticed the bundle wrapped in tarpaulin in the far corner. 'It looks like another vehicle.'

'Oh, that,' said Martha, screwing up her face. 'That's just one of Jack's funny quirks. I wouldn't bother with it if I were you. It's not going anywhere.'

'But what is it?' Juliet pursued. If Martha Johnson had been trying to stem her curiosity, being mysterious about the package was the wrong way to go about it. Juliet was like a bloodhound when it came to sniffing out the unusual.

'It is a vehicle. It's a car,' said Martha slowly. 'It's a kind of collector's item. It hasn't been taxed and I doubt if the engine would start. It hasn't been out on the road for a very long time. As I said, it's just one of Jack's quirks.'

Juliet walked over to the car. The tarpaulin was bound round it tightly and secured with ropes and masking tape. Juliet traced her fingers along it, trying to make out the shape of the car beneath.

'It's probably a small domestic car. An old one. I'd say a Morris Minor, something like that.'

Martha Johnson's eyes widened.

'That's clever of you.'

'Not really. They're a very distinctive shape. And there's quite a market for the reconditioned ones. I think there's someone local who does them up.'

'I wouldn't know about that. Anyway, this one hasn't been reconditioned. Jack just keeps it like this.'

'I'm no expert, but I doubt if the tarpaulin's helping to preserve it. The bodywork would probably survive better if it was open to the air. Under cover, I mean, but not wrapped up.'

'I think Jack would be.... superstitious about exposing it.'

'How do you mean?'

Martha Johnson took a deep breath.

'Jack's owned it for a long time. I don't know how he came by it, but one of his ideas was to open a museum of vehicles that had been used in serious crimes. A sort of Chamber of Horrors, but it never got off the ground. That was because this car was the first one he bought for it, and then it spooked him. That's why it's covered up. It's got a hold over his imagination. He doesn't like it, but he doesn't want to let it go.'

'Where did it come from?'

'I told you, I don't know.'

'I didn't mean that. I meant, which crime was it used in? Presumably it was a well-known one?'

'Have you heard of the A6 murder?'

'Yes. Most people who've studied criminal law must have done. James Hanratty was one of the last people to be hanged in this country, for murdering a scientist and wounding his mistress so that she was paralysed for the rest of her life. I don't know the date, but I do know it was early in the 1960s. The woman's name was Valerie Storie – it sticks in the mind, because she continued to pop up in the media at intervals right up until her death. I can't remember the scientist's name.'

'Michael Gregsten.'

'That's right. Are you telling me this was Gregsten's car? The car in which he was sitting when Hanratty murdered him?'

'What are you lot doing in here?' An angry voice came booming through the shed, drowning the beginnings of Martha Johnson's reply. She ceased speaking swiftly and turned to face the newcomer.

'Hello, Josh,' she said quietly. 'It's all right: one of the policemen who was here yesterday came back with a colleague, to talk to us about security.'

'What do they want to talk to you about security for? You don't know owt about it. You'd do well to stop meddling.'

'We asked Ms Johnson to help,' said Juliet. Her mobile began to ring.

'Could you just wrap up here?' she said to Ricky. 'I need to take this. I'll come back when I've finished talking,' she added, glancing at Martha. She thought the girl might have been cowed by Josh Marriott's rough way of speaking, but she seemed serene enough.

'Armstrong!' Superintendent Thornton's voiced thundered

out at her, as belligerent as Josh Marriott's had been a few minutes earlier, though Juliet knew from experience that the Superintendent tended to sound like this when he was panicking. 'I need you here at once. I've told Yates to get back, too. Pronto. There's been another murder, right here.'

CHAPTER THIRTY

S imon Smythe was a gay man of a certain age. He'd been a child when homosexuality ceased to be a crime, so by the time he was an adult he didn't have to fear reprisals from the law. There were still compelling reasons for keeping his orientation a secret, however: he came from a family of staunch Fenland Methodists who regarded even heterosexual sex with distaste, only to be tolerated if practised as joylessly as possible for the purposes of procreation.

Simon had nursed both his parents through long illnesses until they'd died just a few months apart, both still believing that their only son had so devoted himself to them that he'd had no time to select the mother of their future grandchildren. Once on his own, he'd retrained as a social worker, specialising in caring for children at risk. He'd also been free, at last, to form relationships with other men and although none of these had lasted more than a few months he'd found each one fulfilling. The break-ups had been amicable and he still had high hopes of discovering a permanent partner. He had 'come out' now and felt happier – and even younger – with each year that passed.

He'd also developed a taste for experimentation. Although

his goal was always to establish a meaningful relationship, he'd also needed to find other outlets for the frustrated fantasies that he'd nurtured for decades. Coached by some of his partners, he'd discovered how to pick up trade in clubs and bars. At first, he'd travelled to larger towns and cities for this purpose, but more recently he'd found that Spalding had its own small but buoyant 'gays-for-pay' community.

He'd finished work early on the Wednesday and gone home to shower. He lived in a small but comfortable flat above a shoe shop in the town centre. He kept the flat neat, but before his shower he took the trouble to tidy away a pair of shoes and a few books and magazines. It wasn't his habit to take his pick-ups home with him, but he'd met a guy the previous weekend whom he was very taken with. He knew that many of the trade gays weren't gay at all, just doing it for the money, but this guy was different. He was certainly not merely pretending to enjoy the sex and he and Simon hit it off in other ways, too. Despite the fact that their relationship was at present purely transactional, Simon had hopes of it turning into something more intimate. He even entertained some diffident hopes that François could be 'the one'.

He combed his wet hair, which was greying now but still wavy and luxuriant, back off his forehead and secured it in a neat, short ponytail at the nape of his neck. His wardrobe was modest in size, but contained only pieces that he liked, some of which had been costly. The previous weekend he'd been wearing a red plaid shirt and a pair of J Brand jeans, his favourites. François had told him how nice he'd looked, so he decided to choose the same outfit again. He'd washed the shirt since then and had the jeans dry-cleaned (he never washed his jeans – it pulled them out of shape).

They'd agreed to meet in a small bar in Double Street, a quiet road only a few hundred yards from Spalding town centre, at 7.30pm. Simon set off soon after 7pm; Double Street was only a few minutes' walk from his flat, but after years of ensuring that first his parents and then the children under his care never missed appointments, he was, as he often ruefully acknowledged, 'pathologically early'. The evening was turning cool, so he'd knotted a Burberry cashmere jumper round his shoulders in case he needed it later on. He'd bought a small gift for François, a box of Belgian shell chocolates, which he carried in a Burberry tote.

The evenings had begun to draw in, but it was still quite light. There wasn't much traffic about. He passed a few pedestrians as he walked through the town, but when he turned into Double Street he saw no one except a man on a bicycle heading towards the High Street bridge. The man glanced at him briefly but did not respond when Simon called out 'Evening!'

Looking ahead, he saw the street wasn't as deserted as he'd first thought. A slight figure up ahead of him was just disappearing round the corner that led into the lower part of the street, where the Quaker chapel stood. He was certain it was François, a wiry little Frenchman who loved bright colours: this man was wearing a turquoise-and-purple striped rugby shirt and maroon corduroy trousers and, although Simon hadn't yet seen François dressed like that, the clothes were just what he'd have expected the Frenchman to choose.

Evidently François, who was new to the town, had walked straight past the bar, which was very discreet. It stood well back from the pavement and wasn't well-lit. Simon hesitated to shout out to François: this was a residential area, and he knew the owner of the bar was careful to keep on the right side of his neighbours. Instead, he broke into a run, hoping to catch up before François reached the end of the street and lost his bearings completely.

Simon had run only a few steps – he was just beginning to pick up speed – when suddenly he tripped across an obstacle on the pavement, lost his footing and fell headlong. The tote bag containing the chocolates slid out of his grasp and was pitched into the gutter. His first thought was to retrieve it, but when he tried to move his breathing became ragged and he could feel a sharp pain in his chest. He hoped he had just winded himself, nothing worse. His chin was hurting. Gingerly, he raised the trembling fingers of his right hand to touch it. Even before he could inspect them he knew they would be bloody.

He was trying to haul himself into a sitting position when he felt someone grab the collar of his shirt. For a few brief seconds he thought himself fortunate: the person must have witnessed the accident and come to help him. He tried to twist his head round so that he could see who it was.

The grip on his collar tightened.

'You don't need to look at me,' said a soft voice. 'I'm not very interesting. But you do need to do exactly what I tell you.'

CHAPTER THIRTY-ONE

Tim and Juliet drove to the murder scene together, having both first called in at the station for some terse instructions from Superintendent Thornton. Tim had arrived before Juliet, so had been cursorily briefed. The Superintendent didn't want to waste time on briefing Juliet, too. Tim told her the few details he knew as they made the short journey to Double Street.

The victim's body had been found in the dark narrow alleyway known as the 'Butter Market', a dank and insanitary cut-through between the street and the central marketplace which was little used except by the stallholders who on market days were obliged to avail themselves of the grim public toilets situated there. Otherwise, the passageway exhibited no features except the gaunt windowless walls of the tall buildings on either side of it.

The body had been left in a shallow recess halfway along the alley, laid on its side to face the wall. It looked as if it had been dumped after death rather than that the victim had crawled there to die: its position was contorted and unnatural. The clothes the corpse was wearing were streaked with dirt.

The recess where it lay was immediately opposite the public toilets. The spot was permanently filthy because of the lack of drains and the foul seepages issuing from the lavatories, which dated from the 1930s and were not well-maintained.

'I take it he hasn't been moved yet, so no one's got a good look at his face. Yet you say we're certain of the identity?' asked Juliet, bending down to take a closer look. The victim was of medium height and powerfully built; his face was obscured.

'He hasn't been formally identified, but the guy who found him is sure he's Simon Smythe. He is – was – a social worker.'

'Has he been reported missing?'

'Not that I know of.'

'So we don't know who saw him last?'

'No, but the bloke who found him had arranged to meet him last night and apparently got lost. He tried to call Smythe and couldn't get a reply.'

'But I thought the body was found this morning?'

'It was. This friend tried to call him again today and when he still couldn't get a reply decided to retrace his footsteps. He'd located the bar where they should have met meantime – says he must have walked straight past it yesterday. He found a bag in the road that belonged to Smythe, apparently, which led him to search the Butter Market.'

'Sounds a likely story to me. Who is this "friend"?'

'His name's François Fabron.'

'Pull the other one! Don't you think he's just made that up for our benefit?'

'Maybe, but he is French, according to Thornton. And new to the area. That's why he failed to find the bar where he was meeting Smythe last night.'

'Still sounds suspicious to me. Could he have been the murderer? And where is he now?'

'He's been taken to hospital, suffering from shock. He could be the murderer – that'll be one of our first lines of enquiry. According to Thornton, though, Fabron's little and weedy: it's unlikely that he'd be able to overpower a bloke of Smythe's build. If he *is* the killer, it's an open-and-shut case, but Thornton doesn't think so. Otherwise he wouldn't be making such a fuss about it.'

'Ironical that he's called Fabron,' said Juliet. 'Why do you say that?'

'It's French for 'blacksmith'. It doesn't sound as if he takes after his ancestors.' She became brisker. 'We need to be able to examine the body properly. When are we going to be able to move it?'

'It's in an awkward position and, as you can see, rigor mortis has set in. Professor Salkeld's been called. I don't know when he'll get here. He won't want us to move it until he's seen it.'

'There's not much we can do until then, is there, except secure the scene? And it looks as if the uniforms have done a pretty good job on that already.'

'It's pretty disgusting in here. Fancy going for a coffee?'

'If you think we should. I haven't had any lunch – not that I want any now – but a warm drink wouldn't go amiss. Did you say Smythe was a social worker?'

'Apparently Fabron said he was. Why do you ask?'

'Oh, I may know someone who knows him, that's all.'

'Okay. Well, that could be useful. When we've got a positive identification, you might like to ask her if they knew him.'

'It's a man, actually.'

'Oh? Do I know him, too?'

'Yes, but I don't know if you remember him. It's Jake Fidler.'

'Guy from the children's home? Of course I remember him. I didn't know you'd kept in touch.'

'Well, we have,' said Juliet uncomfortably. Tim understood that tone of voice: it said: 'Back off.'

'Tea or coffee?' he asked innocently.

They were still sitting in the café when a tall spare man with greying hair appeared in the doorway.

'Professor Salkeld!' said Tim, standing up. 'Can I get you anything?'

'Not now,' growled the pathologist. 'There's work to be done. And if I may say so, I'm feeling a bit overloaded at the moment. Three cadavers in Lincoln and now one here.' The professor frowned, as if the discovery of so many murders in the space of a couple of days had been contrived as a personal affront to him.

'We're grateful to you for coming so quickly. We know we don't have a prior claim over Lincoln.'

'You do and you don't. You probably stand a better chance of catching the perpetrator of this one, which is why I've hot-footed it over here.'

'Why do you say that?'

Professor Salkeld gave Tim an old-fashioned look.

'You're supposed to be the copper. Haven't you always told me that the first twenty-four hours are the most crucial in a murder investigation? Well, there's no chance you'd have got anywhere near that for the lassies you pulled out of the canal, is there? Even the wee girl had been dead for several days when I saw her. So I presume their killer's trail has gone a bit cold. Whereas this latest bastard's could still be red hot.' The professor winked ironically.

'Let's go, then,' said Tim, aware that the professor was beginning to attract the curiosity of some of the shoppers patronising the café. 'I must warn you, the area surrounding the body is not very salubrious.'

'Ye're right, it stinks here,' said Professor Salkeld, as he entered the Butter Market. 'Reminds me of the bogs at my primary school,' he added, snapping on some latex gloves as if they could act as a prophylactic and removing the lens cover from his camera.

When he reached the body, he took a few close-up shots of it where it lay. Then he turned it over gently, holding it by the shoulder.

'Could you just put a plastic sheet under there for me?'

Tim did as he asked. The professor eased the body on to the sheet. Juliet was used to seeing corpses and not particularly squeamish, but what she saw made her flinch. The victim's head had been badly beaten.

'Someone didn't like the fella,' the professor observed. 'He's taken a fair beating.'

'Is that what killed him?'

'Maybe, but I doubt it. He's been beaten about the head, but I don't think the skull's fractured. We shall see. I can't do much here: I need to take a few more pictures in situ and then get him to the morgue. The ambulance service won't want to do it. Have you got an undertaker on standby?'

'One of the local undertakers has been asked to help. They have a spare van today. They can be here in a matter of minutes. Presumably we need to get him into a body bag?'

'That's going to be difficult, in his present condition. I think he'll have to be put on a stretcher and bound round with plastic. Tell the undertaker we need a stretcher. We should be able to do the rest ourselves. Look here,' he added, bending down. 'There's a clue for ye.'

'What is it?' asked Tim.

'It's pretty bloody, but unless I'm mistaken, it's a Gay Pride badge.'

CHAPTER THIRTY-TWO

Giash Chakrabati had been instructed to drive François Fabron to the hospital and wait there until he was fit to be taken back to the station for questioning. Tim and Juliet were surprised to see Giash's car turn into the station just before they themselves reached it. Tim had thought it likely he'd be detained by a wait at the hospital of many hours and that Fabron might be declared unfit for questioning at the end of it – or himself engineer such a diagnosis.

'I'd let them get settled before we set up the interview,' said Juliet. 'We don't want to spook him.'

'Fine,' said Tim, who had been about to leap out of the car. 'We'll give them a few minutes. You could call Jake Fidler while we're waiting.'

He stared at Juliet beadily. She looked uncomfortable and flushed scarlet. Tim was immediately repentant.

'Sorry, that was unfair of me. None of my business, but has Jake Fidler become your "significant other"?'

'You're right, it is none of your business; but since I know you won't let it rest until I tell you, the answer is 'maybe'.'

'Right. That does sound like telling me to mind my own business.'

'Guilty conscience. I mean what I say: I'm not sure.'

'Right,' said Tim again. It was on the tip of his tongue to mention Juliet's previous girlfriends, but he thought better of it. 'I can see you won't want to call him while I'm sitting here.'

'Correct,' said Juliet crisply. 'Shall we go in now?'

François Fabron was skinny to the point of emaciation. Swarthy-skinned, he had a pointed, rather crow-like face and jet-black hair which was thick and greasy and fell in an untidy cowlick over his eyes. The eyes themselves were his finest feature: large and soulful, they were a deep nut brown. He fixed them on Tim dejectedly as he entered the interview room and half stood when he saw Juliet.

'Good afternoon, Mr Fabron. Please don't get up,' said Tim. 'You've had quite an ordeal. I hope you're feeling better now.'

Fabron turned to Giash Chakrabati, who had remained standing.

'He doesn't speak much English, sir. Perhaps best to talk in short sentences and not use unusual words. The hospital says he's all right. His heart was beating very fast when he came here this morning, and his skin was clammy, but the doctor diagnosed only mild shock. He's been given some tranquillisers.'

'Thanks. Has he said much to you? About discovering the body, that is?'

'I've tried not to raise the subject, sir. He got very upset when Superintendent Thornton was speaking to him earlier.'

'Okay. I'd like you to stay while we interview him, if you don't mind. He seems to like you.'

'Do you want me to speak to him in French?' said Juliet.

'I hadn't thought of that. Probably because my own French isn't good enough. It should be, of course.'

'Not a subject you chose to apply yourself to?'

'You could say that.'

Half an hour later, Juliet had extracted all the information she could from François Fabron and Giash Chakrabati had been detailed to take him back to his lodgings. He was staying in a cheap bed-and-breakfast place out on West Marsh Road, one of several that accommodated migrant workers at the food-packing plant. When asked about his occupation, however, he had been cagey.

'Gay as a coot,' had been Tim's comment, when Juliet had explained the many points in their conversation that he hadn't understood.

'Being gay isn't an occupation,' said Juliet.

'In his case, I'd say it probably is. He has pimp written all over him.'

Juliet tried to keep her voice even.

'You may be right. He says he met Smythe on a dating site. They were both fascinated by people with double initials, apparently. 'SS' and 'FF'.'

'How sweet! Did he tell you why he was meeting Smythe last night?'

'Just for a drink, he said. They were planning to go to the Yellow Tulip. It's a bar on Double Street.'

'I know it. Quite a posh establishment. It used to be renowned as a gay bar and pick-up joint, but it's cleaned its act up a bit recently. Tries to have a broader appeal now. Never crossed swords with us as far as I know. The owner likes to stay on the right side of the law. I suppose we ought to question him, ask if his staff saw anything.'

'Superintendent Thornton has started door-to-door enquiries in Double Street. They're bound to include the Yellow Tulip. I'm not sure if the staff there will know much, though, since apparently neither Smythe nor Fabron made it through the door.'

'Yes, but they may know Smythe – or Fabron, I suppose, though that's less likely, if he genuinely couldn't find the place. Or one of them could have been sneaking a fag outside and seen something.'

'Do you want me to give the door-to-doors some special instructions for the Yellow Tulip?'

'Can't hurt, can it? We need to find out more about Smythe. It was Thornton who said he was a social worker. I wonder how he found that out?'

'Speaks French, probably.'

'I'll ask him. He hasn't found out who Smythe worked for yet. It wasn't the council.'

'Professor Salkeld's probably gone through his pockets now. He must have been carrying a wallet, so there'll be something in it that will identify him. I'll call him. And I'll give Jake a call now, too.'

'Thanks,' said Tim. 'Stay in here to make the calls, if you like. It'll be quieter than the main office.'

Juliet stifled a smile. Tim's efforts at diplomacy could be very amusing when they didn't irritate her with their clumsiness.

CHAPTER THIRTY-THREE

Tim had put Juliet in charge of the door-to-door enquiries and managed to wheedle a promise from Superintendent Thornton to stump up the budget to draft in extra help from another police force if he could persuade Michael Robinson, now in danger of permanently losing the support he was receiving from South Lincs, to share the costs. The prospect of a long night with little or no sleep seemed inevitable. Tim had no intention of leaving his team to it while he went home to rest, but, glancing at his watch, was just debating whether he could spare a few minutes to nip home to see Katrin and say goodnight to Sophia when his phone rang.

'DI Yates?'

Tim recognised Professor Salkeld's voice immediately.

'Professor! I wasn't expecting to hear from you again so soon.'

'Aye. Well, I didn't expect ye to, either. But for once my job's been made easier than I expected. I can tell ye now the likely reason for death of the laddie in the alleyway: his body's been punctured with multiple stab wounds.'

'Like the young girl at the Fossdyke!'

'Precisely like that. Strange, don't ye think?'

'But that means that the girl's murder may be linked to Smythe's; and it makes it less likely that she and the other two women in the Fossdyke were killed by the same person!'

'As I've said before, ye're the detective. I'm just giving you the facts. Bear in mind I've just given you the likely reason for his death so far; ye'll have to wait a bit longer for the actual cause. Punctured one or more of the internal organs, is my guess.'

'Bang goes Michael Robinson's theory about copycat murders!'

'With regard to the other two women, I wouldn't rule anything out yet. I'm doing my best to establish a cause of death for them, but it's not easy. Decomposition is very far advanced.'

'But what do you think, Professor? The murders at the Fossdyke had so much in common with the Jenkins murders that DI Robinson wasn't the only person to guess that they were copycat crimes.'

There was a pause at the other end of the phone. Then the Professor could be heard tutting.

'If you really want me to teach you your job, I'd say there were three possibilities: if they're copycat murders, either Jenkins killed a middle-aged male as well and it was never discovered; or your copycat criminal has got the wind up and decided to commit another crime to lead you off scent.'

'Makes sense. And the third possibility?'

'That the crimes aren't linked.'

'But you don't believe that, do you, Professor?'

'I try to keep an open mind. It's my job to do so. But since you ask, like yourself, I'm inclined to be suspicious of coincidences. So, no, I don't believe they're unrelated. And if they aren't, there's someone very dangerous out there who's on a bit of a killing jag at the moment.'

Having exchanged farewell pleasantries, Tim put down the phone. A crisis point had been reached; now he must think very clearly about what to do. The police urgently needed to warn the public of the danger, but what form should the warning take? Tim had successfully tackled killers on the loose before, but they'd never chosen such a diverse set of victims. If this was a single killer, his or her victims had been two young women, a child and a middle-aged man. Was there a link between their deaths, or had they simply been chosen at random? Alternatively, was it possible there were two or even three killers at work? The two women whose bodies had been hauled from the Fossdyke Canal must have been murdered by the same person, but the killer of the girl and Smythe could have been someone different, or, less probably, two completely separate people. Should the public at large be warned that everyone was in danger? Tim knew this wouldn't work. Unless he could say that specific groups of people were at risk, it was unlikely that anyone at all would heed the warnings.

His need to see Katrin had become urgent now. She'd be able to look at the whole thing objectively, perhaps spot some links that he was missing, help him to narrow down the killer's profile. For the first time, he admitted to himself that the course she was studying had its uses.

He was about to go in search of Juliet to say that he was nipping home for half an hour when his phone rang again.

'Hello, Timmo.'

'Michael? How's it going? I'm sorry I had to rush off, but I did warn you that Superintendent Thornton might see my secondment as a very temporary arrangement. I'm afraid it doesn't look as if I'll be coming back to you soon, if at all.'

He had made a snap-second, very ungallant decision not to tell DI Robinson any details about the Spalding murder. Let him hang on to his copycat theory for a bit longer, perhaps get egg on his face!

'No, I guessed that. But I'd still like to ask for your help unofficially, if you don't mind.'

Tim had already been preoccupied when he'd first taken the call and therefore was not paying much attention to Robinson's tone, but now he focused on it more closely and detected the note of panic there. The annoying uppitiness Robinson had exhibited earlier in the day had vanished.

'I'll do my best,' he said carefully. 'I don't have much time, as you know.'

'I've had a visitor. About the Fossdyke murders,' Robinson began, his voice shaking slightly.

'Oh, yes? A witness?'

'Not exactly. Someone who says they're from the Roma community.'

Tim pricked up his ears. This could be more interesting than he'd expected.

'What did they want?'

'They said they'd been looking for a girl who disappeared a few days ago.'

'Sounds promising! Go on.'

'Apparently this girl sometimes mixed with the estate kids who go down to the Fossdyke to muck around.'

'This gets even better, Michael. Who is this person? Is it a parent?'

'No, just a woman who says she takes care of the Roma kids sometimes – or tries to – while their parents are out 'working'. She hasn't told me much about the girl she's been looking for.'

'Have you asked her to bring the parents in? See if they can identify the girl in the morgue?'

'No, not yet.' Robinson's voice had almost dropped to a whisper.

'Well, why the hell not, Michael? This could be our – your – best lead so far!'

'I don't know if she's above board. But she did tell me that she'd been to the Fossdyke Canal to look for the girl. At night.'

Suddenly, Tim understood.

'Which night? The night the bodies of the two women were found and the Fossdyke Canal was left without police guard? Michael, is she trying to blackmail you?'

'I don't know. What do you think?'

'I don't know, either. But you can't afford to pass up on this lead just because you're afraid someone in the press might accuse you of negligence. You won't put her off by ignoring her, in any case. If she's hoping to squeeze something out of you, she'll keep on until it either works or you get shut of her. Surely you know that. And you also know you can't afford to let it work. You haven't broken the law by being negligent, but if you succumb to blackmail, God help you!'

'I know,' said Robinson miserably.

'Is that the favour you wanted to ask? Just for me to listen?'

'Well, actually, no, I...'

'Go on,' said Tim, trying to sound as off-putting as he could.

'I wondered if you'd come over to interview her with me. I'd appreciate your opinion. You'll have a better sense of if she's above board than I will.'

Tim was in no mood for flattery.

'You mean, if she's thinking of blackmail she won't dare try it on with me?'

'If you want to put it like that, yes. Can you spare the time?'

'The answer to that is no. But I will come if I can – only because I'm interested myself in whether she has any genuine information. When can you get her back in?'

'She's here now. I've asked her to wait.'

'Christ, Michael, I've had a beast of a day. There's a new

185

murder here to solve and I haven't had chance to speak to Katrin since yesterday. I was just about to nip home now...'

'I'd do it for you, Timmo.'

Tim was amused by the blatant lie. He almost let out a shout of laughter.

'I'm quite certain you wouldn't, Michael. But okay, you win. I'll be with you shortly.'

CHAPTER THIRTY-FOUR

Juliet hesitated before calling Jake Fidler. It wasn't that she still felt awkward with him – the conversation he'd initiated about the future of their relationship had helped her to relax, so that now she felt she'd be entirely easy in his company and certainly not shy of asking him for a favour. Her diffidence stemmed from the fact that, although they'd originally met through their respective jobs, since they'd started seeing each other the context had been entirely social. More than anything, Juliet wanted a private life, an existence unrelated to her work. Involving Jake in this new murder enquiry seemed like a violation: it would mean allowing the murk and graft of her job to intrude into what was still a fragile friendship. She felt superstitious about it, as if the very act of involving Jake in the Smythe murder, however tangentially, could damage their regard for each other.

She was upset that Tim had found out about Jake: although she thought she could rely on his discretion, he'd put her on the spot by assuming that her personal friends were at the beck of the force. It was annoying.

She was still deliberating with herself when she

remembered that she'd promised to call Jake that evening. He answered on the first ring.

'Juliet? It's great to hear you. I've heard they've found a body in the town centre. I thought you might not have time to call.'

'Hello, Jake. That's nice of you. I wish I could say I wasn't putting my job first, but I'm ashamed to admit that it's about the murder that I've called. And because I promised I would,' she added. She knew it sounded like an afterthought.

'So it was a murder! On the news it just said the body was found in "unexplained circumstances".'

'That's what we tell them to say, until we know for sure. And until we know who the victim is. Otherwise we'd have people turning up from far and wide, worried about someone who's gone missing even if that person doesn't remotely fit the description. What exactly did they say on the news?'

'Just that the body of a middle-aged man, believed to be local, had been found in the Butter Market in unexplained circumstances.'

'Well, that's accurate, anyway. They didn't try to guess who it was?'

'No. Is that why you're ringing? Is it someone I know?'

'It may be. Have you ever come across a social worker called Simon Smythe?'

'No, can't say that I have. But I'd probably only have known him if he'd worked with one of the children here.'

'I knew it was a bit of a long shot, asking you, but worth a try. He doesn't seem to have any next of kin we can contact.'

'If he was an official social worker, he'll have been registered with the Health and Care Professions Council.'

'Thanks, I should have thought of that. Don't mention this to anyone else, by the way. There's an outside chance that the man we found isn't Simon Smythe, but I think it's unlikely.'

'I should hope you already know me better than that. Talking of which, is there still a chance of seeing you this weekend, now you're involved in this murder case?'

'I'll do my best to get away for a few hours if I can. It might be during the day, though.'

'That's fine by me, especially if it's on Sunday. I've got one of my rare weekends off – there's a relief manager coming on Saturday morning; she's staying until Monday morning.'

'To what do you owe that privilege?'

'They still haven't found a deputy for me. I've been running the home on my own ever since I took over as warden. I get the odd day off, as you know, but the regular staff aren't qualified to be left in charge overnight.'

'I see. That's great,' said Juliet, trying not to sound strained. There was an uncomfortable silence.

'Not that I need to stay out overnight,' said Jake brightly. 'It's just nice to know that I have the option, for once.'

CHAPTER THIRTY-FIVE

A s soon as he saw the woman, Tim doubted she was a blackmailer. She had a long, sallow face and black corkscrew curls which hung around her face and were escaping from the untidy bun on top of her head. Her eyes were dark and sad and when his own green eyes met them she returned his gaze unflinchingly, but her stare was not bold. He judged her reluctant to look away because she was willing him, beseeching him, even, to give her good news about the missing child, or at the very least a firm promise of help.

She was seated at a table in the interview room into which Michael Robinson had led Tim as soon as he had arrived. She made no move to stand up, but locked eyes with Tim as soon as he took the chair opposite her. Robinson had moved to the back of the room, where he remained standing, shifting from one foot to the other and fidgeting with the string on the window blind. Tim found his behaviour exasperating, at once hostile and nervous. Maybe Robinson's craven behaviour indicated a fear of something worse than a dressing-down for neglecting to station a guard at the murder scene; alternatively, perhaps he was heading for a breakdown. He was obviously having a bad effect on the witness. Noticing the woman's frightened glances in his direction, Tim was about to suggest to her that she might feel more comfortable if he asked a policewoman to sit in on the interview when she started talking.

'You will help us to find her, won't you?' she said. She spoke with a Geordie twang.

'The girl you were looking after? That's why I'm here.' He realised Robinson had omitted to tell him who the woman was. 'I'm sorry, I don't know your name?'

'Penelope. Penny.'

'And the girl's name?'

'Selina.'

'What is your relationship with Selina?'

'I'm not related to her. She's one of the kids I look after sometimes when their mums are working.'

'You're Romany?' She nodded.

'What's your other name?'

'Green. We're staying in Appleby.'

'The horse fair's over, isn't it?'

'There's an Appleby in Lincolnshire as well.' Michael Robinson's voice, from the back of the room, was impatient.

'Sorry, I didn't realise,' said Tim. He turned back to the woman. 'Tell me about Selina.'

'She's one of the Petts. They've got three girls. Selina's the oldest. I've been minding the other two this week and thought nowt of it when she didn't turn up. She's fourteen now. But the others tell me she hasn't been home for three nights.'

'Why haven't her parents reported her missing?'

Penny shrugged. For the first time Tim thought she looked shifty. She chewed over the question before she answered him, choosing her words with care.

'They're away... on business. I said I'd keep an eye on the girls.'

'What does that mean?'

'What it says.' She was more defiant now, but Tim sensed it was a defiance born of fear. 'I see them off to school, they drop in on me when they get back to tell me they're all right, I help them with shopping, that kind of thing.'

'I see,' said Tim, wondering for how long the parents' business kept them 'away'. 'So they don't stay with you? Or you with them?'

'No. There's no need. Annie, the youngest, is ten and Janice is twelve. They're grown up, really.' She didn't sound very convincing. Tim knew his face would show that he certainly wasn't convinced. He didn't want to needle the woman, however. He could detect in her a deeper-than-average mistrust of the police, something he'd encountered before when questioning Romanies and travellers. He didn't want to frighten her into silence.

'Where do the girls go to school?'

'North Kesteven – Selina and Janice, that is. Littl'un's still at first school.'

'Which first school?'

'I'm not sure.' Penny looked uncomfortable.

'You're not sure? As the youngest, isn't she the one that needs most looking after?'

'Yes, but the other two does that. They drop her off of a morning. Anyway, she's not the one who's gone missing.'

Tim might have lost his temper at this irresponsible piece of logic had the woman not looked so wretched. She had put her hands to her forehead and was squeezing it, as if to exorcise some terrible pain.

'Okay,' he said more gently, 'tell me about the last time you saw Selina.'

'It was on Sunday. She didn't come with the others on Monday to tell me they were on their way to school.'

'Did you ask them where she was?'

'Yes. They said she'd gone on ahead, didn't need to see me.'

'Didn't you find that worrying? Considering she's the eldest and supposed to look after her sisters?'

'Janice is old enough to see to Annie,' said Penny defensively. 'Besides, I didn't like to pry. I thought Selina might've...'

'Go on,' said Tim. 'What did you think Selina might have done?'

Penny looked down at her hands, now twitching uneasily in her lap.

'Ms Green, what did you think Selina might have done? It's important that you tell us. Her life could be at risk.'

Penny was close to tears.

'I thought she might have decided to bunk off, go and earn herself a bit of cash somewhere. She isn't all that sold on school and I can't say as I blame her. Nothing there for her, really, is there?'

Tim didn't answer the question.

'When you saw her on Sunday, did she seem all right?'

'Yes. They all did. I think they like it when their ma and da go off. Gives them a bit of freedom.'

'Can you remember what she was wearing?'

'Not really. Jeans, probably. That's what all the kids wear, isn't it? Nothing as stood out, anyway.'

'And when you say you thought she might have gone to earn "a bit of cash" somewhere, exactly what do you mean by that?'

Penny suddenly jerked her head up and looked Tim in the eye again.

'Oh, I didn't mean – what I think you might mean. She wouldn't go with men.'

'Why did you think I might mean that?' said Tim, although it was precisely what he had been thinking.

She dropped her eyes.

'Anyway, what I meant was that she might have gone to earn herself a few quid on the land somewhere. Still a few casual jobs at this time of year.'

Tim nodded.

'When are her parents coming back?'

'Next week, sometime.'

'Can you get in touch with them?'

'That wouldn't be easy.' Penny was getting agitated again.

'Why wouldn't it be easy? Don't they tell you how to get hold of them? If one of the girls is ill, say?'

Penny's face twisted into an ugly grimace of misery.

'Yes but... they'll blame me if Selina's missing.'

'Their daughter's their responsibility, not yours,' said Tim. Penny stared at him blankly. He understood: what difference would the law make to their attitude to her?

'Can you give us the address they're staying at? Or better still, a number to call?'

'I ain't got no address. They'll be moving around, probably. Bill left a mobile with me. Said to call it in emergencies.'

'Where is this mobile?'

'Back in my van. Do you want me to fetch it?' Penny was already standing up. Tim motioned to her to keep her seat.

'One of us will take you to get it. I just want to ask you a couple more questions first.'

She slumped down in the chair again, as if exhausted. 'DI Robinson tells me that you went to the Fossdyke Canal to look for Selina. Why did you go there, in particular?'

'It's where I found her a few weeks ago when she didn't come back. Littl'uns told me that was where she'd be. She was hanging out with some other kids.'

'But you went there at night, long after dark. Surely you didn't expect to find kids playing there at that time.'

'I was worried. I'd watched the news: that the woman was dragged from the canal.'

'Did you think that might have been Selina?'

'No. They said the woman was older – in her twenties or older than that, even. But trouble often strikes more than once in the same spot, don't it?'

Tim sighed. A self-declared hater of coincidences, he was about to contradict her when he realised that, on this point at least, she'd been absolutely right.

'Let's go and get that phone,' he said kindly. 'Selina's mum and dad need to come home straight away.'

Penny seemed to shrink into herself. She was mumbling almost incoherently, not directing her words at either of the two policemen.

'They'll blame me for it,' she said. 'Jesus God, they're sure to blame me.'

CHAPTER THIRTY-SIX

I t was hideously late by the time Tim reached home. His house was in darkness. He opened the front door as quietly as he could and tiptoed into the kitchen. Everything was switched off, the working surfaces all pristine. Ever the optimist, he opened the oven door to check that Katrin hadn't left something to warm for him on a low light, but found nothing but the roasting tin that was kept there when the oven wasn't in use. He pulled a Peroni from the fridge, snapped off the cap and began to drink it as he prepared a peanut butter sandwich. It was unsatisfying fare, but at least it plugged the growling void in his stomach.

When he'd wolfed down the sandwich, he took the rest of the beer and went to sit for a while in the living room. He was dog-tired, but he needed some time to unwind before he went to bed.

Unwinding proved next to impossible: his head was buzzing with the case – or cases. How many separate cases were there now? The murders of the two women found in the Fossdyke Canal must have been linked: that was obvious. Was the young girl's killing associated with theirs, or, as was looking more likely, with Smythe's? Or were hers and Smythe's separate murders, unrelated both to the Fossdyke mutilations and each other? Were there three separate murderers operating in Lincolnshire at the same time? That almost beggared belief – yet what were the connections between them? Smythe and the girl had been stabbed in a similar way, it was true, but stabbing was a common enough way of committing murder and, *pace* Professor Salkeld, he wasn't sure he believed in 'gentle' stabbing: to him it seemed to be a contradiction in terms. Smythe was – reputedly, they still had to verify that – a social worker, but unless the girl had recently lived in South Lincs he was unlikely to have come into contact with her. He was also gay, but there was no evidence either way to suggest he'd been the victim of a gay hate attack. François Fabron was still a suspect, but Tim was unpersuaded of his guilt. The Frenchman was of limited intelligence: it would have taken a much better actor than he to feign the shock he'd shown when he'd first discovered the body. So, probably three separate perpetrators, certainly two; and four people murdered. And, apart from Fabron, no leads.

Then there were the fucking vehicle thefts – he hadn't thought about those much since they'd been handed over to Ricky, but they came back to haunt him now. No leads there, either. Thornton would be doing his nut: in charge of a police force rapidly gaining a reputation for its inability to solve any type of serious crime. The vehicle thefts had been depressing Tim for weeks, but he'd rarely felt as despondent as he did now.

The effects of the beer and the sandwich started to kick in and he told himself that low blood sugar levels and sheer bloody fatigue were largely responsible for his mood. The frustrating evening he'd just spent on fruitlessly trying to track down the parents of the Roma girl had also played its part. His was a naturally sanguine nature, but his worst enemy couldn't accuse him of patience and his had run out considerably before the utter failure of his repeated attempts to get a reply from the mobile Penny Green had produced. The phone had contained a sim card and there was a single number programmed into its directory, but this number appeared to be out of use. Asked if she had more information about Selina's parents' whereabouts, Penny Green could only say vaguely that they were 'in Ireland'. She thought the name they were using was Wood, but she didn't seem too certain. Tim didn't question her about why the surname was different from their daughters'. There could have been another explanation, but he was pretty certain this meant they used more than one name. He didn't want to frighten Penny by enquiring further into why this might be. They had let Penny go then, after she'd promised to spend the night with the two younger children. They'd have to send someone from the social services department to the camp the next day, but they decided not to do anything to alarm the girls that evening.

Michael Robinson had set someone to work tracking the mobile and discovered that it had been reported stolen several months before and not used since. Another dead end. All they could do was contact the Irish police and ask them to have broadcast an emergency message to 'Bill and Rosa Wood, believed to be travelling somewhere in Ireland'. As they hadn't yet given a reason for wanting to talk to the couple, Tim doubted this would produce any results, though there was an outside chance they'd call the mobile, which Michael Robinson had kept in his possession, or try to get in touch with their daughters. That was if they heard the radio message: it was anybody's guess what they were doing and how remote from normal media channels this activity took them.

'What a fucking pig's ear,' said Tim under his breath, as he picked up the empty Peroni bottle and deposited it in the kitchen. He didn't know what tomorrow would bring, but of one thing he could be certain: Thornton would be on the warpath. From an outsider's perspective, who could blame him?

To his surprise, Tim slept reasonably well. He was woken early by Sophia coming into the bedroom to show him the clothes she'd chosen for pre-school that day.

'Where's Mummy?' he asked groggily.

'She's getting the breakfast ready.'

Tim looked at his watch and groaned.

'It's only half-past six.'

'It's a college day,' Sophia said reprovingly, as if Tim should have known this already. Perhaps he should, he thought.

'I forgot! Okay, I'll get up now. Tell Mummy I'm coming. You look lovely,' he added as a perfunctory afterthought. Sophia cocked her head on one side and grinned ironically. Tim smiled broadly himself. *Her mother's daughter, through and through,* he thought. He'd better be careful: he'd stand no chance against the united wit of both.

He made it to breakfast just as Katrin was helping Sophia put on her coat. He gave them both a kiss.

'See you this evening!' he said cheerfully, and, in a lower voice to Katrin, 'I'm sorry about last night. I was trying to help Michael Robinson out of a mess he'd got himself into.'

'Was it worth it?'

'Probably not,' said Tim. 'Anyway, I missed our evening together. I really wanted to talk to you.'

Sophia was standing on tiptoe, reaching up for the door handle. Katrin opened the door for her and she went bouncing down the path. Katrin went outside, too, but as she was standing on the doormat she looked back at Tim and said, 'There's no college this morning. I only have to go in this afternoon. If there's something you really need to talk to me about, I'll be back in twenty minutes.'

'Great!' said Tim. 'Thank you for that. I'll be waiting for you.'

He turned back into the house, uneasily aware – as he so often was – that he didn't deserve Katrin. While in the act of fixing himself some toast, he decided to call Thornton and make his late appearance at work official. He looked at his watch. It was barely 7am. Thornton usually got in to work early, but he probably wouldn't arrive at the station for another half hour or so. Tim left a message on the Superintendent's office phone and, as an afterthought, on his mobile, too. He knew for a fact that Thornton wouldn't check the latter, but at least Tim would then have covered all bases. He told Thornton he was following up a lead and would be at the station mid-morning at the latest. He fervently hoped Katrin would produce some good ideas to validate this statement when she returned.

He watched her as she breezed up their short garden path in a few elegant strides, her camel coat flying open, her hair ruffled by a slight wind. She looked almost the same as the girl he'd married nine years before, though he fancied her face was more contoured, the look in her eyes, though still mischievous, flecked with a kind of wisdom. His mood lifted. Murderers, vehicle thieves, Superintendent Thornton! Bring them on, as long his home life was intact.

'Coffee?' said Katrin, arching her eyebrows just enough to indicate that Tim should already have made it.

'Thanks, I could murder some. I'll do it,' Tim added ineffectually.

'No, you clear the table. Then we'll have somewhere to sit, if we want to look at our laptops.'

'I wasn't thinking of...'

'Just in case,' said Katrin briskly. 'You never know.'

A few minutes later, they were installed side by side at the dining-room table, each holding a mug of freshly-ground coffee.

'I heard about the murder in the Butter Market,' Katrin said. 'There was a short piece about it on the local news. That's why I wasn't surprised when you didn't come home when you said you would.'

'I meant to. I wanted to talk to you about that murder. It wasn't because of that I was late; it was because I had to go to Lincoln to help Michael Robinson interview a witness.'

'So you said. Tell me about this latest murder. No connection to the others, I take it?'

'Not that I can see. That's why I wanted to talk to you. Did Stephen Jenkins commit any other murders?'

'None that were discovered. The police had their suspicions at the time about various other women who'd gone missing in the area where he lived. There was one case in particular: the woman had been stabbed and her murderer had made a clumsy attempt at hacking off her head. It was never pinned on Jenkins, but it seems likely he did it.'

'Serving his apprenticeship in decapitation?' Tim smiled grimly.

'If you want to put it like that.'

'Any evidence that he killed or tried to kill men?'

'Not that I know of. He was one of those killers who become fixated with a hatred of prostitutes. As I told you, he may have killed the girl because she discovered something. She probably wasn't part of his plan, whatever that was – punishing prostitutes, clearing the area of them, who knows?'

'I just wondered if he had a thing about gays.'

'I haven't read anything to suggest that. I suppose he could have borne a grudge against prostitutes in general, including males. Any chance your victim was a gay prostitute?'

'I don't think so. It's more likely that his boyfriend was one.'

'Mistaken identity?'

'Not unless the murderer didn't know what he looked like. Smythe was quite a hefty bloke – not fat, but broad and muscular. The boyfriend's a little weedy guy and a gaudy dresser, which Smythe wasn't. And French, too.'

'You mean the boyfriend's French?'

'Yep. No idea what he's doing in Spalding, unless it's just to ply his trade. He's got digs out in West Marsh Road, but I don't think he works at any of the factories there. I'm pretty certain he's unemployed.'

'Now that is interesting!' said Katrin thoughtfully. She powered up her laptop.

'What do you mean? What are you talking about?' said Tim impatiently.

'Wait a minute. Just let me do this, will you?'

Tim edged his chair nearer to hers and watched while she searched for a website. After a few minutes, she found what she was looking for and read aloud:

'A middle-aged male, later identified as George Gordon, was found murdered in an alleyway in Alachua County, June 1995. Cause of death: multiple stab wounds. Main suspect was a Quebecois, name of Philippe Pacquet, who was an associate of Gordon's. Pacquet was released after providing a watertight alibi. The killer has never been found. A cold case enquiry in 2007 yielded no new evidence.'

'Interesting,' said Tim, although he was clearly disappointed. 'But Gordon was killed more than twenty years ago, and in – where did you say?'

'Alachua County. It's in Florida. This is an official police website listing unsolved crimes in Florida. I've been using it for an assignment.'

'Right. Are you suggesting Smythe's killer came over here

from Florida? That it's the same guy who killed this George Gordon twenty-three years ago?'

'No, Tim, of course I'm not saying that. Can't you see the similarities between the crimes? Gordon was killed in an alleyway, Smythe in the Butter Market, which is what an American would call an alleyway. Both were stabbed to death. Both had a younger male lover who spoke French.'

'It doesn't say that Pacquet was Gordon's lover.'

'No, but what do you think 'associate' means? Americans can be very squeamish: they're more prone to using euphemisms than people think.'

'How do you know Pacquet spoke French?'

'I don't; but the odds are in favour of it. He was Québecois. They tend to hang on to their mother tongue.'

'Okay, so Gordon, a middle-aged man, was killed in an alleyway, but not by his much younger French-speaking male lover; and Smythe was killed in an alleyway, also, in all probability, not by his much younger French-speaking lover. I'm sorry, I must be missing something: I can't see where you're going with all of this.'

'It's only a theory – or a hypothesis, I should say. But I'm suggesting that maybe the murders are all connected. Perhaps they're all copycat crimes. The killer of the two women and the young girl in the Fossdyke Canal was copying Stephen Jenkins; and Simon Smythe's killer was copying whoever killed George Gordon.'

'You're suggesting a serial copycat killer?'

'Yes.'

'Is there any previous record of such a person?'

'There have been lots of copycat killers. But the ones I've read about have all based their murders either on one previously-committed murder or the career of a previous murderer. I've never heard of a copycat killer who copied the crimes of several different murderers.'

'That doesn't make it impossible. But what evidence is there besides the similarities you've mentioned? I hate coincidences, as you know, but the Jenkins crimes and the Florida murder are so far apart in time and place that we could be looking at coincidence here.'

'I agree it's perfectly possible, but the most striking thing about both the murder of the girl thrown into the Fossdyke Canal and Simon Smythe is these so-called 'gentle stab wounds' that Professor Salkeld described. As if the killer's just going through the motions, not stabbing with any conviction – or rather, not enough conviction to drive him into the kind of frenzy that murderers usually need to see them through. As if he's not engaged in the actual act so much as the game of following someone else's actions.'

'I think you're on to something,' said Tim. 'Well done! We'll keep this to ourselves for a while, until we've had more time to think it through.'

'There's just one other thing,' said Katrin. 'If this killer kills as a sort of intellectual exercise to prove that he can get away with copying crimes for which someone has been convicted and jailed in the past, like Jenkins, or others for which, like the original killer, he remains unapprehended, that means he doesn't have a single modus operandi. And that, in turn, means he may be responsible for other killings – either detected or undetected. Murders or disappearances that we'd never link him to because they don't bear any resemblance to these other crimes.'

'Christ!' said Tim. 'You're right. But if the murders don't resemble each other, how can we possibly identify that they've been committed by the same person?'

'There must be a link,' said Katrin. 'There always is a link.'

'Hmm,' said Tim. 'Perhaps. And perhaps that criminology course is teaching you to look for patterns where none exists.' He regretted the snub as soon as the words had left his lips. The smile disappeared from Katrin's face; her brow creased in a light frown.

'Anyway,' Tim finished lamely, 'I'll settle for finding the killers of Smythe and the three females first. Then we can think about casting our net further. And thank you.'

'Don't mention it,' said Katrin wryly, as she gathered the coffee mugs and disappeared with them into the kitchen.

'By the way,' Tim called after her, 'has Thornton picked up on the copycat idea with you? Michael Robinson spotted the similarity between the Fossdyke Canal deaths and the Jenkins murders, too. He told me he'd asked Thornton if you could do a bit of research on them.'

'He hasn't mentioned it yet. But if he does, I've mostly dug out all I can about Jenkins now.'

'And I suppose you'll have to hand it over to him. But don't tell him about this serial copycat idea yet, will you?'

CHAPTER THIRTY-SEVEN

Tim arrived at the station just before 10.30. He headed straight for Superintendent Thornton's office, thinking about the myriad things on which he needed to update his boss: Professor Salkeld's views on the Smythe murder, the interview with the Roma woman and the lead she had offered about the murdered girl's identity, the fruitless attempts to contact Rosa and Bill Wood.

He paused when he reached the open-plan area. He'd better check that the Woods had not been located overnight. Juliet was already sitting at her desk.

'Have you been in touch with Michael Robinson this morning?'

'Yes, he called to tell you that they've made no further progress in getting hold of the parents. I said I'd give you the message. From what he said, you've managed to identify the girl thrown in the Fossdyke Canal?'

'Only tentatively; well, probably, I suppose. But we need her parents to come back to give a positive identification. They're travelling in Ireland, apparently. Courteous of Michael to keep me informed. I didn't expect it, I must say.'

'Well, he wanted to ask a favour as well. He needs a responsible adult – someone who's an expert in child interrogation – to help him interview the two Roma children. I recommended Tom Tarrant.'

'He's a good choice, if he's available. But isn't Michael being a bit precipitate? We don't know if the murdered girl is Selina Pett yet.'

'No, but Selina's gone missing, whether she's been murdered or not. I'd say that was a good enough reason to interview her sisters.'

'I guess you're right. Tom will help Michael to do it properly. I thought Michael was bloody intimidating during the interview with Penny Green yesterday.'

'Is she the Roma woman?'

Tim nodded.

'Superintendent Thornton asked me to let you know he's upstairs and he'd like to see you.'

'In a mood, is he?'

'Not that I noticed; but he does have a visitor. It's Jack Fovargue.'

'Really? I'm intrigued. Fovargue's the last person I'd have expected to come here voluntarily.'

'I don't think he was expecting him. Fovargue turned up about half an hour ago. He's been with the Superintendent ever since.'

'Thanks,' said Tim. He removed his coat and draped it over his chair. He took the stairs one at a time, slower than usual, as he turned over in his mind what Fovargue might want. He hoped the man wasn't there to register a complaint of some kind. When he reached the landing that led to the Superintendent's office, he smoothed down his hair, then ducked to peer through the window set into Thornton's door. Thornton must have been looking out for him because he waved him in. Tim tapped on the door lightly and entered the room.

'Take a seat, Yates. You know Mr Fovargue? He's come to report a rather... hmm, hmm... (the Superintendent cleared his throat)... ah... delicate matter.'

Tim helped himself to one of the metal and plastic chairs that Thornton kept in a stack in the corner of his office. He placed it next to the chair on which Fovargue was seated and sat down himself. Fovargue had been studiously keeping his back turned to the door, but now Tim was alongside him he was shocked to see his ravaged face. Fovargue had obviously been crying, and recently.

'Are you all right, sir?' he said.

'Don't fuss the man, Yates. He's in a bit of a distressed state, as you can see. No need to draw attention to it.'

'I'm sorry,' Tim muttered. He was at a loss to explain why Thornton was behaving so ebulliently. Surely Fovargue's "distressed state" couldn't trigger some kind of gratification in his boss? It wasn't unheard of for Thornton to be insensitive, but he usually managed to present a mask of concern to members of the public.

'Mr Fovargue has come here to report a missing person,' said the Superintendent.

'Oh?' said Tim. Not another one, he thought, praying more fervently than he'd thought he knew how. 'Who is it? The missing person, I mean.'

'Someone you've met recently, Yates, I believe. A young woman named Martha Johnson. She's been working for Mr Fovargue at his experimental soil station. Do you remember her?'

'Yes, I remember her,' said Tim. He turned to Fovargue. 'Forgive me for saying this, sir, but one of your other employees indicated that Martha isn't particularly industrious. Are you sure she hasn't just decided to take the day off without telling you?'

A dull flush gradually burnished Fovargue's narrow features an unattractive brick red. He met Tim's steady green-eyed gaze with his own now sodden blue eyes. His fury was unmistakeable.

'Who said that? You'd better tell me, I'll have them sacked. Martha is the most intelligent worker I've ever employed. The rest of them are just jealous because...' he stopped short, evidently regretting that he'd embarked on this final sentence.

'Because what, sir?'

'Now, Yates, let's take it easy, shall we? One step at a time. Mr Fovargue was very frank during the conversation we had just now. The fact is that he and Ms Johnson are... er... in a liaison together.'

Fovargue's gaze shifted to the floor.

'Really?' said Tim noncommittally. 'Well, I suppose it would have come out in the end if you're asking us to try to find her. But it's early days yet. How long has Ms Johnson been missing?'

'She was at work yesterday morning,' said Fovargue. 'Your DC McFardle and the lady copper downstairs saw her. Josh Marriott was there, too.'

'We can check with DC MacFadyen and DS Armstrong, ask them if there was anything unusual about her behaviour. And Mr Marriott, if it comes to that. Did anyone else see her while she was there?'

'I believe Nathan was hanging around some of the time yesterday. He may have bumped into her.'

'The tanker driver?'

'Yes.'

'As I said, we can check with all these people, see if they can suggest why she didn't come to work today. But I think it's too early to assume that she's really missing. She's been with colleagues in the last twenty-four hours and she isn't a minor. How old is she, Mr Fovargue?'

'Twenty-six.'

'And you've tried to call her, presumably?'

'I've done more than that, I've been to her house. I was supposed to be picking her up on our way to see the organisers of a harvest festival fete. We wanted to know if we could exhibit with our soil appreciation stand. That's why I know something's happened to her.'

'I'm not sure I follow,' said Tim.

'Martha would have been there. She'd have made sure of it. She's always there when I invite her to do something with me. And if she'd somehow been delayed she'd have been sure to call me.'

'I see,' said Tim.

'You must admit, Yates, it looks as if something might have happened to the young lady,' said Superintendent Thornton, steepling his fingers and regarding Tim through the prism he'd just made.

'Today we'll make some preliminary enquiries of the kind I've just indicated,' said Tim. 'If she hasn't turned up by tomorrow lunchtime, we'll launch a full-scale search.'

'Will you be acting quickly enough?' Fovargue demanded aggressively.

'I can't answer that question, sir, but what I've described is standard procedure for a missing adult unless we have reason to believe she's in danger. I take it you don't know of any particular reason why she might have come to harm?'

'No,' said Fovargue uncertainly. 'The work we do with the soil is unpopular with the local farmers, of course.'

'Unpopular enough for someone to attack or threaten Ms Johnson?'

'No, I don't suppose so.' In the act of standing, Fovargue paused uncomfortably. 'You'll keep this under your hat, won't you?'

'What do you mean, sir?'

'Don't be obtuse, Yates. Mr Fovargue means he doesn't want us to let the media publish some lurid story about his relationship with Ms Johnson.' Superintendent Thornton was smirking. He had a salacious gleam in his eye. Tim recognised it as Thornton's 'man of the world' look. He tried not to sigh.

'Quite,' said Jack Fovargue. 'You'll keep me informed?' He leant across the desk to shake hands with Superintendent Thornton.

'Nice man,' said the Superintendent when he'd gone. 'Now, Yates, we need to concentrate on those murders. Tell me where you're up to with the Smythe investigation. And Michael called to say he'd made progress with identifying the young girl – do you know anything about that?'

'Yes,' said Tim shortly. Could Thornton really gloss so glibly over the fact that if Martha Johnson didn't reappear in the next twenty-four hours they'd have to deploy officers to a major search initiative as well as coping with Smythe's murder, hunting for the vehicle thieves and helping Lincoln with the three Fossdyke murders?

CHAPTER THIRTY-EIGHT

Just over an hour after Fovargue's visit, Juliet and Ricky had returned to Silverdale Farm to interview Josh Marriott and Nathan Buckland.

'I didn't expect to be back here again so quickly,' said Ricky. 'It would be neat if they've had some vehicles nicked – or we can spot some of the ones that are missing. It would help me to tie up a few loose ends.'

Juliet laughed despite herself. She was beginning to appreciate Ricky's black sense of humour.

'Very funny. But we mustn't be flippant about it. It's possible that something horrible has happened to Martha Johnson.'

'I wasn't being flippant – or not very. I'm sick of this fucking vehicles case. I can't make any headway with it at all. And yeah, something might have happened to her, but I think it's equally probable that she saw the light and decided to dump that sleazeball. Or Fovargue's wife "persuaded" her to dump him.'

'You may have a point there: keep hold of that idea. Let's go and find Marriott. I can't say I'm particularly relishing this interview. Whether he has any information to help us or not, you can bet he won't be co-operative.'

They got out of Juliet's car and started to walk down the track towards the shed that contained the office. Juliet glanced across at the farmhouse as they passed it. There was no sign of life there. She wondered where Fovargue had gone after he left the police station. According to Tim, he'd been very upset, so it would be surprising if he'd gone off somewhere to work. Perhaps he'd made a very rapid recovery.

Ricky was still talking about Marriott.

'He's one of those people who are automatically suspicious of the police. I meant to look him up, see if he's done time. In fact, DI Yates suggested it when we first came here.'

'Not a bad idea. Isn't that him now, coming towards us?'

A well-built man had just emerged from the narrow walkway between the two largest sheds. He waited by the one that contained the office. As they moved closer to him, Juliet saw that he was smiling. He extended his hand in turn to her and Ricky.

'This is a rum do,' he said. 'Didn't expect to see you back again this quick.'

'That's just what we were saying. Can you spare us a few minutes?'

'Yeah, sure. The boss rang to say he thought Martha Johnson had gone missing, so I was expecting you.'

'Where is Mr Fovargue?'

'He had an appointment to keep. Something about taking the stand to a village fete. As I've told you, I don't get mixed up in that soil malarkey.'

'Quite,' said Juliet. Whether or not he was acting callously, Fovargue's plans for the day evidently tallied with what he'd told Tim earlier.

'Anyway,' said Marriott, 'do you want to come into the office? It's warmer in there.'

Juliet and Ricky followed Marriott into the office where they'd last seen Martha Johnson. He gestured to Juliet to take the chair behind Martha's desk and fetched another rather grimy chair for Ricky from the main warehouse area. Juliet noticed that the desk looked different today. She cast her mind back to the previous day and tried to visualise what it had looked like then. Most of it had been covered with test tube racks, each one containing six glass tubes half-filled with soil and neatly labelled. There had been a small contraption next to them which Juliet thought might have been a PH soil testing kit. And a notebook, she was pretty sure: a rather suave red Moleskine notebook with an elegant silver and gold pen lying across it. Now the desk was covered in lever arch files, some of them very dusty. The other paraphernalia had been moved.

'When did you last see Ms Johnson?' Juliet asked.

'Same time as you did, yesterday. I didn't see her after that.'

'So you didn't see her leave the office?'

'No. She said she was knocking off early, so I assume she went just after you did.'

'Where were you yesterday afternoon, Mr Marriott?'

'I took one of the tankers out. It was a little job that Nathan was supposed to be doing, but he said he felt ill. Vomiting bug. It can happen: it goes with the territory.'

'He looked all right when we saw him,' said Ricky.

'Aye. Well, that's how it takes you. One moment you're right as rain, the next you're puking your guts up.'

'So what happened to Nathan? Did he go home?'

'Yeah. I dropped him off when I took the tanker out.'

'Is he here today?'

'Nah. Still off sick. Must be a bad'un – it's not like him to skip work.'

'We'll need to talk to him. Do you have his address?'

'Sure. He lives in Bourne. Out on West Road, not far from the woods.'

'Can you give us the number?'

'Not offhand. It'll be in the files.' Josh Marriott gestured at the pile of lever-arch folders on Martha Johnson's desk. 'I can take you there if you like.'

'Thanks, we'll probably be able to find it. Nathan's name is Buckland, isn't it? There can't be too many Bucklands living on the same street.'

'Lives with his mum and dad, I reckon. Don't know what they're called.'

'If it isn't Buckland, we'll come back to you. Thanks for the offer.' Juliet paused to draw breath while thinking rapidly. She hadn't known whether to ask the next question or not. She decided she'd risk it.

'You don't like Martha Johnson very much, do you, Mr Marriott?'

Marriott's heavy face split into a huge grin.

'Now what makes you say that?' It was his turn to pause. He's teasing me, thought Juliet, vaguely annoyed. 'Course I don't like her,' he continued. 'Flouncy little madam with her airs and graces. Coming between the boss and Susie.'

'Who told you that?'

'I dint need telling. Fucking obvious, isn't it? He hangs around her like a pet dog. Just because she pretends an interest in what he does.'

'Why do you think she's pretending?'

'I know the type. Butter wouldn't melt. But she's just after what she can get. I feel sorry for Susie, the way she's worked for him and put up with all his funny ideas, having that little bitch stick her nose in and try to take him away from her.'

'Has Mrs Fovargue ever discussed Martha Johnson with

you?'

'No. I shouldn't think she'd let herself down like that. But I can see how unhappy she is sometimes.'

'Do you know where Mrs Fovargue is today?'

'No. If she's not in the house, she's probably out on one of her school visits. Does all that for him, too. I'm not sure she believes in it.'

'Believes in what?'

'The 'look after the soil or we're all doomed' crap.'

'All right. We'll go and see if we can catch her now. Thank you, Mr Marriott, you've been very helpful. We'll let you know if we can't find Nathan Buckland.'

As they came out of the shed, Ricky slipped on the wet surface of the forecourt. It had rained the night before and the tarmacked area, which the previous day had been pristine, was now streaked with mud. He looked at the area in front of the bigger shed, the one that housed the vintage vehicles, and saw tyre tracks leading out of it and back in again.

'Has someone been test-driving one of the old vehicles?' he asked.

Josh Marriott shrugged.

'Don't ask me. It's not my problem. I have my hands full with the farming – the proper farming, I mean, not the experimental stuff. And the tankers.'

He watched them head back towards Juliet's car before he turned away and disappeared into the shed again.

Juliet and Ricky walked across the muddy lawn and knocked on the door of the farmhouse. They weren't surprised when there was no reply. Juliet had raised her arm to knock again when she heard the sound of a phone ringing inside the house. She moved her head closer to the door to listen; the ringing stopped after three ringtones. Either someone had answered it, or the farm's answerphone had a very short kick-in period. She waited for a while but could hear no further sounds. She knocked again and again they waited.

'Let's have a look at the back of the house,' said Ricky. 'We haven't been there yet, have we?'

'Okay,' said Juliet.

There was a narrow path encircling the house. Once they'd turned the corner and started walking along the side of the building, they saw that it led through a five-barred gate, past a haystack covered with tarpaulins, to a private area at the back. The gate was closed but not locked. Ricky unlatched it and held it open for Juliet, closing it quietly behind them. It wasn't until they had passed the haystack that they realised how much land there was to the rear of the house. Beyond the haystack was a substantial kitchen garden. To the right of it, immediately behind the house, was a large paved area on which stood Susie Fovargue's Smart Car and a massive pantechnicon. The latter was inscribed with the words 'Silverdale Soil Appreciation Society'.

Juliet continued to follow the path until she reached the back door of the house. She knocked on it gently but no one answered. Following a hunch, she tried the door handle: the door was not locked.

'What now?' Ricky whispered. 'Shall we go in?' Juliet shook her head.

'We don't have a warrant,' she said. 'We'd be trespassing – and for all we know the door's been left unlocked by mistake. There may really be no one here.'

'Pull the other one,' said Ricky. He took a few steps backwards and looked up at the first-floor windows. There was no sign of life.

'Let's get back to the station,' said Juliet. 'We can get a warrant if necessary, but at the moment there's no point in hanging around here.'

CHAPTER THIRTY-NINE

Tim had just taken a call from the Health and Care Professions Council. The woman he spoke to confirmed that Simon Smythe had been a registered social worker for four years. He worked mainly with the probation service. She provided Tim with the address of the Magistrates' Court in Peterborough, which was where she said Smythe was based. Tim asked her if she could supply a photograph of Smythe and she agreed to email one. It had just come through on his laptop. Opening it up, he saw at once that the man who'd died in the Butter Market was Smythe. Despite the lacerations and bruises that had disfigured the dead man's face and the fact that the photo showed an unsmiling mugshot, the likeness was unmistakeable.

That Smythe had been based in Peterborough explained why Jake Fidler didn't know him. Tim wondered why he had chosen to live so far away from where he worked. Circumstances, perhaps; or maybe he liked to keep his private and professional lives quite separate.

There'd been no wallet on Smythe's body, which Tim had thought was odd, particularly as his pockets had contained no cash, either. Smythe must have been carrying money or some means of paying if he'd intended to take François Fabron for a drink. Had the murderer kept the wallet as a trophy? It was possible, but Tim thought it unlikely. It was much more probable that Fabron had lifted it before he reported the murder. Fabron would have to be interviewed again, but he'd wait until Juliet came back from Silverdale Farm; she was the only person who could get any sense out of the guy.

Tim's phone rang.

'Hi, Timmo.'

'Hello, Michael. How's it going?'

'The Irish police have found Selina Pett's parents.'

'That's great news. When are they going to come home?'

'That's why I've called you. I've hit a bit of a brick wall.'

'Go on.'

'They didn't contact the police; the police apprehended them.'

'You mean they're in custody?'

'Yes. And the Paddies aren't being very co-operative.'

Tim cringed. He hoped Robinson hadn't been openly exposing his prejudices to the Irish police.

'Won't they release them to identify the body? Have you said it's on compassionate grounds? Or guaranteed their secure return to Ireland?'

'I... no. To tell you the truth, I lost my rag a bit. I thought you might be able to help.'

'Okay, give me the details of the person you spoke to. I'll see what I can do.'

'Thanks. It's Superintendent Francis Donnelly. His number is...'

• • •

A few minutes later, after he'd prised out of Michael Robinson the gist of his conversation with Superintendent Donnelly, Tim was talking to the man himself. At first, Donnelly's manner was peremptory.

'Good morning, Superintendent Donnelly. It's DI Yates of South Lincolnshire Police. I've been working with a colleague in Lincoln, DI Michael Robinson...'

'Good morning, DI Yates. I know what DI Robinson wants – I've spoken to him already. The answer is no. We've been trying to apprehend Pett and his wife for some time. We're not about to let them go now.'

'So you do know them as Pett? We thought they might be travelling under the name of Wood.'

'So DI Robinson said. Pett has a number of names he goes by, I believe, but he's calling himself Pett at the moment.'

'That makes it more likely that he and his wife are the couple we're looking for. Did DI Robinson explain what it was about?'

'He said that a girl's gone missing who could be their daughter. In my experience Roma girls go missing all the time. I wouldn't put it past Pett to have told her to make herself scarce in case we arrested him. It would be a good ploy to get himself shipped back to the UK on compassionate grounds so that he can do one of his disappearing acts.'

'May I ask what the charge against him is?'

'Grand larceny. We think he's behind numerous vehicle thefts here. There's been a spate of them every few months, each time when Pett's been in the Republic.'

Tim pricked up his ears. 'What kind of vehicle thefts?'

'All sorts. Bikes and quads, mostly, but there's been stolen farm machinery that we think is linked to Pett as well.'

'Do you think he takes the vehicles out of the country?'

'We haven't got that far yet. I suspect the answer is that he does get them out of the country, but he doesn't do it himself. He must have accomplices. Or some kind of network.'

'I see. What makes you so sure he's the culprit?'

There was a long silence.

'I have my sources. I know what you UK cops think about informers, but they're very useful here. Indispensable, in fact.'

'I'm not averse to using informers when the occasion warrants,' Tim said mildly. 'I want you to know how welcome this conversation is. We've been trying to track down the perpetrator of a series of agricultural vehicle thefts here for most of this year. Can I ask you what you think Pett's MO is?'

'How do you mean, his MO? He takes the bloody vehicles, doesn't he, presumably to sell on.'

'Yes,' said Tim patiently, 'but *how* does he do it? That's what's been puzzling us. In Lincolnshire, no one's as much as seen one of these vehicles disappearing into the distance since the thefts started.'

'He's got contacts in the horse-racing world. We think someone lends him a horse box, or something resembling a horse box from the outside. Not a small one, one of the big ones that takes several animals. He or one of his accomplices drives the stolen vehicle into it and closes the door. Then they drive off. Simple but effective. No one would bat an eyelid at seeing a horse box round here. We suspect the vehicles are then loaded on to a ship, probably one heading for the Continent.'

'Superintendent Donnelly, you've probably just helped me to make a major breakthrough. I can't thank you enough. I'd like to meet you to discuss your case, see how many more similarities there are with ours.'

'You're very welcome. Come over to see us any time.'

'Thanks. I will. But first can I ask you if you'll reconsider your decision not to let Bill and Rosa... er, Pett... come back to the UK? Even if we provide a police escort and return them to your custody? You see, I'm not sure that DI Robinson explained the whole situation. We're not just investigating a missing girl – we've also got a body that we think tallies with her description. Did DI Robinson mention that?'

'No, but maybe I didn't give him the chance. He put my back up straight away. A bit jumped-up, isn't he?'

Tim smiled into the phone.

'You could say that.'

'And you'll pay the costs for an escort both ways? It's important because we're strapped for cash here.'

'Of course,' said Tim, rapidly thinking that he'd have to make Michael Robinson pay the costs. The murder was on his patch, after all. However much he might like Robinson, Thornton wouldn't be pleased by having to foot one of his bills. Was there a police force that wasn't 'strapped for cash'?

CHAPTER FORTY

I t wasn't difficult to find Nathan Buckland's house. It was a pristine 1930s bungalow set in a smallholding plot which had been turned into a very well-organised junkyard. It was the last house in the street: beyond it was a straggly coppice, a ragged herald of the adjacent, sprawling Bourne Woods. A bright yellow and blue sign set just inside the front wall proclaimed 'Buckland's Scrap Merchants. Best Prices Offered for Silver, Copper, Lead and all Iron and Steel Items'.

Juliet and Ricky had stopped at the top of West Road to ask a man standing in his garden if he knew where Buckland lived. The man gave a few perfunctory directions, but, as he pointed out, it was impossible to miss the scrapyard sign. Pulling up by the sign, they saw there was also a smaller 'No Parking' sign in front of the main entrance to the yard. Juliet parked her car beyond it, on the edge of the coppice, and she and Ricky walked back to the gates.

Despite the jaunty, well-kept appearance of the house, there was something about it that Juliet found disquieting. With its long wooden verandah and shuttered windows, all painted dark green, and sand-coloured bricks it seemed like a fake house, a cottage plucked from the pages of a children's story book.

'The gingerbread house,' said Ricky, as if reading her thoughts.

'Hansel and Gretel?' said Juliet. 'Do you think there's a wicked witch inside?'

Ricky chuckled. He followed Juliet down the path to the door.

It was opened before she could reach it by a youth of about fifteen. Juliet caught only a glimpse of him before he disappeared, leaving the door open. A woman came to stand in the space he'd vacated, framed squarely in the lintel. She was big rather than fat, but she had no waist. Her swarthy olive complexion was crowned by a wreath of dark plaited hair showing grey at the roots. She was not smiling.

'If you've come to see Reg, he's out,' she said.

'DS Armstrong, South Lincs police,' said Juliet, showing her warrant card. 'It's actually Nathan we've come to see. Nathan Buckland. Is he your son?'

'Yes. What has he done?'

'Nothing as far as we know, Mrs Buckland. We just want a word with him. Is he here?'

'Yes, but he's sickly. He's in no fit state...'

'It's all right, Ma.' Nathan Buckland appeared behind her, clad in a T-shirt and boxers. He donned a pair of grey tracksuit bottoms as he talked, hopping nimbly from one foot to the other. Dressed but still barefoot, he pushed his mother gently to one side.

'What's up?' he said. Juliet saw that his face had a green-ish tinge and his eyes were bloodshot. It looked as if he had genuinely been unwell.

'May we come in, Mr Buckland?'

'No,' came his mother's voice from the recesses of a room beyond the hallway. 'It ain't convenient.'

If Nathan Buckland was embarrassed by his parent he didn't show it. He looked Juliet boldly in the eye and shrugged.

'What's it about?'

'It's about Martha Johnson, Mr Buckland. When did you last see her?'

'When she was talking to you yesterday. Why?'

'She's been reported missing. Probably nothing to worry about: it's not been twenty-four hours yet.'

She was watching Buckland's face closely. It was already pale and drawn. Did she imagine a flicker of trauma pass across his features?

'She works odd hours. You talked to the boss?' Nathan swallowed.

'Yes. It was Mr Fovargue who reported her missing.'

'Well, I don't know owt about it. Sorry.'

'Thank you, Mr Buckland. Will you be back at work tomorrow? Do you work Saturdays?'

'Yes. Why?'

'We have to know where to find you. In case we need to talk to you again.'

'You're best off talking to Josh, then. He's the one as keeps the work schedule. I'll like as not be out somewhere.'

'Thank you, Mr Buckland, we'll bear that in mind.'

'Is that all? Because I'm catching my death out here.'

'Yes, thank you, we won't trouble you further.'

As Juliet turned away from the door, a red pick-up stopped in the road outside the house. Two men climbed out of it, one in his twenties, the other middle-aged. The younger man took one look at them and disappeared behind one of the neat stacks of scrap metal. The middle-aged man came striding up the path towards them. He wasn't tall but quite thick-set and his manner was pugnacious.

'What's going on here?' he said.

'Nowt, Dad, it was just summat to do with work,' said Nathan Buckland. His manner towards his father was deferential, even cowed.

'Aye, well don't bring your work troubles here. I don't know why you wanted to cut adrift, anyway. You'd be better off working with us.' He glowered at Ricky, ignoring Juliet.

'Coppers, are you?'

Ricky stared at him.

'Wondering how I know? I've seen plenty of your kind in my time. Has the lad got himself into some sort of trouble?'

'Not that we know of, Mr Buckland. Someone he works with didn't turn up for work today, that's all. It's caused a bit of concern, but it's probably nothing to worry about. We just wanted to know when your son last saw her.'

'Right,' said Reg Buckland, pushing past Juliet to go into the house. Nathan Buckland had already disappeared again.

Reg Buckland closed the door firmly behind him.

'You're very quiet,' Ricky said to Juliet as they drove away. 'Was there something about that little do that bothered you? Apart from just being pissed off by the rudeness, I mean.'

'Rudeness doesn't get to me these days. Water off a duck's back.'

Ricky tried to look as if he believed her. They drove on in silence for a few minutes before Juliet suddenly spoke again. Her voice was sharp.

'Did you get a look at the kid who went back inside the house before Nathan Buckland showed up?'

'Yeah, looked just like him, didn't he? They both remind me of someone else I've seen recently, too.'

'I'm pretty certain that kid was my peeping Tom.'

'What peeping Tom? I didn't know about that?'

'I'd forgotten that I didn't tell anyone. At the station, that is,' said Juliet, with her usual scruple to tell the truth. 'There was a kid leering through my window at me after I took a shower the other evening.'

'What happened?'

'I screamed and he disappeared.'

'You should have reported it.'

'Like you were keen to report that you'd been mugged? You know as well as I do it could've caused more trouble than it was worth.'

'Didn't it shake you up?'

'A bit. But I had someone with me.'

Ricky grinned.

'I see,' he said.

CHAPTER FORTY-ONE

Katrin's imagination had been gripped by her conversation with Tim earlier that morning. After he'd gone, she searched the Holmes database for accounts of murders of gay men. She was looking particularly for crimes that had already been attributed to a serial killer or murders that shared similar characteristics, even if these had yet to be recognised. She trawled through many accounts of gay murders but found no others that matched Steve Smythe's. Most were hate crimes, often the result of street brawls, or killings that had taken place at private addresses. The latter tended to have been caused by sex games that had gone wrong or perpetrated by a serial killer who had deliberately lured the victims to their deaths. Dennis Nilsen's crimes were the most prolific of these. Katrin knew that Nilsen had inspired copycat killers, if inspired was the right word, but she could see no resemblance between Smythe's murder and Nilsen's killings.

She returned to the account of the Florida killing, looking for more details about George Gordon, but the description on the website was sparse, amounting to only a few hundred words. There was no information about Gordon's occupation or circumstances, or Pacquet's, for that matter. Other searches yielded no further results. Pacquet would himself be middle-aged now. She could find no address for him in Florida. She guessed that he'd probably returned to Quebec and tried searching telephone directories there, but so many Pacquets were listed that she gave up.

Turning back to the Alachua County entry describing the murder, Katrin noticed something that had previously slipped her attention: Gordon's and Pacquet's first names and surnames both began with the same letter. The point had eluded her because the name 'George' had a soft 'g' and the 'Ph' of 'Philippe' was also soft.

François Fabron had said that he and Smythe had first got together because they were fascinated by the fact that both their first names and their surnames began with the same letter. Had Smythe been targeted by his killer to create a cynical parody of the Alachua County murder? If so, had the killer deliberately researched obscure murder cases to carry out a copycat murder that wouldn't be recognised as such? Katrin thought that, though unlikely, it was a possibility. But if this theory was correct, Smythe's killer must also have known that he and Fabron shared names in which the initial letters of the first name and surname were duplicated. This was much harder to explain, because their relationship was such a new one: she'd suggest that Tim checked, but she thought it unlikely that Smythe would have confided about Fabron to friends and colleagues. Fabron himself had indicated that they'd kept it a secret. That meant that the killer had not only encountered them when they were together – which must have been very recently – but that he also knew both their names.

Katrin was quite aware that she could be barking up the wrong tree altogether; but if she wasn't, it would cut down the possible identity of the murderer from hundreds, even thousands, to a handful of individuals.

Assailed by a sudden pang of hunger, Katrin glanced at the time on her laptop and saw it was almost 2pm. It would be too late to get to the college in time for her lecture now. She was annoyed with herself: this would be the first class she'd missed. She recovered her equanimity quickly, however. Delving into the history of past crimes or working on hypothetical cases could hardly compare with helping Tim to solve a live crime; and Sophia would be pleased to see her if she turned up at the pre-school early. She'd make herself a sandwich and give Tim a call.

CHAPTER FORTY-TWO

It was 1.30pm when Juliet and Ricky returned to the station. 'Any joy?' Tim asked.

'Not really,' said Juliet. 'Josh Marriott wasn't very cooperative, but I didn't get the impression that he knew anything about Martha Johnson. Ricky and I both thought he might have something else to hide, though.'

'I'm going to do some checks on Marriott,' Ricky put in. 'I meant to do it the other day, after we visited the first time. I swear he's got form; I'd stake my life on it.'

'Marriott told us how to find Nathan Buckland,' Juliet continued. 'Buckland was decidedly unhelpful, but his tale of having had to go home sick seemed to hang together.' She paused, hoping that Ricky wouldn't tell Tim about the peeping Tom, before adding, 'Do you know anything about the Buckland family? They seem a strange lot. The house is immaculate, but they're quite rough and very hostile. They run a scrap metal business.'

'I think they're a travelling family that's put down roots,' said Tim. 'You're right, they do run a scrap metal business, but as far as I know it's all above board. I'm not surprised they weren't pleased to see you: a hangover from their traveller days, probably – inbred mistrust of the police.'

'Them and ninety per cent of the rest of the population,' said Ricky. 'I'm going to find some lunch. Then I'll do those checks on Marriott. Want anything?' he said to Juliet.

'A sandwich would be great, if there are any left.'

'I've asked Andy to bring Fabron in again,' said Tim, as Ricky disappeared. 'I want you to do another interview with him. There was no wallet on Smythe's body and he must have been carrying one. We need to get a more coherent statement from Fabron in any case.'

'You think Fabron took Smythe's wallet?'

'I wouldn't put it past him. He's lost what could have been a nice meal ticket now, hasn't he?'

'Yes,' said Juliet. 'I'll interview him. But what are we going to do about Martha Johnson? It's twenty-four hours since she was last seen now. You can bet Jack Fovargue'll be on your tail again shortly. Besides which, we should be getting worried about what may have happened to her, shouldn't we?'

'Christ! You're right,' said Tim. 'I'd better go and tell Thornton we need to start searching for her now. He's not going to be pleased. I've never known a time when cases kept on multiplying like they are at the moment. I still want you to interview Fabron next.'

Tim's mobile rang at that moment.

'Katrin, hi, everything all right? I thought you were at college today.'

Tim listened intently while Katrin spoke, at one point smiling and saying: 'Well, I suppose one lecture won't hurt.'

He was silent again while Katrin carried on talking.

'Well, it does sound far-fetched, I agree, but if you're right it'll give the investigation a massive boost. As it happens, Juliet's going to interview Fabron again shortly. Shall I hand you over to her?'

He passed his mobile to Juliet: 'It's Katrin. She's got some ideas about the Smythe murder. It might help to hear what they are before you speak to Fabron again.'

CHAPTER FORTY-THREE

It had been some time since Juliet and Katrin had last met. As Katrin threw open the door in welcome, Juliet was impressed by how much Tim's wife had changed during the intervening period. Katrin had clearly been rocked by Sophia's birth; even after she'd recovered from post-natal depression, she seemed for years to have lost her confidence and that glossy, put-together look that might have inspired sour remarks from other women if Katrin hadn't been so unassuming. Juliet knew that Tim must have regretted profoundly the loss of Katrin's dry humour and the diminution of her deftly capable ways.

Now, as Katrin rushed to meet her, Juliet thought that she looked better than she ever had, even in the pre-Sophia years. It wasn't just that she'd regained her sleek, well-groomed appearance, matched by a figure that was yet svelter than before she was pregnant: there was an energy coming from her, a buzz that proclaimed both confidence and love of life. Perhaps the deep inner fulfilment that motherhood was supposed to confer had merely been delayed, and Katrin was experiencing it now. Juliet felt a sharp pang of envy that she knew to be ridiculous, and quickly stifled it.

'Tea?' Katrin asked. 'Or perhaps you'd prefer coffee? I can't drink it in the afternoon, but you're very welcome to have some.'

'Coffee would be great. I don't seem to manage to sleep much these days.'

Katrin gave her a keen look.

'We've had this conversation before, so sorry for repeating it: but if you let the job take you over, you won't get any thanks for it.'

'You of all people must know that there's often no option. Tim's been working like a demon for the past six months. There's been no let-up in his efforts to put a stop to these farm vehicle thefts and we've got nowhere with them. It's really got to him.'

'I know. But Tim's very resilient – I'm not saying you aren't, but he can bounce back like a Kelly doll. It's a strange thing to say, and I wouldn't risk it with anyone else, but having the murders to deal with as well has lifted his spirits.'

'You and I can understand that, though it might infuriate an outsider. It's because he has more chance of making progress with the murders. There's nothing more draining than a case that just keeps going round in circles – especially if the Chief Constable's on your tail.'

'I didn't know about that. Tim's certainly not at his best when he's being challenged from above. It brings out the bolshie in him. But talking of the murders, I assume that's why you're here? Tim said he'd ask you to come.'

'He said you've had a brainwave, if you don't mind sharing it with me.'

'I don't mind sharing my idea, but I wouldn't describe it as a brainwave. You can feel free to write it off as barmy straight away.'

'I doubt I'll think that. You've always been brilliant at thinking outside the box. Let's give it a try.'

'Come in properly first,' said Katrin. 'I didn't mean to keep you standing here in the hall! Go through into the sitting-room and I'll bring the coffee.'

Some minutes later, when they were seated, Katrin emphasised again the speculative nature of her thoughts.

'You must remember my views are bound to be coloured by the criminology course I'm taking. I see conspiracy theories behind every lamp post!'

'The crime rate in this area has burgeoned so much lately that you might be right to! Go on.'

'Tim's probably told you that I thought the Fossdyke Canal murders could be copycats of the Stephen Jenkins murders – Jenkins decapitated two women and threw them into a canal, which the Fossdyke killer's now also done. Subsequently, Jenkins also killed a young girl, but without decapitating her.'

'Yes, I knew you'd thought of that. Michael Robinson spotted the similarities, too.'

'Tim said he had – then he said that the Butter Market murder had put him off the idea.'

'Tim and I have discussed whether the murders are all by the same killer or not. Unless it was never detected, Jenkins didn't commit a crime like that. But I've got an open mind on whether all the murders are connected or not.'

'I'm convinced they are,' said Katrin. Although her voice was quiet, she sounded confident rather than diffident.

'How can you be so sure?'

'The murder of Simon Smythe bears a number of similarities to the murder of a homosexual male in Florida in the 1990s. The victim – his name was George Gordon – had been planning an assignation with a new lover, just like Smythe. The killer was never found – though it has to be said that the cops in the rural America of the day probably didn't consider it worth over-exerting themselves to catch the murderer of a "faggot". I can show you the police reports of the case if you like.'

'Sounds fascinating! But – sorry to be thick – I can't work out how that establishes a link between the killings.'

'It's the copycat element, don't you see?' said Katrin, her voice rising as she became more animated. 'If I'm right, this killer kills as a kind of intellectual game. He alternates between crimes that have been solved and ones that haven't. He probably copies the ones that haven't been solved more exactly than the ones that have. For those where the killer was caught, he deviates from those aspects that led to the arrest.'

'Jenkins' mistakes were legion. He cut off the women's heads in his flat. Although he cleaned up thoroughly, of course it's next to impossible to remove blood stains completely. Then someone saw him digging a hole on the banks of the canal, so that was how the police knew to look for the heads there afterwards.'

'Exactly. And I'd bet a thousand pounds that they won't find the heads of the two women pulled from the Fossdyke buried on the towpath there. They're bound to have been looking.'

'You say he 'alternates' between types of killing. What makes you think he's committed other crimes?'

'I'm pretty certain he will have. The Fossdyke murders were very accomplished – as was Smythe's, in a different way. And I think they were discovered exactly when the killer intended them to be. This isn't a murderer who's just begun to cut his teeth. He's killed before and he'll do it again. Unless I really am barmy – you decide!'

Juliet's face froze. Katrin's hypothesis didn't seem 'barmy' to her; on the contrary, it was the most plausible explanation anyone had yet come up with. Its implications chilled her to the core.

'You're saying that we could be looking for a prolific killer? One who's been operating for a number of years?'

'Yes.'

'If he's as clever as you think, what are our chances of catching him out?'

'I can't answer that – otherwise I'd be able to catch him! I can try to help, if you like.'

'I'd love you to help, but you're not a policewoman.'

'No, but I'm a police researcher. I could ask Superintendent Thornton to let me trawl back across recent murders and see if there are any unsolved ones which match them.'

'Why only the *unsolved* ones?'

'Because if I'm correct, they'll be like the originals in almost every respect. The ones that don't match – where he altered the MO to avoid trapping himself – will be more difficult to spot. What strikes me about the Fossdyke murders is that he seems to be taunting us with them. Jenkins' crimes were so distinctive that the link was obvious to anyone who knew about them. Even Michael Robinson noticed it.'

Juliet grinned.

'Are you saying the killer's giving us easier clues than in the past?'

'Yes, in a way. I think the murders must be getting more frequent. One of the reasons the copycat link hasn't been noticed before is probably that the earlier crimes were committed further apart in time. Now he's spelling it out to us, daring us to catch him before he does it again. He's got a big advantage over us: usually serial killers perfect an MO. They're looking for the same type of victim and kill in the same kind of way. This killer has a huge repertoire to choose from – of both the types of victims and how they're killed. The only constant is that a victim similar to the one he selects has been killed in a similar way at some point in the past.'

'Serial killers do get more accomplished, as you say. They also get careless. That's usually how they're picked up.'

'I know. And although ours is certainly a controlled and calculating killer – not what the textbooks call a 'disorganised' one – I think the desire to murder is taking him over. As with other serial killers, what began with an experiment and continued to feed a habit is now spiralling into an uncontrollable binge. I don't think it'll be long before he chooses his next victim. He may have done so already.'

'Oh, God,' said Juliet. 'I think you're right. And I think we know who she is: her name's Martha Johnson.'

CHAPTER FORTY-FOUR

François Fabron was becoming ever more mutinous as the interview went on. A small man who looked as if he was perpetually sucking in his cheekbones, so gaunt was his face, he had been reasonably appealing in a gamin sort of way when he'd first presented himself at the police station, distressed and anxious to co-operate after his discovery of Smythe's corpse. Now, his brow was furrowed and his face wore a thunderously sulky expression – any semblance of personal charm had vanished. As suspicions were cast on his respect for the truth, his features grew more simian by the minute.

Ever conscientious, Juliet was aware that she wasn't in the best mood for conducting the interview. When she'd returned to the station, she'd managed to snatch a few brief moments to tell Tim of her meeting with Katrin and she'd been irritated when he'd barely listened. He didn't show any particular surprise when she'd said she thought Martha Johnson might already have become the killer's next victim. He'd told her he'd already launched a full-scale search for Martha: later, there'd be a televised request for information about her whereabouts after midday the previous day and a direct appeal to Martha herself to contact police if she could. No doubt, Tim had added, the Superintendent would want Juliet to help draft the announcement – a touch sardonically, she thought. Or had she imagined that?

She chivvied herself to focus on the task in hand and turned her attention to Fabron again. Andy Carstairs was also in the interview room, taking notes. Under pressure, he'd admitted to having learnt French at school, though he claimed not to have enough confidence to speak it. Juliet's own grounding in French was no better, though she acknowledged that Andy was probably correct in his opinion that she would have applied herself more assiduously than he had. She hoped they'd be able to make sense of his transcript. The interview was being taped as well, but Andy had offered to transcribe it into English as it happened, to save time.

They'd been lucky to have found a duty solicitor who spoke French without having to cast the net wider. The first name to come up on the duty rota was that of a woman called Sandra Hicks; Juliet had never seen her before, but it turned out that Ms Hicks spoke perfect French.

Juliet decided to take a sterner approach than she had so far.

'Mr Fabron, I'm going to put the question to you again. When you found Mr Smythe's body in the alleyway, did you take anything from it? His wallet, for example?' She allowed her tone to soften again. 'It would be understandable if you'd wanted to remove the wallet for safe-keeping: so that no one else could take it, I mean, while you went to get help. I know discovering the body was a very traumatic experience for you. Perhaps you forgot to alert us that you had the wallet? Perhaps you forgot to give it to us afterwards?'

François Fabron's dark eyes flashed.

'But you are not listening to me, or you do not believe me. I did not take this wallet. I would never have taken this wallet!'

He brought his bird-like fist down hard upon the table. The resulting dull thud failed to create the éclat that he'd intended.

'DS Armstrong,' Ms Hicks said quietly. 'My client has denied having taken the wallet several times. I don't see what you're hoping to achieve by pursuing this line of questioning. As you are aware, it's making M'sieur Fabron very agitated.'

She turned to Fabron and repeated what she'd just said to Juliet in fluent French. He gave a wry smile as he shrugged; then, unexpectedly, he exploded into a torrent of words, speaking so rapidly that Juliet couldn't follow him. When, finally, he stopped talking, she turned to Sandra Hicks.

'I'm sorry, I didn't get half of that,' she said. 'Would you mind translating for us?' She glanced across at Andy, who had given up on his task and put down his pen.

'Certainly. He says he did not steal the wallet and he doesn't understand why you're persecuting him by suggesting that he did. You have no right to assume he is a thief. Your behaviour is barbaric, especially after all he has gone through. Are you prejudiced against gay men? If so, he wants to be questioned by someone else. And besides, even if he had been tempted by it, he wouldn't have taken the wallet. He has a terrible aversion to the sight of blood. Don't you understand? He is totally repelled by blood. He could never touch a man who had been bleeding.'

'Thank you,' said Juliet. The last part of Fabron's outburst carried the ring of truth. She felt inclined to believe he hadn't stolen the wallet, but, if it wasn't him, who had it been? Perhaps the wallet had already been removed when Fabron had discovered Smythe.

Juliet resolved to talk to Katrin again about the Florida murder she had mentioned. Had that victim's wallet also disappeared? And if so, did the police ever find out what had happened to it? But first she must help Tim with the search for Martha Johnson.

CHAPTER FORTY-FIVE

'What's the verdict on Fabron?' Tim asked after Juliet had seen the Frenchman and his solicitor out.

'I think he's probably telling the truth about the wallet. I'm sure he has plenty to hide – he strikes me as being quite shifty and he's brighter than I first thought. He certainly knows how to press his solicitor's buttons. But my instinct is to believe his story about how he found Smythe and that he didn't take the wallet. He's probably scared we're going to find out other details about his life: stuff that we're not actually interested in.'

'If Smythe's killer kept his wallet, that may be our first real lead. Robbery seems an unlikely motive, though. How much was Smythe likely to have had on him when he was just out for a few drinks?'

'I agree. And I've talked with Katrin now. She says that the Smythe killing bears some resemblance to the murder of a gay man in the USA more than twenty years ago. I've asked her to find out if his wallet was stolen. If it was, Smythe's wallet may have been taken in emulation.'

'The copycat notion again? It's intriguing! But copycat or not, the wallet still exists somewhere.'

'Unless the killer's destroyed it.'

'You're right; but I've got a feeling we may be after a trophy hunter.'

'Interesting. If it's true, that could be the link between the murders that we're looking for. Katrin's theory is that we're dealing with a copycat killer who keeps on copying different murderers, making him hard to catch because he doesn't use the same MO twice. If he collects trophies, that could be his Achilles heel.'

'It's an idea that's worth pursuing. Can you keep in touch with Katrin about it?'

'Of course. But isn't Martha Johnson the priority at the moment?'

'We're doing everything we can to trace her. She lives in a terrace in Sleaford. The local cops have broken into the house but there was no sign of a disturbance. Her father came to meet them there, but he wasn't much help, either: he couldn't say whether anything had been stolen – he was actually quite uninformed about everything, as if he had no close contact with her – but it looks as if the place is just as she left it yesterday, even down to the crockery in the sink. Her handbag and mobile aren't there. We can't trace the mobile: it's not giving a signal. But the search didn't yield much. The uniforms have interviewed her neighbours: no one seems to have seen her for a day or two. She hasn't been into the college this week, either. As you know, we've sent out messages on the media asking her or anyone who knows her whereabouts to contact us. But her scooter is missing.'

'Has Jack Fovargue been involved in any of this?'

'Not so far. I'm not sure how to play that. I think that officially we're not supposed to know that he's having an affair with Martha. It's tricky because Thornton doesn't want us to do anything to compromise his relationship with Susie. God knows how he thinks we're going to protect Fovargue's privacy: the media are bound to get hold of the story sooner or later.'

'We can't allow that to impede the search. And I'm convinced her disappearance has something to do with Silverdale Farm. It's obvious that neither Susie Fovargue nor Josh Marriott likes her, for a start: Susie probably because she knows about the affair already. I think we need to interview both of them again.'

Ricky MacFadyen had been listening. He butted in suddenly.

'You ought not to go there alone. I've checked out Marriott now and, as we suspected, he's got form. He was convicted of GBH – admittedly when he was much younger – and served three and a half years of a five-year sentence. He's also done time for receiving stolen goods. Only a year, but the judge clearly thought it was the tip of the iceberg – that he was into something much bigger. There just wasn't sufficient proof.'

'Who did he assault?'

'His ex-wife and her boyfriend. Nearly killed the boyfriend, apparently. The sentence would have been tougher if his lawyer hadn't made a good case for provocation.'

'What about the stolen goods? What kinds of goods?'

'Whole ragbag of stuff, apparently. The linking factor was that it was all stolen to order. The prosecution thought he must have been co-ordinating quite a sophisticated network of people to spirit the stuff away and then redistribute it. He was caught by chance when his van broke down on the motorway. The cop who went to help him recognised that some of the items he was carrying had been listed on police stolen goods reports. One or two of his immediate accomplices were also prosecuted, but, as I said, he was suspected of being in charge of a much bigger outfit.'

'Wow!' said Tim. 'How long ago?'

'He was released from Lincoln Jail twelve years ago.'

'Find out what he did after that. Who he worked for, where he lived, anything you can dig out about him, especially after he started working for Fovargue. And where he lives now.'

'Wouldn't it be quicker just to ask him?' said Juliet. 'He hasn't absconded, as far as we know. And are you saying that he's a suspect? Of what? Martha's abduction? Her murder? Or maybe that he's an all-purpose perpetrator of all the crimes we're investigating? It would be convenient if we found out that he was responsible for the vehicle thefts, too!'

Tim grinned. Juliet had nailed the reason for his optimism: but his suspicions sounded absurd when she put them into words.

'Too convenient, I agree! But there's no guarantee that he'll tell us the truth and, if he is mixed up either in Martha's disappearance or the vehicle thefts, I'd rather not alert him that we're on to him.'

'Okay, but he'll already know we're investigating her disappearance; also that we know he's one of the people who saw her last. He won't be surprised that we want to question him. We can ask him directly how long he's worked for Fovargue and where he lives now. We can verify what he tells us later if we need to.'

'Perhaps you're right,' said Tim. 'But what Ricky says is true: you can't go there alone. I'm coming with you.'

CHAPTER FORTY-SIX

The front door of Silverdale Farm was wide open when Tim and Juliet drew up at the top of the track. As they were getting out of Tim's car, a small boy came racing across the lawn, followed by a toddler who had little chance of catching him up. The boy crossed the track and cannoned breathlessly into Tim.

'Steady on!' said Tim, taking hold of the child's shoulders. 'You need to be careful when you're crossing this road.' He looked across at the toddler, who had stopped running and was standing in the middle of the lawn viewing them both apprehensively.

'Is that your little brother?'

'Yes,' said the boy. 'He's called Alfie.'

'What's your name?'

'I'm Joe and he's Alfie.'

'Is your mum in?'

'Yes, but she's busy with Daddy. Dilys is looking after us.' He pointed at the house, from which a heavily-built middle-aged woman was just emerging, pushing back untidy grey hair from her eyes.

'Come here Joe, Alfie,' she called. 'You're not to run off like that.'

Alfie turned immediately and headed towards her. Joe hesitated. Tim took his hand and crossed the lawn with him. By the time they'd reached the woman, she had bundled Alfie back inside the house. She was standing in the doorway with her arms folded. She wasn't exactly glowering, but neither was she trying to look hospitable. Juliet caught up with Tim and Joe.

'Go inside and play with Alfie, Joe,' she said. Then, addressing Juliet rather than Tim, 'And who might you be?'

'DS Armstrong, South Lincs CID,' said Juliet. 'And this is DI Yates. You'll know that Martha Johnson has been reported missing?'

'It's hard not to know with all the fuss being made on the wireless. Nothing to do with me or the children, though, is it?'

'We didn't come to see you. We'd like to have a few words with Josh Marriott, if you know where we can find him. And since Joe says his mum's here, perhaps she wouldn't mind talking to us, too,' said Tim.

'Susie's round the back loading up for the Lincoln show,' said the woman. 'As for Josh, I don't have anything to do with the businesses. That man is a law unto himself and…'

'DI Yates!' A rough voice intruded suddenly. Tim turned to see Josh Marriott standing to his right. Somehow, he had managed to join them without being seen, although there was no foliage in the vicinity of the house.

'Mr Marriott. Just the person we were hoping to see.'

'Aye, I thought it wouldn't be long before you beat a path to my door.'

'Well, you've got what you wanted now,' said Dilys. 'If you'll excuse me, I need to look after the kids.' She gave Tim and Juliet a brief nod that seemed not to include Marriott.

'Thank you very much Mrs…'

'It's Miss. Miss Pacey. Dilys.'

'Thank you, Miss Pacey,' said Juliet. 'We'll let you know if we need your help again.'

Dilys Pacey raised her eyebrows as she retreated into the house, closing the door firmly behind her.

'When is the Lincoln show?' Juliet asked Marriott.

'Tomorrow. The boss and Susie are both going.'

'So they're here for the rest of today?'

'No, they'll be off shortly. I've had the stand loaded into the van. They're just picking up some leaflets and that. Then they'll go to Lincoln to set up.'

'We'd like to speak to Mrs Fovargue before they leave,' said Juliet, looking at Tim. He took the hint.

'Why don't you go to see her while I talk to Mr Marriott?' he said.

Juliet nodded and gave him a quick smile. Tim could be obtuse sometimes when it came to catching her drift. Today he was in good form.

Juliet followed the narrow path round the side of the house to the courtyard at the back. The huge pantechnicon was standing on the paved area, its doors wide open. She observed that strips of metal and a canvas awning had been neatly ranged around the sides of its interior and at the back, leaving a huge space in the middle. She could see no one inside the vehicle. She was about to walk to the front of it in case the Fovargues were already sitting in the cab when she heard raised voices. Listening carefully, she decided they were coming from the house. They were very clear: either the kitchen door or one of the windows must have been left open. Fovargue was reasoning with his wife.

'I admit I made a mistake,' he was saying. 'It was wrong of me. But you're wrong about the rest of it. Of course I wouldn't have left you.'

'Oh, a moment of madness, was it? Spare me!'

'No, it was more than that. I admit it. But nothing and no one would have come between us. Not permanently. We share too much.'

'Damn' right we do! Don't you see that by letting that little bitch in you exposed us?'

'What do you mean? She doesn't know about anything except the soil business. She isn't interested in anything else.'

'Except you, of course. Besides, how do you know what she is – or was – interested in?'

'What do you mean, 'was'? Did you send her away, Susie? Did you make her leave?'

There was a long silence. When the reply came, it was barely audible: subdued, defeated, quite unlike the shrill screeching that had preceded it.

'How could I have? She wouldn't have listened to me.'

'Susie...'

'Let's drop the subject, shall we? Help me get this through the door.'

Nimbly, Juliet doubled back on her footsteps. As if just arriving, she was rounding the corner of the house again when the Fovargues emerged, carrying between them an elaborate spinner stacked with leaflets about soil management. Susie Fovargue was first to hear Juliet approaching and turned sharply, placing her end of the spinner on the ground. Fovargue hoisted the contraption upright and stood it on the paving stones.

'DS Armstrong,' he said tonelessly. 'We're just going out. Is there any news of Martha Johnson?'

'Unfortunately not.'

'Well, I've told you all that I know.'

'I realise that, sir. It's Mrs Fovargue I've come to see.'

'Me? I didn't have anything to do with the... with her.'

'I appreciate that, but you were here when she was talking to us yesterday. Therefore, along with Mr Marriott and DC MacFadyen and myself, you were one of the last people to see her before she disappeared.'

'Purely by chance. I didn't see her again. As you've just said, I left her with you.'

'How would you describe your relationship with Ms Johnson?'

'I have no relationship with her. She is one of Jack's employees. That's all. I don't have much to do with most of them.'

'But she does work in the same part of the business as you do, doesn't she? The soil appreciation stuff?'

'Not exactly. She does the testing. I go out to see people – mainly schoolchildren – and take the stand to shows.'

'Oh? I thought she did go out with Mr Fovargue sometimes. In fact, I thought she was due to accompany him yesterday.'

'I just asked her to keep herself free as a backstop, nothing more,' said Fovargue quickly. 'Just in case Susie couldn't make it.'

Susie Fovargue stared at him, disbelief etched on her every feature.

'I see. Well, thank you for your time. I hope the show is a success. When will you be returning?'

'Tomorrow evening. It's only a one-day show.'

'Excellent, because I must ask you to keep us informed of your whereabouts, in case we need your help again. We'll be sure to let you know if we make any progress. I have your mobile number.'

Fovargue nodded curtly and took hold of the spinner again, rolling it towards the pantechnicon while Susie stood, her arms folded, watching him.

CHAPTER FORTY-SEVEN

Complying with Tim's request, Josh Marriott led the way to the office where Martha Johnson worked. The desk was clear apart from the pen tidy that had been pushed into the far right-hand corner. Rows of test tubes in racks were arranged on the table that stood at right angles to the desk, each tube labelled in a bold, faultless script.

'It's very tidy in here. Does Ms Johnson always leave her office looking so neat?'

Marriott gave an unhelpful shrug.

'How should I know? I hardly ever come in here.'

'Any particular reason for that?'

'I don't make any secret of the fact that I don't like her. I think she's a waste of space – and dangerous with it.'

'Dangerous? In what way?'

'She's a mischief-maker. Got her claws into the boss. Now she's setting her cap at Nathan. Boy's fool enough not to see through her.'

'Are you certain of that?'

Marriott paused before he answered.

'No, not certain. But she talks to him quite a bit when he's here. And I thought I saw them out together once.'

'Out together? Where?'

'Just in Bourne. Coming out of a shop.'

'Nathan lives close to Bourne. They could have just met by chance.'

Again the pause and slow reply. 'Aye, 'appen you're right.'

'Mr Marriott, where do you think Martha Johnson is now? Do you think something's happened to her?'

'How should I know? Done a bunk? Rediscovered her Christian roots and seen the error of her ways?'

'When we met at the door of Silverdale Farm just now, you said that you thought we'd come looking for you. Why did you think that?'

'Stands to reason, dun't it? Someone disappears, first thing you cops do is cast around looking for someone to blame. Don't tell me you haven't latched on to my time in clink.'

'We do know you have a criminal record, yes. We'll try not to jump to facile conclusions, though. Is there anything you want to say about your convictions?'

Marriott fixed Tim with a surly eye.

'What do you want me to say? I was guilty and I got caught. I did me time and learnt to be a bit smarter.'

'Meaning?'

'Meaning that I made up me mind to go straight. I got the job here and made a go of it.'

'Mr Fovargue knows about your... past history?'

'Course he does. He judges me on results, not on what I did before. I've worked hard for him, helped him build these businesses up. It was a great little set-up...'

'*Was* a great little set-up? Why do you say that?'

'Things haven't been so good lately, what with the boss mooning after Martha and Susie in a perpetual bad mood.'

'I'm going to ask you this outright, Mr Marriott: did you play any part in Martha Johnson's disappearance?'

'You mean did I top her? I'd be mad to do that. Risk spending the rest of me life inside? Not likely. She isn't worth it.'

'Can you tell me what you were doing yesterday afternoon and evening?'

'I was working in the afternoon. At home in the evening, until I dropped into the Brownlow Arms for a drink about tennish.'

'Do you live alone?'

'No. Girlfriend works at the Brownlow. That's why I went there: to fetch her home.'

'What time did you get home yesterday evening after you finished work?'

'Around half six. Later than usual. Nathan was off sick and I'd to do some of his work.'

'What's your address?'

There was a light knocking at the office door.

'May I come in?' asked Juliet.

'Of course. I was just asking Mr Marriott for his address. Have Mr and Mrs Fovargue gone now?'

'Yep.' Juliet nodded. Tim divined the interview with them had not been satisfactory.

'It'll be easiest if I write the address down for you,' said Marriott, suddenly co-operative. He took a pen from the desk tidy and scrabbled among the files on the shelf above the desk, evidently searching for scrap paper.

'Those lever arch files were piled up on Martha's desk last time I was here,' said Juliet.

'Happen they were. It wouldn't surprise me. They're none of her business, but that wouldn't stop her.'

'What are they for?'

'They're mostly journey records for the businesses. Log sheets that say when the vehicles were taken out, where they went, when they came back, how many miles covered. That sort of thing. And the petrol receipts. Other receipts, too, if there were any: meals in cafés, car park tickets, that sort of thing.'

'Who tidied them up, put them back on the shelves. Do you know?'

'Well, it wasn't me, if that's what you're thinking. Most likely Martha herself, I'd say. Could have been the boss, I suppose. Or Susie.'

'I think we need to take a look at those files,' said Juliet.

'You can look at them if you like, but if you're thinking of taking them away I can't give you permission. You'll have to ask the boss for that.'

'I think we should take them now,' said Juliet, looking at Tim for approval.

'Where's your search warrant?' said Josh Marriott.

'We can get a warrant, but we need to take the files now.'

'We're allowed to take any evidence we find during the routine investigation of a crime scene,' said Tim, thinking quickly. He didn't know why Juliet was making such an urgent play to retain the files, but her reason was bound to be a good one.

'Who says it's a crime scene?'

'It's the last place Martha Johnson was seen alive. I'm empowered to call it a crime scene.'

'I just hope you're right about that,' said Marriott. 'I'm not going to try to stop you, but you can bet the boss will have the law on you if you're wrong.'

Tim smiled wryly at the irony of the comment. He forbore to mention that Jack Fovargue hadn't been particularly keen on using the law to his advantage when he was mugged.

'How many files are there?' he asked Juliet. Then, turning to Marriott, 'We'll give you a receipt for them, naturally. They'll be returned as soon as possible.'

'There are ten,' she replied. 'One for each year, going back to 2008.'

CHAPTER FORTY-EIGHT

'What do you want all these files for?' said Tim, as he helped Juliet carry them back to his car. 'They go back much further than Martha Johnson's connection with this place.'

'I admit it's a long shot,' said Juliet, 'but if I'm right they'll help the work Katrin's doing, looking for relevant unsolved crimes. It'll still be like looking for a needle in a haystack, but if we can find just one 'coincidence' it'll be worth it.'

'You know I don't believe in coincidences.'

'Precisely. Neither do I.'

'And you're planning to land Katrin with all of them?' Tim gestured at the files, which were now scattered across the back seat of the car.

'I don't mind helping her with them. I'll talk to her about it – I think we'll agree on the sort of thing we're looking for. And we need to send someone to check out what the Fovargues get up to at the Lincoln show. Starting from now, if we can.'

'Christ, do we really have to do that? We're stretched to the limit for personnel as it is.'

'Up to you, sir,' said Juliet briskly. 'I'm convinced the

Fovargues are involved in at least one of the crimes we're investigating. We may be able to prevent another if we act now.'

Tim groaned.

'You win, on one condition.'

'What's that?'

'That if Marriott – or Fovargue – complains that we took these files without permission, you explain it to Thornton.'

'Done,' said Juliet.

'Does Fovargue know Andy Carstairs?'

'Unlikely,' said Juliet. 'It's mostly Ricky he's had dealings with. He may have caught a glimpse of Andy when he came to the station, but I doubt it registered.'

CHAPTER FORTY-NINE

Superintendent Thornton was not in a good mood when Tim and Juliet returned to the station.

'Where the hell have you been, Yates? There's a couple of Irish policemen here. They've brought in someone called William Pett. He's already in custody in Ireland and they say you want him for questioning here. We've put him in the cells for now. Can you tell me what this is about? They seem to think we're paying their travel expenses, as well!'

'I'm sorry, sir. I did ask Superintendent Donnelly to let us interview Pett. The Irish police have only just apprehended him – they've been after him for a long time. I had to say we'd pay them to escort him. Otherwise they wouldn't have been happy to risk losing him again.'

'And you omitted to mention this to me?'

'I'm sorry. It must have slipped my mind.'

'Typical, if I may say so. Why are you so keen to talk to this Pett? It'd better be worth the expense!'

'He's the father of the girl who was found in the Fossdyke Canal.'

'Oh, so it's Michael who should be footing the bill.'

'We can ask DI Robinson to share the costs if you like. But you should also know I now have another reason for being interested in Pett: the Irish police think he's involved in a series of vehicle thefts over there.'

Superintendent Thornton changed tack immediately. He emitted a low whistle, which almost reduced Juliet to giggles.

'You think he might be responsible for taking vehicles here, too?'

'I think it's likely he's mixed up in it. I'm not sure he's the mastermind.'

'Well, get on and interview him, Yates. Do you want to take Armstrong with you?'

'DC MacFadyen has been detailed to assist DI Yates with the theft case,' said Juliet quickly. 'I'd like to concentrate on Martha Johnson's disappearance, if that's okay.'

'Fine by me,' said Tim. 'Do you want to start working through those files?'

'Yes,' said Juliet. 'I might need some assistance. It'll involve going out for a while.'

'See you later.'

Superintendent Thornton was still hovering.

'Do you want me to sit in on the interview with Pett?' he asked. Tim's heart sank.

'That's generous of you, sir, but DC MacFadyen is completely up to speed with the case. If you could keep tabs on the door-to-doors for the Smythe murder I'd be grateful. We're going to have to issue a press release about Martha Johnson later, too.'

'Drat it, you've just let Armstrong leave. I'll have to draft the press release myself now. There's no news of the Johnson woman, I suppose?'

'No.'

'Well, I'd better get on with it. Assure the public that no stone is being left unturned and we're doing all we can to help the family, etcetera. Talking of which, go easy on Pett, won't you? Remember he's just been bereaved. I don't want him kicking up a stink because we haven't handled him sensitively enough.'

William Pett was something of a surprise. Tim had imagined he'd be big and beefy, with muscular arms and a beer gut, but instead the man standing before him bore a strong resemblance to a very well-dressed leprechaun. His face was gaunt and rather aristocratic-looking, while there was such fluidity to his movements that he almost seemed to be dancing. Only his high colour suggested that Tim might have been right in one respect: Pett had the complexion of the habitual heavy drinker.

One of the Irish policemen was sitting with Pett; the other was guarding the door. Pett stood when Tim and Ricky entered the interview room and the seated policeman automatically stood up with him, revealing that they were handcuffed together. Superintendent Donnelly had obviously instructed his team that Pett must be given no opportunity to escape. There was no solicitor present, which Tim thought odd, until he remembered that ostensibly Pett was being questioned only about his daughter's disappearance and murder. He sighed inwardly. Pett would be unlikely to pass up on the chance to delay the interview by demanding legal representation if its subject switched to the stolen vehicles.

'Mr Pett,' said Tim. 'Thank you for coming here.'

Disconcertingly, Pett broke out into a high-pitched laugh.

'Didn't have much choice, did I?' He raised his fist,

displaying its shackle, and gestured at the policeman at the door with his free hand. He sounded amicable enough, Tim thought ... and as tricky as a nest of snakes.

'Please, sit down.' Tim gestured at the chairs that Pett and the policeman had just vacated. 'This is DC MacFadyen. I'm afraid we need to ask some questions about Selina. First, I'd like you to know that we're very sorry for your loss.'

Pett's leprechaun eyes darted and twinkled.

'Ach, the good Lord was ready to take her, so she went. Some childer are destined to die young. It's in their stars.'

'It wasn't fate that took your daughter, Mr Pett. She was murdered.'

'Aye, so you say. Her mother will believe you.'

'Where is your wife?'

'She's been kept by your crew in Ireland. They wouldn let us both out of their sights together. Just as well, maybe. She wouldn have wanted to see the body.'

'Penny Green has already identified your daughter – we're satisfied that she was the girl pulled from the Fossdyke. But you'll want to see her for yourself, of course.'

Pett sat up straight in his chair and flicked his bright eyes around the room. His twinkling, genial demeanour had evaporated in a flash.

'Penny has a lot to answer for. She'll be sorry when I catch up with her.'

'Ms Green was doing her best to look after your daughters. You and your wife left them in her care.'

'Aye, because we trusted her with them,' said Pett, eyeballing Tim and spraying him with spittle.

'My understanding is that Ms Green wasn't asked to sleep under the same roof as them. She could hardly be held accountable for their actions when you gave them that degree of freedom.'

'That's as maybe. There'll still be trouble when I see her.'

'I must warn you that this conversation is being recorded. If you or anyone else threatens Ms Green, the recording may be used as evidence against you.'

Pett fell silent and stared at the floor. Tim allowed him time to collect himself before he continued.

'Your wife's name is Rosa, right?'

Pett nodded.

'Why did you and Rosa leave three young girls only semi-supervised? You must have had a powerful reason to do such a thing.'

''Twas for business. To make the money to get us through the winter.'

'And Rosa had to go with you, too?'

'She helps me.'

'What kind of business is it, Mr Pett?'

'I'm a trader.'

'What do you trade?'

'This and that. I look out for stuff for people, take it to them if I can get them a deal.'

'I see. So "people" ask you to get things for them?'

'That's about the size of it.'

'Does it include vehicles?'

'It might do. Look, what is this? I came here to talk to you about Selina and the bastard that killed her. It isn't about me and what I do.'

'Agreed, Mr Pett. I apologise. We'll leave it there, perhaps come back to this discussion another time, when it will be your right to have a solicitor present. I'll arrange for you to visit the morgue now. Just one more question, if I may. Does the name Josh Marriott mean anything to you?'

Tim was scrutinising Pett closely. Pett met his eye boldly and took his time to answer.

'No. Why? Should it do?'

'No particular reason. What about Jack Fovargue?'

'No,' said Pett, more quickly this time. He yanked at the handcuff and he and the Irish policeman stood up together.

If Tim was sure of anything, it was that Pett was lying.

CHAPTER FIFTY

Something had been nagging at the back of Juliet's mind since she and Katrin had talked about the likelihood of there being a multiple copycat killer. She pushed it away while driving the short distance to Katrin's office and instead started thinking about Jake Fidler and the promise she had made to meet him at the weekend. Guiltily, she glanced over her shoulder at the files from Silverdale Farm, which were sitting on the back seat of her car, now neatly packed into two cardboard boxes. She doubted she'd be able to keep that promise now.

The nagging feeling pushed itself to the surface again as she turned over in her mind all that had happened during the evening she'd spent with Jake. Every memory of it was crystal clear. She relived their conversation, recalling almost the exact words each had uttered. Mentally she retraced the time they'd spent in her flat together and the progress of their journey to Cambridge. She'd overreacted when she'd seen the roadside shrine dedicated to the Polish woman. She'd been afraid that she'd spoilt the evening by introducing too much of the cop into it and then... she returned again to what she'd said to Jake as they'd passed the shrine.

'She got off the bus at the wrong stop and vanished.'

Katrin had said she'd look for unsolved crimes and then try to pair them with similar crimes that had been committed prior to them, because the copycat killer would be likely to have replicated an unsolved murder more closely than a solved one. Juliet wondered if Katrin had found police accounts of the Polish woman's disappearance and if so whether she'd considered that case worth adding to the list. But she knew that, officially, the Polish woman had been declared missing; although both the police and the media had long ago assumed she was dead, probably murdered, her husband had clung on to the slender chance that she might still be alive. He'd refused to have her classified as 'presumed dead'. Katrin would probably not have found the right sort of information to be able to single her out.

She parked the car in front of the early Victorian building that housed Katrin's office and was opening the nearside back door to retrieve the two boxes when Katrin herself emerged from the building, wearing her coat.

'Juliet! I didn't expect to see you again today. Were you looking for me?'

Juliet glanced at her watch.

'God! I had no idea it was so late. I've brought some files from Silverdale Farm. The missing woman I told you about – Martha Johnson – hasn't turned up and we've launched a massive search for her. The files contain transport records – they detail movements of the vehicles belonging to the farm. I want to work through them to see if they offer any clues to Martha's disappearance. I was going to ask you to help me, partly because they might throw some light on the work you're doing, too. But it's the weekend now: don't let me fuck yours up as well as my own. If I still need some help, I'll come back on Monday, shall I?'

'I don't think I'll be getting much of a weekend. Tim's already told me that Martha Johnson is now officially missing and a big search is under way. That's on top of the two murder enquiries – but I don't need to tell you about it. I'll be surprised if I see much of Tim over the next two days. I'll have to look after Sophia, of course, but she's out at a party tomorrow afternoon and I can call in a few favours with other mums to get her invited on play dates at least some of the time on Sunday. If you're prepared to have a bit of an interrupted schedule, we can take the files back to mine.'

'If you're sure that's okay, it would be great.'

Juliet slammed the rear car door shut and opened the passenger door for Katrin. She noticed that Katrin herself was carrying a bulky wad of papers.

'Let me hold those for you while you strap yourself in.'

As Juliet started the car, she looked at the bundle of papers again.

'Have you found some cases that might fit with our theory?'

'There are five unsolved murders or permanent disappearances that I think might yield something. I know I won't find 'twins' for all of them – maybe even for none of them, but I'll try. They bear no obvious similarities to each other, but there is one thing that's curious about them.'

'Go on.'

'Chronologically speaking, the locations get progressively closer to South Lincolnshire, ending with the Butter Market murder. Steven Smythe was killed in Spalding – that's right in the middle of the South Lincs police patch. The Fossdyke Canal murders are in North Lincs territory. Last year, there was a case of a girl who disappeared in Worksop. Those are the ones nearest to us. The others are further away, both in time and distance – the disappearance of another girl in the Midlands, two murders in Newcastle, one in Wales.'

'Have you found any earlier crimes that match them?'

'Not yet. I was going to do some work on that over the weekend. I'll be lucky if I find any matches, even if there are some.'

'Why did you pick these cases in particular?'

'They all seem like motiveless crimes. No one can come up with an explanation for any of them. And once I started looking at the detail, I found the strange fact that they seem gradually to home in on this area – almost as if the murderer's taunting us, daring us to find him.'

'You think he might live in Spalding?'

'That depends on how reckless he is. If I were him, I'd take care not to foul my own doorstep. But as you know, some serial killers have a kind of death-wish; subconsciously or not, they want to be caught.'

'Hm, I'll keep an open mind on whether he lives in Spalding or not. I don't want to get obsessive about Silverdale Farm, but I'm convinced that something very nasty has been going on there. And Martha Johnson worked – or, should I say, works – there. There's nothing to indicate that Spalding's the end of the trail.'

'I guess you're right. Anyway, I can start by looking for similar cases or first help you wade through those files, whichever you think will be most help.'

'Looking for the similar cases might be the best bet – it'll be more interesting than the files, too. I'll have to keep my wits about me while I sift through a mountain of pedestrian mileage accounts. I reckon boredom's the leading cause of missing clues in paperwork.'

Katrin laughed.

'I'm sure Tim would agree with that. I'll keep you supplied with coffee.'

Juliet had just swung the car into Edinburgh Drive. She

could see Tim's car standing outside the dormer bungalow he shared with Katrin.

'There's Tim's car now,' said Juliet. 'Perhaps I'd better come back tomorrow. I didn't realise he would be home this early. I'm sure you'd like a to spend some time alone with him.'

'He's parked on the street. That means he's not planning to stay for long. He's probably just popped in to see Sophia.'

'Where is she?'

'She's with the child-minder who picks her up after pre-school. She lives in the next street. I'll walk round to fetch Sophia. You go in and make yourself at home. See if Tim'll make you a cup of tea.'

'Thanks.' Juliet nodded, thinking Tim was far more likely to suggest that she made one for him. She'd probably do it, too: she still felt uncomfortable about intruding on his private space.

As Katrin hurried away, Juliet remembered that she hadn't raised with her the disappearance of the Polish woman. She'd bring it up later. It was true it wasn't surprising the woman didn't feature on Katrin's list, but the more Juliet thought about it, the more she thought her disappearance fitted with the theory.

CHAPTER FIFTY-ONE

Andy Carstairs had spent a mildly interesting couple of hours at the Lincoln showground watching farmers, agricultural machinery manufacturers and assorted local artisans setting up their stands. There was a St John Ambulance first aid post near the entrance to the ground and Andy had struck up a conversation with the man and woman on duty, explaining that he was a plain-clothes police officer on the look-out for undesirables. Luckily for him, they'd attended another show a few weeks before at which some of the stands had been damaged and visitors endangered by a group of motorcycle joyriders speeding through "for a laugh", as the man put it contemptuously. Andy's mission sounded plausible, therefore, and they made him welcome, even providing him with tea.

Lincoln wasn't one of the big shows – plots had been marked out for perhaps two dozen stands. From his vantage point, Andy was able to keep watch on the Fovargues, who had a pitch in the central row. They seemed to be working together harmoniously enough, erecting the stand with a practised skill. It took them about ninety minutes to complete the job. They spent some time after that walking round the other stands and talking to their owners. Most were affable enough and happy to engage in conversation – one or two were gruff and got rid of them with a short couple of words, but Andy didn't think such brush-offs were significant. This was Lincolnshire, after all: some people didn't like being interrupted when they were busy and Lincolnshire folk weren't usually slow to tell it how it was.

He thought he saw Susie Fovargue glance across at the first aid post a few times as if she had clocked him, but since they'd never actually met, he was probably imagining it. Jack Fovargue, having immersed himself in his own particular brand of bonhomie, didn't look at him once.

After three quarters of an hour or so, Susie had had enough of the niceties. She said something to Fovargue and gestured towards the pantechnicon, which they'd parked at the end of their row of stands. Fovargue nodded and, after chatting for a few more seconds with one of his neighbours, followed Susie across the grass to the vehicle. He manoeuvred it round the edge of the field with considerable dexterity. As it neared the first aid post, Andy walked away so that Fovargue wouldn't see his face. He listened to the chug-chugging noise it made as Fovargue steered it through the narrow entranceway and only turned back to look at it once it was out on the road. It appeared to be heading out towards Scampton.

Andy called Tim on his mobile.

Tim put down the cup of tea that Juliet had just made for him. He switched the phone to 'speak'.

'Hello, Andy? Are you still at the showground?'

'Yep. But the Fovargues have just left. They're on the A15, on the Scampton road – going in the opposite direction to Silverdale Farm.'

'Hi, Andy, it's Juliet. That's not a surprise. Susie told me they were staying overnight somewhere near to the show. There's a local woman looking after the kids.'

'Can you follow them, Andy?' It was Tim again.

'If I go right away, probably. They can't be moving very fast in that thing he's driving.'

'Get after them, then, will you?'

'Sure. And then what? Do you want me to keep tabs on them for the whole night?'

'No, that shouldn't be necessary. Just wait until you think they've settled down for the night. If it's only a guest house they're staying in, they might go out to dinner.'

'All right. I'd better get going.'

Andy cut the call. He'd left his car parked on the main road, as close in to the verge as he could get it. Another car had now parked in front of his. As Andy reversed back a few yards to pull in front of it, a motorcyclist shot past him.

'Christ, mate, slow down, will you!' Andy muttered as he swung the car out into the road and followed the bike.

He'd almost reached Scampton before he rounded a bend and saw the pantechnicon just ahead of him. To his surprise, the motorcyclist was riding behind it. Having roared past Andy like a bat out of hell, the rider had slowed to the sedate speed of 35mph. Andy tried to see beyond the lorry. The road ahead appeared to be both straight and clear; overtaking the giant vehicle in a car might be tricky, but it shouldn't have presented too much of a problem to an accomplished biker.

The motorcyclist looked over his shoulder. As far as Andy could tell, it was no one he knew, but he decided to hang back and allowed another car, a red Honda, to occupy the space between them. It was unlikely he'd lose the pantechnicon now. The whole group trundled on for a few miles, eventually losing the Honda when it turned into the yard of a pub. The pantechnicon halted at the junction of the A15 and the A1103 and turned left towards Gainsborough. The motorcyclist followed. Andy drew closer to the bike and memorised its registration number, then dropped back again.

Andy's mobile sang into life.

'Andy? Did you catch up with Fovargue?'

'Yes, and I'm still following him. He's just turned left on the A1103, heading for Gainsborough.'

'That's probably where he'll be staying, then. Remember what I said.'

Andy rolled his eyes.

'Yes, boss. One other thing: a motorcyclist may be following him as well. He came haring past me at the showground, but since he caught up with Fovargue he's stayed behind him.'

'Strange. You don't know who it is?'

'I don't think so, but his face is covered by a visor.'

'Could just be a coincidence, but go carefully, Andy. Don't get involved in anything. If you need to apprehend anyone, send for backup first. I'll alert DI Robinson, ask him to have a patrol car ready to come out from Lincoln to support you.'

'Thanks,' said Andy. 'Look, I'm going to switch you off now because...' He'd missed the click. Tim had already terminated the call.

Tim was still at home. He'd put Sophia to bed and had been sitting in his living room with Juliet when Andy called.

'You don't believe in coincidences,' she said.

'No, and I don't believe in lone coppers getting done over, either. Andy's got to ask for help if he wants to do anything more than just watch. Give him another call in fifteen minutes or so, will you? He should be in Gainsborough then, if that is where the Fovargues do intend to stay. Right, I'm going back to the station now. Thank you for staying to help Katrin.'

'It's the other way round: Katrin's helping me – us, I should say.'

'Well, thanks, anyway.'

He went into the kitchen, where Katrin was stirring bolognaise sauce.

'Sophia go off all right?'

'Yes.'

'God, that smells nice!'

'Stay for some, then. The pasta's almost ready.'

'Sorry, got to go. Don't wait up!'

He gave her a quick kiss on the lips. Juliet, who'd just come to stand in the doorway, retreated, at once embarrassed and assailed by a sharp pang of envy.

CHAPTER FIFTY-TWO

Andy continued to follow Fovargue and the motorcyclist. The motorcyclist was keeping plumb in the middle of his side of the road, riding close up to the pantechnicon. He didn't try to pull out or hang back so that he could see beyond the vehicle. Fovargue had fitted extra-large wing mirrors on both sides of it, but Andy still thought it unlikely he'd be able to see a motorcyclist who was keeping to that position.

Fovargue headed out beyond the town, taking a narrow lane that was barely wide enough for the pantechnicon to negotiate. After rounding a sharp bend, he pulled up at a red-brick farmhouse. A sign standing in the field opposite announced it as *Marston Farm. Bed & Breakfast. Children and Dogs Welcome. Evening Meals by Arrangement.* There were two entrances to the farm, with a turning circle linking them, one gated, the other open. Fovargue steered the lorry into the open entrance so that it was almost off the road but standing parallel to it. The motorcyclist halted after he turned the bend, got off his bike and propped it up under some trees. Andy stopped his car and reversed it back round the bend. He couldn't tell whether either the motorcyclist or Fovargue knew that he had been following them.

Juliet called him at that moment. Andy considered ignoring her, then thought better of it.

'Juliet, hi, I can't stop – Jack and Susie Fovargue have just rolled up to a farmhouse that does bed and breakfast. The motorcyclist followed them all the way and he's dismounted now. I should go and see what's happening.'

'Where are you?'

'On the other side of the bend in the road before the farm. I reversed when I saw they were stopping.'

'Do they know you're there?'

'Perhaps the motorcyclist does. As I told you, he turned round to look at me just after he passed me at the showground. He may have been aware that I didn't turn off after that. It's less likely the Fovargues have noticed me.'

'Tell me which road you're on and the name of the farm. I'll work out the compass co-ordinates and send them to DI Robinson. He's on standby to provide backup.'

'I'm on a road called Marston Common Lane. I've just passed an airfield. The B & B is at Marston Farm.'

'Brilliant. Wait where you are for backup.'

'But they'll probably...'

'Wait for backup, Andy. Tim's orders.'

Andy could hear raised voices. A man with a rough Lincolnshire accent was shouting. A woman started screaming.

'I'm sorry, Juliet, I'm going to have to deal with this now. I can hear a woman getting hysterical. Most likely it's Susie Fovargue. Someone may have been hurt.'

'Andy...'

Andy left the phone on, putting it in his pocket, and scrambled out of his car. As he turned the bend he saw Jack

Fovargue lying on the ground. The motorcyclist was standing over him. As soon as Fovargue had hauled himself back on his feet, the motorcyclist landed another punch straight in the centre of his face. Fovargue staggered and fell down again. The motorcyclist kicked at him viciously.

The woman screamed again. It wasn't Susie Fovargue, who was leaning out of the cab window of the lorry. She was shouting 'Mr Shucksmith! Mr Shucksmith!'

Andy ran down the road towards the motorcyclist.

'Police!' he shouted. 'Stay where you are! Don't lay hands on him again!' In his pocket he could feel his phone vibrating.

The motorcyclist was still wearing his helmet. He stood stock-still in the road until Andy reached him.

'I am arresting you...' Andy began. The motorcyclist landed him a powerful left hook, turned and sprinted to where his motorcycle was standing under the trees. Andy staggered against the back of the lorry. He put his hand to his face and then inspected it: his nose was bleeding. Taking a few seconds to recover, he launched himself back on his feet and started pursuing the motorcyclist, but his head was spinning and he found himself incapable of running. He had moved only a few yards before the motorcyclist had reached his bike, jumped on it and ridden away.

Andy sat down by the side of the road and took the mobile out of his pocket. Not surprisingly, Juliet had hung up. He called her again.

'Andy? Are you okay?'

'I think so. I've just been punched in the face by that motorcyclist, but it seems to be nothing worse than a nose bleed. Jack Fovargue's more seriously hurt – the guy floored him twice and then kicked him.'

'There's a patrol car coming from Lincoln.'

'Get them to send an ambulance, will you?'

'Sure. Did you get the number of the bike?'

'Yes. It's FT17 OGS.'

'I'll have it checked.'

'Right. I'm going to see how Fovargue is. He's sitting up now, but he hasn't managed to stand yet.'

'Get yourself checked out when the ambulance comes, will you?'

Andy cut the call. He scrambled to his feet and walked back to where Fovargue was sitting with his back propped against the nearside rear wheel of his vehicle. Susie had climbed out of the cab. She was crouching beside him, talking to him in a low voice, and with a vehemence that didn't suggest her first concern was for his welfare.

Andy hadn't quite reached them when a man wearing a checked flat cap appeared from the direction of the farmhouse. He was carrying a shotgun, though he had broken it and was holding it over the crook of his arm: it didn't look as if he was about to shoot someone. He strode up to the Fovargues. Like Susie, he didn't seem inclined to show much sympathy for Fovargue's injuries.

'What the hell is going on here?' he demanded. 'Just what do you think you're doing? You've upset Rita now. You know her nerves are bad.'

Andy continued to approach them; belatedly, the man noticed him and swung round.

'And who the fuck are you?'

'DC Carstairs, South Lincs Police,' said Andy. He fumbled for his identity card. The man snatched it from his hand, then gave it back to him. 'May I ask who you are, sir?'

'Name's Shucksmith. This is my farm. Wife runs a B & B. More trouble than it's worth, as you can see. These are tonight's 'guests'.' He didn't try to conceal the sneer in his voice.

Susie Fovargue had stood up when Shucksmith appeared. Fovargue found his feet more slowly.

'Why are you here?' he asked Andy. 'Don't tell me you were just bloody well passing by!'

It wasn't a question Andy had prepared himself for. Trying to think on the hoof, he was saved by an interjection from Susie.

'Lucky for you he did come,' she said ironically.

'There's an ambulance on its way,' said Andy.

'That's quite unnecessary,' said Fovargue, suddenly agitated. 'All I need is a hot bath and a decent meal. And perhaps a glass of wine or two.'

'You're planning on staying, then?' said Shucksmith without enthusiasm. 'Better check first that Rita's still up for it.'

'I'll come in and talk to her,' said Susie.

'Please come back when you've seen her,' said Andy. 'I'll need you to answer a few questions.'

'Why don't you all come inside and use the visitors' lounge,' said Shucksmith. 'You can't keep on standing out here making an exhibition of yourselves.'

'We'll wait here until the ambulance has arrived,' said Andy. 'Mr Fovargue can sit in my car. I'll go and fetch it.'

'How do you know my name?' said Fovargue obstreperously. 'And where is your car? I don't see one.'

Andy debated with himself: he could say that the name Fovargue was painted clearly on the side of the pantechnicon. It wouldn't wash: Fovargue would still have had to swallow too many coincidences.

'DI Yates detailed me to drop in at the showground, make sure you were all right, sir. He was concerned for your safety after the assault the other day. I watched you leave and then I saw the motorcyclist come helling past. I thought he might be following you, so I decided to follow myself.'

'I suppose you think I should be grateful.'

'Not really, sir. We don't expect much gratitude in this job. Let me fetch the car. It's just around the corner. You'll be all right for a couple of minutes?'

'Yeah, yeah.' Fovargue flapped the air with one hand, as if to brush away any concerns. 'Your nose is bleeding,' he added with faux concern. 'It's dripping on to your shirt.'

Annoyed with himself for feeling embarrassed by Fovargue's taunt, Andy found a crumpled tissue in his pocket and dabbed at his nose.

'I'll be right back,' he said over his shoulder. He felt giddy as he retraced his steps, challenged by the slight incline in the road.

He'd rounded the corner when he saw a patrol car come speeding towards him. He tried to flag it down, but either the driver didn't see him or decided to ignore him.

'Fuck!' he muttered to himself. He didn't want the plods to get to Fovargue – or Susie – before he did. Belatedly he realised he should have asked Juliet to tell them to call him when they were close to the farm. He made a final painful push for his car and was starting the engine when a paramedics' first response vehicle zoomed past him. He drove the car back to the farmhouse as quickly as he could.

Two policemen and two paramedics, one of the latter a woman, were gathered round Fovargue, who was leaning against his lorry with as nonchalant an air as he could muster. The female paramedic was taking his pulse.

'Ah, here comes the detective now,' Fovargue said. 'I told you he wouldn't be long.'

'DC Andy Carstairs,' said Andy shortly. 'I believe DS Armstrong sent for you. You passed me on the road just now.'

'Sorry, sir, I didn't realise it was you. I thought you looked a bit... ruffled. Are you all right, sir?'

'Yes, I'm fine,' Andy snapped. 'Can we just get on with questioning Mr Fovargue now?'

'We have to check him over first,' said the male paramedic. 'I don't think we'll need the ambulance, though. I'll cancel it.'

'Best let me check your pulse, too,' said the female paramedic to Andy. 'And here's some lint to hold to your nose.'

'Look,' said Andy, 'I have just prevented a very serious incident. There was a guy going for this gentleman as if he wanted to kill him. Can we please drop the trivialities?'

The two paramedics looked offended.

'No harm in letting them take a look at you,' ventured one of the policemen.

'All right,' said Andy. 'I'll do that if you'd do me the favour of taking some notes. I want to question Mr Fovargue while the attack is still fresh in his mind.' He turned to Fovargue and registered the amused glint in his eye.

'Mr Fovargue, did you know your assailant?'

'Hard to say, but I don't think so. He kept his helmet on, but I didn't recognise him.'

'Do you think it was the same man who assaulted you last Monday?'

'If you think about what I've just said, it should be obvious to you that the answer to your second question is also that I don't know.' Fovargue had recovered his urbane manner, but there was more than a hint of testiness in his words. 'Besides, I didn't see the person on Monday at all clearly. As I've already said in my statement.'

Mr Shucksmith appeared again.

'For Christ's sake, what is this, a party?' he said. 'Unless you're going soon, I must insist you all come inside. I've got staff and the neighbours to think about.'

Andy caught the eye of the policeman who'd spoken to him

and they exchanged an amused glance. Country people often considered it shameful to be associated with the police.

'Is that all right with Mrs Shucksmith?' he asked.

'What? Oh, Rita's all right. Tends to make a fuss about nothing. Anyway' – turning to Fovargue – 'your wife has quite charmed her. And to tell you the truth, I think Rita's interested in hearing about what happened herself.'

CHAPTER FIFTY-THREE

J uliet sighed deeply as she put down her phone after fielding a long succession of calls. She was kneeling on the hearthrug in Katrin's living room with the files from Silverdale Farm spread around her. Katrin was sitting on the sofa, trawling reports of missing persons and unsolved murders on her laptop. She could see that Juliet's nerves were getting frayed and decided against making vacuous comments about the number of interruptions they'd had since they'd started work after supper. It was almost 9pm.

'More coffee?'

Juliet looked at her watch.

'I ought to be going soon. Sorry: this evening's been a bit of a wash-out.'

'Well, I'm not going to stop work yet. I don't normally go to bed until about eleven. I'll probably carry on for another couple of hours. You're welcome to stay. Stay the night if you like. You don't have to keep on working. Help yourself to a drink – there's wine in the fridge, or maybe you'd like a gin and tonic? And it hasn't been a wash-out for me: I'm glad of the company.'

'Thanks. I won't stay the night, though – I don't want to

intrude too much on you and Tim and, besides, I ought to get back to my flat. I've hardly been there since Monday. But you have spurred me on to work a bit longer.'

Juliet returned to the file she'd been working on. All the Silverdale Farm files were overstuffed with papers, making it hard to turn the pages without removing them from the binder rings. She was therefore lifting the documents out of each file, turning them over so that the one dated latest was at the bottom of the pile and then replacing them in order after she'd examined them. As she'd predicted, the task was mind-bogglingly dull. Someone had meticulously filed the bills of sale, petrol receipts, service documents and repair dockets for all the Fovargue vehicles, using date sequences rather than devoting sections of the files to each vehicle. It was not the first set of business records she'd had to plough through and she recognised these were an accountant's dream: they were almost too perfectly kept. Perhaps she was barking up the wrong tree. She eyed the seven unexamined files with distaste. Was she wasting her time on this when perhaps she could be helping Tim to make a more crucial breakthrough?

Katrin set down a mug of coffee beside her, standing it on the hearth. She looked over Juliet's shoulder.

'What's that?' she asked.

'What's what?'

Katrin bent to point to a large piece of buff card that had been stuck to the back board of the file Juliet had just emptied. 'It's a pocket for loose papers – like the ones they put in posh notebooks and organisers.'

'Like Moleskines, you mean?'

'Yes. I haven't seen cardboard pockets in files like this before, but each of the files has one. Must be the way this make of file is designed. They haven't been used much – I think they're meant to hold receipts and other small documents that aren't easy to punch holes in, but whoever kept the accounts stapled all the receipts to sheets of paper. There were far too many to make use of the wallets.'

'I think I can see something in that one, though.'

Juliet looked again at the wallet. She could see now that it wasn't lying entirely flat. She nipped at its edges to open it up and withdrew a yellowed sheet of newspaper which had been neatly folded into eight. She spread it out carefully on the hearthrug, trying to smooth the folds without damaging it. It had been torn from a tabloid and its condition was fragile.

'It's just an old advert for agricultural vehicles.'

'I suppose that figures. Disappointing!'

'What were you hoping for? A signed confession?'

Katrin laughed.

'There's no need to mock. It's worth taking a look at the other side, though. Just to see if someone had a reason for keeping it.'

'Other than fancying a new tractor, you mean?'

Juliet turned over the sheet of paper.

'Looks like a digest of the news in other parts of the country,' she said. 'It's a local paper – it only deigns to give the national news one page.' She lifted the sheet of paper carefully and passed it to Katrin. 'Have a read if you're interested. I was going to say be careful, as it's in danger of disintegrating, but I don't suppose anyone is going to bring a charge against us for damage to a fragment of old newspaper.'

Katrin sat down again.

'God,' she said. '13th May 2010. David Cameron and Nick Clegg in the rose garden at Downing Street. That seems a long time ago. Iraqi insurgents kill 100 people and injure 200 others. Amazing how these local rags devote the front page to the opening of a new factory out in the sticks or some minor royal attending a village garden party and relegate stuff like this to a few paragraphs hidden among the adverts.'

'You don't know what was on the front page of this issue. It could have been...'

'Aaagh!'

'Katrin? Are you all right?'

Katrin sprang up from the sofa.

'Juliet, listen to this. "Police investigating the disappearance of fifteen-year-old paper girl Debbie Wicks have held a press briefing where they issued a statement saying there are no further leads to explain what has happened to Debbie or where she is now. It is three days since Debbie vanished while completing her paper round in Smethwick. Her bicycle was found in the grounds of Brooks' paint factory, site of her last delivery. There was no sign of Debbie or the canvas bag in which she carried the newspapers. Speaking at the briefing, DI Ron Blackman said that there were now grave concerns for Debbie's safety and appealed to anyone who might have information regarding her movements, however trivial it might seem, to contact the police on..." and it gives the number.'

'Is Debbie Wicks the girl in the Midlands you told me about? One of the cases you're trying to find lookalikes for?'

'Yes.'

'It was quite a long time ago – longer than I realised. Are you saying this is the copycat, or the original murder?'

'Does it matter? The fact is that someone at Silverdale Farm kept this cutting...'

'...and they could have kept it because they were interested in tractors, or David Cameron in the rose garden, or what was going on in Iraq.'

'Yes, but you don't really believe that, do you?'

'I'm going to keep an open mind. This may be significant, but we shouldn't get carried away. The first thing I'm going to do is check the rest of these brown cardboard pouches, see if I can find anything else in them. But thanks for some great work, Katrin – I'd certainly have missed that cutting. What did I say about getting bogged down in the detail?'

'I can't remember, but how about changing your mind about the gin and tonic?'

'Okay. Let's take a break. There's something else I want to run past you. Do you remember the disappearance of a Polish woman just outside Cambridge a few years ago?'

CHAPTER FIFTY-FOUR

The paramedics had left Marston Farm. They'd advised Fovargue to rest up the following day and told Andy to have his nose X-rayed to check for a possible fracture. Irritatingly, Andy found himself united with Fovargue in rejecting their advice: he had no intention of attending A & E and Fovargue clearly wasn't going to pass up on the Lincoln show.

The female paramedic picked up their mutinous attitude and rolled her eyes.

'Suit yourselves,' she said. 'We can't make you do as we say. It's your funeral.'

The paramedics didn't wait for the tea and cake which Rita Shucksmith brought into the visitors' sitting room. Fovargue, Susie and Andy weren't interested in the cake, either, but the policemen from Lincoln did it justice.

Andy had asked Fovargue a few more questions before handing over to them. Since Fovargue had been reluctant to admit a possible link between this assault and the one on the previous Monday, the Lincoln police had treated it as a separate incident. They'd taken statements from Jack Fovargue,

Susie Fovargue and Rita Shucksmith. All were equally unhelpful when it came to attempting to identify the assailant. Fovargue and Susie were adamant that they didn't know who the motorcyclist was and thought it unlikely they'd ever seen him before. He'd had his face turned away from Mrs Shucksmith, who had glimpsed his back view only from a window and then from the doorway of her house. She didn't know any bikers and said they were a rarity in the area. None of them would say they could recognise the man if they saw him again.

Andy could see that the Lincoln police thought they were wasting their time. He doubted that they'd follow up on the case unless someone prodded them into it.

When they'd gone, Mrs Shucksmith bustled off to make the Fovargues' dinner. Fovargue's pretence of not having suffered much from the assault was becoming difficult for him to maintain. Several times, his eyelids drooped before he juddered awake again. Susie had perched herself on the arm of a shabby brown sofa, a curious expression on her face. Andy couldn't decide whether she was feeling ill-at-ease or simply irritated by his own presence. It was clear that both Fovargues wanted to get shut of him.

Excusing himself, he went into the garden. Dusk was approaching. For a few seconds he watched, fascinated, as three bats circled an outside light. He noticed a bench on the far side of the parking area and calculated that it was beyond earshot of the house, even if someone happened to be standing at one of the open windows. He sat down on the bench. A sharp shooting pain in his knee made him wince: he must have fallen more awkwardly than he'd realised. Suddenly, he felt inexpressibly weary.

He direct-dialled Tim's number and was relieved to discover that Juliet had already provided his boss with an account of the events up to the motorcyclist's escape. Briefly, he added details of the interview with the Fovargues and Mrs Shucksmith.

'Doesn't sound as if you achieved very much there,' said Tim.

Andy bit back a stinging retort.

'No. It's hard to tell whether the Fovargues really don't know the attacker or are just stone-walling.'

'How badly hurt is Fovargue?'

'The paramedics said his injuries are pretty superficial, but he's quite shaken up. He's more shocked by the attack than he's letting on. He's supposed to be having dinner, but my guess is that he'll head for bed pretty quickly if I say I'm leaving.'

'Are you planning to go soon?'

'That's why I've called you. You said I didn't need to continue with the surveillance once I was sure the Fovargues were settled for the evening. Does that still stand now that Fovargue's been attacked?'

'What are the chances of his attacker returning?'

'Nil, I'd say. The bloke clearly didn't want anyone to know who he was. And he may have seen Shucksmith when he turned up with his shotgun.'

'Well, if you don't think the Fovargues will go out again tonight and that the attacker won't come back, there's no point in your hanging around. I could certainly use you back here.'

Andy groaned inwardly; he'd been hoping for a hot bath and a mindless half hour in front of the box nursing a beer before bed. Perhaps he should have taken the paramedic's advice.

CHAPTER FIFTY-FIVE

K atrin listened, fascinated, while Juliet outlined the story of the Polish woman.

'Can you remember her name?'

'Not her surname. I know that her first name was Irina and her husband was called Feliks. I remember being disturbed by the case at the time. I was reminded of it again when I was in Cambridge a few days ago. There's a shrine dedicated to her at the spot where she disappeared. We passed it.'

Her curiosity instantly kindled, Katrin wondered if the 'we' was a slip. She didn't comment on it.

'Shouldn't be too difficult to find something about it online. I'll try googling it first. If I draw a blank, I'll carry out a search in the archives I've been using.'

Katrin returned to her laptop.

'Here it is,' she said after a minute or two. 'Irina Grzegorzewski. That's probably not how you're meant to pronounce it. What a mouthful! Husband's name was Feliks, as you said. This is quite an unfriendly article about him. It looks as if he was a suspect for a while.'

'The media were very keen on pinning it on him – probably in part because the local police were insensitive when they took him in for questioning. It became apparent pretty quickly that he couldn't have killed her and then pretended she'd disappeared. He could account for his movements at the crucial times and there was precise information about hers, too, because she vanished after getting off a bus.'

'Another vanishing act. As you say, it fits the theory. I'm surprised I overlooked it.'

'That's why I wanted to talk to you about it. Her disappearance has never been formally logged as a murder because Feliks wouldn't allow it. Believing that she was dead was too much for him to bear. She's still officially a missing person. She's therefore not in the records as a murder victim.'

'She disappeared more than four years ago. I'm going to look for some similar disappearances prior to that. Ones that weren't necessarily considered to be murders, though that will make it much more time-consuming.'

'It's too late to start doing that now. We both need to get some rest. I'm going to have one more look at the stuff in this file, then put back these papers and go home. I'll come back in the morning, if that's all right.'

'Sure. And I suppose you're right. Even though I'm intrigued by this new lead.'

'It may not be a lead. We're clutching at straws here because it's all we have.'

'I know. But I think...'

'Ouch! Now why didn't I find that before?'

Katrin had refolded the piece of newspaper and was returning it to the cardboard pocket when she caught her finger on something sharp. Inspecting it, she found beads of blood collecting in a small cut. She sucked the wound clean, then felt more cautiously in the pocket and pulled out a receipt. She'd cut her finger on the staple attached to the top of the receipt.

She smoothed out the narrow oblong of yellowing paper.

'9th May 2010,' she read. 'Westcross Service Station. 6.10am. 48 litres.'

'Where's Westcross Service Station?'

'I don't know. Google it for me, will you? There may be hundreds of them!'

'No, I can only find one,' said Katrin after a few seconds. 'It's in Smethwick.'

'That's where Debbie Wicks had her paper round.'

'Yes, but the newspaper article is dated 13th May. You said she disappeared on the 9th.'

'I know. But it says she'd been missing for three days. Allowing for the fact that the article is reporting the previous day's news, that would make the day she disappeared 9th May – the same as the date on the petrol receipt. Am I right about the 9th?'

'I'm just checking. Yes, it was the 9th. The exact time she disappeared isn't known, but it was probably around 7am. Her bicycle was discovered by the canteen cook, near the entrance of the factory where she delivered the last of the papers.'

'At what time?'

'About seven forty-five.'

'So the killer could have purchased petrol at 6.10am.'

'He could have. He'd have had quite a long wait afterwards, if it was specifically Debbie he was looking for.'

'I think he's a highly-organised killer. He'd have to be, to copy all these different MOs. It probably matters to him that he gets the details of each copycat crime as close to the original as he can. He may have been following Debbie until she arrived at a place that was similar to the scene of crime he was copying.'

'That makes my blood run cold. If you're right, it's even more calculating than most premeditated crimes.'

'If I'm right, the killer is or was an employee at Silverdale Farm. I think we need to call Tim.'

CHAPTER FIFTY-SIX

T im took one look at Andy and told him to go home.

'I thought you needed me here?' said Andy, perversely aggrieved now that he was no longer wanted.

'You didn't tell me you'd been beaten up. And I seem to remember that I told you not to get into any trouble.'

'Well, what would you have done, boss? The guy was out to kill Fovargue.'

'Point taken. Superintendent Thornton would have been annoyed if you'd let that happen,' said Tim sardonically. 'You and Ricky are a right pair, though. How have you both managed to be done over in the same week?'

'Probably because we both tangled with the same guy.'

'I think you're right – and Fovargue is the common denominator.'

Andy looked blank for a second.

'You mean he was there both times?'

'Not only that, but he really seems to get up this bloke's nose. I wonder what the connection is between the attacker and Fovargue.'

'Fovargue says he doesn't know the guy and he can't say whether it's the same person who socked him one on Monday.'

'Who does he think he's trying to kid? He's supposed to be a local blue-eyed boy, pillar of the community, interested in conservation and preserving the environment for future generations. Why would someone like that get beaten up at all, let alone twice in the same week? And if the two incidents are unconnected, why does he have so many enemies? Anyway, you need to go home. Get some sleep.'

'Thanks. I could do with it. I'll be in bright and early tomorrow.'

'If you feel up to working tomorrow, I'd like you to go back to Lincoln.'

'And watch Fovargue again, you mean? But he knows who I am now.'

'That'll make it easier, then, won't it? You've got a legitimate reason for watching him: it's in case the biker comes back.'

'Not exactly a DC's job...'

'No, but he doesn't know that.'

'What time should I get there?'

'Whenever the show starts. 9 o'clock, probably. You can check it out online. In fact, if you're awake early enough, you could go back to that farmhouse, watch Fovargue and his wife leave. You can speak to him if you like. No need to be hole-in-the-corner about it.'

'All right,' said Andy. He calculated that he'd have to have to be on his way by 6.30 at the latest the following morning if he was going to catch the Fovargues eating their breakfast. So much for a good night's sleep.

Juliet's call came shortly afterwards.

'Tim? I'm still with Katrin. We think we've made a breakthrough.'

'Great if you have, because we're making absolutely no progress here. Except that Fovargue's been beaten up again, if you call that progress. But you know about that.'

'Did they catch the motorcyclist? And is Andy all right?'

'No, and yes, I think so. Tell me about your breakthrough. If I may say so, you don't sound very convinced.'

'Oh, we're convinced enough – it's just that we've come to this by a roundabout route. It might be hard for us to convince other people.'

'Try me.'

'Could you come back here? It's difficult to explain on the phone.'

Tim glanced across at Ricky, who was busy taking routine report-backs from the uniforms searching for Martha Johnson.

'Can I leave you to it for a while? Juliet thinks she's found something.'

While Tim was on his way, Juliet took yet another call.

'You're absolutely sure?' she said.

Katrin was curious. She'd heard Juliet use this tone of voice before: vehement, yet almost unable to believe her luck.

'Wow!' Juliet put down her mobile.

'Well, tell me what it was about. The suspense is killing me!'

'It's the motorbike – the bike that Fovargue's attacker was riding. Its registered owner is Mr T R Pack.'

'*The* Mr T R Pack?'

'The same. It's one of the vehicles that was stolen from him earlier this year.'

'Great, but I don't understand why you're so pleased about

it. The biker got away, didn't he? So you're no closer to restoring Mr Pack's property to him.'

'True, but, don't you see, there's a pattern emerging here? You know I teased you earlier when I said perhaps you hoped we could neatly tie all these crimes together. The way things are looking, we might be able to do just that.'

'You're several steps ahead of me. Let's wait until Tim comes, then you can explain. But solving the vehicle thefts surely isn't as important as finding Martha Johnson?'

'I'm thinking she's connected to them.'

'And the serial killings – if they are serial killings? You're not suggesting that Martha Johnson is a serial killer?'

'I think she was probably on to a serial killer. That's why she disappeared.'

'You think she's dead, then?'

'Yes. Don't you?'

CHAPTER FIFTY-SEVEN

It was just after midnight when Tim finally reached home again. The curtains of the sitting room had been drawn, but the electric light was shining through them. Katrin and Juliet were still waiting for him.

He sighed. He knew he was being defeatist, but all he wanted to do was crawl into his bed and pitch himself into the sort of black, dreamless sleep that only came when he was totally exhausted.

Katrin came to the door to greet him.

'Gin and tonic?' she said cheerfully. 'We're having one.'

'Yes, thanks. On second thoughts, I won't. I'm bushed. If I have anything at all to drink, I probably won't be able to think straight.'

'Okay. Juliet's still here.'

'Is she staying the night?'

'I've told her she's welcome...'

'That's very kind,' Juliet called from the room beyond, 'but I really must go home when we've done here.'

'Doesn't seem much point, really,' said Tim, entering the sitting room himself. 'But your decision.' He sat down heavily on the sofa. 'Tell me about this discovery that's got you so excited.'

Half an hour later, when Katrin and Juliet had finished explaining their theory, Tim was wide awake and, if not bursting with energy, certainly no longer exhausted.

'It's an ingenious idea... or set of ideas,' he said. 'Improbable, I grant you, but not impossible. And it's more logical than anything else we've managed to come up with so far. You may be right that Martha Johnson's the key to all of it, though I'm a bit more sceptical about that. The vehicle thefts have been going on a long time – if they all connect back to Silverdale Farm, I think she'd have found out about them before now, given that Fovargue seems to trust her with absolutely everything. And she's such a goody two shoes, I can't imagine her condoning grand larceny.'

'And obviously not murder!' said Juliet. 'But remember she only works part-time. And we don't know when she began the affair with Fovargue. It may only have been very recently.'

'Okay, assuming she discovered someone at Silverdale Farm was involved in the vehicle thefts, how would that tie in with the murders? And even more to the point, *whom* do you think she suspected? Surely not Fovargue himself?'

'We know she had those vehicle records on her desk around the time she went missing. Something made her want to work through them. We do have a clue about what that was, though it's only a slender one.'

'The newspaper clipping about Debbie Wicks,' Katrin put in.

'On its own, it's very slight. And that clipping could just have been saved for the farm machinery advert.'

'Agreed, but someone – probably Martha – found a petrol

receipt that matched the date of Wicks' disappearance. And all those files had cardboard pouches fastened into the back of them, all empty except for that one. Maybe there were other newspaper clippings, other petrol receipts, too.'

'So someone's moved them?'

'I think that either someone caught Martha looking at them, or she challenged that person herself. As you say, she's quite prim, but she's also surprisingly confident. One of those religious types who instinctively know their way is best.'

'Okay, so I come back to my second question: if Martha suspected someone of theft and/or murder, who was it?'

'Josh Marriott would be the obvious candidate,' said Juliet. 'There is no love lost between them. He doesn't even try to disguise his dislike for her. And she either ignores him or treats him with contempt.'

Tim was thoughtful.

'He assured me that he'd been going straight since he last served time.'

Katrin let out a peal of laughter. Juliet restrained herself and simply smiled.

'All right, I know that sounds very naïve,' said Tim, 'but somehow I believed him. I may not always be a good judge of character, but I can usually tell when old lags are swinging the lead. Of course, there may be other pressures on Marriott.'

'Such as?'

'He may be covering for someone else. He told me he was pretty happy with the life he's carved out for himself. Perhaps he saw that something – or someone – was threatening it.'

'Whether you realise it or not, you're making a good case for his having killed Martha. You asked him for his address, didn't you?'

'Yes, and he gave it to me. He lives with his girlfriend.'

'It's just possible Martha's still alive. I think we should arrest him.'

'On what grounds?'

'Abduction. Unlawful detention. Or suspected murder, if you prefer.'

'I'm not sure that we can justify any of them.'

'Let's just take him in for questioning, then. We can hold him for twenty-four hours. If we still think he's detaining Martha somewhere, we can follow him when we let him go.'

Tim blinked. He was dubious about such an enterprise. But Juliet was more often right than wrong.

'Okay, I'll agree to that. I'll go and challenge him. I'll get a uniform to come with me.'

'I'd like to come with you.'

'Marriott might turn violent.'

'I can take care of myself. And I doubt if he'd be stupid enough to lash out – it would be tantamount to admitting he's guilty. But it's probably wise to take a uniform, too. A hefty one. There's no reason why I shouldn't come as well, is there?'

Tim grinned.

'Half a dozen reasons, off the top of my head – getting some sleep being top of the list. But I can see you're not going to give in. Why so keen?'

'I think I'll know if Marriott's lying,' said Juliet. 'And even if he's such a good liar that I can't see through him, there's the girlfriend to consider, too. She might give something away.'

CHAPTER FIFTY-EIGHT

Tim and Juliet had to wait only a few minutes for the patrol car they had requested to arrive. Tim was amused to see Giash Chakrabati step out of it.

'What did you say about needing someone hefty?' said Tim sotto voce as they went to meet him. 'He's the thinnest copper I know.'

'Maybe, but he's got a black belt in karate,' said Juliet.

'You're just jealous!' said Katrin, who had accompanied them as far as the gate. Tim's grin faded a little. He was conscious that he'd developed the beginnings of a small paunch, the consequence of many nights working late, sometimes snatching stodgy food, since the missing vehicles investigation had started.

'Where's Verity?' Juliet asked Giash.

'Gone to get some sleep. I'd just dropped her off when DC MacFadyen called me for this job. He said I wouldn't need a partner because there'd be the three of us.'

'That's right,' said Tim.

'But we're sorry you drew the short straw,' said Juliet. 'Another five minutes and you'd have been off duty yourself?'

Giash shrugged and smiled. Never mind being the thinnest copper in the force, thought Juliet: he was certainly the politest.

'Where does this guy live?' he asked.

Tim took out his notebook. The scrap of paper on which Marriott had written his address was still tucked inside it.

'He lives at Twenty Drove, out beyond Bourne,' he said. 'According to Marriott, the house has no number. It's called Beet House.'

'Shouldn't be hard to find, sir. There aren't many houses out that way. We can be there in twenty minutes or so.'

'You want to sit in the front with Giash?' Tim said to Juliet. 'I might try to get a power sleep.'

It was dark – there was a moon, but obscured by cloud. The street lights petered out once they'd left Spalding. Tim closed his eyes and tried to rest. That he was able to relax cleared his head, but he was very far from being able to sleep. His conversation with Josh Marriott returned with astonishing clarity: 'Things haven't been so great lately, what with the boss mooning after Martha and Susie in a perpetual bad mood.'

Susie Fovargue, thought Tim. They hadn't really considered her except as Fovargue's wife, helper and, they now knew, female cuckold. Cuckquean, he thought the correct term was. He'd come across it in a history book and the word had intrigued him.

Fovargue had been terrified that Susie would find out about his relationship with Martha, but in practice she must have known of it. Why else would she have been so hostile to Martha? And if Marriott recognised that she was in a 'perpetual bad mood', Fovargue would have noticed that, too.

It beggared belief that Susie Fovargue was the mastermind behind the organised vehicle thefts. Perhaps Juliet was wrong about the thefts being mixed up in some way with the murders. She'd almost succeeded in convincing Tim that

Silverdale Farm was at the heart of the crimes, but nevertheless he retained a lingering belief in Marriott's assertion of his own innocence. If neither Susie nor Marriott was the vehicle thief, the other likely candidates were Fovargue himself and Nathan Buckland, whom Marriott seemed to hold in inexplicably high regard. If Martha had been killed but not by Marriott, Susie was her most likely murderer. Of the people they knew at Silverdale Farm, that was; there were other people working there, too, that they hadn't met. Or maybe between them she and Katrin had invented it all and none of the crimes had anything to do with Silverdale Farm. Except Martha's disappearance, if it was indeed the result of a crime.

Tim sighed. For a few exuberant seconds he'd believed he was getting somewhere: when he was half asleep the answer to the whole conundrum had appeared to be within his grasp; now it was slipping away again.

'Just waking up?' said Juliet, turning round to peer at him.

'I've been thinking, not sleeping,' said Tim crossly.

'Sounds nasty,' said Juliet. 'Anyway, we're here now.'

Giash had pulled up outside a neat brick house with no front garden or fence. The front door was protected by a porch, but otherwise opened straight on to the road. Tim stepped under the porch, which was dimly lit by an electric lantern. A black ring-shaped doorknocker had been fastened to the door. He took hold of it and rapped it fairly gently a couple of times. As he did so, he heard the sound of a catch being released and noticed there was a small square glass window set above the knocker. He recognised it as a type of spy-hole; it was protected on the other side by a shutter, which someone had just pulled open.

'Who is it?' Unmistakeably, the voice was Marriott's.

'Police,' said Tim. 'It's DI Yates and DS Armstrong.'

Heavy bolts were drawn back and a double lock released. Marriott clearly took no chances when it came to security.

Marriott half-opened the door and himself stepped into the porch, almost closing the door behind him. He was fully dressed, not in the work gear that he'd been wearing earlier that day, but in a pair of smart chinos and a Pringle sweater. Tim stepped back on to the road to give him some space.

'DI Yates,' he said, echoing Tim's words as if he didn't believe them. 'It's a bit late for bothering folk, in't it? Can't it wait until morning? Have you come to tell me you've found the girl?'

'Unfortunately not, Mr Marriott. We're sorry to disturb you at this hour – as you say, it's very late. But we need to ask you some more questions. You'll know that every minute counts after someone's first reported missing.'

'That's as maybe. It took you long enough to decide that she *was* missing, didn't it?'

Tim ignored the comment.

'I'm glad you're still up because we do need to talk to you. May we come in?'

'I don't know about that. The girlfriend's had a tough time at work and she's to get up in the morning. Can't we talk out here?'

'Most people prefer conversations with the police to be as private as possible.'

Marriott chuckled and stretched his arms as wide as the porch would allow.

'Nothing to bother my privacy here,' he said. 'As you can see, we've got no neighbours.'

'We could sit in the patrol car to interview you,' said Juliet.

'Aye, let's do that,' said Marriott, with some alacrity.

'I'll stand in the doorway, sir,' said Giash.

'No need for that,' said Marriott quickly. 'The girlfriend doesn't need guarding.'

'Nevertheless, it's not a bad idea of PC Chakrabati's. It'll be cramped in the car if we're all there.'

Marriott shrugged and sullenly accepted one of the back seats. Tim climbed in beside him, while Juliet resumed her place in the passenger seat. Both Tim and Juliet noticed that Marriott was uneasy. He kept flicking glances at Giash, as if afraid that the policeman might try to enter the house.

'Now, Mr Marriott,' said Tim, 'take your time to answer these questions. We need you to be as accurate as possible. We may want you to think back a few weeks. Do you think you can do that?'

'It depends,' said Marriott gravely. 'I'll do me best.'

'Good. Now you'll remember that earlier today I removed some files from the office at the farm. You didn't want me to take them. Did you have any particular reason for that?'

'I told you, they weren't mine to lend.'

'Was that your only reason?'

Marriott nodded.

'You knew what was in the files?'

'Course. All the vehicle records. The vehicles we use, I mean. Not the ones for sale.'

'Are you responsible for helping to keep those records?'

'No. All I do is hand over the receipts. Same as the others in my team.'

'And they're mainly receipts for fuel?'

'Not just fuel. Services and repairs as well. Sometimes bills for food or overnight stays, but we don't often do those.'

'And you've never filed the receipts yourself? Not at any time in the past?'

'No, that's always been Susie's job. She's good at that sort of thing. She's got a tidy mind. Trained as an accountant, too.'

'Have you ever taken an interest in those files? Looked through them yourself? I want you to think carefully, now.'

Marriott pantomimed deep concentration with an intensity that forced Tim to suppress a laugh.

'Can't say I have. I may have checked the odd sheet with Susie when she wanted me to explain something, but not looked through them, no. I don't take no interest in the paperwork if I can help it.'

'Each of those files has a cardboard pocket fixed to the inside of the back cover. Did you notice that?'

Marriott furrowed his brow.

'I can't say as I did. I've told you, I don't really handle the files.'

'Okay. So it was always Mrs Fovargue – Susie – who looked after them?'

'Yes.'

'But when DS Armstrong was in the office, she thought the files were piled up on Martha's desk.'

'They could of been. Poke her nose into anything, she would. Owt except getting on with her own business.'

'You don't like Martha much, do you?'

'I've told you I don't. I don't make no secret of it.'

'You said it's because you feel she's upset things at Silverdale Farm and it doesn't run as smoothly as before she came?'

'That's about right, yes.'

'Susie doesn't like her either, does she?'

'Well, you can't hardly blame her, can you? That mealy-mouthed act didn't fool Susie, or me, for that matter. She was...'

There came an urgent tapping at Tim's window. He opened the car door.

'PC Chakrabati, is everything all right?'

'I'm not sure, sir. I thought I heard a door slam at the back of the house and when I came out of the porch I could see a light moving across the fields. Do you think we should go in, see that the lady's okay?'

Tim sprang out of the car and peered into the darkness in the direction in which Giash was pointing. Two small points of light could be seen disappearing at some speed into the gloom.

'What do you think it is, sir? Someone on a motorbike?'

'No,' said Tim. 'That vehicle has two rear lights, not one. And from the speed at which it's travelling over rough land, I'd say there's only one thing it could be: it's a quad.'

CHAPTER FIFTY-NINE

Reluctantly, Marriott allowed them into the house. The rooms at the front were in darkness, but the lights had been left on in the small kitchen. He led them there now.

'Take a seat,' he said, gesturing at four chairs arranged with almost mathematical precision, one on each side of a square deal table. 'I'm going up to see the girlfriend. I don't want her to be frightened.'

'We'd like to talk to her, too, if she doesn't mind coming downstairs. Does she have a name?' said Juliet.

Marriott threw her a withering look.

'Course – it's Kezia. I doubt she'll want to come down, though. She doesn't like people seeing her without her make-up on.'

He returned quickly, but not before Tim had noticed that three mugs had been left to soak in the kitchen sink.

'Kezia says she'll be with us when she's had chance to get dressed.'

'That's good of her,' said Juliet.

Only Juliet was seated. Tim had propped himself against

the sink and Giash Chakrabati was standing beside the back door.

'Would you like to sit down, Mr Marriott?'

'No, I'll stand.'

'As you wish. That was a quad that we saw driving away from this property, wasn't it?'

'It sounded like one, yes.'

'Do you own a quad yourself?'

'I don't *own* one, no. I've shown you the old one we use at the farm. That's good enough for me. I can borrow it when I want.'

'Did you borrow it this evening?'

'No.'

'But you had a visitor?'

Marriott hesitated. Tim moved to one side of the sink so that the dirty mugs were in view.

'Yes.'

'And your visitor was still here when we arrived?'

'Yes.' Marriott's mood was hard to gauge. He seemed subdued, rather than truculent.

'And now he's gone. That was your visitor we saw driving away on the quad, wasn't it?'

'Yes.'

'Mr Marriott, I don't understand why we're having to drag this information out of you bit by bit, but I can tell you it isn't making a good impression. Who was your visitor? And why didn't you want us to know he was here?'

'It was Aaron, my brother. Well, half-brother, if we're splitting hairs.'

The words were spoken by the woman who had just entered the room unobserved. The three police officers all turned to look at her. She was a large-boned woman of about forty, her mass of dark hair tied back with a red scarf. She was dressed in jeans and an immaculate white shirt.

'You're Kezia?' said Juliet. 'Thank you for getting up again. I'm sorry we've had to disturb you.'

'What's your brother's surname?' Tim asked.

'It's Buckland. Aaron Buckland.'

'He's Nathan Buckland's brother?'

'Yes. Aaron's older than Nathan. He works for his dad. He's been in trouble with the police – some time ago, it wasn't serious – but Josh says it freaked him out when you came. He must've thought you'd gone when he left.'

'So you weren't with him while we were outside with Mr Marriott?'

'No. I went to bed earlier. I was still up when he got here.'

'Is your name Buckland, too?'

'No. Same mum, different dads. My name's Pett. Kezia Pett.'

CHAPTER SIXTY

'We can't knock the Bucklands up in the middle of the night,' said Tim, as Giash was driving them back to Spalding. 'We've got no reason to suspect them.'

'Aaron Buckland was behaving very strangely. So was Marriott, for that matter.'

'I agree, but Kezia's explanation rang true. Old lags are always suspicious and nervous around coppers.'

'What about her? It can't be a coincidence that her name is Pett. That's one of Bill Wood's aliases, and Selina Pett's surname.'

'I know. I decided not to draw attention to that. We can't be sure that Selina was killed by the same person who topped the two women in the Fossdyke. She could have been the victim of some kind of family feud.'

'I thought you were thinking that,' said Juliet.

'You'll stay the night with us, now, won't you? What's left of it, anyway. There's not much point in going home for a few hours if you're going to be working with Katrin again tomorrow.'

'I don't have any clothes...'

'I'm sure Katrin can find you some.'

Juliet gave Giash a sidelong glance. He was plainly exhausted. Making the additional detour to her flat would cost him another fifteen minutes.

'Very well,' she said. 'Thank you.'

CHAPTER SIXTY-ONE

K atrin had waited up for them.
'I'm so pleased you've decided to stay,' she said to
Juliet. 'The bed's already made up. I've put a towel and some
toiletries on it. Is there anything else you need?'

'Just a glass of water,' said Juliet. 'I can fetch it for myself.'

'Time we were in bed, too,' said Katrin after Juliet had left
them.

'Yep, too much for us all to do tomorrow. No point in being
knackered as well. You know, when I was dozing in the squad
car earlier I almost thought I'd worked it all out. It's gone again
now.'

'It'll come back to you,' said Katrin.

Tim had nodded, but retrieving the idea that had almost
surfaced continued to niggle away at him as he lay in bed. It
destroyed any prospect of sleep.

He tried to recall the conversation he'd had with Martha
Johnson. Suddenly he sat up in bed.

'That was it!' he exclaimed.

'Oh, Tim, for goodness' sake, what now?' said Katrin,
grumpy at being roused from sleep.

'Sorry, I didn't mean to wake you. I was just thinking back to when I spoke to Martha Johnson. She said there was an old cesspit under her office. It slipped my mind because we talked about cesspits every time we went to Silverdale Farm – one of the Fovargue businesses involves emptying them.'

'I'm sorry, I really don't see why that's significant.'

'She said Fovargue wanted to preserve the cesspit. Josh Marriott was there at the time. He said it ought to be filled in.'

'I'm still not with you.'

'We'll have to uncover that cesspit tomorrow. I think Martha Johnson may have been buried there.'

CHAPTER SIXTY-TWO

B leary-eyed and feeling less rested than when he'd fallen into bed a few hours previously, Andy rose at 5.45am on the Saturday of the Lincoln show. He showered quickly and, after a very brief breakfast of a glass of milk and a handful of cookies, set out once more for Marston Farm.

He decided not to bother the Shucksmiths again, but, following Tim's advice, he didn't try to conceal his presence from the Fovargues. He parked his car behind the pantechnicon. As he waited for Fovargue and Susie to emerge, he eyed up their vehicle and thought it had been moved slightly. The difference in its position was almost imperceptible, but he was sure that it was nearer in to the entrance of the farm than when he'd been talking to Fovargue the evening before. He got out of his car to see if he could find two rows of track marks, but the ground was hard and dry and his inspection yielded nothing.

He was still standing in the road when Fovargue came hurrying out of the guest house and climbed into his cab. He started the engine immediately and would have driven off without noticing Andy if Andy hadn't nipped round the side of the giant lorry quickly enough for Fovargue to catch sight of him in the wing mirrors.

Fovargue turned off the ignition and opened the cab door. The bruise on his face had darkened overnight, giving him a sinister look. He appeared to be flustered, almost distracted.

'Good morning, sir. How are you feeling today?'

'I'm fine,' said Fovargue shortly. 'What do you want now?'

'DI Yates asked me to accompany you to the showground, keep an eye on you in case that ruffian showed up again.'

'That's very kind of DI Yates – and you – but I don't need your protection.'

'Is Mrs Fovargue not coming with you, sir?'

'Oh, Susie's had to go home. One of the kids is ill. I'll be doing the show without her.'

'I'm sorry to hear that. How did she get home?'

'What? Oh, I called Josh, asked him to come and fetch her.'

'Do you know roughly when that was, sir?'

'I can't be exactly sure. Around midnight, I think. Now, if you'll excuse me, I have quite a lot to do now that I'm working on my own.'

'I don't want to stand in your way, Mr Fovargue. I'll see you at the show.'

Fovargue opened his mouth as if to argue, then changed his mind, climbed back into the cab, started the vehicle again and drove away without saying another word.

CHAPTER SIXTY-THREE

Tim had indeed slipped into the deep, dreamless sleep that he'd hoped for, but he still awoke early, long before the rest of his household was beginning to stir. He raised himself on one elbow and looked at his watch. It was 6.45am.

Out of the blue, like a blow between the eyes, came the certain if inexplicable knowledge that there was an urgent need for him to visit Silverdale Farm immediately. He had to go there now. There was no time to assemble a team.

Katrin, as usual sensitive to the slightest sound, turned on to her side to face him and lifted her head from her pillow.

'Tim? What's up?' she asked groggily.

'Yes. I'm just wide awake, that's all. I've had quite a good night, but I know I won't get any more sleep now. I think I'll get up, go in to work, perhaps, and see how the search is going.'

He'd intended his words to sound casual, but Katrin was at once suspicious. She roused herself quickly and sat up in bed.

'You aren't thinking of driving out to look at that cesspit on your own, are you?'

'Not really.'

'Look at me, Tim: promise me you won't do that. If you're

right and the cesspit's significant, you shouldn't be alone at that farm.'

'I promise. I'll go in to the station first, see who can come with me.'

'Aren't you going to wait for Juliet?'

'No, let her sleep. Besides, you know she's keen on getting back to her flat. She's probably got a date lined up for later.'

'A *date*?'

'I don't have time to explain now. Don't mention to her what I've just said – I'll tell you what I know when I come home.'

Tim's remark helped to throw Katrin off his case. Fifteen minutes later, he'd showered and shaved and was driving his car to the station. He'd almost reached it when Andy called.

'He's lying,' Tim said, when Andy had repeated what Fovargue had said. 'We were with Marriott at his house shortly after midnight and we've good reason to believe he'd been there for some time before that, probably most of the evening, or at least from soon after the pub where his girlfriend works closed. Follow Fovargue to the Lincoln show and make sure you know where he is at all times, even when he's at the showground. We'll have to try to find Susie now. There's every chance she isn't at home with the kids, like Fovargue said.'

'What are you going to do next?'

'There's a disused cesspit at Silverdale Farm. Martha Johnson told us about it. I'm convinced it's connected with her disappearance. Examining it is our first priority. If Susie Fovargue is at the farm, that'll be a bonus. If she isn't, we'll be mounting a search for her straight away.'

'Do you think she's a killer?'

'No. I think she and Martha Johnson are both victims of a killer. It's likely they're both dead.'

'And Fovargue's the killer?'

'Either that or it's someone who's working for him.'

'Marriott?'

'Possibly. But I still feel uneasy about pinning it all on him.'

Tim reversed the car into a side street and turned it round. When he'd made the promise to Katrin, it was before he'd discovered that Susie Fovargue hadn't spent the night at the guest house. Katrin would understand that the situation had changed. Besides, he'd be sure to call for backup: they wouldn't be long in coming.

CHAPTER SIXTY-FOUR

When Tim reached Silverdale House the day had dawned, although the light was still greyish. He parked his car at the top of the drive and climbed out cautiously. The lawn was in its usual rundown state, but the toys that had previously lain scattered across it had gone. Perhaps the stand-in nanny had cleared them away.

The house itself had a closed-up look, as if its owners were on holiday. All the windows were shut. No electric lights were burning, either in the downstairs or the upstairs rooms, although he remembered that the kitchen was a gloomy room in which the light had been switched on when he and Ricky had first met Fovargue there.

When he reached the door, he could hear no sounds coming from the inside. It was nearly eight o'clock now: surely the two Fovargue children weren't still sleeping? He didn't fancy tackling the nanny again – she'd been sullen and uncooperative when he'd met her the day before – but he guessed he would have to, unless by some miracle Susie herself answered the door. But Tim was convinced this wouldn't happen.

He was about to ring the bell when he realised that he

hadn't thought about what he was going to say. He'd ask for Susie, of course, but whether she was there or not, he wanted someone to let him into the soil appreciation shed so that he could examine the cesspit. Susie herself would probably have reservations about giving him access, but the nanny would be an even worse bet: he doubted she understood the security arrangements or would know where to find the keys. Even if she did, she had "jobsworth" written all over her: she'd be unlikely to let him into the shed while the Fovargues were away.

He turned slightly as he paused, still trying to work out his best plan of action, and glanced across at the two big sheds. There was a long, narrow gleam of light shining underneath the one containing Martha's office – the one where the cesspit was also concealed. He tried not to raise his hopes unduly: the most likely explanation was that they had forgotten to switch off the light the previous evening. It was just possible, however, that someone had turned up early and let themselves into the shed.

He decided not to try to raise anyone at the house, but instead make straight for the shed itself. He knew he'd have to take care: at best he would be an unwelcome visitor. If he was right about the cesspit, the situation could get tricky.

The garden was bare of foliage: it offered no cover from shrubs or even a hedge. He moved across to its left-hand perimeter, which was near to the road, a rough wooden fence acting as the boundary, and crept alongside the fence, taking advantage of what meagre protection it offered, until he could cross the track and reach his car again. There were no weapons as such in the car, but he took a military-style torch from the glove-box and put it in his pocket. He removed his phone from his inside jacket pocket, debating whether to call for backup now – he'd forgotten to do it earlier – or wait until he was certain that the circumstances merited it. He told himself he didn't have time to enter into a tedious explanation with

Superintendent Thornton now and that, besides, someone at the farm might hear him talking. It would be better to press on. He replaced the phone.

He ran along the left-hand edge of the road in a crouching position, trying to keep in the shadows as much as possible, until he reached the shed. The door had been opened, but not by much: if someone was inside the shed now, they had squeezed through a gap that was only a few inches wide.

Tim looked at the gap. He was confident he'd be able to get through it, but it would be impossible to do so without alerting anyone who happened to be on the other side unless they were right at the back of the shed or in the office. He took a deep breath and sprinted through the gap as silently as possible, taking cover in a kind of shallow alcove in the right-hand wall as he entered. He looked around him, adjusting his eyes to the sudden shadows, looking out for signs of movement.

The shed was barer than he'd remembered: Fovargue and Susie had taken some of the stuff normally stored there to Lincoln with them. There was now a big, empty expanse in the middle of the main part of the building which would be impossible to cross unseen, even though it was quite dark in the further reaches of the shed. Only the first bank of lights, the ones that illuminated the doorway, had been switched on.

Tim could still hear no sound within the building, but he had a nagging hunch that he wasn't its only occupant. He edged along the wall until he reached the glass and wood structure that was Martha Johnson's office. He ducked down below the level of the glass and crawled along the floor until he reached the office doorway. The door was not fastened shut, but it was almost closed. He wouldn't be able to see if there was anyone inside the office without pushing it further open. He stood up as noiselessly as he could, flattening himself against the door lintel in what he knew was a futile attempt to conceal himself if someone inside the room happened to be looking out.

There were no lights on in the office, but a skylight set in the sloping roof of the shed enabled him to make out the shapes of the furniture it contained. Tim moved to his left so that he could get a view through the glass unimpeded by the door. Although he'd thought he'd prepared himself for this, he was both astonished and appalled by what he saw.

Inadvertently, he moved back a couple of steps, knocking wide the door as he stumbled clumsily and noisily against it. The sound of it banging open reverberated throughout the shed.

CHAPTER SIXTY-FIVE

Juliet woke with a headache. She could hear voices coming from just beyond her door and guessed immediately that she'd overslept. She squinted at the clock on her bedside table and groaned. It was almost 8am.

She rubbed her eyes and sprang from the bed, throwing on Katrin's borrowed dressing gown as she headed out to the bathroom. Thankfully, it was free. She showered quickly, doing her best to keep her hair dry. She would have no time to tame the frizz if she got it wet.

Normally, she would have found it distasteful to have to dress in the previous day's clothes, but today she was in too much of a hurry to bother. Returning to her room, she flung them on as rapidly as she could and was still dragging her comb through her hair when she entered Katrin and Tim's kitchen.

Sophia was sitting at the table. Katrin stood beside her, pouring milk on to a bowl of cereal. She turned to smile at Juliet.

'Good morning! Cup of tea? It's only just been made.'

'Where's Tim?' Juliet asked, without ceremony.

'He woke up early and went to the station. He said we should leave you to sleep.'

'Fuck!' said Juliet, and immediately covered her mouth with her hand. Sophia regarded her with large, solemn eyes.

'Sorry!' Juliet said to Katrin, who shrugged. 'Tim hasn't gone to Silverdale Farm by himself, has he?'

'I don't think so. I made him promise he wouldn't. He must have intended to go to the station to get a team together because he said visiting the farm was his first priority.'

'I'd better go now. I want to be there, too, if they haven't left without me.'

'At least have a cup of tea first.'

'Sorry, Katrin, there's no time. Thank you for the hospitality: you know I appreciate it. I'll come back later or call you to let you know what's happening if I'm delayed.'

'All right,' said Katrin. 'Sophia has a party later. I'll get on with the research while she's out.'

As soon as she was in her car, Juliet called Ricky. 'Where are you?' she asked abruptly.

'At the station. Where do you think?' he replied, equally testily. He'd been up most of the night and was in no mood to humour her.

'Have you seen Tim?'

'Tim? No. I thought he was doing something with you. He's not been back here today.'

Juliet cut the call and speed-dialled Andy's number.

'Hello, Andy, are you at the showground?'

'Yes, I've been here for half an hour or so. Fovargue's here, too. Tim told me not to let him out of my sight.'

'What about Susie?'

'She went home last night. According to Fovargue, one of the kids was ill and she had to leave the guest house. Didn't Tim tell you?'

'I haven't seen Tim this morning,' said Juliet shortly. Then, in a strained voice, 'But thanks, Andy. And good luck.'

She cut this call, too. She deliberated for less than a minute on what she should do next. There was no time to wait for anyone else. But she would ask for backup. Starting the engine of her car, she called Ricky again.

CHAPTER SIXTY-SIX

Tim edged cautiously into the office. Searching each of the walls quickly, he saw that he was alone, at least within the confined space of the small inner room: he was unable to shake off the uncanny feeling that someone else was hiding close by, awaiting his or her moment.

Taking the torch out of his pocket, he played it first across the stack of floorboards which had been levered up and placed in a neat pile against one wall and then over the gaping hole at his feet. The cesspit was roughly round in shape and deeper than he had expected: he calculated it to be one and a half times his own height. It was lined with large red bricks, most marred with efflorescence and flaking in places. It looked like a waterless well. Although it had clearly not held sewage for many years, a strong and unpleasant smell was rising up from the cavity: a mixture of sour earth, damp and something harder to define. It was an odour he'd encountered before, reminiscent perhaps of rotting mushrooms.

A short metal ladder had been fixed to the lip of the pit. Tim shone the torch on it. It consisted of four or five rungs extending to about three feet above the floor of the pit. It was designed to make both descending into the pit and returning to the surface easy to accomplish.

Tim crouched at the edge of the pit and pointed the torch at its floor. He could see that a number of items had been placed there, but the torch wasn't powerful enough to pick them out in detail.

Tim looked over his shoulder, then at the ladder. His hunch about the cesspit had been right so far: someone had spent some time uncovering it, which meant it was important to them. He was now convinced that the pit held the clue to Martha Johnson's disappearance, perhaps some of the other crimes he was investigating, too. He was torn between his desire to descend the ladder to find out what had been left there and the knowledge that once inside the cavity he would be trapped if someone were to attack him.

He'd promised Katrin that he wouldn't get into such a situation, but he was here now. He reasoned that there was still an outside chance that Martha Johnson was alive and being held somewhere against her will. If he climbed into the pit, he might discover the information that would set her free. Really, he had no choice.

He slipped the ring at the end of the torch over his thumb and grabbed hold of the top of the ladder, carefully edging himself down into the darkness. When he reached the final rung, he jumped the remaining few feet. It had not been a difficult exercise, but the pungent smell hit hard now he was at the bottom: it was strong enough to make him want to retch. Taking off his jacket, he tried to hold part of it bunched over his face, but found he was unable to do this and direct the light of the torch as well. He decided to alternate the two actions.

From the top of the pit, he'd spotted what had looked like a heap of rags. He'd seen they were nearest the ladder and he poked around for them first. He located them quickly. Tucking his jacket through one of the rungs of the ladder, he shone the torch on the rags and gingerly touched the item on top. It was a scarf or bandana, a man's neckerchief, perhaps. It was caked with some substance that had caused the fabric to mass into a long, rope-like coil. Tim tried to smooth it flat, holding the torch close to it, and realised that the disfiguring substance was dried blood. Disgusted, his instinct was to toss it away from him, but mindful that it constituted evidence he laid the scarf carefully to one side and picked up the next item, a bright pink jumper which appeared to be undamaged. He put that next to the scarf and continued to work methodically through the pile. In a couple of minutes he was surrounded by a random agglomeration of articles of clothing, including a pair of over-the-knee boots, a mini-skirt, a raincoat and a woman's headscarf. At the very bottom of the pile he found a large canvas bag.

He knew that from the top of the pit he'd seen other things down here besides the heap of clothes. He pressed on by moving methodically around its perimeter, shining the torch on the lower half of the wall and the floor in front of it as he went. He'd proceeded only a few steps when he noticed the flat edge of an object that had been pushed into a crevice in the wall. He grabbed it and pulled. It yielded so easily that he'd exerted too much strength on dislodging it and almost lost his balance. He turned it over, scrutinising it by torchlight. It was a black leather wallet embellished with some writing in gold or silver. 'Michael Kors', Tim read. He opened the wallet. It contained two twenty-pound notes, several credit cards and an ID badge. The photograph on the ID badge had been scored through, almost certainly deliberately, but the name printed on the badge and the credit cards was intact: Steven S. Smythe.

Tim drew a deep breath, oblivious now to the foul smell. He had no doubt that all the items in the cesspit were trophies of some kind, but the wallet was the first definitive link he could make with one of the murders.

He thought he heard a cracking sound and looked up fearfully at the dark-rimmed circle that had become the top of the cesspit. He turned off the torch and waited. All above was silent: he must either have imagined the noise or it was just the normal creaking of an agricultural building. After listening for a couple of minutes, he set the torch again and continued his circuit.

It didn't take him long to find what he was looking for.

CHAPTER SIXTY-SEVEN

Juliet had been driving for only five minutes when her mobile rang.

'Hello? Ricky?' she said.

'It's not Ricky, Juliet, it's me: Jake. I know it's early, but I wondered if you've had any thoughts about today. I'm free the whole day. I know you're busy with your investigation: just saying I'll fit in. Even a quick coffee would be nice.'

'Oh... Jake...'

'What's the matter? You don't sound very pleased to hear me!' He said it laughingly, but even through her anxiety Juliet could hear the hurt in his tone.

'It's not that... I'm sorry, Jake, it's not a good time. I think Tim may have done something stupid and put himself in danger.'

'You mean DI Yates?'

'Yes, of course I do,' said Juliet testily.

'Juliet, tell me what you're planning on doing. You're not going to put *yourself* in danger, are you?'

Juliet hesitated.

'Just promise me you won't try any heroics, especially on

your own. You won't help DI Yates by getting trapped in the same situation.'

'I've asked for backup,' said Juliet defensively.

'Good. Wait until it comes. And Juliet?'

'Yes?'

'I won't say I love you, because I know it'd make you run a mile. But just understand I wouldn't get over it if...'

'Thank you, Jake,' said Juliet. 'Please don't say any more. I have to go now.'

She cut the call, livid that her eyes had filled with tears.

CHAPTER SIXTY-EIGHT

A ndy was roosting at the St John Ambulance station again, even though today Jack Fovargue was now aware of his presence and there was therefore no need to conceal himself. He enjoyed the company of the two first aiders, who were assiduous dispensers of tea. Besides, it was better for both Fovargue and himself if he carried out his surveillance from a distance.

If Fovargue had felt self-conscious about being watched by a policeman, which Andy doubted, any awkwardness was quickly dissipated as soon as he was approached by the punters. At present, these consisted only of a few of the most eager show-goers and the occasional fellow stallholder. The latter were probably motivated as much by boredom as curiosity, but Fovargue loved playing to the gallery, even if he could muster an audience of only one or two individuals at a time.

There was a sudden roaring sound. Everyone looked skywards. A fighter jet came powering across the sky and boomed off into the distance. Dazed by both the noise and the brightness of the sky, Andy was still struggling to refocus his eyes when a second plane burst upon his senses.

'F-35s,' said the St John Ambulance man knowledgeably. 'On manoeuvres.'

Andy nodded and clasped his hand to his forehead, light-headed from the unexpected intrusion and lack of sleep. His face began to throb lightly from the previous day's assault.

'You all right, mate? Here, take a seat and I'll fetch you some water.'

Andy sat down heavily on a folding plastic chair. His head was spinning. He closed his eyes and briefly fell into a strange waking sleep – he was still conscious, but the darkness seemed to be closing in on him from all sides.

'Head between your knees, now. Easy does it,' said the St John Ambulance man.

Obediently, Andy did as he was told. It was an unpleasant posture and he felt a bit of an idiot – he was vaguely aware that a couple of kids had halted nearby, presumably to stare at him. However, after a short time the fog that had seemed to envelop him cleared. He sat up again, his face flushed.

'Drink some of this now,' said the St John Ambulance man. 'And sit there for a while. Don't try to get up too soon or suddenly.'

Andy took the glass. He glared at the kids, who wandered on, disappointed, probably, that there hadn't been more of a drama. There was a slight breeze, which he found refreshing, and by the time he'd drunk the entire glass of water in slow sips, he was feeling much better. He glanced across at Fovargue's stand and could see no one gathered there. This was surprising, because, as he'd already observed, Fovargue usually managed to command an audience of some sort. He stood up and saw that the stand was deserted – Fovargue himself had disappeared. In a rush of panic, he took a few steps forward and saw the pantechnicon was still standing where Fovargue had parked it, at the edge of the field, the same spot he'd chosen the day before.

Andy breathed a sigh of relief. Fovargue couldn't have gone far; he must just have taken a toilet break.

'Have you seen the soil appreciation bloke walk past?' he asked the St John Ambulance man, as casually as he could.

'Jack Fovargue, you mean? We know him quite well – he comes to a lot of these dos. He's gone off on that little KTM Enduro bike he has. Probably to get some grub or something. He usually travels with it in the lorry – I think that's why he drives such a bloody great big thing. His wife's got one, too. Come to think of it, I haven't seen her today. She was here yesterday. It's not like them to leave the stand unmanned.'

'Christ!' said Andy.

'Is something the matter?'

'I don't know. But probably.'

He whipped out his phone as he hurried round the back of the first aid post to get some privacy and called Tim.

CHAPTER SIXTY-NINE

T im shone his torch on the two packages, which had been placed together almost in the centre of the cesspit floor. They were of a similar size. Both were tightly bound in turquoise plastic. Tim recognised it as the stuff farmers used for wrapping hay bales.

Despite the secure packing, a sticky dark liquid was seeping from the bottom of each of the two bundles. For the past few minutes he'd been too engrossed in his search to notice the foul smell, but now the vicious odour returned to assail him with redoubled force. It was strongest in the area surrounding the packages.

He wasn't carrying a knife. Casting around for a suitable implement, he picked up some loose shards of brick from the floor and tried them one by one against the tape that secured the top of the nearer of the bundles. His first two efforts failed, but his third attempt was with a blade-like piece of brick that crumbled as he worked with it but nevertheless enabled him to sever the tape. Impatiently, he pulled the plastic apart and held the torch over the aperture he had created.

The smell had become overpowering, but it wasn't because

of it that Tim started gagging. Standing back from the package, he vomited on to the floor of the pit. He was intensely conscious of the noise he was making. What he'd seen in the torchlight had shocked him to the core. It had revealed the top of a decomposing skull, its rotting flesh slippery and stinking but still capped with a mass of dark hair.

Tim had been afraid of getting trapped all the time he'd been in the cesspit, but now he was stricken with the overwhelming realisation that his life was in danger. He made a scramble for the ladder and hoisted himself on to the bottom rung. Knocking both knees hard against the ladder as he went, he clambered to the top with ungainly speed and drew breath only when he'd reached the relative safety of Martha Johnson's enclosed little office.

His first thought was to get out of the shed as quickly as possible, run for his car and call for backup. He cursed himself for having failed to do so previously.

Standing at the office door, he peered into the main shed and tried to calculate how long it would take him to cross the floor if he ran for it instead of edging round the walls, as he had when he arrived. It was then that he noticed that the bank of four lights at the top of the shed had been switched off. Worse, the massive shed door was no longer partially open. It had been closed, and – he'd stake his life on it, he thought with no little irony – also locked. Making a dash across the shed only to get trapped with no cover would be foolhardy in the extreme.

He made a quick reckoning of the resources at his disposal. The torch was heavy – his initial thought when he'd taken it from the car was that it could serve as a weapon – and he still had his phone. He'd switch it to silent and text Juliet for help. As he took the phone out of his pocket, the display screen suddenly lit up. Andy Carstairs' number flashed into view and the phone started ringing. Made clumsy by panic, Tim swatted at the red button and instead of shutting off the noise dropped the phone, which continued to blare its jaunty tune for several seconds until he'd dived to retrieve it.

'DI Yates, good morning,' came a soft voice from the shadows of the office. 'Is this what you're looking for?'

Someone was standing to the left of him. A gloved hand passed him a folder.

'I'll give you just thirty minutes to look through it,' said the voice, 'so that you can admire our handiwork. Then I'm going to give you a little demonstration.'

A figure stepped from the shadows. He still couldn't see its face. It was brandishing what at first looked like a crude mediaeval weapon. Tim recognised one of the old billhooks he'd seen on the wall with the other farming tools.

'You must have wondered how we took their heads off, but I doubt if you thought we'd used one of these. On both occasions, they were already dead. It'll be my first time with a live body. A little bit of one-upmanship on which to finish.'

CHAPTER SEVENTY

J uliet saw Tim's car as soon as she rounded the final bend in the road that led to Silverdale Farm. Deciding to park her own car on the roadside rather than within the farm's boundaries, she manoeuvred as much of it as she could on to the soft grass verge.

She took out her mobile and called Ricky.

'Following my request for backup, I'm now at Silverdale Farm and can confirm that DI Yates's car is here. DI Yates is not with his car and there's no sign of activity at the farmhouse. I can't see the other buildings from my current position. I want to repeat the request for backup.'

'Backup's on its way,' said Ricky. 'Do you need an armed response unit, too?'

'No,' said Juliet. She paused. 'On second thoughts, yes. We don't know what we're going to find here.'

'That'll take a bit longer. Backup should be with you in ten-fifteen minutes. Suggest you stay put until they arrive. With respect, DS Armstrong,' Ricky added. His final comment was no doubt tongue-in-cheek, but Juliet appreciated the concern that lay behind it.

'Thanks, Ricky,' she said. 'That's good advice.'

It was broad daylight. She got out of the car and walked a few paces towards the entrance to the farm lane. The farmhouse looked deserted: it had that shut-up look that was so often a giveaway to thieves when the owners of a property were on holiday. Crossing the lane, she stood opposite the farmhouse and scrutinised the two big sheds and the tanker lorry yard. The sheds both seemed to be closed and locked up, too, and the tankers were standing in a neat row like three elephants frozen in motion, as if about to perform a circus trick but waiting for their handlers to arrive.

It was a Saturday, after all. Juliet had a vague recollection from their conversations with Josh Marriott that some of the employees worked on Saturdays, but probably not at this time of year.

Where was Tim, in that case? From where she was standing, she couldn't see the Dutch lights. It was possible Tim had gone to explore them, though she could think of no plausible reason unless it was to speak to someone there. Beyond lay the fields Fovargue owned, which they'd discovered were more extensive than they'd first been led to believe. Would Tim have wandered off in that direction? Juliet doubted it.

Tim had been convinced that the cesspit Martha Johnson had mentioned held clues to her disappearance, so he'd have tried to get access to the second of the big sheds. Juliet tried to recreate his thought processes. He knew that he needed the key to the shed and also the security pad code. He'd have been reluctant to call at the house for help, but he'd probably have decided there was no option but to do so. She guessed he'd drawn a blank there, however. What would he have done next? Almost certainly, he'd either have tried to get into the shed without a key or walked round the property to see if someone was there who could produce one.

She'd been standing by the roadside for five minutes now and Tim still hadn't appeared. If he'd been on a fruitless errand he would have turned up again by now. All her instincts told her that Tim was already in the shed, but if that was so, why hadn't he contacted anyone? Even Tim wouldn't be so pig-headed as to try to conclude the investigation single-handed; besides, he'd promised Katrin that he wouldn't do that.

Susie Fovargue was the answer. Andy must have told Tim that Susie hadn't spent the night at Marston Farm after he'd left for the station. That was why he'd changed his plans and broken his promise to Katrin. He'd decided he had no time to lose; and the fact that his car was here told Juliet that examining the cesspit was still his 'first priority'. He must have found a way into the shed. She was reluctant to call his mobile in case he'd forgotten to switch it to silent, but she thought she could risk texting him. *I'm at Silverdale Farm. Where can I find you?*

She knew Tim would reply immediately if he was able to, perhaps call her. She waited a couple of minutes for a response. When she didn't get one, she knew that Tim was either in trouble or had become separated from his phone.

Ricky's advice had indeed been sound but, like Tim a while before, Juliet felt prudence was a luxury she could no longer afford. She would have to find a way into the shed immediately.

She ran back to the farm lane and had begun to hurry down it when she heard the gnat-like whine of a moped approaching. She moved to the side of the track before she turned round, her heart in her mouth.

Nathan Buckland drew up alongside her. '

Is summat up?' he said.

'Sorry?' said Juliet.

'I said, is summat up? Is something going off?' he added, obviously humouring her.

Juliet thought furiously. She had no idea whether she could

343

trust Nathan. He'd been uncooperative when she and Ricky had visited him at home, but both Josh Marriott and Martha Johnson had seemed to rate him – if that was a recommendation. More to the point, what alternative did she have?

'What are you doing?' she asked cautiously, her eyes intent on his face as if to gauge his honesty.

'I'm working today. Mekkin' up for the time off in the week. Why?'

'I just wondered. Do you have a key to that shed? The one where Martha's office is, not the other one? And the security code?'

'Only Josh and the boss has them. And Susie. And Martha, now,' he added. 'Why? Do you want to get into the shed? I can give Josh a call. He said he'd be coming on later, anyway.'

'It's urgent,' said Juliet. 'There's no time to wait. I think DI Yates might be trapped in there.'

'*Trapped?*' repeated Nathan incredulously. 'How'd he manage that, then?'

'I can't explain – I don't know the details myself. Is there any quick way you can get hold of a key?'

Nathan sized her up in much the same way she'd tried to gauge him a few moments before. Evidently he'd noted the panic in her voice. It was clear he was taking her seriously.

'There's a door at the back,' he said, after a pause. 'It was meant to be a fire exit – to fit in with safety regs – but boss didn't like it. Said it was a security risk, so no one uses it. It's locked up, but just with an ordinary lock. It'll be easier to break open than the door at the front. It'll make a bit of a row, mind you, but you say it's an emergency...'

'Thank you,' said Juliet. 'Will you help me with it?'

Nathan shrugged.

'I suppose so,' he said. 'If you explain to boss afterwards. I'll fetch a crowbar from the yard. It'll make less mess than an 'atchet.'

CHAPTER SEVENTY-ONE

Constantly threatened by the billhook, Tim had done as he was ordered and sat down on the office floor with his back to his adversary, who had fastened his right arm and his right ankle with long cable ties to the big old desk. The fingers that had grabbed his wrist were strong but the hand itself felt slight. The touch was impersonal, almost professional, like a doctor's. The cable ties hadn't been secured tightly enough to cause him pain.

He'd dropped to the ground the folder that had been passed to him. A booted foot now kicked it towards him. It was a safety boot, black and bulky, but its shortness indicated the foot inside it was quite small. The low, soft voice was deepish – it could have been male or female and may have been disguised deliberately – but Tim was now practically certain his assailant was a woman.

'Read,' the voice commanded.

He opened the folder with his left hand. A lamp on the desk was switched on.

The folder was crammed with a series of cardboard pockets containing folded papers. The papers that protruded appeared to be mostly news clippings. The first pocket was less bulky than the others. Twisting his hand awkwardly to get a purchase on its contents, he pulled from it a printed sheet of A4 that had been folded in half and a single sheet torn from the *Lincolnshire Free Press*, also folded.

It was relatively easy to flick open the A4 sheet, which was made of printing paper and not flimsy newsprint. Bending his head as low as he could to examine it, Tim at once recognised the content. It was an article he'd seen recently, printed out from a website: the article that he and Katrin had looked at together, lamenting the tantalisingly sparse details it recorded about the murder of the American George Gordon and the wrongly-accused Philippe Pacquet. Tim didn't need to waste time reading it again. He grabbed at the sheet of newspaper and after some fumbling managed to open it out, too. It was from the current week's edition. It did not astonish him to see it was an article covering the information the police had so far released about the murder of Simon Smythe.

The next cardboard pocket was much bulkier, packed so tightly with papers that he struggled to release them.

'Get on with it!' said his attacker. The attempt at disguising the voice had been abandoned; it was quite clear now that it belonged to a woman. Tim detected the kind of strain that precedes hysteria in her latest words. It set off alarm bells in his head; he knew that panic was just as dangerous a catalyst of violence as anger.

He scrabbled at the wad of papers and eventually dislodged them. They'd been folded into neat little squares which would be awkward to open out. He was sweating profusely, aware that the woman was losing patience, perhaps also her nerve.

He pushed at the edges of the first piece of folded paper until he'd partially unwrapped it. Yellowed and crisp with fragility, inadvertently his action had made it stand up like a tent, but the headline stood out clearly. 'Stephen Jenkins', he read. He didn't need to see any more.

'Okay,' he said. 'You've made your point. I don't need to open the rest of them to understand what you're telling me. We were on the right track: we were already on to the idea of unrelated copycat crimes.'

There was a silence.

'I don't believe you!' she burst out.

'Believe me or not as you choose, it's true,' said Tim.

'It's not very smart of you to throw away some of your half-hour by giving up on the reading, is it, DI Yates? Technically there are still fourteen minutes left.'

'We can spend the rest of the time talking,' said Tim evenly. 'If you're really planning to kill me, there'll be no record of what you say to me. You can afford to indulge my curiosity. You may as well know that I think your method is an ingenious one: copying murders from different points in time, using different MOs. I'm sure there are lots of crimes in that file that we wouldn't have had the remotest chance of solving. There's one thing that puzzles me: you've exercised the greatest care to not get caught for many years and, until recently, the murders were well spaced out. What made you get careless – or maybe that's the wrong word? Perhaps I mean reckless?'

She began pacing the room, at first up and down the confined area behind the desk, but eventually moving on past Tim so that she was standing in front of him. She wore a hooded jacket and her face was covered with a dark scarf, but neither hid completely the luxuriant red curls that poked out in several places. Until this moment she had still been clutching the billhook, but in her agitation she placed it on the desk. She was unarmed now. Tim furiously tried to concentrate on how he might capitalise on this fact while he kept her talking.

'Well?' he said. 'What was it that changed?'

She was pushing her hands up under the black scarf. He realised that she was crying.

'You think you're so clever, but you don't really get it, do you? This was our secret. It was more than a secret, it was our bond: to plan and carry out a series of perfect crimes. Motiveless, beautifully-executed murders that no one even suspected were murders; and copycat murders we allowed to be detected to show we hadn't made the same mistakes as the original killers – for those who looked for the link, anyway. Each killing was a separate feat and also part of a set, like diamonds in a necklace. We could have gone on for ever: we were complete soul mates, two halves of the same person.'

Tim's attention was fully engaged now, the danger still threatening him pushed to one side of his mind.

'You mean there are two of you?'

CHAPTER SEVENTY-TWO

Unable to reach Tim, Andy had called the station. Ricky put him through to Superintendent Thornton.

The Superintendent, who had been informed of the assault on Fovargue and Andy the previous evening as well as the likelihood that the occupants of Silverdale Farm were responsible for some of the crimes under investigation and also that Tim and possibly Juliet were currently in jeopardy at the farm, had rapidly abandoned his tolerant view of Fovargue. Fovargue was no longer Jack the Lad but Jack Be Nimble, a sly and devious evader of the law, a possible murderer. Swayed by local opinion, he'd given the man the benefit of the doubt, but he'd thought there was something shifty about his character right from the start. Catching Fovargue was now his priority: road blocks would be set up. Descriptions of Fovargue would be sent to all the police forces in the country.

'...and in the meantime, Carstairs,' the Superintendent concluded, 'keep a strict eye on that vehicle until we can get some uniforms there to impound it.'

Andy, uneasy and distracted by the fear that his call to Tim might have created problems for his boss, answered semi-automatically, "Yes, sir". He was annoyed that Superintendent Thornton would bother him by fussing about the pantechnicon at such a time, a concern which in any case was faintly ridiculous. Who was going to try to steal that bloody great monstrosity?

He emerged from behind the St John Ambulance station and looked across at the lorry. Hardly able to believe his eyes, he saw that someone was in the driver's seat putting it into reverse, presumably in preparation for taking it out of the field.

'Hey!' he shouted. He sprinted up the alleyway created between the double row of exhibitors' stands, finally rounding Fovargue's, which stood at the end of the row. The lorry was now facing the road. Today, it was the only vehicle that had been parked on the far side of the field: other, smaller vehicles had either been left in the visitors' car park or tucked in behind their owners' stands. No obstacles now stood between the lorry and the gate.

For a mad moment Andy considered standing in front of the monster, his arms stretched wide, to order it to stop. The notion must have flashed across his face, because the St John Ambulance man, who had followed him, came to grab hold of his arm.

'Not much point in arguing with that, is there?' he said.

'I suppose not,' said Andy. The lorry was level with him now. He looked up at the cab and saw the driver was wearing a motorcyclist's helmet. He was all but certain it was the motorcyclist who'd followed and attacked Jack Fovargue the previous evening.

Ungraciously, he shook free his arm.

'There's going to be an unholy row about this,' he muttered, more or less to himself.

351

'Not your fault, was it?'

'That's a matter of opinion,' said Andy. He took out his mobile and called Superintendent Thornton again.

CHAPTER SEVENTY-THREE

'You don't know very much at all, really, do you?'
Tim was certain of the identity of his captor now. The plummy, rather supercilious county drawl was distinctive.

'As you say,' Susie Fovargue continued, 'no one else will know what we've been talking about. I don't fancy Jack's chances of getting away with it, though, do you?'

'Getting away with what?' Tim asked, bewildered. Surely she wasn't suggesting that she and Fovargue would be able to wriggle out of being sentenced for the murders, after all the evidence she'd just revealed. Was she mad enough not only to kill Tim but to imagine that he hadn't told anyone of his whereabouts? Or that she could replace the floorboards and cover over their grisly secret?

It struck him with a massive pang of guilt that he hadn't, actually, told anyone else that he was heading for the farm. Juliet would have been sure to guess, though, after their discussion yesterday evening. Wouldn't she?

'Killing that stupid girl,' said Susie, finally ripping the scarf from her face and shaking her mane of hair free from the hood.

'I'd gladly have done it with him: dispatching her was long overdue. But he had to do it on his own, without me. After he'd let her violate our trust in each other, too.'

Tim could see her eyes now. In the shadowy artificial light, she looked half-crazed.

'Are you trying to tell me that your husband has killed Martha Johnson?'

'Oh, well done, DI Yates. I knew you'd get there at last! Yes, that's what I *am* telling you – not *trying* to tell you. He's denying it, of course. I told him I'd get even with him over it.'

Tim was assailed by a sudden terrible thought. 'Where are your children, Susie?'

'What? Oh, I asked the nanny to take them to stay with her in the village. She does that sometimes. They seem to enjoy it, for some reason.'

His words seemed to disorient her, as if he'd reminded her that she inhabited two unimaginably separate worlds. Suddenly, she lost some of her energy. Tim cursed his fetters. If he could only free himself, she'd be easier to overpower now.

Susie Fovargue looked around her uncertainly, then glanced at her watch.

'Time's up, DI Yates,' she said, obviously attempting to recover some of her former aplomb. 'Would you like me to blindfold you? The others were already dead, but I believe it's the done thing when the accused is still alive.'

'What's that noise?' said Tim. He'd said it to stall her, but as he spoke he could genuinely hear something: a sharp splitting sound.

She stopped to listen. The noise came again, closely followed by another, different, sound: the distinctive din of a door being kicked in, a door closer to them, Tim would swear, and less robust than the giant armoured portal that fronted the building.

Susie Fovargue seized the billhook from the desk.

'Watch out! She's armed!' Tim shouted, as two figures came rushing into the room.

Susie lashed out. The smaller of the two figures let out a yell and slumped to the floor. The other, a muscular young man, seized Susie's wrist and twisted it viciously, forcing her to drop the billhook. He kept hold of her wrist and held her other arm against her upper back, immobilising her. She made a feeble attempt to kick his ankle, but he retaliated by kicking her own ankle much harder.

Juliet had fallen just a few feet from Tim. Slowly she got to her knees, holding one side of her face tight with both hands. Blood was coursing across her clenched fingers.

'Juliet!' Tim shouted.

She couldn't answer him.

'She needs an ambulance!' Tim shouted. 'Call for an ambulance now!'

'Do you want me to let Susie go?' said Nathan Buckland.

'Can you cut my hand free without releasing her?'

'What the bloody hell's going on here? And what's that stink?'

Josh Marriott had appeared in the office doorway. No one had heard him enter the building. He was clearly bewildered by what he saw.

'Susie?' he asked questioningly. 'Nathan?' Although he didn't understand the situation, it became apparent that of the two, it was Nathan Buckland whom he trusted. He made no attempt to free Susie Fovargue from Nathan's grasp.

'Get an ambulance!' Tim repeated. 'Now!'

Josh took a closer look at Juliet. His face set grimly. 'I'll get a better signal outside.'

Fleetingly, it crossed Tim's mind that Marriott might decide to do a bunk. But he knew from experience the signal from within the shed would be weak. Besides, his only option was to trust the man.

CHAPTER SEVENTY-FOUR

D I Michael Robinson was feeling rather pleased with himself. The start of his working day had unexpectedly become more interesting after he'd himself been selected to co-ordinate the North Lincs search for the pantechnicon in response to the call Superintendent Thornton had put out to all adjacent police forces. It got better: twenty minutes later he received the message that one of the North Lincs squad cars had apprehended the vehicle as its driver tried to manoeuvre it down a narrow lane. Robinson anticipated that he would be rewarded with much kudos, even though the effort he'd expended had been modest. He was looking forward to the conversation with Dennis Thornton as he picked up the phone.

'Dennis? It's Michael here. I think we've got your lorry. And the driver. His name's Aaron Buckland. He's got form, though it's not recent. We nabbed him in twenty minutes. Not bad, eh?'

Superintendent Thornton was worried about Tim and Juliet. Usually he appreciated DI Robinson's larger-than-life bumptiousness, but under the circumstances he thought such joviality more than a little uncalled-for.

'Did Buckland come quietly?' Superintendent Thornton

asked, deliberately refraining from showering DI Robinson with the gratitude he was so obviously angling for.

'Relatively quietly, I believe. I daresay he realised the game was up. But really, Dennis, how could your lot lose such a thing as that lorry? Wasn't it big enough for them to be able to see it properly?' Robinson chortled down the phone.

'My 'lot', as you put it, are out risking their lives to catch a murderer who's been operating on your patch. I'm grateful for your co-operation, Michael, but you're forgetting it's a two-way street,' said the Superintendent stiffly.

'Ouch! Sorry, I'm sure!' said DI Robinson, in a tone that suggested otherwise.

'Yes, well, I'm busy now, Michael. I'll call you later. We'll want to interview Buckland as soon as possible. We may need you to have him brought here.'

'No problem,' said DI Robinson, 'We can...'

Superintendent Thornton had already put down the phone.

CHAPTER SEVENTY-FIVE

Guided by Josh Marriott, PC Giash Chakrabati crossed the big shed and cautiously entered the small office. Tim had always liked Giash, but he'd never been as pleased to see him as he was now. PC Verity Tandy followed close behind. Seeing Juliet kneeling on the floor, obviously wounded, Verity hurried to crouch down beside her. Juliet's hand was still clamped to her face. She met Verity's eyes. Verity saw they were stricken with pain. She wanted to hug Juliet but was afraid of hurting her more. She patted Juliet's free arm.

'Don't worry, you're going to be okay,' she said. The words sounded thin and facile. It was the type of thing police officers always said to victims of accidents or violent crime. Juliet might be contemptuous of the inadequate sentiment and find it hollow, but Verity fervently hoped that she would know it was genuine.

'The ambulance is almost here,' she said, and, turning to Tim, 'The armed response team had already asked for it.'

'Armed response team?' said Tim.

'DS Armstrong called for them. They'll be here any minute.

We were sent separately as backup by Superintendent Thornton,' said Giash. 'Would you like me to cut those ties, sir?'

'Can you make sure she's secured first?' said Tim, indicating Susie Fovargue with a toss of his head. Nathan Buckland had fastened Susie's hands together using the same type of cable ties she had herself used on Tim. Susie seemed utterly deflated, almost demented. She hadn't resisted when Nathan pushed her on to the chair behind the desk while he fixed the ties. Now she remained slumped there, vaguely looking down at the floor, not attempting to communicate with anyone.

'I don't think she'll get out of those in a hurry,' said Giash, inspecting her wrists. Approaching Tim, he took out a penknife and deftly cut through the ties that tethered him to the desk.

'Thanks,' said Tim, wincing as he stood up. 'Can you go back outside to meet the armed response team? There's no point in having them bursting in here now. When they come we'll ask them to escort Mrs Fovargue to the station.'

He turned to where Juliet and Verity were huddled.

'Do you want to show me the wound?'

Juliet shook her head slightly.

'Probably wise. You're right to hold it together. Just hang in there, for God's sake. You'll be safe in hospital soon.'

Tim turned his back, the lump in his throat threatening to choke him.

Nathan Buckland had gone to stand next to Josh Marriott.

'What do you want us to do now?' Josh asked gruffly. 'Carry on with us work? Or go home?'

'I'm afraid neither is possible. This shed – in fact the whole farm – is now certainly a crime scene. We want you to touch as little as possible from this point and not move or use anything. We'll be asking you each for a statement as soon as we can organise it.'

'You still haven't found the lass, have you?'

'No,' said Tim. 'We still haven't found her, but unfortunately we think we know what's happened to her.'

He looked across at Susie Fovargue. She gave no indication of having heard his words. She remained sitting, motionless, in the office chair, her eyes wandering dully across the floor.

CHAPTER SEVENTY-SIX

The ambulance came and took Juliet to the Peterborough City Hospital. Tim offered to accompany her, but she indicated she'd prefer Verity. Tim knew Juliet well enough to understand that she wanted to leave him free to get on with the case. He didn't try to argue with her.

Susie Fovargue was cut free of the plastic ties and handcuffed. She was taken to Spalding police station and detained in one of the cells.

Using the keys and barcodes and other practical knowledge supplied by Josh Marriott and Nathan Buckland, members of the armed response unit had helped Tim to search and secure the buildings at Silverdale Farm. They were obliged to break into the farmhouse itself – Marriott did not have keys to it – and searched it, but, as Juliet and Tim had both surmised, it was deserted.

Tim called Superintendent Thornton and gave him a brief update. With similar – and uncharacteristic – brevity, the Superintendent told him of Fovargue's disappearance.

Four members of the response unit stayed to guard the crime scene until South Lincs Police could take over. Tim knew they must deploy SOCOs as soon as possible to examine and analyse the contents of the cesspit. He hoped Patti Gardner would be spared its horrors but knew this was unlikely: she'd already helped with the Fossdyke murders so she'd be the logical choice to lead the SOCOs at Silverdale Farm.

Tim himself drove Josh Marriott and Nathan Buckland to the station. Both were subdued, but Marriott seemed stunned by what he'd witnessed. Tim led them to an interview room and arranged for them to be supplied with water and hot drinks while he went for a quick debriefing with Superintendent Thornton. He was carrying the folder Susie Fovargue had flung at him.

The Superintendent was in an unforgiving frame of mind. Like the mother of a child who's frightened her by wandering off, his relief that Tim was safe was mixed with anger at his impetuous behaviour.

'There's no excuse for the way you acted, Yates, you do understand that, don't you?'

'Yes, sir, but...'

'No buts. It's because of you that Armstrong's been injured. And you could both have been killed.'

'I know that, sir.' This time Tim didn't try to retaliate. Thornton had hit him where it hurt hardest. He knew he'd always blame himself for Juliet's injury. He hoped to God she wouldn't be permanently disfigured.

'Is there any word from the hospital?'

'Not yet. I've asked them to call me. I'm pretty certain she'll need an operation.'

Even the Superintendent, whose strong suit was not emotional intelligence, couldn't fail to see how stricken Tim felt. He decided to be magnanimous.

'Well, we'll leave it at that for the moment. I can't make any guarantees, you understand. Disciplinary action may have to be taken. Armstrong herself may press for compensation, though arguably neither of you was following good working practice.'

'Yes, sir.' Not Juliet, he thought. She wouldn't sue the police force.

'Do you believe Mrs Fovargue's assertion that she and her husband are joint murderers?'

'I have no reason not to believe her. We'll know more when Forensics have examined the stuff in that cesspit. And when we've worked through the contents of this.'

Tim placed the folder on the Superintendent's desk. He was reluctantly impressed when the Superintendent drew on a pair of latex gloves.

'No doubt your prints are all over it already, Yates, but we won't add mine as well. There are probably some more interesting daubs on it than yours, so let's try to preserve them. This is extraordinary,' he added, as he turned the cover and pulled out the first sheaf of papers. He skim-read the *Free Press* account of Smythe's murder and the print-out from the website. 'Is it really the true record of a series of murders?'

'Innocent people have been known to confess to being serial killers, from some warped notion that it's glamorous, I suppose. But I think we'll find the people named in here once owned the trophies in that cesspit. With a bit of luck, there'll be some DNA evidence as well, or, as you've pointed out, fingerprints. Even without them, I think we've got a watertight case against the Fovargues – if it transpires it really was both of them.'

'Smythe's murder is the first to appear here. Does that mean he was their last victim?'

'We need time to work through the folder properly, but I think they're filed in reverse chronological order, like accounts. Susie Fovargue was – is – an accountant.'

'Do you think that means they haven't killed Martha Johnson? Or simply that they hadn't opened a file on her?'

'According to Susie, Fovargue killed Martha Johnson without consulting her. That was what made her flip – the fact that he did it on his own, when all their previous murders had been planned and shared together.'

'But that doesn't add up, does it, Yates? You saw the man when he was in here. I don't think he was putting on the distress he felt at Johnson's disappearance. In fact, now I look back on it, I'd say it was more than ordinary distress – more as if he were afraid of something. That his wife had killed Johnson, perhaps?'

'You've got a point there,' said Tim. 'But that doesn't explain why Susie opened up the cesspit. I think she did it because she believed Fovargue had killed Martha Johnson and hidden something of hers in there. She may even have thought he'd put the body in it. And Fovargue had got over his hysterics by the time he was preparing for the Lincoln show. Perhaps by then he knew what had happened to Martha?'

'Perhaps. Or perhaps he'd calmed down because he knew she was dead. Perhaps he'd been worried that Johnson would expose them – and that was why he was distressed when he came to see me. He took matters into his own hands and sorted out the threat.'

'I certainly think Martha was on to something,' said Tim. 'There's evidence the news clippings were originally stored in the accounts files – they mainly contained receipts for fuel and other vehicle expenses. I think Susie – or Fovargue – moved them into this folder because Martha went looking into the accounts files, which strictly speaking were none of her business, and found something that made her suspicious. One of the clippings was left in the accounts files – Juliet and Katrin found it when they were working through them last night.'

'You're beginning to lose me now, Yates. You'll have to put all of this in a report so we can consider the implications properly. The point I'm trying to get at now is whether I should scale down the search for Martha Johnson or not. It seems to me there's a chance she's still alive, even if it's a remote one. Should we keep on with the full-scale search for at least another day?'

'I'd certainly prefer to do that.' Tim tried not to show his surprise: it was unlike Thornton to miss an opportunity to save police money. Perhaps Martha Johnson *was* still alive.

'Now,' said the Superintendent, standing up and looking businesslike. 'I've asked Michael Robinson to have Aaron Buckland brought here for questioning. Do you want to do it, or shall I?'

'*Aaron Buckland?*' said Tim. 'Why do we want to question him?'

'Oh, did we forget to tell you, Yates? After Fovargue did his bunk, Buckland showed up and tried to steal Fovargue's vehicle – a damn big truck, from what I hear. Some of Michael's team caught up with him with commendable speed and arrested him.'

'Christ,' said Tim, his mind whirring with possibilities. 'That is a turn-up for the book. And, God, we'll have to be careful. We've got Nathan Buckland here to give a statement about how he helped arrest Susie Fovargue and now Aaron Buckland under arrest for vehicle theft. I suppose it was theft – Fovargue didn't ask him to take it?'

'What do you think, Yates? According to Carstairs, Aaron Buckland's the person who assaulted Fovargue yesterday evening. He'd hardly invite the man to borrow his lorry after that, would he?'

Tim's mind whirred faster. His reply was directed to the Superintendent, but in reality he was talking to himself.

'So he has a grudge against Fovargue, if it was Buckland who hit Fovargue yesterday – and we think Monday's attacker was the same bloke. If it was Buckland, Ricky should be able to recognise him.'

'Right, well, I'll leave you to it,' said the Superintendent.

'Let me know if you need me when Buckland gets here. By the way, Yates...' Tim noted the change in tone and gave his boss his full attention.

'...I don't remember authorising you to ask Katrin for the information she gathered on this case?'

It was a parting shot. The Superintendent sat down at his desk again and, still wearing the latex gloves, began to work through the file in earnest. Tim understood that he had been dismissed.

CHAPTER SEVENTY-SEVEN

Before he was escorted from Lincoln police station, Aaron Buckland told Michael Robinson that he knew his rights; he wouldn't consent to be interviewed without a solicitor. Robinson had relayed this to Superintendent Thornton, who'd asked for the duty solicitor. It turned out to be Sandra Hicks again. She arrived shortly before Buckland was expected. Tim briefed her quickly.

'Naturally you'll allow me some time to talk to my client before the interview begins?' she said in her no-nonsense way.

'Naturally,' Tim agreed. If she detected the irony in his voice she didn't show it.

Aaron Buckland was due to arrive sooner than he'd first thought. He debated whether to keep Aaron waiting until after the interviews with Marriott and Nathan Buckland were over but decided against it. Aaron might be able to give them clues to Fovargue's whereabouts; and there was also the tantalising possibility that he was somehow mixed up in the other vehicle thefts. They'd have to make sure that Nathan Buckland didn't know his brother was in custody. Nathan had been helpful – in fact indispensable – so far, but blood was thicker than water.

Tim asked for sandwiches to be sent in to Nathan and Marriott; the desk sergeant was detailed to sit with them in the interview room and make sure they stayed put.

Buckland arrived wearing his motorcycle leathers. Bizarrely, his helmet was swinging from one hand. The other was handcuffed to DI Robinson, who flashed Tim a sly, conspiratorial wink.

Tim tried not to show his astonishment in front of Buckland. Michael Robinson, carrying out mundane escort duties! He led them both to Interview Room 2, where Sandra Hicks was waiting. Michael Robinson unshackled himself and cuffed Buckland's hands behind his back.

'Are the handcuffs really necessary?' asked Sandra Hicks with a frown.

'I'm afraid so,' said Tim. 'For now, anyway. We'll give you five minutes to talk to Mr Buckland before we come back to interview him. Is that all right?'

'I expect so. I'll ask if I think we need more time.'

'I'm sure you will,' said Tim. She didn't miss the irony this time. She flashed him a look of disapproval.

He took Robinson into the kitchen.

'Tea?' he said. 'I'm amazed to see you here. It's very good of you to bring Buckland yourself, but don't you have better things to do?'

Michael Robinson clapped him on the back. It was an unsettling gesture, almost rough.

'I thought I ought to be in on the action. Dennis tells me you think you've caught our murderer. It's a bit unsporting of you not to have told me yourself. When can I see her?'

'I would have told you, of course I would. But there's no prospect of your seeing her today. From what we can tell, she's had a complete mental collapse. We've asked for a doctor to assess her.'

'I understand you think there might be two killers?'

'Susie Fovargue has implicated her husband in the crimes. We haven't had time to work through the evidence yet, so we don't know if it's true.'

'The guy's scarpered, though, hasn't he? It doesn't look good.'

'I agree; and as you know, we're still searching for Martha Johnson. According to Susie, Fovargue killed her, working on his own. That's what pushed Susie over the edge.'

'Hmm. Not sure I buy that. How does Buckland fit in?'

'All we know so far is that he tried to steal the vehicle he was driving when your cops caught him.'

'But you think there's more to it than that?'

'Possibly,' said Tim. He was reluctant to share his ideas with Robinson; he knew from experience that in short order they would become Robinson's own.

'Mind if I sit in on the interview with Buckland?'

'I was going to ask Ricky...' Tim began. However, Ricky had his work cut out co-ordinating the search operation and Tim also wanted him to identify Buckland. If Ricky said Buckland was the man who'd assaulted him the previous Monday, Hicks would be sure to kick up about his being in on the interrogation.

'Okay. That would be helpful. As you know, we're pretty stretched here.' Tim looked at his watch. 'I think they've had their five minutes now, don't you? Let's get on with it.'

As they emerged from the kitchen, they bumped into Superintendent Thornton.

'DI Robinson, what brings you here?' Tim noted the lack of warmth in Thornton's greeting.

'Hello, Dennis. After you'd filled me in I thought I'd come down, see if I could help,' said DI Robinson guilelessly.

'Oh. Yes. Well, don't get in DI Yates's hair, will you? He's a busy man, and he's had a pig of a day already. And by the way, I think we should preserve the formalities when we're on duty, don't you? Observe rank and title and so on?'

The Superintendent brushed past the two DIs and disappeared into the kitchen, clutching his mug.

'I wonder what's eating him?' said Michael Robinson, clearly disconcerted.

'I wouldn't worry,' said Tim, trying not to laugh. 'He's probably in a bad mood because he's having to make his own tea.'

CHAPTER SEVENTY-EIGHT

Aaron Buckland was taller and several years older than his brother Nathan, but the family resemblance was striking. Both had the chiselled good looks and olive-coloured skin often associated with Roma heritage. Both were muscular and physically powerful men.

'Mr Buckland, you already know DI Robinson, of the North Lincs Police. DI Robinson and I will interview you together. We will tape the interview. For the benefit of the tape, the interview is commencing at 15.09 hours on Saturday 30th September.'

Sandra Hicks immediately wrote something on a piece of paper and shoved it in front of Buckland, who nodded.

'Mr Buckland, you were apprehended by PC Mark Rawlings and PC Justin Smith in Wood Lane, near Lincoln, this morning, in a vehicle that was not your own. Can you provide an explanation for this?'

Buckland eyed Tim warily.

'I was borrowing it.'

'You were borrowing it. That implies that the owner, Mr Jack Fovargue, gave his permission for you to take it. Is that the case?'

'No, but he wouldn't of minded. We've got an agreement.'

'What kind of agreement?'

Buckland paused. He glanced at Sandra Hicks, who shook her head.

'No comment.'

'Okay. Mr Buckland, you are probably aware that we're looking for Mr Fovargue ourselves. He disappeared from the Lincoln showground immediately before you took his lorry. Do you know where he is now?'

'No,' said Buckland, with some force.

'Have you been in contact with him at all today? Say, by mobile phone?'

'No,' Buckland repeated defiantly, scowling.

'How did you know that Mr Fovargue wouldn't be nearby when you approached the vehicle?'

'It wouldn't of mattered if he was. As I said, we've got a deal.'

'So it was a coincidence that you came along just a few minutes after he left the showground?'

Buckland whispered to Sandra Hicks. She nodded.

'All right, I was watching him. I saw him go.'

'Where were you when you were watching him?'

'On the other side of the 'edge, near to the road.'

'How did you get to the showground?'

'On my bike.'

'So your bike will still be there now?'

Buckland bristled.

'It had better be. If someone's nicked it, there'll be 'ell to pay.'

'It's all right, Mr Buckland,' Michael Robinson put in smoothly. 'I'll ask my officers to fetch the bike and put it in the police pound. If you'd like to write down the registration number, I'll get on with it now.'

Buckland suddenly became evasive.

'Don't worry,' said Tim. He didn't want to tackle Buckland about the stolen motorbike just yet. 'It will do later. I'm sure no harm will come to it. But while we're talking about motorbikes, a motorcyclist attacked Mr Fovargue outside the guest house where he was staying yesterday evening. One of my officers was there and attacked as well. Were you the motorcyclist?'

Buckland set his jaw. Once more he turned to Sandra Hicks for support. She certainly had the knack of gaining the trust of her clients rapidly.

'DI Yates,' she said severely, 'I consider the attack you mention to be outside the scope of this interview. The brief you gave me concerned the theft of the vehicle only.'

Tim swallowed. He'd planned the inquiry about the assault as a lead-in to a much bigger question. He anticipated she was preparing to close down the interview, perhaps demand Buckland's release on the grounds that there was no proof Fovargue hadn't lent him the lorry. It was now or never.

'Mr Buckland, you must be aware that there's a massive police search under way for a young woman called Martha Johnson. She worked at Mr Fovargue's farm. Do you know her?'

Sandra Hicks put her hand on Buckland's sleeve, but he angrily shook himself away from her.

'Yes, I know her,' he said.

'Did you play any part in her disappearance?'

'DI Yates, I really...' Sandra Hicks began. Aaron Buckland cut her off, raising his voice to shout over her objection.

'No, I didn't!' he spat at Tim. 'I wouldn't harm a 'air of her 'ead. And if that bastard's done something to her, 'e won't be long for this world 'imself, let me tell you. If it wasn't for needing the lorry, I'd've done for 'im meself already.'

'What did you need the lorry for, Mr Buckland?'

374

'You don't have to answer that question,' Sandra Hicks said urgently.

'What's the use of not saying? What's the use of any of this?' said Buckland bitterly. 'It's a racket. We started it in a small way and we was struggling to make it work. I knew quite a bit about how Josh had done it years ago, but not enough. I tried to talk to him about it, give him a cut, but he wasn't having any. It was Kezia who said we needed a big vehicle. She said Jack Fovargue had just what we wanted.'

'We're talking about shifting stolen vehicles, aren't we?'

Buckland nodded.

'So you went and asked Fovargue to lend you his lorry so that you could transport stolen vehicles in it?' said Tim incredulously.

'It wasn't like that. I went to take a look at it at one of them shows. I couldn't understand why they needed such a big brute for the stuff they carried around with them. To be honest, it struck me that Jack was up to some kind of scam himself. So, when I got chance, I followed him. Turns out he kept a nifty little bike in the lorry and went out picking up tarts after he'd been to a show. I saw him at it once, in Mansfield it was.'

'Was Susie with him?'

Buckland let out a short laugh.

'What do you think? No, of course she wasn't.'

'How long did you stay?'

'In Mansfield, you mean? Long enough for him to agree a price with the tart. I took photographs to prove it.'

'And then you blackmailed him into letting you borrow the lorry when you're out stealing vehicles?'

Again, the short bark of a laugh.

'Call it blackmail if you like. I'd call it a business arrangement. And not when we're stealing them – we'd soon be caught in a bloody great thing like that, wouldn't we? But afterwards, when things have died down. The deal is we take the lorry out overnight from wherever Jack and Susie are staying, return it before they want to leave the next morning.'

'Does Susie know about this 'deal'?'

'She doesn't know the reason for it. She knows we borrow the lorry sometimes, that's all. She'd shop us to you lot as soon as look at us if she'd known. I'm not sorry Jack's been cheating on her. She's a first-class bitch. But he had to put his filthy paws on Martha, too.'

'Why do you mind about it so much? Was Martha your girlfriend?'

'I wish! No, but I thought I was in with a chance there. Until Gentleman Jack muscled in on her, that is.' Buckland's features were distorted into a sneer.

'How did you know her?'

'Her dad's a vicar. He visited me when I was inside – he came to the prison regularly. He kept in touch when I got out and she was with him when he met me sometimes. I couldn't believe my luck when she said she was going to work at Silverdale. But then it was all about Jack. Jack, Jack, bloody Jack.'

'Her choice, though.'

'Yes, but he was making her miserable. He had her right where he wanted her – she'd do owt for him. It wasn't the right kind of life for her. She'd tell Nathan about it sometimes. Promise me you'll catch that bastard. If 'e's 'armed her I'll catch up with 'im if it's the last thing I do.'

'I think we should terminate this interview now,' said Sandra Hicks. 'I need to talk to my client.'

'Agreed,' said Tim. 'Interview formally terminated on Saturday 30th September at 15.43 hours. There's just one more thing. I'd like to ask Mr Buckland to stay there for a minute while I introduce him to someone.'

'Is that okay with you?' Sandra Hicks asked Buckland.

He shrugged. 'I suppose so.'

Tim went to the door. Ricky was waiting outside.

'Afternoon, Mr Buckland,' he said, as he entered the interview room. 'I think we've met already.'

CHAPTER SEVENTY-NINE

'Well, that was quite a session,' said Michael Robinson. 'I'm pleased I was able to catch him for you.'

Tim barely answered. Increasingly, it seemed that all the crimes they had been investigating were interconnected in some way – the neat solution they'd dreamed of, but now it was turning into a nightmare. He doubted they'd ever be able to unravel all the crimes completely or catch everyone who'd been involved.

Worst of all, Fovargue was still free – and, if what Buckland said was true, he'd carried out at least some of the murders alone. Was Susie actually party to any of the killings, or were her assertions the product of a deluded brain, or even misplaced loyalty to Fovargue? She hadn't sounded very loyal when crouched over that cesspit, though: more like she hated her husband's guts. And she'd known what the cesspit was used for. When she'd uncovered it, she'd been looking for something: probably something of Martha's or Martha's body.

Martha Johnson had known about the cesspit, too – it was she who had told them about it. Had she discovered – or guessed – its grisly secrets? Or had she just been prattling in her inconsequential way when she mentioned it? And had Fovargue really made her unhappy, as Buckland asserted? Tim had seen no evidence of it.

'Excuse me, Michael,' he said curtly. 'If there's been no word from the hospital, I need to ring to see how Juliet is.'

'Has she been injured?' Michael Robinson asked, his voice edged with alarm. 'I hope she's okay!' For the first time, Tim was convinced he was being sincere.

'Susie Fovargue slashed at her with a billhook. I don't know how bad it is. Give me a couple of minutes, will you? Then if you like you can help me interview Marriott and the other Buckland. Just witness statements, at least for now.'

'Sure. You'll let me know how Juliet is?'

Tim nodded. Across the room he could see Ricky gesturing. He wanted to shake Robinson off.

'I'm sure Superintendent Thornton would appreciate a chat,' he said.

'I'm not so sure about that, but I'll give it a try.'

'DS Armstrong's been sedated,' said Ricky quietly, as Tim went to sit alongside him. 'They've stopped the bleeding and cleaned the wound. It's deep, apparently. She's going to need plastic surgery.'

'Oh, God,' said Tim. 'Is anyone with her? Can we visit her?'

'As I said, she's been sedated. PC Tandy's volunteered to spend the night at the hospital. If the doctors think she's strong enough, they may let us see her for a few minutes tomorrow.'

'She doesn't have any next of kin, does she?'

'Not in this country. Is there anyone else we should inform?'

'No, I don't think so – but wait, there is one person. I think his number's still programmed into my phone.'

Tim kept his call with Jake Fidler short. He'd only met Jake professionally and just on a few occasions; he was uncertain whether Juliet would welcome the intervention or not. Fidler was equally reserved when they spoke, but he seemed grateful.

For privacy, Tim had shut himself into the kitchen. As he re-emerged into the open-plan area, DI Robinson came flying down the stairs.

'Come quickly, Timmo, you've got to listen to this.'

Annoyed that Robinson was once again in the thick of it, Tim followed him up the stairs to Superintendent Thornton's office. Thornton was speaking to someone on the phone. As soon as he saw Tim, he gestured him to his side.

'DI Yates is here, now,' he said. 'I'm sure he'd like to speak to you.' He handed Tim the phone.

'Who is it?' Tim mouthed.

'Martha Johnson,' Thornton mouthed back.

'Martha?' said Tim into the phone. 'Where are you? Are you safe?'

'I'm at my father's house.'

'Where's that?'

'North Hykeham.'

'Is your father with you?'

'Yes. He persuaded me to come here. When he found out about Jack, he made me see that what I was doing – what Jack and I were doing – was wrong.'

'But, Martha, you must be aware that there's a massive search going on for you. Your father certainly knows – he came to your house to meet us.'

'I know. I'm sorry. But when I told Jack I was thinking of leaving he seemed so... intense, like a stalker, that I was afraid of him. He could be... harsh when he wanted his own way. I thought he'd come after me. And then I came to Dad's and the whole thing just snowballed. I'm still worried Jack's trying to find me.'

'Did you have any specific reason for not trusting him? Did you find something suspicious?'

'I don't understand what you mean. Suspicious? What kind of thing?'

Tim sighed. He hated leading questions, but he was inexpressibly weary and time was short.

'There was a pile of files on your desk. Had you been searching through them?'

'Those were Susie's files. Someone left them there; I suppose it was her. They were of no interest to me, but I didn't like to move them. It didn't take much to upset her where I was concerned. I decided to work around them until she took them away again. Listen, I know you're after Jack and he's on the run. I'm really scared that he's going to come here.'

Michael Robinson tapped Tim on the arm.

'May I?' he said, holding out his hand for the phone. Tim passed it over.

'Martha, this is DI Robinson. I'm a colleague of DI Yates. North Hykeham's on my patch. I'm going to send a squad car to fetch you now. I'll make sure that one of the officers is a policewoman. I'll ask her to bring you here – to Spalding. There's nothing to be afraid of. We can talk some more when you get here.' He handed the phone back to Tim.

'Goodbye for now, Martha. We'll see you shortly.'

'Any chance that Fovargue is on his way to North Hykeham?' asked the Superintendent.

'I doubt it, unless he's gone by a very roundabout route. It's barely ten miles from the Lincoln showground,' said Robinson. 'My guess is that he's put as much distance between himself and Lincolnshire as he can. He could be in Scotland by now.'

'If Martha really didn't suspect anything, Susie must have engineered the thing with the files,' said Tim. 'She said she was angry with Fovargue for killing Martha without her, but perhaps she was really trying to provoke him into killing her. And Fovargue panicked because he thought Susie had killed Martha. Unhinged or not, Susie was right about one thing: once the trust between them was broken, they were bound to come unstuck.'

'Thank God for that,' said the Superintendent piously. Then, more briskly, 'But if both of them are killers, that's small consolation while Fovargue himself is still at large.' He stood up and walked out of his office, as if personally affronted by the idea.

'Ever the master of the obvious statement,' said Michael Robinson.

Despite himself, Tim laughed.

CHAPTER EIGHTY

Jack Fovargue was apprehended trying to board the Liverpool to Dublin Ferry. He gave himself up without a struggle. His phone records showed that Susie had called him shortly before he left Marston Farm.

CHAPTER EIGHTY-ONE

Tim and Katrin visited Juliet in hospital every day. She'd had an operation to tidy up the wound. She'd have to wait until it had healed before plastic surgery could be attempted. The dressing on her face made it difficult for her to talk and, on Sunday and Monday, she was weak and tearful, obviously still in great pain. They sat with her and talked to her about everyday things.

By Tuesday, some of her usual verve had returned. The dressing on her face had been changed; its replacement was smaller. Although still very tired, she was sitting up and able to speak.

'How are you?' Tim asked.

'I'm getting there. But for God's sake, Tim, tell me more about the case. I know you arrested Susie. Have you got Fovargue as well?'

'Yes, both of them. Did you hear any of what Susie said before you broke into the shed?' Tim asked.

'Some of it; enough to persuade Nathan Buckland of her guilt. We heard her say Fovargue had killed Martha and that they were both killers. I can't remember her exact words. Have you found Martha?'

'Yes; and Susie was wrong. Fovargue didn't kill her. He may have thought Susie had. But she's still alive.'

'Is there enough evidence to sew up the investigation?'

'I think so – and the vehicle thefts, too. But it's going to be complicated.'

'So we were right about the connection with the vehicle thefts!' Juliet exclaimed, leaning forward. 'Tell me about it. All of it. In a nutshell.'

Tim made a wry face.

'In a nutshell? It's the most complicated case I've ever worked on. But here goes: Jack and Susie Fovargue are serial killers: enough evidence has already been analysed to show they were both involved in the murders, though it's possible Jack carried out some on his own. The motive appears to have been satisfying an intellectual challenge and the pleasure of working together to keep a diabolical secret: as you and Katrin had already surmised, the murders all parodied earlier ones, most of them recent but some decades old. Jack had a roving eye and always went for women who looked like Susie. Normally Susie put up with this, but Jack was getting far too close to Martha Johnson. Susie thought Jack might leave her for Martha or even that he'd shared the secret with her – God knows why, Martha would have run a mile – but jealousy or guilt were clouding Susie's mental faculties by this time. Bizarrely, after she confronted Jack, she believed he'd killed Martha without involving her and, at least temporarily, he thought Susie had murdered her. Martha had in fact got the wind up and run away.

'Aaron Buckland, who'd been in prison with Josh Marriott, decided to mastermind the same kind of scam that had put Josh there. Josh refused to have anything to do with it – he liked the life he'd carved out for himself at Silverdale Farm – but he certainly knew about it and his girlfriend, who is related to Aaron, persuaded him to give Aaron advice from time to time. Aaron was running a big network of thieves and fences, some of them based in or prepared to travel to Ireland. Bill Wood or Pett or whatever he calls himself was part of this network. From Ireland, some of the vehicles were shipped to Europe.

'Aaron was blackmailing Josh Fovargue to make him lend his pantechnicon for moving the smaller vehicles that his lot nicked around the country. He'd seen Fovargue picking up a prostitute and threatened to tell Susie, but you can bet Susie knew all about it and the prostitute was one of their victims. Fovargue will have gone along with it because he didn't want Aaron to delve any further. The bigger vehicles – like Mr T R Pack's combine harvester – were kept in storage for months, until everyone had forgotten about them, and then moved on. We think some of the vehicles were stolen to order, others just on the off-chance.'

'Where did he store them?'

'In a disused airfield. It's near Scampton – not the RAF base, a private one.'

Juliet laughed out loud.

'What's so funny?'

'When I first got involved with the case and Ricky was telling me how frustrating it was not to be able to locate the vehicles, this was what he said: 'Where are they, then? In a bloody great aircraft hangar that nobody has noticed?' He meant it sarcastically, of course. He had no inkling he was right!'

'Well, that's it in a nutshell. There are dozens of lines of enquiry to pursue, as you can imagine, and I've got a list of questions I want to answer as long as your arm.'

'What about Josh Marriott and Nathan Buckland? Are they innocent?'

'Nathan is, almost certainly. That's going to make life difficult for him in the community he lives in – particularly when they find out that he helped you. As I said, Marriott certainly knew something about what Aaron was up to. I believe he was a very reluctant accomplice, but technically he's guilty of a felony – aiding and abetting, accessory after the fact, something like that. We'll have to report him to the CPS and see if they decide to prosecute. Personally, I hope they decide they've got bigger fish to fry, but they could argue that the thefts wouldn't have gone on so long without his advice.'

'Give me some of the questions on your list.'

'I've actually solved one of them myself. As you know, we thought it was odd that Mr Pack was the only big landowner to have been targeted by the thieves. Both the combine harvester and the motorbike were stolen from him. It turns out Aaron bore him a grudge because he was the foreman of the jury that convicted him.'

'Well done. What's top of the list?'

'How did Fovargue and Susie find out that Steven Smythe, whose first name and last name initials were the same, was dating a bloke who also had such initials?'

'Internet chat rooms? Lonely hearts adverts in the paper?'

'Thanks for that,' said Tim. 'We can talk to Fabron again, see if he can throw any light on it.'

'Next one!' Juliet was clearly enjoying herself.

'Did Fovargue and Susie know of the connection between Selina Pett and Aaron Buckland – in other words, was Selina chosen deliberately – or was she just in the wrong place at the wrong time?'

'I can't answer that. It'll take some very skilful interrogation to prise that out of them. Particularly as the Petts are bound to have contacts on the inside, so they'll be reluctant to admit they targeted Selina. Go on!'

'Just a minute,' said Katrin. 'We're not supposed to be discussing the case at all, let alone wearing you out. Besides, Tim's got something important to say to you.'

Tim looked grave.

'Yes,' he said. 'I have. I owe you a huge apology – in fact, to apologise is far too feeble, but I don't know what else to do. You're in here because of my stupidity. As Thornton put it, I behaved like a fucking idiot when I went to the farm alone.'

'Did he really say that?' Juliet asked, amused.

'Well, words to that effect. You probably saved my life and I know there's no way of making it up to you.'

'But you can try,' said Katrin. She turned to Juliet. 'If I were you, I'd be compiling a list of my own. Stuff that Tim can do for you.'

'I was a fucking idiot, too.'

'Yes, but only because Tim pushed you into being one.'

'Okay,' said Juliet. 'I'll need some time to think about it. But there's one thing you can do for me straight away.'

'Go on,' said Tim.

'Let me back on the case as soon as you can – like, now. I can at least do some of the follow-up stuff before I'm signed off.'

'Done,' said Tim.

'Only if the doctors let you,' said Katrin. 'And only for an hour or so at a time at first.'

CHAPTER EIGHTY-TWO

When Juliet was alone again, her sanguine mood evaporated. She knew she'd have to suffer long months of pain and probably multiple operations before she could begin to think about putting the attack behind her. She had never been vain, but neither was she confident in her looks. If she were badly disfigured it would be a massive burden to carry and certainly affect her professionally. She didn't even want to consider what it might do to her private life.

She was still occupying a side ward. It contained two beds, but she'd not been asked to share it with another patient. She'd just fallen back against the pillows when there came a tap at the door. Jake Fidler came in, carrying books and a newspaper.

'I didn't know what to bring you,' he explained. 'I didn't think you were the floral type.'

'I'm not,' said Juliet, 'and I'm not sure flowers are allowed in hospitals these days.'

'I visited on Sunday, but you were sleeping and they only let me stay a little while. I couldn't get away yesterday, unfortunately.'

'But you did call to ask how I was,' said Juliet. 'The staff nurse told me.'

'They said you were groggy yesterday. How are you today?'

Juliet was furious with herself when her eyes again filled with tears.

'Just ignore me,' she said, brushing them away. 'It's a side effect of the drugs they're giving me: they play havoc with your emotions.' She paused. 'Did they tell you that my face is likely to be scarred? They'll do their best with plastic surgery, but there are no guarantees.'

He took her hand.

'You're the most beautiful person I know.'

She attempted a smile.

'Gentleman Jake,' she murmured.

'What was that?'

'Nothing,' she said. 'I was just playing with words.'

THE END

ACKNOWLEDGEMENTS

First of all, I owe a massive debt of gratitude to Betsy Reavley and Fred Freeman, of Bloodhound Books, for believing in the DI Yates series; and to Tara Lyons and Hannah Deuce for their unstinting guidance and support and very hard work.

The Yates novels would be nothing without their readers. From the bottom of my heart I'd like to thank all of you, including those whom I've met in person, those of you who have taken the trouble to 'meet' me or review my books with such generosity on blogs and social networks, and everyone who has bought or borrowed my books to read. You are a constant source of inspiration to me.

Equally important is the growing list of booksellers and librarians who support my novels. You are too many to name, so please don't be offended if I have missed you out. Among booksellers I owe very special thanks to Sam and Sarah and their reading groups at Bookmark in Spalding; Tim Walker and Jenny Pugh of Walker Books in Stamford; and the legendary crime buff Richard Reynolds, of Heffer's Bookshop in Cambridge and his colleague Kate Fleet, whose knowledge of crime writing and support of crime fiction writers is second to none.

Among librarians, Jane Barber at Stamford Library, Alison Cassels at Wakefield One, Lynne Cook at Gainsborough Library, Jude Hall at Woodhall Spa Library, Sharman Morriss at Spalding Library and Nicola Swann, who works for Cambridgeshire Libraries, have been particularly outstanding.

I'd also like to thank Judith Heneghan, who was for several years the distinguished director of the Winchester Literary Festival, for inviting me to speak and take part in author 'surgeries' several years running; Carla Green of BBC Radio Lincolnshire and Chris Ilsley of Lincoln City Radio, who continue to provide generous air time whenever a new Yates is published; and Yusef Sayed, editor of *Lincolnshire Life*, whose enthusiasm for Yates and South Lincs police has influenced many new readers.

There are many other people whom I ought to thank here. As always, it's impossible to mention everyone, but I must pay tribute to those staunch friends who wait impatiently for the next book to come out and always promote it with enthusiasm, especially Madelaine and Marc, my chief champions in Lincolnshire and their friend Anthony; Pamela and Robert, who provided invaluable advice on cesspits and tanker lorries (as well as excellent rhubarb gin); and to long-suffering Sally, who has never failed to offer a bed and wit and wisdom over a bottle of wine when I've needed to stay in London. (Sadly, Covid has made this impossible for the past two years, but I hope it is a tradition we shall start again shortly.)

The members of my family continue to overwhelm with their unique style of support. James and Annika have once again checked the final draft and picked up inaccuracies and inconsistencies with hawklike precision, assiduously checking on my behalf the details of such matters as how the road systems operate around Cambridge, how long a bicycle wheel can keep turning when the bike is lying on the ground and how much work anyone, even Tim Yates, can be expected to fit into one day. Emma continues to surprise and delight with her mastery of language and her impeccable approach to logic. Chris wins a line to himself for bestowing the occasional word of praise, appreciated not only for its rarity but because he always 'gets' what each book is really about.

My very sincere thanks to you all.

Christina James

ABOUT THE AUTHOR

Christina James was born in Spalding and sets her novels in the evocative Fenland countryside of South Lincolnshire. She works as a bookseller, researcher and teacher. She has a lifelong fascination with crime fiction and its history. She is also a well-established non-fiction writer, under a separate name.

A NOTE FROM THE PUBLISHER

Thank you for reading this book. If you enjoyed it please do consider leaving a review on Amazon to help others find it too.

We hate typos. All of our books have been rigorously edited and proofread, but sometimes mistakes do slip through. If you have spotted a typo, please do let us know and we can get it amended within hours.

info@bloodhoundbooks.com

Lightning Source UK Ltd.
Milton Keynes UK
UKHW011848100123
415128UK00001B/175